WHEN STRANGERS MARRY

Also by Lisa Kleypas
in Large Print:

Lady Sophia's Lover

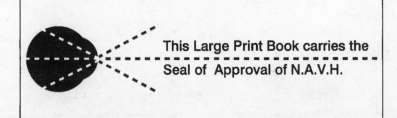

WHEN STRANGERS MARRY

Lisa Kleypas

WHEELER
PUBLISHING

Published in 2003 by arrangement with Avon Books, an imprint of HarperCollins Publishers, Inc.

Wheeler Large Print Romance Series.

The text of this Large Print edition is unabridged. Other aspects of the book may vary from the original edition.

Set in 16 pt. Plantin by Minnie B. Raven.

Printed in the United States on permanent paper.

Library of Congress Cataloging-in-Publication Data

Kleypas, Lisa.
    When strangers marry / Lisa Kleypas.
        p. cm.
     ISBN 1-58724-407-1 (lg. print : hc : alk. paper)
     1. Natchez (Miss.) — Fiction.   2. Large type books.
 I. Title.
PS3561.L456W47 2003
  813'.54—dc21   2002192258

To my father, Lloyd Kleypas,

For always believing in me,
and encouraging me to do my best . . .
for being someone I can
always trust and count on . . .
and for making me feel strong
even when I am leaning on you.

I am so proud to be your daughter,

With love always,
L.K.

PROLOGUE

NATCHEZ, 1805

The room was filled with the sound of fists pounding flesh. Lysette huddled in a ball with her arms covering her head, while smothered cries were torn from her raw throat. Her rebellion had been crushed until all that remained was the will to survive her stepfather's assault.

Gaspard Medart was a short but powerfully built man, with a bullish strength that was often used to compensate for his lack of intelligence. When he was satisfied that Lysette would offer no further resistance, he straightened with an angry grunt and wiped his bloody fists on his waistcoat.

It took a full minute for Lysette to realize Gaspard was finished. Cautiously she unwrapped her arms from around her head and turned her face to the side. He was standing above her, his hands still clenched. She swallowed, tasting blood, and pushed herself up to a sitting position.

"Now you have learned the price of challenging me," Gaspard muttered. "And from now on, each time you give me so much as an impertinent glance, I'll repay it with *this*." He held his clenched hand in front of her face. "Do you understand?"

"*Oui.*" Lysette's eyes closed. *Let it be over,* she thought feverishly. *Let it be over.* . . . She would say or do anything just to make him go away.

She was vaguely aware of Gaspard's snort of contempt as he left the room. Her head swam as she crawled to her bed and pulled herself to a standing position. She raised a hand to her bruised jaw, testing it gingerly. A salty taste filled her mouth, and she spat thickly. The door creaked, and she glanced toward it warily, fearing that her stepfather had returned. However, it was her aunt Delphine, who had cowered in another room during the worst of Gaspard's rage.

Delphine was referred to by everyone as *tante,* one of that category of luckless spinsters who had not caught a husband in her earlier years and therefore was relegated to living on the uncertain charity of reluctant relatives. Her plump face was creased with concern and exasperation as she stared at Lysette's battered face.

"You think I deserve to be punished," Lysette said hoarsely. "I know you do. After all, Gaspard is the head of the house . . . the only man. His decisions are to be accepted without question. Isn't that right?"

"It is fortunate that he did not do worse," Delphine said, managing to sound both pitying and self-righteous. "I did not believe you would take it so far." She approached Lysette and took hold of her arm. "Let me help you —"

"Go away," Lysette muttered, shaking off the plump hand. "I don't need your help now. I needed it ten minutes ago, when Gaspard was beating me."

"You must accept your fate and not be spiteful," Delphine said. "Perhaps it will not be as terrible as you anticipate, being the wife of Etienne Sagesse."

Lysette's breath hissed though her teeth as she climbed painfully onto the bed. "Delphine, you don't believe that. Sagesse is a mean, self-indulgent pig, and no one with any wits would dispute that."

"*Le Bon Dieu* has decided for you, and if it is His will that you be the wife of such a man . . ." Delphine shrugged.

"But it wasn't God who decided." Lysette glared at the empty doorway. "It was Gaspard." In the past two years, he had gone through every cent of the money her late father had left them. To replenish his accounts and restore his credit, Gaspard had arranged a marriage between Lysette's older sister Jacqueline and a wealthy old man three times her age. Now it was Lysette's turn to be sold to the highest bidder. She had thought that Gaspard could not possibly find a worse husband for her than he had for Jacqueline, but somehow he had outdone himself.

Lysette's husband-to-be was a planter from New Orleans named Etienne Sagesse. He had justified her worst fears during their one encounter, behaving in a condescending and crude manner, even going so far as to grope the front of her gown in a drunken attempt to feel her breasts. Gaspard had seemed amused, proclaiming that the disgusting creature was merely full of masculine spirit.

"Lysette?" Delphine hovered over her, annoying her beyond reason. "Perhaps some cool water to bathe your —"

"Don't touch me." Lysette turned her face away. "If you want to be of use, then send for my sister." The thought of Jacqueline filled her with a tremendous longing for comfort.

"But her husband may not give her permission —"

"Tell her," Lysette insisted, lowering her head to the brocaded counterpane. "Tell Jacqueline that I need her."

There was an unnatural silence after Delphine left the room. Licking at her swollen, cracked lips, Lysette closed her eyes and tried to make plans. Gaspard's abuse had only intensified her determination to find her way out of the nightmare she was in.

Despite the pain of her bruises, Lysette dozed until the afternoon sun had faded and the room was dark with evening shadows. When she awakened, she found her sister at her bedside.

"Jacqueline," she whispered, her lips pulling into a crooked, aching smile.

Once, Jacqueline might have wept over Lysette's pain and held her close to comfort her. But the Jacqueline of the past had been replaced by a brittle, unnaturally self-contained woman. Jacqueline had always been the prettier of the two sisters, her auburn hair smooth whereas Lysette's was frizzy, her skin pale and perfect as opposed to Lysette's flurry of amber freckles. However, Lysette had never been jealous of her older sister, as Jacqueline had always been maternal and loving to her. More so, in fact, than their own mother, Jeanne.

Jacqueline rested a slim, perfumed hand on the counterpane. Her hair was fashionably arranged and her face carefully powdered, but no artifice would hide the fact that she had aged greatly since her marriage.

"Jacqueline . . ." Lysette's voice cracked.

Her sister's face was taut but composed. "Has it finally come to this? I've always feared you would push Gaspard too far. I've warned you not to defy him."

Lysette unburdened herself eagerly. "He

wants me to marry a planter from New Orleans . . . a man I *despise*."

"Yes, Etienne Sagesse," came the flat reply. "I knew about it even before Sagesse arrived in Natchez."

"You knew?" Lysette frowned in bewilderment. "Why didn't you warn me about what Gaspard was planning?"

"From what I've heard, it's not a bad match. If that is what Gaspard wants, then do it. At least you'll be free of him."

"No, you don't understand what this man is like, Jacqueline —"

"I'm certain that Sagesse is no different from any other man," Jacqueline said tonelessly. "Marriage is not so very difficult, Lysette — not compared to this. You'll have your own house to manage, and you won't have to wait on Maman hand and foot. And after you bear a child or two, your husband won't visit your bed as often."

"And I am supposed to be content with *that* for the rest of my life?" Lysette's throat tightened unbearably.

Jacqueline sighed. "I'm sorry if you find me poor comfort. But I think you need the truth more than platitudes." She leaned over to touch Lysette's sore shoulder. Lysette winced in discomfort.

Jacqueline's lips thinned. "From now on I hope you'll be wise enough to hold your tongue around Gaspard. Can you try to give at least a pretense of obedience?"

"Yes," Lysette said grudgingly.

"I am going to see Maman now. How has she been this week?"

"Worse than usual. The doctor said . . ." Lysette hesitated, her gaze fixed on the swath of patterned damask hanging over the headboard. Like the other furnishings in the house, it was frayed and grimy with age. "By now Maman couldn't get out of bed if she wanted to," she said dully. "The past years of playing invalid and never leaving her room have weakened her. If it weren't for Gaspard, she would be perfectly healthy. But every time he begins to shout, she takes another dose of tonic, closes the curtains, and sleeps for two days. Why did she marry him?"

Jacqueline shook her head thoughtfully. "A woman has to make the best of what she is offered. By the time Papa died, Maman's youth was gone, and there were few suitors offering for her. I suppose Gaspard seemed the most promising match."

"She could have chosen to live alone."

"Even a bad husband is better than living alone." Jacqueline stood and straightened her skirts. "I'll go to Maman now. Is she aware of what happened between you and Gaspard?"

Lysette smiled bitterly, thinking of the commotion they had raised. "I don't see how she could have avoided it."

"Then she is upset, I'm certain. Well, per-haps, with both of us gone, there will be more peace around here. I hope so, for Maman's sake."

As Jacqueline left, Lysette stared after her older sister and turned to her side. It even hurt to breathe. "Somehow," she muttered wryly, "I was expecting a bit more sym-pathy."

Closing her eyes, she began to plan fever-ishly. She would *not* become Etienne Sagesse's bride . . . no matter what she had to do to avoid it.

CHAPTER

1

NEW ORLEANS

Philippe and Justin Vallerand wandered through the woods and down to the bayou, finding their way around mud holes, pines, and sycamore trees. The boys were tall for their age, lanky and thin, not yet having attained their father's heavily muscled build.

Their features were stamped with the inborn arrogance of all the Vallerands. Heavy black hair fell over their foreheads in untidy waves, and their blue eyes were framed with long dark lashes. Strangers were never able to tell them apart, but inwardly they were as different as it was possible for two boys to be. Philippe was gentle, compassionate, someone who followed rules even when he didn't fully understand the reasoning behind them. Justin, on the other hand, was ruthless, resentful of authority, and proud of it.

"What are we going to do?" Philippe asked. "Should we take the pirogue and look for pirates downriver?"

Justin gave a scornful laugh. "You can do

as you like. *I* plan to visit Madeleine today."

Madeleine Scipion was the pretty black-haired daughter of a town merchant. Lately she had displayed more than a casual interest in Justin, although she was aware that Philippe was smitten with her. The girl seemed to delight in pitting one brother against the other.

Philippe's sensitive face revealed his envy. "Are you in love with her?"

Justin grinned and spat. "Love? Who cares about that? Did I tell you what Madeleine let me do to her the last time I saw her?"

"What?" Philippe demanded with rising jealousy.

Their eyes locked. Suddenly Justin cuffed him on the side of the head and laughed, fleeing through the trees as Philippe gave chase. "I'll make you tell me!" Philippe scooped up a glob of mud and threw it at Justin's back. "I'll make you —"

They both stopped short as they saw a movement near the pirogue. A small boy dressed in ragged clothes and a floppy hat was fumbling with the craft. The tethering rope dropped from his hands as he realized he had been found out. Quickly he picked up a knotted bundle of cloth and fled.

"He's trying to steal it!" Justin said, and the twins ran after the vanishing thief with warlike yells, their quarrel with each other discarded.

"Head him off!" Justin ordered. Philippe swerved to the left, disappearing behind a cluster of cypress trees that trailed their moss down to the soft, muddy brown water. Within minutes he succeeded in cutting the boy off, coming face-to-face with him just beyond the cypress grove.

Seeing the boy's violent trembling, Philippe grinned triumphantly, drawing a forearm across his sweaty brow. "You'll be sorry you ever thought of touching our pirogue," he panted, advancing on his prey.

Breathing heavily, the thief turned in the opposite direction and ran into Justin, who caught him with one arm and held him dangling sideways. The boy dropped his bundle and gave a high-pitched scream, which caused the twins to laugh.

"Philippe!" Justin cried, fending off the boy's feeble blows. "Look what I've caught! A little *lutin* with no respect for others' property! What should we do with him?"

Philippe regarded the hapless thief with the censuring stare of a judge. "You!" he barked, swaggering before the wriggling imp. "What's your name?"

"Let go of me! I've done nothing!"

"Only because we interrupted you," Justin said.

Philippe whistled as he saw the red welts and bleeding scratches that covered the boy's thin arms and neck. "You've been a feast for the mosquitoes, haven't you? How long have you been in the swamp?"

The flailing child managed to kick Justin in the knee.

"Ah, that hurt!" Justin shook the black hair out of his eyes and glared at the boy. "Now I've lost my patience!"

"Let me go, you mongrel!"

Annoyed, Justin raised his hand to box his captive's ears. "I'll teach you manners, boy."

"Justin, wait," Philippe interrupted. It was impossible not to feel sympathy for the child caught so helplessly in his brother's grasp. "He's too small. Don't be a bully."

"How soft you are," Justin mocked, but his arm lowered. "How do you suggest we make him talk? Dunk him in the bayou?"

"Maybe we shouldn't . . ." Philippe began, but his brother was already heading to the edge of the water, dragging the screaming child behind him.

"Are you aware there are snakes in here?" Justin said, swinging the boy up, preparing to throw him in. "Poisonous ones."

"No! Please!"

"And alligators, too, all waiting to snap up a little bite like . . ." His voice trailed off into silence as the boy's floppy hat dropped into the bayou and drifted gently away. A long, frizzled red braid swung over the child's shoulder, her delicate features no longer concealed by the hat.

Their thief was a girl, a girl their age or

18

perhaps a bit older. She threw her slim arms around Justin's neck, clinging as if he held her over a pit of fire.

"Don't throw me in. *Je vous en prie.* I can't swim."

Justin shifted her in his arms, staring down at the small, dirty face so close to his. She looked like an ordinary girl, pretty but not remarkably so, although it was difficult to tell beneath the mud and mosquito bites. "Well," Justin said slowly, "it seems we were mistaken, Philippe." He shook the protesting girl to quiet her. "Hush. I'm not going to throw you in. I think I can find a better use for you."

"Justin, give her to me," Philippe said.

Justin smiled darkly and turned away from his brother. "Go amuse yourself somewhere else. She's mine."

"She is just as much mine as yours!"

"I'm the one who caught her," Justin said matter-of-factly.

"With my help!" Philippe cried in outrage. "Besides, you have Madeleine!"

"You take Madeleine. I want this one."

Philippe scowled. "Let *her* choose!"

They stared at each other in challenge, and suddenly Justin chuckled. "So be it," he said, his fierceness mellowing to lazy good humor. He jostled the girl in his arms. "Well, which one of us do you want?"

Lysette shook her head, too weak and exhausted to understand what he was asking. She had traveled through the swamp for two terror-filled days, wet, filthy, and certain that at any moment she would be killed by an alligator or poisonous snake. The steamy heat had been bad enough, but the proliferation of insects had nearly driven her mad. They had bitten and stung through her clothes until every inch of her skin itched and burned. Lysette had even begun to entertain the thought that she would not survive the hellish journey she had undertaken, and it hadn't mattered. Anything, even a nasty death in a Louisiana bayou, would be preferable to a lifetime of Etienne Sagesse.

"Come, don't take all day," the boy named Justin said impatiently Lysette struggled against him, but his lanky arms were surprisingly strong. He tightened his grip until she subsided with a gasp of pain.

"*Mon Dieu,* it's not necessary to hurt her," Philippe said.

"I didn't hurt her," Justin replied indignantly. "I just squeezed her a little." He gave Lysette a warning glance. "And I will do it again if she doesn't make up her mind now."

Numbly Lysette looked from the imperious dark face of the boy who held her to the lighter one of the boy nearby. They were identical twins, she realized. The one called Philippe seemed a little gentler, and there was a trace of compassion in his blue eyes that she sensed was absent in the other. It was possible that she could convince him to release her.

"You," she said desperately, looking at Philippe.

"*Him?*" Justin scoffed, letting her feet drop to the ground. He shoved her toward his brother with a contemptuous snort. "There, Philippe, do as you please. I didn't want her anyway." He scooped up the bundle on the ground and searched through it, discovering a handful of coins tied in a handkerchief, a rolled-up dress, and an amber comb.

Unable to stop her momentum, Lysette staggered against the other boy. His steadying hands came to her narrow shoulders. "What is your name?" he asked.

His voice was unexpectedly kind. Lysette chewed the insides of her cheeks and shook her head, while her eyes stung with sudden tears. She despised herself for the moment of weakness, but she was exhausted and starving, and she was nearly at her wits' end.

"Why were you taking the pirogue?" Philippe asked.

"I'm sorry. I shouldn't have. Let me go — I won't bother you again."

Philippe's gaze took a detailed tour from her head to her feet. Lysette withstood the inspection with resignation. Even at her best, she had never been called a great beauty. Now, after her sojourn through the swamp, she was muddy and strong-smelling.

As the boy gazed at her, he seemed to come to a decision. "Come with me," he said, grasping her wrists. "If you are in trouble, we may be able to help you."

Lysette was filled with instant alarm. She suspected the boy intended to bring her to his parents. Then it would only be a matter of hours before she was delivered to the Sagesse household. "No, *please*," she begged, pulling at her imprisoned arms.

"You have no choice."

She shoved at him as hard as she could, jabbing with her elbows and knees. He defeated her with humiliating ease. "I'm not going to hurt you," Philippe said, swinging her over his shoulder and locking his arm behind her knees. She gave a scream of mingled rage and despair as she flailed helplessly against his back.

Justin watched his brother with a sardonic frown. "Where are you taking her?"

"To Father."

"*Father?* What are you doing that for? He'll only make you let her go."

"It's the right thing to do," Philippe said matter-of-factly.

"Idiot," Justin muttered underneath his breath, but he followed reluctantly as his brother carried their new acquisition from the bank of the bayou.

Lysette went limp halfway up the incline,

deciding it would be wiser to save the strength she had left to face whatever fate was in store for her. There was no way she was going to escape the clutches of these two arrogant boys. She closed her eyes, feeling sick.

"Don't carry me upside down," she said thickly. "I will be ill if you do."

Justin spoke up from behind them. "She does look rather green, Philippe."

"Really?" Philippe stopped and let Lysette's feet slide to the ground. "Would you like to walk?"

"Yes," Lysette said, stumbling a little. The brothers each took an arm, guiding her forward. Dazed, she looked from right to left, realizing the boys must belong to a family of great wealth. Like other plantation homes in the exclusive bayou district, the house faced the Bayou St. John, a finger of water that extended from Lake Pontchartrain to the Mississippi River. The lazy afternoon sun glared on the main house's white and pale gray exterior. All three stories of the home were surrounded with wide shaded verandas framed by sturdy white columns. Abundant groves of cypress, oak, and magnolia trees had been planted around the chapel, smokehouse, and what appeared to be slave quarters.

Lysette's stomach churned unpleasantly as the boys propelled her up a flight of steps leading to the main door of the house. They passed through a dark, cool entrance hall lined with narrow mahogany benches.

"Father?" Philippe called, and a startled dark-skinned woman gestured to a room just beyond one of the twin parlors bordering the hallway. Smugly the boys paraded their charge into the library, where their father sat at a massive mahogany desk. The room was splendidly furnished, the chairs upholstered with rich yellow silk that matched the yellow and lapis lazuli print on the walls. Heavy swags of scarlet wool moreen framed the windows.

Lysette's attention moved from the room to the figure at the desk. He faced away from them as he worked. He wore no waistcoat, and his white shirt clung damply to the outlines of his powerful muscular back.

"What is it?" came a deep voice that sent an unsettling thrill of awareness down her spine.

"Father," Philippe said, "we caught someone by the water trying to steal our pirogue."

The man at the desk shuffled papers into a neat pile. "Oh? I hope you taught him the consequences of tampering with Vallerand property."

"Actually . . ." Philippe began, and coughed nervously. "Actually, Father . . ."

"It's a *girl*," Justin blurted out.

Evidently that was enough to attract Vallerand's attention. He turned in his chair

24

and stared at Lysette with cool curiosity.

If the devil ever decided to assume a human guise, Lysette was certain that he would look exactly like this . . . dark, handsome, with a bold nose, a hard sullen mouth, and wicked dark eyes. He was a rampantly masculine creature, possessing the swarthy tan and the obvious physicality of someone who spent much of his time outdoors. Although Lysette was taller than average, Vallerand's dominating presence made her feel almost tiny. Rising to his feet, he leaned back against the desk and surveyed her lazily, seeming less than enthralled by the sight of a mud-encrusted girl in his library.

"Who are you?" he asked.

Lysette met his assessing gaze without blinking, while she considered various ways to deal with him. He did not seem to be the kind of man who would be moved by tearful pleading. Nor would he be impressed with threats or defiance. There was a possibility that he was acquainted with the Sagesse family, perhaps even was close friends with them. Her only hope was to convince him that she was not worth the trouble of bothering with.

Justin spoke eagerly before Lysette could reply to his question. "She won't tell us, Father!"

Vallerand pushed away from the desk and approached Lysette. She was not aware of backing away until she bumped into Philippe's solid form behind her. When Vallerand reached her, he slid his long fingers beneath her chin, tilting her face upward. Carefully he turned her face from right to left, dispassionately surveying the damage wrought from her journey along the bayou. She swallowed hard against the callused pads of his fingers. His deep chest was level with her face, the shadow of black hair visible beneath the thin lawn of his shirt.

Now that he was standing so close, she saw that his eyes were a very dark brown. She had always thought of brown as a warm color, but those eyes provided definite evidence to the contrary.

"Why take the pirogue?"

"I am sorry for that," she said hoarsely. "I've never stolen anything before. But my need for the pirogue was greater than yours."

"What is your name?" When she didn't reply, his fingers urged her chin up a fraction of an inch higher. "Who is your family?"

"You are kind to be concerned, monsieur," she parried, perfectly aware that kindness was the last thing that motivated him. "However, I have no need of your help, and I do not wish to trouble you. If you would release me, I will go on my way and —"

"Are you lost?"

"No," she replied shortly.

"Then you're running from someone."

Lysette hesitated just a little too long. "No, monsieur —"

"From whom?"

She pushed his fingers away from her chin, while a sense of hopeless defeat began to creep over her. "You don't need to know," she said curtly. "Let me go."

He smiled as if the flicker of spirit had pleased him. "Are you from New Orleans, mademoiselle?"

"No."

"I didn't think so. Have you heard of the Vallerand family?"

She had, actually. As Lysette stared at the stranger's lean, dark face, she tried to recall what had been said about the Vallerands. The name had been mentioned at the supper table, when Gaspard and his friends had discussed politics and business. Several Louisiana planters had become some of the richest men in the nation, Vallerand included. If she remembered correctly, the family owned huge tracts of land on either side of New Orleans, including the forest just beyond Lake Pontchartrain. Gaspard's friends had said with some resentment that Maximilien Vallerand, the head of the family, was a friend and advisor to the new governor of the Orleans Territory.

"I've heard of you," Lysette acknowledged flatly. "You are an important man in New Orleans, *n'est-ce pas?* No doubt you have many other things to concern yourself with. I apologize for my little transgression, but obviously no harm was done. Now, if you don't mind, I would like to leave."

Holding her breath, she turned away, only to have his large hand close gently around her upper arm. "But I do mind," he said softly.

Although his touch was light, he happened to grasp one of the more painful bruises Gaspard had inflicted. Lysette inhaled sharply and felt herself turn white, while her entire arm throbbed with agony.

Immediately Vallerand's hand dropped, and he stared at her intently. Lysette straightened her spine, doing her best to conceal the pain he had caused. When Vallerand spoke, his voice was even softer than before. "Where were you planning to go in the pirogue?"

"I have a cousin who lives in Beauvallet."

"Beauvallet?" Justin repeated, staring at her with contempt. "That's fifteen miles away! Haven't you ever heard of alligators? And river pirates? Don't you know what can happen to you in the swamp? What do you think you are?"

"Justin," Vallerand interrupted. "Enough."

His son quieted instantly.

"Traveling such a distance by yourself is an ambitious undertaking," Vallerand commented. "But perhaps you were not planning to go alone. Were you planning to meet with

28

someone on the way? A lover?"

"Yes," Lysette lied. Suddenly she was so tired and thirsty and distressed that silver sparks danced before her eyes. She had to get away from him. "That is exactly what I have planned, and you are interfering. I will not stay here any longer." Blindly she spun around and headed for the door, consumed with the desire to escape.

Vallerand caught her instantly, one long arm sliding around her front, the other grasping her nape. Lysette clenched her teeth and let out a dry sob, knowing that she had finally been defeated. "Damn you," she whispered. "Why won't you just let me go?"

His soft, deep voice tickled her ear. "Easy, I won't hurt you. Be still."

He glanced at the twins, who were watching the pair of them with fascination. "Leave, both of you."

"But why?" Justin protested hotly. "We were the ones who found her, and besides —"

"Now. And tell your *grand-mère* I wish her to join us in the library."

"He has my belongings!" Lysette said, throwing an accusing stare at Justin. "I want them back!"

"Justin," Vallerand said in a low voice.

The boy grinned, pulling the knotted handkerchief of coins out of his pocket and tossing it to a nearby chair. He slipped out the door before his father could reprimand him.

Left alone with Vallerand, Lysette twisted helplessly in his grasp. He contained her easily. "I told you to be still."

She went rigid as she felt him tug the hem of her shirt upward, exposing the tender flesh of her back. "What are you doing? Stop that! I will not be abused like this, you high-handed, arrogant —"

"Calm yourself." He stuffed the hem of the shirt into the back of her collar. "You have nothing to fear. I have no interest in your . . ." He paused and added sardonically, "Feminine charms. Besides, I usually prefer my victims to be somewhat cleaner than you before I molest them."

Lysette gasped and dug her nails into his hard forearm as she felt the touch of his hand on her back. The tiny hairs on the nape of her neck rose and prickled in response to the brush of his fingers. Deftly he located the tail end of the binding cloth that had been tucked underneath her right arm.

Realizing that no amount of resistance would stop him from doing as he wished, Lysette spared herself the effort of fighting him. "You are no gentleman," she muttered, flinching as he loosened the binding.

The comment did not deter him. "That is true." He unwound the coarse length of cloth that had flattened her breasts beneath the shirt.

Despite her distress over being stripped

half naked by a stranger, Lysette could not prevent a sigh of relief as the tight, itching binding was removed from her sore back. Cool air swept over her moist skin, making her shiver.

"Just as I thought," she heard him murmur.

Lysette knew exactly what he was seeing, the week-old bruises left from Gaspard's beating, the welts of insect bites, the mess of smarting scratches and scrapes. She had never been so humiliated, but somehow, as the silence lengthened, she stopped caring what he thought. She was too weary to stand on her own. Her chin lowered until her cheek rested against his shoulder. She couldn't help noticing his fragrance, the scent of clean male skin mingled with the hints of horses and tobacco. The utterly masculine smell was unexpectedly appealing. Her nose and throat opened, drawing in more, while she began to relax against the solid weight of his body.

A strange shiver went through her as his fingertips descended to her back, moving in a delicate trail over her spine. She wouldn't have expected such a large man to have such a light touch. It became hard to think, the entire scene covered in a thick fog that promised oblivion. She struggled to stay conscious, but she must have fainted for a few seconds, because she had no memory of him pulling her shirt back down over her back, and yet suddenly she was covered and he had turned her to face him.

"Who did it?" he asked.

She shook her head and spoke through dry, cracked lips. "It doesn't matter."

"Mademoiselle, you are in no condition to defy me. Don't waste my time, or yours. Just tell me what I want to know, and then you can rest."

Rest. The word made her entire being surge in longing. Clearly he was not going to let her go, and there was little point in resisting him. Later, she promised herself. Later she would consider what to do next and make a new plan. In the meantime, she had to regain the strength she had lost.

"My stepfather did it," she said.

"His name?"

Tilting her head back, she stared into his dark eyes. "First promise me that you won't send word to him."

A brief laugh caught in his throat. "I'm not going to bargain with you, *petite*."

"Then you can go to hell."

His teeth flashed in a grin. Clearly he was amused rather than annoyed by her defiance. "All right, I promise that I will not send word to him. Now tell me his name."

"Monsieur Gaspard Medart."

"Why did he beat you?"

"We have come from Natchez for my wed-

32

ding. I despise my fiancé, and I have refused to honor the betrothal agreement my step-father made."

Vallerand's brows raised slightly. Until a Creole girl was wedded, her father — or stepfather — was considered to be her master, every bit as much as her husband would be. To defy a parent's wishes, especially in the area of marriage, was unthinkable. "Most people would not censure a man for disciplining a rebellious daughter in such circumstances," he said.

"And you?" Lysette asked dully, already knowing the answer.

"I would never strike a woman," he said readily, surprising her. "No matter what the provocation."

"That . . ." Her voice seemed to stick in her throat. "That is fortunate for your wife, monsieur."

He reached out and pushed back a straggling lock of her hair with gentle fingers. "I am a widower, *petite*."

"Oh." Lysette blinked in surprise, wondering why the information caused a queer little pang in her midriff.

"Where is your stepfather staying?"

"At the home of Monsieur Sagesse." Her attention was caught by the sudden gleam that entered his eyes.

He was silent for several moments, before speaking in a soft, almost velvety voice. "Your betrothed is Etienne Sagesse?"

"*Oui.*"

"And your name?" he prompted.

"Lysette Kersaint," she whispered in defeat. "I suppose you are acquainted with the Sagesses, monsieur?"

"Oh, yes."

"You are friends?"

"No. There is bad blood between us."

Lysette considered the information. If Vallerand disliked the Sagesses, it would be somewhat easier to enlist his help.

"Max? *Qu'est-ce qu' il y a?*" An elderly silver-haired woman, beautifully dressed in lace-trimmed lavender muslin, entered the library. She frowned in consternation as she saw Lysette's bedraggled form.

"This is Mademoiselle Lysette Kersaint, Maman. A visitor from Natchez. Apparently she has become separated from her family. The boys encountered her outside and brought her to me. Have a room prepared, as she will be staying with us tonight." He gave Lysette an inscrutable gaze. "My mother, Irénée Vallerand," he murmured. "Go with her, *petite.*"

Although Irénée was obviously curious, she forbore comment and extended a hand of welcome to Lysette. New Orleanians were an innately hospitable people, and she was no exception. "*Pauvre petite.*" She clicked her tongue sympathetically. "Come, I will have a bath readied, and then you must eat and sleep."

"Madame," Lysette began in a wavering voice. "I must —"

"We will talk later," Irénée said, and moved forward to take her hand. "*Allons,* child."

"*Merci,* madame," Lysette murmured in agreement, and went willingly, more than eager to escape Maximilien Vallerand's presence. She intended to regain her strength as quickly as possible and leave the plantation at the first available opportunity.

Two hours later, Irénée approached her son with trepidation. Max stood at the window of the library with a drink in his hand.

"How is she?" he asked without turning.

"She has bathed, eaten a little, and now is resting. Noeline put a paste on the scrapes and insect bites." Irénée joined him at the window and contemplated the sleepy bayou. "I remember making the acquaintance of Lysette's mother, Jeanne, many years ago. Jeanne is one of the Magniers, a fine family that once lived in New Orleans but regrettably produced no sons to carry on the name. I remember Jeanne was an exceptionally beautiful woman — it is unfortunate that her daughter has not inherited her beauty."

Max smiled absently, recalling the girl's freckled face, defiant blue eyes, and disheveled red braid. Clearly Lysette Kersaint was not a conventional beauty. However, there was something about her that made him want her. Not casually, not superficially, but with a hunger that pervaded his entire being. She promised something unusual: an intensity of sensation, a fulfillment that might finally satisfy the longing that had tormented him for so long.

Beneath the desire, Max had been aware of the insistent pull of curiosity. He wanted to know her, to uncover the facets of a girl more outspoken and determined and desperate than anyone he had ever met. He was going to have her. God knew she would be wasted on Etienne Sagesse.

"Do you know who she is betrothed to, Maman?" he asked.

Irénée's fine dark brows pinched together in a frown. "*Oui,* she has told me about the arrangement with Etienne Sagesse."

"Yes, the man who brought dishonor on my wife, and on my name. I think it fitting that I repay Sagesse by taking his fiancée."

His mother stared at him as if he had become a stranger. "What do you mean, 'taking'?"

"And then," he mused, "a duel will be inevitable."

"No, I will not allow it!"

He cast her a mocking glance. "How do you plan to stop me?"

"You would ruin an innocent girl merely to

36

strike at Etienne Sagesse? Lysette Kersaint has done nothing to harm you. Would you have her on your conscience for the rest of your life?"

"I have no conscience," he reminded her dryly.

Irénée took a sharp breath. "Max, you must not do this."

"You would rather see her married to a man like Sagesse?"

"Yes, if the only alternative is to see her ruined by you and cast into the streets!"

As he saw the horror in her eyes and knew that she believed the worst of him, Max was bedeviled by the urge to prove her right. "She will not be cast into the streets," he said coldly. "Of course I will provide for her afterward. A small price, considering the opportunity she has afforded me."

"Her stepfather will certainly challenge you."

"It would not be the first duel I have fought."

"*Alors,* you intend to violate Lysette's innocence, establish her in a residence where she will be scorned by all decent society, and duel with an aging father trying to avenge the honor of his ruined daughter —"

"Stepfather. Who beats her, I might add."

"That doesn't justify *your* behavior! How can I have raised such a wicked man as you?"

Max's better nature — what little was left

of it — stirred uncomfortably at her words. However, the prospect of finally having revenge on the man who had ruined his life was too much to resist. He could not stop himself from seizing the opportunity any more than he could stop his own heart from beating.

"I warn you, Maman, don't interfere. I've waited years for this chance. And your sympathy is wasted on the girl. I guarantee that she'll be well compensated when it's over."

CHAPTER

2

The gown Lysette had carried with her was irreparably stained by her journey through the swamp. The morning after her arrival, Irénée provided a pale blue gown that fit well, although the high-collared, intricately tucked style was rather matronly for a young woman of her age. Still, Lysette was grateful for the older woman's kindness and generosity. It was a relief to wear clean garments and to be rid of the filth and stench of the bayou.

"You look much better, *ma chère*," Irénée said kindly.

Lysette murmured her thanks, wondering how such a gentle woman had raised a son like Maximilien Vallerand. He must have been an aberration — surely the rest of the family could not be like him.

"Madame Vallerand," she asked, "do you have other children?"

"*Oui,* I have two younger sons, Alexandre and Bernard, who will be returning soon from a journey to France." Irénée leaned nearer and added conspiratorially, "I have a cousin there with five pretty daughters, all unmarried. I encouraged them to go for an extended visit, hoping that Alexandre or Bernard would take an interest in one of the girls and return with a wife." She frowned. "However, either the girls are not as attractive as their mother claimed, or my stubborn sons are determined never to marry. They should return in two months."

Seeming to read Lysette's mind, Irénée added, "I can assure you, they are very different than their brother. But Maximilien was not always this way. It is only in the last few years that he has become so embittered. He has suffered much tragedy in the past."

Lysette repressed a disbelieving snort. Suffered? That splendidly healthy, self-assured male she had met the previous day did not appear to have suffered unduly. Now, after a good night's sleep, she was fully prepared to deal with him. Vallerand would not take advantage of her again. One thing was certain — no matter what she had to do, she would not be returned to Gaspard Medart's guardianship and then passed along to Etienne Sagesse.

Her mother had often told her that it was a woman's lot to suffer and endure whatever *le Bon Dieu* sent her way. And in the past Tante Delphine had said that even the worst of husbands was better than no husband at all. Well, that was fine for some girls, but not for her.

Lysette's heart thumped faster as they entered the parlor, a small but airy room decorated in pink, brown, and cream-flowered
brocade. A rich flemish finish covered the
woodwork of white oak. Spotless floor-to-
ceiling windows let in the hazy Louisiana
sunlight. The moss-green chairs and small
baroque sofas were grouped together to invite
intimate conversation. Seeing that the room
was empty, Lysette began to relax.

She heard Vallerand's voice from the doorway behind her.

"Mademoiselle, we have some things to
discuss —" he began, and broke off abruptly
as Lysette turned to face him.

He stared at her with an arrested expression. Lysette returned his gaze coolly, wondering what he seemed to find so fascinating.
Certainly her appearance had improved with
a bath and some much-needed sleep. She had
no illusions that he might find her beautiful,
as even the most vigorous brushing could not
tame her frizzy explosion of red curls, and
the past two days spent out-of-doors had
made her freckles proliferate to an alarming
degree. Her figure was slim but unspectacular, with small breasts and nonexistent hips.
Her features were pleasant, but her nose was
too wide and her lips unfashionably full.

As the silence lengthened, Lysette gave
Vallerand an insolent inspection of her own,
a comprehensive gaze that no lady should

ever give a gentleman. Vallerand was even more striking and virile than she had remembered . . . tanned and muscular and tall, his hair black as pitch, his eyes dark and audacious. He made the young men she had known in Natchez seem immature and callow. Wryly she wondered if Vallerand was a typical example of the New Orleans Creole. God help her if there were more like him roaming through the city.

"Yes, we do have much to discuss," Lysette said decisively. As Irénée seated herself on a brocade-covered settee, Lysette strode to a nearby chair, trying to look more relaxed than she felt. She sat and regarded Vallerand with a challenging gaze. "First, monsieur, I would like to know if you intend to send me to the Sagesse plantation."

Her directness did not seem to offend Vallerand. He leaned a shoulder against the doorframe in a casual posture, watching her intently. "Not if you don't wish it, mademoiselle."

"I do not."

"Why do you object to the match?" Vallerand asked idly. "Many young women would be pleased to marry a Sagesse."

"I object to everything about him. His character, his manners, his appearance, even his age."

"His age?" A frown crossed his face.

"He is in his mid-thirties." Lysette smiled

provokingly as she added, "Quite old."

Vallerand responded with an ironic glance, as it was obvious that he and Sagesse were contemporaries. "A man of thirty-five is hardly teetering on the edge of the grave," he said dryly. "I would suspect that he has a few good years left in him."

"Lysette, if you marry Sagesse, you would certainly be well provided for," Irénée broke in. The comment earned a warning glance from her son.

"That doesn't matter," Lysette said. "I would rather be poor than marry a man I despise. And I have made my objections clear to Monsieur Sagesse. What I don't understand is why he offered for me in the first place. My dowry is negligible, and although I come from a family of good blood, we are hardly aristocratic. And obviously I am no great beauty." She shrugged. "There are dozens of other women who would serve his purpose equally well."

"What of this cousin in Beauvallet?" Max asked. "What did you hope to accomplish by reaching him?"

"Her," Lysette corrected. "Marie Dufour, and her husband Claude." The Dufours were a prosperous farming family. She remembered Marie as a kind and compassionate woman who had eloped with Claude for the sake of love. "Marie and I were fond of each other as children," she said. "I had thought that the Dufours might support me in my refusal of my stepfather's wishes, and perhaps allow me to live with them."

Vallerand's face was a calm mask. "I could buy some time for you," he offered. "Two or three days, at least. You may write a letter to your cousin, explaining your dilemma, and stay here until she replies. If she wishes to help you, I will release you to the Dufours' guardianship before Monsieur Medart can lay a finger on you."

Lysette frowned thoughtfully. "It won't be long before my stepfather and the Sagesses realize that I am here. When they come for me, you won't be able to stop them from taking me."

"We can claim you have fallen ill after your journey through the swamp. The family physician will affirm that it is dangerous for you to be moved until your convalescence is complete."

"But the doctor will know I am not ill."

"He will say what I desire him to say."

Lysette considered the proposal, while Vallerand's keen gaze rested on her. "My mother's presence will ensure that no harm will come to your reputation," he said.

"Why do you want to help me?" she asked warily.

A subtle smile played at the corners of his lips. "Out of the goodness of my heart, of course."

Lysette let out a disbelieving laugh. "Forgive me if I don't believe you. What is the real reason? I suppose it would please you to thwart Monsieur Sagesse from having something he desires?"

"Yes," he said smoothly, "that is precisely the reason."

She met his shadowed gaze, perfectly aware that he was hiding something from her. "What is the cause of the bad blood between you and Sagesse?"

"Nothing that I would care to explain." When Lysette opened her mouth to question him further, he continued brusquely, "Will you write the letter or not, Miss Kersaint?"

"Yes, I will," she said slowly, despite the suspicion that coiled inside her. She did not want to trust Vallerand, but she had no choice. "Thank you, monsieur."

Satisfaction flickered in his dark eyes. "You are quite welcome."

Max accompanied Lysette to the library and seated her at his own desk, setting out pen holders, parchment, and ink. Standing behind her chair, he stared at the top of her head, where her brilliant hair had been pinned in a braided coil. A garish color, many would say, the tightly curled locks containing almost purple lights in the depths of red. He was fascinated by the volatile shade, by the profligate mass of curls that appeared too heavy for her slim neck to support.

The mere notions he'd had yesterday had kindled into white-hot resolution the moment he had seen her this morning. It had been years since he had wanted someone this badly. She was unconventionally, irresistibly beautiful, her allure having nothing to do with something as banal as classical proportions. Her features were strong, the lines of her cheekbones and jaw and throat drawn with decisive purity. And he had never seen anything as inviting as the generous scattering of freckles . . . he wanted to follow their paths all over her body, and touch his tongue to every one of them.

The fact that Lysette was too young for him did not matter nearly as much as it should have. Her self-possession was remarkable for a girl of her tender years. Clearly she was not afraid of him — she treated him as if they were equals, regardless of the years that separated them.

His pulse quickened as sexual images drifted through his mind, and he forced his attention to the task at hand. "Do you require assistance with the letter, Mademoiselle Kersaint?"

Her lush, deep-cornered mouth twitched with amusement. "I can write quite well, thank you."

Max had met many women, far more well bred and blue-blooded than she, who were virtually illiterate. A good portion of Creole society considered that too much education was bad for a woman. He half leaned, half sat against the desk, facing her. "You have been educated, then," he commented.

"Yes, thanks to my father. He hired a governess for my sister Jacqueline and me. We were taught to read and write, and to speak English as well as French. We studied history, geography, mathematics . . . even a volume or two of science. But after my father died, the governess was dismissed." She picked up an engraved silver pen holder, rolling it between her slender fingers. "There wasn't much more she could teach us, anyway. A woman's education is only allowed to go so far, much to my regret."

"What use would you have for more education?" She smiled and returned his provoking gaze without batting an eye. "Perhaps, monsieur, I have ambitions other than serving as a brood mare to some pompous aristocrat who is afraid of having a wife who is smarter than he is."

"You have a high estimation of your own intelligence, Mademoiselle Kersaint."

"Does that bother you?" Her voice was silky soft.

Max was completely fascinated by her, his mind thoroughly engaged, his blood stirring at the challenge she presented. Good Lord, how he wanted to bed her. "No, it doesn't."

She smiled and smoothed the sheet of parchment before her. "If you don't mind, monsieur, I would prefer a few minutes of privacy, while I exercise my inadequate feminine brain to compose a few coherent lines. Perhaps you would be so kind as to check my spelling afterward?"

It wasn't her spelling that he wished to examine. Max managed to produce a cool smile, when his entire body was urging him to flip up her skirts, pull her onto his lap, and ravish her for hours. "I take my leave with all confidence in your abilities," he said with an answering smile, and left her while he was still able.

Max had barely managed to conquer his raging lust by the time he returned to the salon. Irénée greeted him with obvious relief. "I knew that you would not take advantage of her, after all," she said warmly. "Thank heaven you have changed your mind."

He gave her a blank look. "I haven't changed my mind about anything."

Irénée's face fell. "But the letter you are allowing her to write to her cousin —"

"The letter will never be sent. If I'm going to compromise her, I don't want a damned cousin interfering."

She stared at him in surprised dismay. "How could you, Max? I would never have believed you could take advantage of a woman this way!"

48

"You believe me to be capable of quite worse, Maman," he said in a voice edged with sudden bitterness. "Don't you?"

She looked away from him, unable to reply, her face drawn with a helpless regret that filled him with fury.

The Medarts came to the plantation house far sooner than Max had anticipated. Apparently they and the Sagesses were visiting every residence on the bayou road in an effort to ferret out any information about the young woman that had supposedly become lost. When Max and Irénée confirmed Lysette's presence in their household, the Medarts were filled with obvious relief.

Max's already established contempt for Gaspard Medart doubled upon meeting him. Medart was short, muscular, and hard-faced, his eyes like chips of obsidian. The thought that this cold little bully had beaten Lysette filled Max with a hostility that he found difficult to conceal.

Medart was accompanied by a corpulent woman with hair that had been inexpertly darkened with coffee. A frantic look had congealed on her face. The *tante*, Max surmised, suspecting that she had offered little objection to Medart's abuse of his stepdaughter.

"Where is she?" Medart demanded, perspiring profusely. His gaze darted greedily around the room, as if he half suspected she were hiding behind a chair. "Where is Lysette? Bring her to me at once."

Max introduced his mother, and they all sat as the housekeeper, Noeline, brought in a tray of refreshments. It was the Creole tradition that nothing was ever done in a hurry. Visits were conducted at a lazy pace, and almost every conversation began with the ritual of explaining family histories and recounting long lines of ancestors. New Orleanians never trusted a stranger with whom they could not establish at least one common relative. In fact, they were all so familiar with their own pedigrees that at least ten generations of distant cousins and far-removed offspring could be examined meticulously until the desired link was finally established.

Gaspard Medart, however, was too impatient to adhere to tradition. "I want to see my stepdaughter at once," he demanded. "I have no time for idle chatter. Give her to me now."

Irénée gave Max a glance of amazement at the man's rudeness. Max turned an expressionless face to Medart. "Unfortunately, monsieur, I must impart some distressing news."

"She has run away again!" Medart exploded. "I knew it!"

"No, nothing like that. Do not be alarmed. It is only that she has succumbed to a touch of fever."

"Fever!" the *tante* exclaimed, clearly aware of the deadly plagues that occasionally swept the city.

"It seems to be a mild case," Max said reassuringly, "but of course I have summoned the family doctor to examine her. Until he arrives, it would be dangerous to disturb her. She is resting in a guest room upstairs."

"I insist on seeing her now," Medart said.

"Certainly." Max began to rise, then questioned, "I assume you have had the fever before?"

"*Non.*"

"You had better not visit her, then. If your exposure results in fever, it could be life-threatening to a man of your age."

"Perhaps," the *tante* interceded hastily, "we should return tomorrow after the doctor has seen her, Gaspard."

Irénée lent her persuasive voice. "I assure you, Monsieur Medart, we will take excellent care of her."

"But the imposition . . ." Delphine said, her large frame jiggling as she made a helpless gesture.

"It is not an imposition," Irénée replied firmly. "Not at all. All that matters is Lysette's welfare."

"I have no proof that she is even here!" Medart cried.

"She is here," Max assured him.

Medart scowled. "I am aware of your reputation, monsieur. And I know that you are the enemy of Lysette's betrothed. If you are hatching some kind of plot, I will make you pay!"

Irénée leaned forward and said with conviction, "I promise you, Monsieur Medart, that your stepdaughter will be safe with us. No harm will come to her." She glanced at Max and added with a steely edge to her tone, "I will make certain of that."

After further persuasion, the Medarts left, seeming to realize that they had no other choice. Max let out a hearty sigh of relief at the sound of their carriage wheels on the drive outside. "Despicable people," he muttered.

Irénée pursed her lips in displeasure. "They know that we are lying, Max."

He shrugged. "They can't do anything about it."

"I would have given Lysette over to them gladly if it weren't for the bruises on her back. I have no wish to abandon her to more of Monsieur Medart's discipline."

"Now the rumors will begin," Max muttered with dark satisfaction. "I would give a fortune to see Sagesse's face when Medart tells him that I have her."

"Lysette would be safer with Etienne than she is with you," Irénée accused. "At least *he* has marriage in mind for her!"

"She'll find a liaison with me far more

agreeable than marriage to him."

"What a bitter, cruel man you have become," Irénée said in wonder. "And how disappointed your father would be to see it."

Stung, Max sent her a sullen glare. "If he had gone through what I have, he would probably react the same way."

"That shows how little you knew him," Irénée shot back, and left the room with her spine stiff.

Although Irénée was disgusted with her eldest son, she had not yet given up on the possibility of his redemption. While she had breakfast in her room, she discussed the situation with the housekeeper, Noeline. A slim, attractive woman who possessed innate practicality and a penchant for speaking her mind, Noeline had been the housekeeper at the plantation for the past fifteen years. As Irénée had expected, no detail of their houseguest, or Max's intentions toward her, had escaped Noeline's observant gaze.

"I can't believe that he truly means to ruin her," Irénée said, lifting the china cup to her lips. "She is a decent young woman, and she hardly deserves to be caught in the middle of my son's feud with Etienne Sagesse."

Noeline's coffee-colored features were expressionless, but a rueful gleam entered her eyes. "Monsieur Vallerand wants revenge against Sagesse too much to think about anyone else."

"I suppose so," Irénée said reluctantly. "But Noeline, I can't believe that Max would be so wicked as to deliberately seduce an innocent girl."

"He's not wicked," Noeline replied, moving to the dressing table and straightening the tiny flasks and brushes into neat rows. "He's just a man, madame. And you can't keep a man from a pretty girl like that, any more than you could tie up a hound with a string of sausages."

"Do you think Lysette is pretty?" Irénée frowned thoughtfully. "I must admit, at first I didn't think so. But it seems that the longer I know her, the more attractive she becomes."

"She's got *something* Monsieur likes," Noeline observed dryly. "He sizzles like a pan of cracklings every time she comes in the room."

"Noeline," Irénée chided, laughing into her teacup.

The housekeeper smiled as well. "It's true, madame," she insisted. "And when he looks at her, he's got more on his mind than revenge. He just doesn't want to admit it."

When Lysette was assured that her stepfather had left the estate, she went to find Vallerand. He had just finished a cigar and a drink on the front porch, a wisp of smoke rising lazily from a crystal dish. His attention was focused on a magnificent thoroughbred that a stableboy was bringing from the stables. It appeared that Vallerand was going to ride to town.

Hearing Lysette's light footstep on the porch, Vallerand turned toward her. His gaze was heavy-lidded, his mouth holding an almost surly curve that did something very odd to her insides. He made her want to shock him, catch him off guard. . . . She wondered crazily what he might do if she simply walked over and kissed his hard, tempting mouth, and tugged the crisp white cravat from his neck. No man had ever affected her this way before. She wanted to feel the shaven scrape of his cheeks, and gently rub her lips over his, and feel his hot breath against her skin. He seemed to take himself a bit too seriously, as if he badly needed something — or someone — to tease and disarm him. If she were his wife, she would do something about that.

The startling thought made her wonder how long he had been a widower, and how his wife had died. Clearly it was a forbidden subject in the Vallerand household. Even the talkative Irénée was disinclined to respond to Lysette's questions on the subject.

Lysette offered Vallerand a tentative smile. "I suppose my stepfather was very angry when you would not let him see me."

"Very."

"Good." She came to stand near him, and

his height forced her to tilt her head back. Good lord, the man was huge. "Did he believe you when you told him that I was ill?"

"No, he didn't."

"And he left anyway?" She chewed on her lower lip and frowned. "I would have expected him to challenge you."

"Your stepfather is trying to avoid a scandal," Vallerand replied. "He won't challenge me. And as long as you are in my house, no one can forcibly remove you."

"Not even the local authorities?"

He shook his head. "I am closely acquainted with Governor Claiborne."

She laughed briefly. "Clearly I am fortunate to have made friends with such an influential man." Pulling the letter to Marie from her sleeve, Lysette handed the wax-sealed square to him. "My letter. Please have it delivered as soon as possible. It's important."

"I am aware of the letter's importance, mademoiselle."

Lysette regarded him quizzically, wondering why she seemed to make him uncomfortable. Perhaps he did not like her straightforward manner. She supposed he must be accustomed to the refined ladies of New Orleans, who most likely did not rampage through swamps and defy their families. "Monsieur Vallerand," she said gently, "I apologize for the inconvenience I have caused you. In return for your hospitality, I promise to be gone as soon as possible. If my cousin Marie will not take me, I will join the Ursuline convent. You will not have to endure me much longer."

He smiled suddenly, seeming entertained by the notion. "A nun with red witch-curls." An odd, almost caressing note had entered his voice.

Lysette smiled self-consciously, raising a hand to her chaotic pinned-up hair. "No doubt they would insist on shaving off this appalling mess."

"No," he said swiftly. "It's beautiful."

Lysette almost took offense, thinking that he was mocking her. But as he continued to stare at her with that steady dark gaze, she realized that he was sincere. And that led to another, more startling realization . . . that Maximilien Vallerand was every bit as attracted to her as she was to him.

Nothing could or would come of it, of course. However, she found it interesting, all the same. A touch of heat rose in her face, and she averted her gaze hastily. "Good evening, monsieur," she muttered, and strode away so quickly that her skirts nearly tangled around her ankles.

"Back again this evening?" Mariame purred, opening the door wider and welcoming Max into her white one-story house, located in the quadroon quarter of the Vieux

Carré, near Rampart. Her thick lashes lowered as she concentrated on loosening Max's
starched necktie. "I thought I had satisfied
all your desires last night."

Eight years ago Mariame's first protector
had broken off their arrangement callously,
leaving her and their illegitimate child with
no money or home. In despair, she had been
packing her belongings to move back in with
her mother. When Max heard of her lover's
desertion, he did not hesitate to come to her.
She was one of the most beautiful women in
New Orleans, and he had long admired her.

Mariame had been openly astonished by
his offer to become her protector. "Most men
want virgins," she had said. In New Orleans,
there were countless beautiful young girls,
most of them of mixed blood, who were
trained to become mistresses of the wealthy
Creole planters and businessmen who could
afford to keep them. *Placées,* the highly
sought-after girls were called, and most of
them were kept in great luxury.

Max had laughed at her comment. "I don't
give a damn about virginity," he had told her.
"I want the companionship of a beautiful, intelligent woman. Name your terms, Mariame
— I want you too badly to quibble over details."

His admiration had soothed Mariame's
grief and wounded pride immeasurably. She
had heard the ugly rumors about Vallerand,

and had long wondered about their truth. However, as she had seen the loneliness in Max's dark eyes and the gentleness in his manner, she had decided to trust him.

In the eight years since then, Mariame had never regretted her choice. Max was a tender lover, a generous provider, and a caring friend. Although he had taken care never to sire any children by her, he had paid for her son to be educated in Paris. The jewels and clothes he had given her through the years would be enough to keep her in luxury for the rest of her life, and she had no doubt that when he ended their relationship, he would give her an extravagant settlement.

Because Max had been kind to Mariame, she had resolved never to stand in the way of anything he wanted. When he decided to break things off between them, she would let him go without protest. She had no wish to chain him to her, and she had wisely avoided falling in love with him.

Mariame's face lit with a smile as she wrapped her arms around Max's shoulders. Lean-bodied and tall, she found it an easy task to rise on her toes and brush her lips against his. However, tonight Max did not respond as she had expected. He was unusually preoccupied, troubled about something.

"I didn't come here for that," Max said, disentangling himself from her grasp.

Mariame went to pour him a drink. "Then

what are you here for, Max?"

"I don't know." He walked around the room restlessly.

"Sit, please, *ma cher*. It makes me nervous to see you pace like a hungry tiger."

Max complied, sitting on the settee with a brooding, unfocused stare.

Mariame settled comfortably on the sofa beside him, her long, sleek legs dangling carelessly over one of his thighs. She handed him a snifter of brandy. "Perhaps this will help to relax you."

He took the glass and drank deeply, barely noticing the fine vintage.

Mariame's fingers walked up his thigh on a path they had often frequented before. "Are you sure you do not want to —"

"No," he muttered, brushing her hand away.

Mariame shrugged. *"D'accord."* A sly, interested smile touched her lips. *"Alors,* you might tell me more about this woman staying at the house."

Max gave her a sardonic glance, realizing that the rumors had spread even more quickly than he had expected. "The twins encountered Mademoiselle Kersaint as she was trying to flee from an undesired marriage."

"Ah." Mariame's sleek brows lifted expressively. "Not many women would dare to do such a thing. Who is her intended, *bien-aimée?*"

"Etienne Sagesse."

Her playful fingers stilled on the edge of his shoulder. "Sagesse . . . *bon Dieu.* How odd that the girl should come to you, of all people, for refuge. What are you going to do?"

"I'm going to take advantage of the situation, naturally."

Her smooth forehead creased with concern. "Be careful, Max. I know that you would stop at nothing to repay Sagesse for what he did all those years ago. But you would come to regret it if you resorted to abusing an innocent in your care." A fond smile touched her lips. "You do have a conscience, *cher,* though you try to pretend otherwise."

A reluctant grin crossed Max's face. "I'm glad you think so." He leaned his head back and stared at the cypress-paneled ceiling above. "Mariame," he said, abruptly changing the subject, "you know that I would never end our relationship without providing for you."

"I have never feared that you would leave me destitute," Mariame replied calmly. Was this, perhaps, the first sign that his interest in her was waning? "Someday," she continued, "I would like to run my own boardinghouse. I would be quite successful at it."

"Yes, you would."

"Should I begin to make plans for it?"

"Someday. If that's what you want." He caressed her cheek lightly. "But not yet."

Thursday was the Vallerands' usual at-home day, when Irénée's friends and acquaintances came to visit and chat over a cup of strong chicory-laced coffee. Unfortunately Irénée had been forced to turn away visitors because of Lysette's presence.

"I am sorry to disrupt your usual habits," Lysette said.

Irénée shushed her cheerfully. "*Non, non,* we will have coffee together, just the two of us. Right now I find your company far more diverting than that of my friends, who bring the same gossip to chew over week after week. You must tell me all about your mother, and about your friends in Natchez, and about your beaux."

"Actually, madame, I have led a very secluded life. My sister and I were not allowed to have beaux. In fact, we seldom associated with even our male cousins or relatives."

Irénée nodded in understanding. "By standards nowadays, that is an old-fashioned upbringing. But it was that way with me. I never read a newspaper until after I was married. I knew nothing of the outside world. It was frightening when the time came to leave the cocoon of my family and assume my place as Victor Vallerand's wife." Irénée smiled, her eyes soft with amusement as she remembered the girl she had once been. "My *tante* Marie and my mother accompanied me to my marriage bed and left me there alone to wait for my husband. Oh, how I begged them to take me back home! I did not want to be a wife at all, much less the wife of a Vallerand. Victor was a big bear of a man, and very intimidating. I was terrified of what he would require of me."

Intrigued, Lysette set down her cup. "Evidently it turned out well," she remarked.

Irénée chuckled. "Yes, Victor proved to be a kind husband. I soon fell deeply in love with him. The Vallerand men are deceptive, you see. Outwardly they are quite masterful and arrogant. However, when managed by the right woman, a Vallerand will go to any lengths to please her." Picking up an engraved silver spoon, Irénée stirred more sugar into her cup. "There," she said with satisfaction. "I like my coffee black as the devil and sweet as sin."

"Madame," Lysette asked casually, sipping her own coffee, "what was your son's wife like? In your opinion, did *she* manage him properly?"

The question made Irénée visibly tense. She hesitated a long time before replying. "Corinne was the most beautiful and spoiled girl I have ever encountered . . . much too concerned about herself to be able to love anyone else. She did not manage Max well at all. And the pity is, it would have taken very little for her to make him happy."

"It was not a good marriage, then."

"No," Irénée said softly. "I don't believe anyone would say it was."

To Lysette's disappointment, she would reveal nothing further about Vallerand's mysterious late wife.

The entire Vallerand household was disrupted as Justin tried to sneak in the house past midnight, bloodied and battered from a brawl. Max cornered him immediately, dragging him into the kitchen and giving him a scalding lecture. Lysette could hear the clash from her room on the second floor. Overwhelmingly curious, she crept to the top of the stairs and strained to hear their argument.

"You cannot treat me as if I were a child! I'm a man now!"

"So you claim," came Vallerand's biting reply. "But a man does not bully others into fighting merely for his own entertainment."

"It's not for entertainment," Justin said hotly.

"Then why do you fight?"

"To prove something!"

"That you're quick with your fists? That won't take you far, Justin. Soon you'll reach the age when fistfights turn to swordplay, and then you'll have a man's blood on your hands."

"Then I'll be like you, won't I?"

Startled by the words, Lysette sat on the shadowy top step and listened intently.

"No matter how bad I am, I couldn't possibly be worse than you," the boy accused. "I know all about you, Papa. And I know about your plans for Sagesse and Mademoiselle Kersaint."

A long, nerve-wracking pause followed. Finally Vallerand growled, "I have reasons that you know nothing about."

"Don't I?" Justin taunted.

"It seems you've heard the rumors."

"I have heard the truth!"

"No one knows the truth," Vallerand said flatly.

The boy spat out a hoarse word and ran from the room. Lysette leapt from the stairs and fled back to her bed, scurrying to avoid being caught eavesdropping. When she was safely beneath the covers, she stared blindly into the shadows, wondering if she had heard the boy correctly. What was the word he had hurled at his father? It had sounded like *murderer*.

But that couldn't be right, she thought, deeply troubled, and her fists curled tightly against the covers.

CHAPTER

3

Max was gone all the next day, attending to business in town. In response to Lysette's questions, Irénée replied that he was meeting with Governor Claiborne.

"How did Monsieur Vallerand become acquainted with the governor?" Lysette asked, fascinated.

Irénée shrugged. "I am not entirely certain, as Max rarely discusses his political activities with me. However, I do know that when Claiborne first took office, he asked my son to help him negotiate with the Creoles and shape his positions to make them acceptable. Like most Americans, the governor does not always understand our way of doing things. And because Max is owed many favors by Creoles *and* Americans, he is often able to persuade them all to agree to Claiborne's policies. Max also helps to calm unrest in the city when Claiborne has made a misstep." She clicked her tongue as she added disapprovingly, "These Americans — such a troublesome people."

Like most Creoles, Irénée considered

Americans to be barbarians, with few exceptions. Rough and unrefined, Americans were preoccupied with money, fond of drinking to excess, and impatient with the Creoles' leisurely way of doing things.

Only Americans would be tasteless enough to replace the Creoles' quadrille and cotillion with the reel and jig. Only the hypocritical Americans would criticize the Creole habit of relaxing on Sunday instead of sitting in stiff-backed pews from morning till night.

Later in the morning, Lysette explored the plantation at her leisure, shielding her complexion with a parasol to prevent a detonation of more unwanted freckles. However, her usual energy was sapped by the heat, and she soon became aware of a nagging pain in her temples. Retreating to the house, she turned her attention to the light needlework Irénée had provided. Soon the blazing summer heat seemed to invade even the most shadowy parts of the house. Perspiration glued her garments to her skin, and Lysette pulled at her clothes irritably

When Irénée retired to take a midday nap, declaring herself fatigued from the heat, Lysette did the same. She trudged into her own room, stripped down to her undergarments, and stretched out on the cool white sheets. A housemaid unrolled the *baire,* a gossamer net that kept mosquitoes away from the bed. Staring up at the eight-foot-high canopy of the bed, Lysette waited for sleep to overtake her. Although it had been three days since her journey along the bayou, she had still not fully recovered from it. She was exhausted, and she ached down to her very bones.

Quietly Justin slipped into the library, his gaze darting from one end of the room to the other. The library was stuffy in the afternoon heat. Books lined up in endless rows seemed to look down from their shelves like sentinels.

The bulk of Max's staunch mahogany desk, with all its mysterious drawers and cubbyholes, stood between the draped windows. The sight of it sent a shiver down Justin's spine. How often he had seen his father sitting at that desk, his head bent over documents and books. The drawers were filed with keys, receipts, papers, and strongboxes — and, Justin hoped, the object he was looking for. Swiftly he moved to the desk and searched it, his fingers peeling through the contents of each drawer.

Justin used the hairpin purloined from Irénée's room to unlock a small document box. It opened with a protesting click, and he threw a wary glance over his shoulder before looking inside. More receipts, and a letter. An unopened letter. Justin's eyes glittered with triumph. Carefully he tucked it inside his shirt, closed the box, and put it back where he found it. "This," he muttered to himself, "will square my account with you, *mon père.*"

Lysette slept well past the supper hour, and Irénée saw to it that she was not interrupted. When she awoke, the room was dark and the coolness of evening had settled. Sluggishly Lysette dressed in a light yellow gown and went downstairs.

"Ah, you have finally awakened," came Irénée's buoyant voice. "I thought it better to let you sleep as long as you wished. You must be hungry now, hmm?" The older woman took Lysette's arm and squeezed it affectionately. "The twins and I have already eaten. Max arrived just a moment ago and is having supper. You may join him in the *salle à manger.*"

The thought of food made Lysette nauseous. *"Non, merci,"* she managed. "I am not hungry."

"But you must have something." Irénée propelled her toward the dining room. "We have delicious gumbo, and pompano stuffed with crab, and hot rice cakes —"

"Oh, I can't," Lysette said, her throat clenching at the thought of the rich food.

"You must try. You are too thin, my dear."

As they went into the dining room, Lysette could see Max's reflection in the gold-framed mirror over the marble fireplace. He was seated at the table, the lamplight gleaming on his raven hair.

"Good evening, mademoiselle." With the innate courtesy of a Creole gentleman, he stood and assisted her into a chair. "Maman tells me that you have slept for a long time." He gave her an assessing glance. "Are you feeling well?"

"Yes, quite well. Just not particularly hungry."

Irénée clucked her tongue. "See that she eats something, Maximilien. I will be in the next room with my embroidery."

Lysette smiled after the older woman as she left. "Your mother is very strong-willed, monsieur."

"There is no disputing that," he agreed wryly.

A housemaid came to set a supper plate before Lysette. Staring at the steaming fish arranged on fried rice cakes, she felt bile rise in her throat. She reached for a glass of water and took a small sip, hoping it would calm her unruly stomach.

"I've heard that you met with your friend Mr. Claiborne today," she remarked.

"Yes." Max's white teeth bit into a piece of golden-crusted bread.

"What did you discuss? Or would it be too complicated for a mere female to understand?"

Max grinned briefly at her gibe.

"Claiborne's administration is under siege. He is trying to gather all the information he can before his enemies destroy him."

"Who are his enemies? The Creoles?"

Max shook his head. "No, not Creoles. Refugees from France and Santo Domingo, and a small but very noisy handful of Americans. Including Aaron Burr, who is in Natchez at this very moment."

"The former vice president of the United States?"

"Yes. There are rumors that Burr is on a reconnaissance mission to enlist men in a plot to take possession of the Orleans territory."

"That must make the governor quite agitated."

Max leaned back in his chair and regarded her with a lingering smile. "Justifiably so. Claiborne is young and inexperienced. His political adversaries would like to discredit him and separate the territory from the Union."

"Are you one of those who wish Louisiana to attain statehood?"

"I'm counting on it," he replied. "When the Americans took over the territory two years ago, I pledged my loyalty to Claiborne. Unfortunately, the Americans have not kept their promise to admit Louisiana into the Union."

"But why?"

"They claim that our population is not ready for citizenship."

"I don't see why . . ." Lysette began, and broke off as a wave of dizziness swept over her. She shut her eyes, and when she opened them, Max was staring at her closely.

"You're very pale," he murmured. "Do you feel ill?"

She shook her head. "I . . . I'm rather tired, monsieur." Clumsily she pushed back from the table. "If you will excuse me, I will go to my room."

"Of course." He helped her up carefully, his large hand cupping her elbow. "I am sorry to be deprived of such a charming supper companion. For a mere female, you manage to keep up with the conversation quite well."

A brief laugh escaped her, and she smiled into his teasing dark eyes. "I will repay you for that tomorrow, when I am feeling better."

He held her gaze for a moment, and his hand slid reluctantly from her arm. "Have a good rest," he murmured, and remained standing while she left the room.

Lysette's legs felt leaden as she climbed the stairs. As she entered her room, she put her hand to her face, knowing something was not right. Her skin was covered in cold sweat. More perspiration trickled between her breasts and beneath her bodice, and she longed to strip off her confining clothes.

There was a white square of paper on her bed, having been placed carefully against the pillow. Frowning curiously, Lysette picked it up. Her heart stopped beating as she saw what it was.

"The letter," she whispered, suddenly finding it hard to breathe. The envelope trembled in her hands. It was her letter to Marie, unopened, undelivered. Vallerand had assured her that it had been sent. Why had he lied? And what was his purpose in keeping it? Oh, God, she had known she couldn't trust him!

She decided to confront him at once. Her head throbbed with sudden vicious pain, and her back ached from the top of her spine to her hips. White with outrage, she gripped the balustrade in her slippery hand and began the long descent. Halfway down the steps, she saw Vallerand walking out of the dining room.

"Monsieur," she said, her tongue feeling thick in her mouth. "You have something to explain to me."

He came to the bottom of the stairs. "Explain what, mademoiselle?"

She held up the letter. "Why did you lie to me? My letter to Marie . . . you kept it! You never intended to send it." She shook her head impatiently to dispel the ringing in her ears. "I don't understand." She tried to back away as he began to ascend the stairs. She couldn't think above the annoying jangling in her head. "St-stay away from me!"

Vallerand's face was inhumanly calm. "How did you get it?"

"That doesn't matter. Tell me *why. Now,* damn you! Tell me —" The letter dropped from her nerveless hand, fluttering to the steps. "I am leaving. I would rather be with Sagesse than endure another minute with you."

"You're staying," he said flatly. "I have plans for you."

"Damn you," Lysette whispered, her eyes prickling with humiliating tears. "What do you want from me?" She raised her hands to her head in an effort to stop the pounding inside. If only it would stop. If only she could calm herself enough to think.

Suddenly Vallerand's face changed. "Lysette . . ." He reached out to steady her swaying form, his hands closing around her waist.

Wildly she pushed at him. "Don't touch me!"

His hard arm slid around her back. "Let me help you upstairs."

"No —"

Even as she fought to be free, she felt herself slump against him. Her head fell weakly against his shoulder while her arms hung uselessly at her sides.

"Max?" questioned Irénée, who had come out of the salon when she heard the commotion. Noeline was close behind. "Is something wrong? *Mon Dieu,* what has happened?"

Vallerand didn't spare her a glance. "Send for the doctor," he said tersely, and picked Lysette up, hooking his arms underneath her knees and back. He carried her as if she weighed nothing, ignoring her whimpers of protest. "I can walk," she sobbed, prying at his hands. "Let me down —"

"Hush," he said softly. "Don't struggle."

The trip to her room took only a few seconds, but to Lysette it seemed to last forever. Her cheek rested on his shoulder, while her tears dampened the crisp linen of his shirt. She was hot and nauseous, and wretchedly dizzy. The only solid thing in the world was his hard chest. Somehow, in her misery, she forgot how much she despised him, and was grateful for the steady support of his arms.

For a moment she felt better, but as Vallerand lay her on the bed, the room whirled sickeningly around her. She was falling into suffocating darkness. Blindly she reached out in an effort to save herself. A gentle hand smoothed the hair back from her burning forehead. "Help me," she whispered.

"It's all right, *petite.*" His voice was calm and soothing. "I'll take care of you. No, don't cry. Hold on to me."

Fitfully Lysette thrashed to escape the scorching cloud that had descended on her. She tried to explain something to him, and

75

he seemed to understand her frantic babble. "Yes, I know," he murmured. "Be still, *petite*."

Noeline, who had followed them into the room, looked over Max's shoulder and shook her head grimly. "Yellow fever," she said. "It's bad when it comes on this quick. I've seen some walk around healthy one day and drop dead the next." She sent a pitying glance at the suffering figure on the bed, as if a quick demise were a certainty.

Max threw the housekeeper a thunderous scowl, but he was careful to keep his voice even. "Bring a pitcher of cold water, and some of that powder — what was it we gave the twins when they had it?"

"Calomel and jalap, monsieur."

"Be quick about it," he growled, and Noeline left immediately.

Max looked down at Lysette, who was muttering incoherently. Tenderly he disentangled her hands from his shirt and gripped her hot fingers in his.

"Oh, hell," he muttered, his entire being seized with a dread he hadn't felt in years, not since the twins had succumbed to the potentially deadly fever. He smoothed her hair again, feeling how wet it was at the roots, and a violent curse escaped him.

Irénée stood behind him. "Her death would certainly foil your plans, *mon fils*," she said quietly.

76

He continued to stare at Lysette. "She's not going to die."

"The illness has come on too quickly and with too much force," she murmured. "She is already out of her head with fever."

"Don't speak of it around her again," he said curtly. "She is going to be well. I won't allow otherwise."

"But Max, she cannot understand —"

"She can hear what's being said." He stood and glared at her. "Remove her clothes and bathe her with a cool cloth. When the doctor arrives, tell him that he is not to do anything without my permission. I don't want her bled."

Irénée nodded, remembering how they had nearly lost Justin during his bout with the fever, when he had been bled too copiously.

Irénée and Noeline took turns sitting with Lysette the first forty-eight hours. Irénée had forgotten the work and patience it required to nurse a yellow fever patient. Her back ached from hours of leaning over the bed and sponging Lysette with cold water. The violent bouts of vomiting, the delirious raving and nightmares, the pungent smell of the vinegar baths they gave her — all of it was repellent and exhausting.

Max frequently asked about the girl's condition, but propriety barred him from entering the room. Although nothing was discussed or admitted, Max suspected Justin's involvement with the letter, knowing his son's penchant for stirring up trouble. The boy slunk around the house, avoiding his father and brother.

At such times, when the adults were otherwise occupied, the twins usually took the opportunity to run wild, dodge their lessons with the tutor, and sneak off to see friends or cause mischief in the city. Now, however, they were unusually quiet. A fog of gloom seemed to have descended on the house, the silence interrupted only by Lysette's incoherent cries during the worst periods of delirium.

This time, when Lysette's family returned to the Vallerand house, they departed with no doubt that she was indeed extremely ill. Delphine was allowed to visit the sickroom, but the girl did not recognize her. Gaspard was subdued as they left, for it was clear that Lysette's chances of survival were slight.

Succumbing to a fit of melancholy, Justin grumbled about the nuisance it was to have an ailing houseguest. "I wish it would end one way or the other," he said dully, as he and Philippe sat on the stairs. "I can't stand everyone having to walk on tiptoe, and the noises she makes, and the whole house stinking of vinegar."

"It won't last much longer," Philippe commented. "I heard *Grand-mère* say she will not live another day."

They froze as they heard a weak cry from upstairs. Suddenly their father emerged from the library, brushing by them without a word. He went up the stairs two at a time. The twins glanced at each other in surprise.

"Do you think he cares for her?" Philippe asked.

Justin's young face hardened in contempt. "He's only concerned that she'll die before she is of any use to him."

"What do you mean?" Suspecting that his brother was hiding something from him, Philippe caught him by the sleeve. "Justin, what do you know that I don't?"

Justin took his arm free impatiently. "I won't tell you. You'd only try to defend him."

Irénée tried in vain to quiet the girl who twisted and turned in the throes of violent delirium. *"Pauvre petite,"* Irénée exclaimed under her breath. Nothing would bring tranquillity. The girl would neither drink nor rest, and no medicine would stay down long enough to do any good. Wearily Irénée slumped in the chair by the bed, watching Lysette's restless twitching.

"Don't . . . don't let him . . . oh, please, please . . ." The thin voice rose and fell monotonously.

Slowly Irénée began to reach for the sponge and basin, hoping to cool the fever with more water. She fell back in surprise as her son appeared in the darkened room.

"Max?" she exclaimed. "What are you doing? It's not proper for you to be here. She's not dressed."

"I don't give a damn."

He swatted aside the filmy folds of the *baire* and sat on the edge of the bed. His dark head bent over the girl's writhing form.

"Max, this is indecent," Irénée protested. "You must leave."

Ignoring her, Max pulled away the knotted mass of sheets from Lysette's sweating body. Her damp chemise was transparent as it clung to her skin, doing nothing to conceal her nakedness. Max's face was taut and harshly drawn as he pushed back Lysette's matted hair and lifted her into his arms. All the force of his will was focused on the shivering figure folded against his chest. "Shhh," he whispered against Lysette's temple, cupping her head in his hand. "Rest against me. Yes. Hush, *petite*. You're exhausting yourself."

The girl clung to him and muttered incoherently.

Shifting her higher against him, Max reached for the wet sponge. He drew it over her face and chest, squeezing until the cool water ran in rivulets over her skin and soaked his own clothes. "Lysette, be still. Let me take care of you. Sleep. You're safe, *ma chère*."

80

After a while the stroking and the quiet words soothed the girl, and she went limp against him. He took the cup from the bedside and pressed it to her lips. She choked and tried to resist, but he coaxed and urged and insisted until she swallowed some of the medicine.

Gently Max eased her back to the mattress and covered her with the sheet. He glanced at his mother's astonished face. "Tell Noeline to bring fresh linens," he said. "She can help me change the bed."

Irénée finally found her voice. "Thank you for your help, Max. I will see to her now."

Max picked up a comb from the night table and began to work on the mass of snarls in Lysette's hair. "You are exhausted, Maman. Go get some rest. I'll take care of her."

Irénée did not know how to reply to such an outrageous statement. "*What?* What a ridiculous suggestion. Completely out of the bounds of propriety. Besides, men don't know anything about nursing. It is a woman's concern. There are duties required —"

"A woman's body is hardly a mystery to me. As for nursing the fever, I took care of the twins when they had it. Remember?"

That silenced Irénée for a few seconds. "Indeed, I had forgotten," she admitted. "You were very good with the twins when they were ill. But they were your sons, and this an innocent girl. . . ."

"Do you think I'm going to ravish her?" Max asked with a twisted smile. "Even I am not that degenerate, Maman."

"Mon fils," she asked suspiciously, "why do you wish to take this upon yourself?"

"Why shouldn't I? I have a vested interest in her welfare. Now go and rest. I'm capable of looking after her for a few hours."

She stood up reluctantly. "I will tell Noeline to take your place."

However, Max did not allow Noeline or anyone else to replace him. From that moment on, he spent every minute by Lysette's bed, his shirtsleeves rolled above his elbows as he labored to break the girl's raging fever. He was inexhaustible and astonishingly patient.

Irénée had never heard of even a husband doing as much for a wife. It was all too shocking. She was dismayed, but unable to think of a way to intercede. She had no control over Max. Perhaps if his brothers had been home they would have volunteered to coerce him from the sickroom, but day after day went by without their arrival — and Max remained in the girl's bedchamber as if it were his right.

A wolf prowled through Lysette's dreams, stalking until she ran and stumbled to the ground. He loomed closer, his teeth gleaming as he crouched over her prone body, and suddenly he was ripping her to pieces. She screamed as she felt herself being savaged and torn apart. Suddenly the wolf was gone, banished by the sound of a low voice. "I'm here . . . it's all right. Shhh . . . I'm here. I'm here."

She was surrounded by sweltering heat that scorched her skin and blistered her lungs. Crying out in agony, she fought to escape it. She felt a cool hand stroke her forehead. Restlessly she sought more. "Please," she gasped, and groaned with relief as the life-giving caress returned, coolness moving over her body, easing the unbearable fire.

The wolf eyes were watching again, glowing devilishly in the darkness. She whirled away in panic and came up against a man's hard chest and taut arms. "Please help me —"

"You've been promised to me," she heard the voice of Etienne Sagesse, and she looked up at his face in horror. Desire flickered bright in his heavy-lidded eyes, and his lips shone with moisture. She twisted away from him and came face-to-face with her step-father.

Gaspard's face was blotched with rage. "You will marry him!" He struck her and raised his hand again.

"Maman," she cried, seeing her mother nearby, but Jeanne backed away, shaking her head.

"Do what your *beau-père* says. You must obey him."

"I can't. . . ."

The hard rim of a cup pressed against her lips, and she recoiled from a bitter taste. A steely arm behind her shoulders would not let her retreat.

"No," she choked, her head falling back against an unyielding shoulder.

"Don't fight me, *petite*. Drink it all. Good girl . . . just a little more." She opened her mouth with a gasp, obeying the gentle prompting.

She saw the dark shape of a man moving through a thick mist. He would help her . . . he must. Frantically she chased after him, ran and ran until her way was blocked by a tall iron gate. She grasped the bars and shook them violently "Wait! Let me in! Wait. . . ."

The wolf was behind her. She could feel him drawing near. His low snarl pierced the misty night. Terrified, she tugged at the gate, but it would not open. Powerful jaws closed around her neck.

"Hush. Be still, you must rest."

"Don't let him hurt me. . . ."

"You're safe in my arms, *ma chère*. Nothing will hurt you."

A wet cloth stroked over her back, legs, neck, arms. Again the cup was raised to her mouth. "Once more," came a quiet command. "Once more."

She submitted while the wolf circled around her stealthily. He snatched her up greedily in his jaw, dragging her into the shadows while she cried in terror for him to stop . . . but he would not let her go . . . he would never let her go. . . .

Lysette emerged from layers of darkness, struggling upward until she broke through the surface of a deep, dreamless sleep. She was lying on her stomach in a dimly lit room, an amber glow coming from a lamp in the corner. Blinking, she shifted toward the light and rested her cheek on the mattress. Her body and head and arms were as heavy as if they had been weighted with bags of sand. Long, cooling strokes moved over her back, and she made a faint sound of gratitude.

A gentle hand descended to the side of her face, testing the temperature of her skin. "You're much better now," came a familiar voice. "The fever has broken, thank God."

Lysette's eyes flew open in astonishment as she recognized the voice. "Monsieur Vallerand?" she asked groggily. "Oh, no. It's *you*."

Amusement curled through his quiet voice. "I'm afraid so, *petite*."

"But . . . but . . ." She floundered into aghast silence. Who had let him into her sickroom? Surely he had not taken care of her while she was ill. Fragments of memory floated through her tired brain . . . the coaxing voice, the strong arms, the gentle hands that had tended to her most intimate needs. She could not believe it.

It dawned on her that she was naked in bed, with a light sheet draped low over her hips, her back completely exposed. It was too much to comprehend . . . she couldn't think of how to react.

"I'm not dressed," she said plaintively.

Vallerand leaned over her. His shirt was rolled up at the sleeves, the neck open to reveal the startling wealth of black curls on his chest. His tanned face was unshaven, his jaw covered with heavy bristle, and his hair was disheveled. The dark eyes were undercut with deep shadows.

Carefully he tucked a stray curl behind her ear. "I'm sorry," he said, although he didn't sound all that apologetic. "It was easier to take care of you this way."

She stiffened at the touch of his finger on the hot curve of her ear.

"Relax," he murmured. "I'm hardly going to molest a woman in your condition." He paused before adding, straight-faced, "I'll wait until you're better."

Despite Lysette's consternation, a gurgle of amusement escaped her. "How long have I been ill?" she asked thickly.

"Almost three weeks."

"Oh, *mon Dieu*," she said, her mouth going dry. She lurched to her side, fumbling with the sheets, her entire body turning crimson as she realized her breasts were exposed.

Vallerand didn't seem to notice the display as he helped her to turn over. Deftly he pulled the sheet over her chest and tucked it beneath her arms. Lysette stared at his dark face in bewilderment as he arranged the pillows behind her with the expertise of a seasoned nurse.

Seeming to understand her needs without being told, he brought a cup to her lips, and Lysette drank thirstily, letting the cool water ease her parched mouth and throat. When the cup was removed, she settled against the pillows.

"I don't understand why your mother allowed you to take care of me," she said hoarsely.

"Maman didn't approve," Vallerand admitted, straightening the covers around her. "But she was exhausted after the first few days of nursing, and I was very stubborn." He smiled wryly. "And later she sadly decided that since you were probably going to die anyway, it didn't matter who took care of you."

Lysette absorbed his words, filled with a deep inner certainty that she would have died without his inexhaustible, patient, all-encompassing care. "You saved my life," she said faintly. "Why?"

His fingertip trailed over her freckled cheek. "Because the world would be a much darker and duller place without you, *ma chère*."

Lysette watched passively as he straightened the articles on the bedside table. Remembering the day she had fallen ill, when she had found the unsent letter to Marie, she recalled that she had good reason to be angry with him. However, that issue could wait until later. No matter what else Vallerand had done, he had seen her through a terrible illness, and for that she owed him her gratitude.

"If I send for some broth, will you try some?" he asked.

The thought made Lysette grimace. "I can't. I'm sorry, but no."

"Just a little." Clearly he was going to pressure her until she relented.

She frowned and sighed. "A *very* little."

After Vallerand called for Noeline and requested the cup of broth, he returned to the bedside. Lysette toyed listlessly with the edge of the sheet and glanced at him, her gaze traveling from his fur-covered chest to his bristled face. "You're the hairiest nurse I've ever seen," she said.

He grinned, his teeth white in his swarthy face. "You can't afford to be particular," he informed her. "Until you're better, *petite,* you're going to have to tolerate me."

When Lysette had recovered enough to desire a change of scene, Max carried her to the downstairs parlor. The stronger she became, the more troubled Lysette was about their developing intimacy.

In the past three days she had tried to put some distance between them. She no longer allowed him to help bathe her or comb and braid her hair, and only Noeline and Irénée were permitted to help her dress.

However, as Max lifted her in his arms and carried her downstairs, the treacherous feelings of closeness remained. It did not help that he was being so gentle and attentive. She could almost let herself forget that he had betrayed her and was certainly planning to manipulate her further.

Reminding herself that she could not let herself be stupid enough to trust him again, Lysette gave him a suspicious frown.

"What is it?" he asked, shifting her slight weight in his arms. "Are you uncomfortable?"

"No," she replied, keeping her arms linked around his neck. "I am merely wondering what your game is, monsieur."

He gave her a blank look. "Game?"

Lysette rolled her eyes at the show of innocence. "The game I have become a pawn in. The one you are playing with Etienne Sagesse. Clearly you had no intention of letting me appeal to my cousin for refuge. You wanted to keep me here, and you've succeeded. Now tell me what your plan is."

"We won't discuss that until you're better," he muttered.

"You may as well admit it," she said. "I've already figured out what you want, and how you plan to get it."

"Oh?" A hot flicker entered his eyes. "Tell me what you think I want."

Before Lysette could answer, he set her carefully on the settee, and Noeline was there to drape a lap blanket over her knees.

Vallerand began to release her, and Lysette felt a painful tug on her scalp. A few strands of her hair had caught in one of his coat buttons. Realizing what had happened, he and Lysette reached for the button at the same time. Their fingers caught together, and Lysette recoiled in confusion.

The warm puff of his breath against her cheek unloosed a blaze of sensations that stunned her. With a dreamlike slowness she let her hands fall, while her heart hammered in her breast. Carefully Vallerand freed the tiny snarl of hair, dismantling the silken bond that had held them together. His scent floated to her nostrils, the intoxicating salty maleness that made her want to press her open mouth to his skin. Her response to him was so carnal and deep that she shrank away from him, shocked at herself.

Vallerand continued to lean over her, one arm braced on the back of the rosewood settee, the other hand resting close to her hip. "Don't be afraid of me," he said, mistaking the alarm in her gaze.

"Afraid of you?" she whispered dazedly. "You're the last man in the world I would be afraid of."

The words seemed to jolt him. His breath quickened, and he stared at her as if he didn't dare believe her.

Irénée entered the room, her voice penetrating the spellbinding silence. "Lysette, how do you feel this morning?"

Max's peculiar expression vanished. "She's fine," he said curtly, striding to the door. "I'll be in the library."

As he left, Irénée looked after him and shook her head. "He has behaved so oddly of late."

Lysette sighed, reflecting that her illness had been only a temporary reprieve from whatever plans Maximilien had concocted. "Madame," she said slowly, "certainly you must know that Monsieur Vallerand never sent the letter to my cousin Marie."

Irénée frowned. "Lysette, we should wait until you are stronger to discuss —"

"He planned to dishonor me, didn't he?" Lysette laced her fingers together over her midriff. "Well, I have been here long enough to ensure that my reputation is in shreds, re-

91

gardless of your presence. My guess is that no one would believe I could stay under Maximilien Vallerand's roof for this long with my honor intact. Will Sagesse demand a duel now? That is how any Creole would respond, *n'est-ce pas?* Obviously it has all turned out the way your son wanted."

Irénée was silent for a long time. "Lysette," she finally said, "it is still not too late for you to be returned to Sagesse. If that is what you wish, I will see that it is done."

Lysette shook her head. "Good Lord, no. I would become a streetwalker before I went back to him."

The older woman was clearly startled by the frank statement. She was spared from replying by Noeline's arrival in the doorway. "Madame," the housekeeper said, rolling her eyes heavenward, "it is Monsieur Medart — he wants to take Mademoiselle Lysette away with him."

CHAPTER

4

Lysette damned her own physical weakness as her stepfather and Tante Delphine entered the room. The impulse to leap from the settee and run was uncontrollable, but she knew she wouldn't make it five yards before collapsing.

"Lysette," Gaspard said calmly, a smile on his lips. The expression in his eyes, however, was one of undiluted hatred. Her marriage to Etienne Sagesse was the only thing that stood between him and financial ruin, and she had almost succeeded in sabotaging his plans. "You are fortunate, you foolish girl. Sagesse still wants you, regardless of all that has happened. The marriage will take place as planned. Now that you are better, you will come with me."

"The marriage will never take place," Lysette said. "I would have thought that would be clear to you by now."

"Lysette," Tante Delphine exclaimed, hurrying forward in a display of maternal affection. "There, there, *enfant*. We have come to take care of you. Certainly you do not wish to be a burden to these strangers any longer. I would have expected you to be more considerate than that." She caressed the side of Lysette's face with her plump hand and tucked the lap blanket more tightly around her.

Lysette realized guiltily that Delphine had a point. She had indeed been a burden to the Vallerands. Moreover, she had no wish to be the unwitting instrument of Vallerand's destruction. If a duel did result from this, there was a possibility that Sagesse would manage to wound or even kill him. Somehow that thought was too awful to contemplate.

"Lysette," Irénée said sympathetically, astonishing them all, "perhaps you should go with them. It might be the wisest course of action."

"Yes, it would," Gaspard added, his swarthy face losing its thunderous cast. "Your sensible attitude pleases me, Madame Vallerand."

"We must consider Lysette's welfare," Irénée replied cautiously.

"Clearly Madame Vallerand recognizes the impropriety of your presence under this roof," Gaspard interrupted, reaching for Lysette. "*Allons,* Lysette. There is a carriage waiting outside, the finest carriage you have ever seen. The Sagesses have anticipated everything you might require." He picked her up easily, his beefy arms crushing her struggles. Lysette was unable to move or breathe in his crushing hold. "You're going to pay for the trouble you've caused me," he said close to her ear, a mist of hot spittle spraying her skin.

Swamped in despair, she shoved at him. "Max," she cried, wondering frantically why he wasn't there. Hadn't anyone told him that her aunt and stepfather had arrived? "Max —"

The world seemed to tilt crazily, and she heard a strange low growl that most certainly had not come from Gaspard. An unseen force wrenched her upward, away from her stepfather's brutal grasp, and momentum brought her hard against Vallerand's un-yielding chest. She grabbed at him immediately, her arms wrapping around his familiar neck. She buried her face against his throat. "He's going to take me to Sagesse," she gasped. "Don't let him, don't —"

"You're not going anywhere," Vallerand interrupted brusquely. "Calm yourself, Lysette. It's not good for you to become excited." His possessiveness made her strangely giddy. As far as he was concerned, she was his, and no one was going to take her away from him.

Gently Vallerand set her on a chair and straightened, his steady gaze fastened on Gaspard. "Don't touch her again," he murmured. Although his voice was soft, it contained a note that chilled Lysette's blood. "If you so much as disarrange a hair on her head, I'll tear you apart."

"She is mine!" Gaspard exploded, staring at them both in incredulous fury.

Lysette returned his gaze with cool satisfaction. Max was going to take her part in the dispute, because it served his purpose to keep her here. She would let him handle the situation however he liked. She didn't give a damn about her ruined reputation, or about the fact that Max was using her. The only thing that mattered was that she wouldn't have to marry Etienne Sagesse.

Gaspard spoke to her directly, his face apoplectic. "Sagesse has said that if you are not returned by this afternoon, he *will not have you*. He will consider you defiled! Do you understand, you stupid fool? *No one* will want you. You'll be useless to me, because no decent man will ever offer for you. You will not only have blemished your own name, but also Sagesse's honor, and this is exactly what Monsieur Vallerand intends. You are nothing but an excuse for him to finish a feud that began years ago. Once it is done, you will have no hope of anything close to the life you might have led as the wife of a Sagesse. Save yourself, Lysette. Come with me now and end this madness!"

Lysette was suddenly exhausted. Her lips curved with a bitter smile as she spoke to Max. "Monsieur Vallerand, everything he says is true, *n'est-ce pas?*"

He remained facing away from her. "Yes," he said bluntly.

She received the admission without surprise. "What had you planned to do with me when your game is over?"

"Repay you for the opportunity you afforded me," he replied, with no visible trace of shame. "Provide for you in whatever manner you wish. You will find that my gratitude for the chance to duel with Sagesse will prove boundless."

His arrogance was so vast that she could not prevent a wry smile. "What has he done to earn such enmity, monsieur?"

Vallerand did not reply.

Thoughtfully Lysette considered her options. "I am weary of being exploited," she said to no one in particular. Her gaze settled on her stepfather. "*Beau-père,* I'm afraid that you will have to return to Sagesse without me. Now that I have no more value on the marriage market, perhaps you will find some other way to make money. As for you, Monsieur Vallerand . . . you are welcome to your duel with Monsieur Sagesse. Congratulations — you have what you want."

"But what will you do, Lysette?" Irénée asked, her face drawn with concern.

"As soon as I am able, I would like to be taken to the Ursuline convent. Although I have no intention of becoming a nun, I am certain that they will offer me shelter until I

97

decide what to do. I suspect I might be able to find work as governess, or perhaps teach somewhere." She extended a hand to Noeline, who had watched the entire episode from the doorway. "Please help me upstairs," she asked with quiet dignity.

Lysette's hair was still damp after a thorough washing during her bath. Carefully Noeline separated the tangles and began to comb the matted locks, while Irénée sat nearby and looked out the window. The afternoon sunlight shone on the oak trees lining the drive, filtering to the damp ground beneath. Irénée watched as Max rode away from the house on his black thoroughbred. When she was assured that there was no chance of his return, Irénée turned to Lysette and spoke softly.

"You have a right to know, Lysette, what happened between Max and Etienne Sagesse. It will help you to understand my son better, and perhaps even to forgive him a little. He is not nearly as wicked and selfish as he seems. When Max was younger, he exceeded all the hopes his father and I had for him. He was a wild boy, to be sure, often given to mischief, but also warm and kind, and full of charm. Nearly every woman in New Orleans, young or old, matron or maiden, was in love with him. His downfall, *naturellement*, was a woman.

"Corinne Quérand was the daughter of a highly respectable family in New Orleans. Max was your age when he married her. So young, in fact, that he was not able to see the real woman beneath the beautiful facade. The first year of their marriage Corinne gave Max the twins, and he was overcome with joy. It seemed that they would be very happy together, but then . . ." Irénée paused and shook her head regretfully.

"What happened?" Lysette demanded.

"Corinne changed. Or perhaps she now allowed her true nature to be revealed. The beautiful mask dropped away, and she began to discard her morals and self-respect as garments she was simply tired of wearing. Corinne had no interest in her children. She wanted to hurt Max, *alors*, she took a lover. I think, Lysette, that you can guess who that was."

Lysette swallowed hard. "Etienne Sagesse."

"*Oui, c'etait lui.* Corinne flaunted her indiscretion with Etienne in Maximilien's face. She knew Max still loved her, and that drove her to such cruelty . . . *Mon Dieu,* my son suffered as no mother would ever want to see her child suffer. He desired to call Etienne out, but his pride would not let him admit before the world that his wife had been unfaithful to him."

Noeline secured Lysette's hair at the nape of her neck and moved to hand Irénée a handkerchief.

"*Merci,* Noeline," Irénée said, swabbing at her moist eyes. "Anyone could understand why it would happen. Corinne had tortured Max with his own feelings for her, until he couldn't stop himself. It was justified, wasn't it, Noeline?"

"*Oui, madame.*"

"What happened?" Lysette asked, although she already knew.

Noeline was the one who replied. "Madame Corinne was found in the empty overseer's house, set back in the woods. She was strangled."

"Max claimed that he found her that way," Irénée said. "He insisted that he didn't kill her, but he had no alibi. The authorities considered the circumstances and chose to be lenient. They can on occasion be persuaded to look the other way, especially in the matter of an unfaithful wife. The duel with Etienne never took place. Max continued to insist he was innocent, but no one had faith in his claim. His friends proved to be unsteadfast, and Max was left alone with his grief. I was certain that after time had passed he would recover and become something like his former self. But the bitterness consumed him. He became incapable of expressing affection, of trusting anyone, of allowing himself to care for anyone except his sons."

"Madame, do you believe in his innocence?" Lysette asked.

Irénée paused an unbearably long time. "I am his mother," she finally answered.

Lysette frowned, thinking that didn't quite sound like a yes. "Perhaps there was someone else who had reason to kill her?"

"No one else," Irénée said with terrible certainty.

Lysette tried to imagine Maximilien Vallerand putting his powerful hands around a woman's throat and choking the life from her. It was impossible to reconcile that image with her knowledge of the man who had cared for her when she was ill. She could accept that Vallerand was ruthless, not to mention manipulative. But a murderer? Somehow she couldn't make herself believe it.

"Max must be pitied," Irénée said. "Now you understand why Max saw you as the means to force Etienne into a duel. He regards it as his opportunity to avenge the past. I have little doubt that he will kill Etienne. Perhaps then Maximilien will be able to put the entire tragedy to rest."

"Or," Lysette murmured, "your son will simply have more blood on his hands."

Irénée could not help but be gratified by the number of visitors she received on Thursday. All her female friends and relatives came from far and wide, eagerly seeking information on the most thrilling gossip to be passed around in years. The controversy had spread to every corner of New Orleans. It was obvious a duel was forthcoming. Everyone knew that Maximilien Vallerand had virtually stolen Etienne Sagesse's fiancée from under his nose and ruined her.

"The rumors are untrue," Irénée said placidly, reigning over the crowd in the parlor like a queen, handing around plates of cakes and *langues de chat,* tiny pastries that dissolved on the tongue. "How can anyone believe my son could assault the virtue of a girl living under my roof? Not only was I there to chaperone her, but she was ill with fever! I myself nursed her through it!"

Four gray, lace-capped heads nodded together. Claire and Nicole Laloux, Marie-Therese Robert, and Fleurette Grenet were Irénée's staunchest friends, supporting her through the most dire circumstances. Even in the dark days of Corinne Quérand's murder, they had not stopped paying calls and had never thought to withdraw their friendship. Irénée was a gentle and generous woman, and everyone knew her to be a lady of the highest refinement. Her son, on the other hand . . .

Still, most Creoles tolerated Maximilien. The Vallerands had been a significant New Orleans family for decades. Regardless of his shameful past, he was invited to the important social events of the year . . . but not to the small, intimate family gatherings, where

102

real attachments were formed and deepened.

"We all know you would *never* have condoned anything improper, Irénée," spoke up Catherine Gauthier, a young matron who was friends with some of the younger Vallerand cousins. "But the poor girl has been ruined just the same. The fact is, she has spent more than two weeks under the same roof with Maximilien, who is undeniably the city's most notorious . . . gentleman. No one blames Etienne Sagesse for not wanting her now."

Everyone murmured agreement, held out their cups to be filled with more coffee, finished the last crumbs of pastry, and began on a new plate.

"Of course there will be a duel now," Marie-Therese said. "It is the only recourse left to Sagesse. Otherwise his honor would be forever besmirched."

"Yes, everyone knows that," Fleurette said, daintily dabbing at the corners of her mouth with a napkin. She assumed an expression of objective interest. "Irénée, what did Maximilien do to make this girl decide to stay here rather than return to Sagesse?"

"He did nothing at all," Irénée said primly.

Claire and Fleurette looked at each other knowingly. It was obvious the girl had been seduced. Either that or she had been threatened with violence. Maximilien was such a wicked man!

* * *

A native of Virginia, William Charles Coles Claiborne was only eight-and-twenty when President Jefferson appointed him the first American governor of the Orleans Territory. Although Creoles had been opposed to him, it was a coalition of money-hungry Americans and French refugees who constituted the greatest threat to Claiborne's administration.

Among those whom Claiborne wisely considered a danger were Edward Livingston, a New Yorker who had come to New Orleans to make his fortune, and General Wilkinson, the ranking officer of the army and newly appointed governor of the Upper Louisiana Territory. Both men had more or less allied themselves with Aaron Burr, who was encouraging them to stir up strife among the most powerful residents of the territory.

Max had many doubts about Claiborne's ability to weather the events that were taking shape. Although clever and determined, Claiborne was still grieving over the loss of his wife and only daughter to yellow fever the year before. The press attacked him ruthlessly, alleging he was a gambler, a reprobate, and had treated his wife cruelly before her death. Worse still, Claiborne's attention was frequently distracted from the Burr problem by the increasing number of pirates infesting Barataria Bay and the bayous to the south of New Orleans.

"The problem," Claiborne said ruefully to Max as they sat in heavy mahogany chairs and discussed the latest events in the city, "is that the bandits know the swamps better than my own police force, and they are far better supplied and organized. President Jefferson has promised a number of gunboats to help combat the pirates, but I fear they will not be in suitable condition. Nor will there be a great number of enlisted men to choose from."

Max smiled wryly. "I should point out that most Creoles will not be in favor of strong measures to oppose privateering. The local merchants will cause quite an uproar if you remove their access to duty-free merchandise. The fortunes of many respectable families have been founded on smuggling. Here it is not always considered a dishonorable vocation."

"Oh! And which respectable families are you referring to?"

The question, asked in a tone of suspicion, might have caused many to recoil in unease. Max only laughed. "I would be surprised if my own father had not contributed to the pirates' cause," he admitted.

Claiborne looked at him sharply, startled by the bold revelation. "And with whom do your sympathies rest in this matter, Vallerand?"

"If you're asking whether or not I have a

hand in smuggling, the answer is . . ." Max paused, drew on his thin black cigar, and blew out an even stream of smoke. "Not at the moment."

Claiborne was torn between annoyance and amusement at the man's insolence. The latter won out, and he chuckled. "Sometimes I wonder, Vallerand, if I should count you as friend or foe."

"Were I your enemy, sir, you would have no cause to wonder."

"Let us talk of *your* enemies for a moment. What is this my aides tell me of the rivalry between you and Etienne Sagesse over some woman? And some ridiculous talk of a duel? Merely a rumor, I hope?"

"All true."

Surprise appeared on the governor's face. "You would not be so impetuous as to duel over a woman? A man of your maturity?"

Max's brow arched. "I am five-and-thirty, monsieur — hardly in the doddering years of infirmity."

"Not by any means, but . . ." Claiborne shook his head in dismay. "Although I haven't known you long, Vallerand, I consider you to be a sensible man, not a wild-blooded youth who would sacrifice all in the heat of a jealous rage. Dueling over a woman? I would have thought you above such behavior."

Max's lips twitched in amusement. "I am a

Creole. God willing, I will never be above such behavior."

"I have no hopes of understanding the Creoles," Claiborne said with a slight scowl, thinking of his brother-in-law, who had recently been killed in a duel while defending the memory of his sister. "With your women, and dueling, and hot tempers . . ."

"You will discover, Governor, that dueling is an inevitable aspect of life in New Orleans. You might someday find it necessary to defend your own honor in such a way."

"Never!"

Like all Americans in New Orleans, Claiborne did not understand the Creoles' penchant for dueling over what seemed to be trifling matters. Rapiers were the preferred weapon, and the art of fencing was taught by a flourishing group of academies. The garden behind the cathedral had absorbed the lifeblood of many gallants who had sacrificed their lives merely to avenge an imagined slight. Sometimes a single misspoken word or the tiniest breach of etiquette was enough to result in a challenge.

"My God, man," Claiborne continued, "how can you involve yourself in something like this, when you may still be of use to me? You know it is imperative that I avoid antagonizing the population of this city, and if the Creoles' hatred of me worsens —"

"The Creoles do not hate you," Max interrupted matter-of-factly.

"They don't?" Claiborne began to look mollified.

"They are largely indifferent to you. It is your own countrymen who hate you."

"Dammit, I know that." The governor gave him a dark look. "Much help you'll be to me if Sagesse wins the duel."

Max half smiled. "That is unlikely. However, if I prove unsuccessful against Sagesse, my absence will not make as much of a difference as you seem to believe."

"The hell it won't! Colonel Burr is in Natchez at this moment, plotting to stir Louisiana to revolt and wreak havoc on God knows what other portions of the continent. He'll be here in a matter of weeks looking for supporters. By that time you'll most likely be buried at the foot of a tree instead of doing what you can to verify the reports I'm receiving. And if Burr succeeds, your property will be confiscated, your family's wealth plundered, and your desire to see Louisiana attain statehood will never be realized."

A gleam of malice appeared in Max's brown eyes. "Yes, they'll alight over the territory like a flock of buzzards. No one can scavenge and pillage quite like Americans."

Claiborne ignored the observation. "Vallerand, the duel can't really be necessary."

"It has been necessary for ten years."

"Ten years? Why?"

"I must go. I'm certain you can find some-one willing to help you," Max said, standing up and proffering his hand on the short busi-nesslike shake the Americans seemed to prefer to the Creole custom of kissing both cheeks. A strange lot, the Anglo-Saxons — so squeamish, solitary, and hypocritical.

"Why must you go?" Claiborne demanded. "I have more to discuss with you."

"The news of my presence here will have circulated by now. I'm expecting to receive a challenge on your very doorstep." Max gave him a slight, mocking bow. "At your service, as always, Governor."

"And what if you are dead by the morrow?"

Max gave him a saturnine grin. "If you re-quire advice from the netherworld, I'll be pleased to oblige."

Claiborne laughed. "Are you threatening to haunt me?"

"You wouldn't be the first to encounter a Vallerand ghost," Max assured him, replacing the wide-brimmed planter's hat on his dark head and striding nonchalantly away.

As Max reached the outer door of the run-down Governor's Palace, he was ap-proached by a small crowd of men. The air snapped with excitement, for the Creoles had been roused from their leisurely routine by the prospect of a duel involving Vallerand.

"Gentlemen?" Max prompted lazily. "May I be of assistance?"

One of them stepped forward, breathing fast, his gaze riveted on Max's dark face. In a sudden jerking movement, he whipped a glove against Max's cheek. "I challenge you on behalf of Etienne Gerard Sagesse," he said.

Max smiled in a way that sent chills down the spine of every man present. "I accept."

"You will appoint a second to arrange the details of the meeting?"

"Jacques Clement will serve as my second. Make the arrangements with him."

Clement was an agile negotiator who had twice been able to reconcile a dispute before swords were crossed. This time, however, Max had made it clear to him that negotiations would not be required. The duel would be fought to the death, with rapiers, on the shores of Lake Pontchartrain. More privacy would be afforded there, as well as fewer distractions.

"And the doctor?" the second asked. "Who will choose —"

"You appoint him," Max replied indifferently, caring about nothing other than the fact that his revenge was finally at hand.

Excited by the rumors flying through the city, Justin and Philippe tore through the house barefoot, staging mock duels with

walking sticks and brooms and upsetting
small knickknacks from their perches as they
bumped into tables, bureaus, and shelves.
Neither of them entertained any doubt that
their renowned and fearsome father would
best Etienne Sagesse. As they had boasted to
their friends, Maximilien had proved himself
without peer, whether the weapon was pistols
or swords.

Irénée had taken to her room, praying feverishly for the safety of her son on the
morrow, and asking forgiveness for his ruthlessness and unholy desire for vengeance.
Lysette sat in the salon, bewildered and
tense, trying to convince herself she did not
care what happened to Maximilien Vallerand.
She stared out the window at the hazy sky
which gleamed with an opalescent shimmer.
In New Orleans, the moisture in the air was
never completely burned off by the sun,
making the twilights lovelier than any she
had ever seen.

Where was Maximilien now? He had appeared earlier in the day, then left without
partaking of supper. Noeline had hinted
archly that he was visiting his mistress. The
idea had caused a perplexing emotion to spill
inside Lysette's chest. "I don't care if he has
a hundred women," she said to herself, but
the words sounded false to her ears.

She could not stop her imagination from
alighting on thoughts of Max with his mis-

tress at this very moment. What would a man say to a woman when he knew he might die the next day? Lysette's eyes half closed as she pictured a woman with an unseen face leading Max to her bed, her slender hips swaying in invitation, her hand caught in his. And Max looking down with a sardonic smile, his head lowering as he stole a kiss, his hands moving to unfasten her clothes. *I had to spend my last night with you,* he might be whispering. *Put your arms around me. . . .* And as the woman arched up to him, her head falling back willingly, Lysette imagined her own face tilted upward, her own arms stealing around his broad back . . .

"Ah, *Mon Dieu,* what am I doing?" she whispered, pressing her hands to the sides of her head to force out the wicked thoughts.

"Mademoiselle!" Philippe's voice interrupted her, and Lysette looked up as he approached. Justin followed at a slower pace, sauntering in a way that reminded her of his father.

"Why so downcast?" Philippe inquired, his blue eyes dancing with exhilaration. "Are you not pleased that *mon père* will be dueling for the sake of your honor tomorrow?"

"Pleased?" she repeated. "How could I be pleased? It is dreadful."

"But it is the highest compliment that can be paid a woman. Just imagine what it will be like, the clashing swords, the blood, all for your sake!"

"The duel is not being fought for her sake," Justin said flatly, his blue eyes locked on her pale face. "Isn't that true, Lysette?"

"Yes," she said flatly. "That is true."

"What?" Philippe looked puzzled. "But of course the duel is over you. That is what everyone says."

"Idiot," Justin muttered, and sat on the sofa beside Lysette, seeming to understand her fear. "He won't lose, you know. He never does."

"What happens to your father is not my concern," she said calmly.

"Isn't it? Then why are you waiting and watching for his return?"

"I am not!"

"Yes, you are. And you might wait all night. Sometimes he doesn't come back until dawn. You do know who he is with, *oui?*"

"No, and I don't . . ." Lysette's voice trailed off, and she flushed. "Who?"

Philippe broke in angrily, "Justin, do not tell her!"

"He is with Mariame," Justin said, giving Lysette a knowing smile. "She's been his *placée* for years. But he doesn't love her."

Lysette swallowed back more questions with extreme difficulty. "I don't care to hear any more," she said, and Justin gave a jeering laugh.

"You would love to hear more," he said, "but I won't tell you."

Suddenly there was a feminine cry of outrage from upstairs. "Justin! Philippe! Ah, the mischief you have done! Come here *immédiatement!*"

When Justin made no move to rise from the sofa, Philippe tugged impatiently at his sleeve. "Justin, come now! *Grand-mère* is calling us!"

"Go see what she wants," Justin said lazily.

Philippe's blue eyes narrowed with annoyance. "Not without you!" He waited while Irénée called, but Justin continued to sit calmly without stirring. Making an exasperated noise, Philippe left the room.

Lysette folded her arms and regarded the boy in front of her with all the cynicism she could dredge up. "Is there something else you want to tell me?" she asked.

"I wondered if you knew the story of what my father did to my mother," Justin said idly.

He was a wicked boy, Lysette thought, and yet she felt sorry for him. It must be terrible to live with such a suspicion of his own father, terrible to know that his mother had been an adulteress.

"It's not necessary to tell me," she said. "It has nothing to do with me."

"Oh, but it does," Justin countered. "You see, my father is going to marry you."

Her breath was driven out of her lungs in a whoosh. She looked at him as if he'd gone mad. "No, he isn't!"

"Don't be stupid. Why else would *Grand-mère* allow him to compromise you, if she wasn't assured he will make the proper amends?"

"I'm not going to marry anyone."

Justin laughed. "We'll see. My father always gets what he wants."

"He doesn't want me," Lysette persisted. "All he wants is revenge. The duel with Monsieur Sagesse."

"You'll be a Vallerand before the week is out," the boy predicted. "Unless, of course, he is defeated — and he won't be."

The scratch of a quill on thin parchment was the only sound in the room as Etienne Sagesse bent over the small desk. Word after scrawling word filled the ivory sheet, while the face above it turned ruddy with effort.

Carefully he blotted the letter, folded and sealed it, then held it in his hands with exceeding lightness, as if it were a delicate weapon. For just an instant a long-forgotten softness appeared in his turquoise eyes, while old memories danced before him.

"Etienne?" His older sister Renée Sagesse Dubois entered the room. She was a striking woman of unusual height, admired for her self-contained ways, respected for being a dutiful wife and the mother of three healthy children.

For years she had worried over Etienne

every bit as earnestly as their own mother had, and although she turned a blind eye to his misdeeds, she could not help but be aware of his true character. "What are you doing?" she inquired.

He gestured with the letter in response. "In case events do not turn out as I wish tomorrow," he said, "I want this to be given to Maximilien Vallerand."

"But why?" Renée asked with a frown. "What does it say?"

"That is only for Max to know."

Renée came to stand by his chair, resting her long hand on the back of it. "Why must you duel over that creature?" she asked, her voice for once impassioned.

"Many reasons. Not the least of which is the fact that Lysette Kersaint is the only woman I ever wanted to marry."

"But *why?* She is not even pretty!"

"She is the most desirable woman I've ever known. No . . . I am not jesting. She is vibrant and clever and unique. I will enjoy killing Vallerand for taking her."

"Will you be able to live with yourself if he dies?"

An odd smile shaped Etienne's lips. "That remains to be seen. I can be certain, however, that Max will not be able to live with himself if *he* emerges the victor." He set the letter down on the desk. "If that happens, do not forget this note. I will be watching from the grave while he reads it."

Renée's blue eyes crackled with anger. "I have never understood your attitude toward that cruel, embittered man. Maximilien Vallerand is not worthy of a single moment of your time, and yet you insist on risking your life to indulge his need for vengeance!"

Etienne appeared to have only half heard her. "Remember how he was?" he said absently. "Remember how everyone loved him? Even you."

A blush edged up to her hairline, but Renée was too straightforward to deny it. Like so many other women, she had been in love with Maximilien back in the days when he had possessed a boyish gallantry that had set her heart beating all too fast.

"Yes, of course I remember," she answered. "But that was *not* the same man, Etienne. The Maximilien Vallerand whom you go to duel with is beyond redemption."

Lake Pontchartrain was a shallow body of water, perhaps sixteen feet at its deepest. Nonetheless, the seemingly tame lake could turn dangerous. Sometimes a strong wind would flail the surface until the waves grew violent enough to overturn vessels and take the lives of many men.

This morning, however, the water was a glassy gray mirror poised against the pale dawn sky. Only the hint of a breeze skimmed the lake and touched the shore. The duel between Max and Etienne would take place away from the beach, on the edge of a pine forest where the ground was firm and even.

While the seconds and the group of onlookers stood by, Max and Etienne drew aside for a private meeting.

The men were similar in height and reach, both experienced and well trained in the art of swordsmanship. None of the witnesses present would dare to choose which opponent they would rather face, though several had noted that an excess of fine living would soon begin to take a toll on Sagesse's agility, if it hadn't already. He indulged too often in the rich wines and cuisines the Creoles loved, and led a dissipated life that would not long allow him his current preeminence as a duelist.

Etienne Sagesse confronted Max with a faint smile on his coarsely handsome face. "Vallerand," he murmured, "you could have found some other excuse years ago. Why did you use my little fiancée to provoke the duel? There was no need to deprive me of such a sweet tidbit."

"It seemed appropriate."

"I suppose it might have seemed appropriate to you, but it was hardly an equal exchange. Lysette was chaste and modest, of far greater value than your harlot of a wife."

Max drew in his breath. "I'm going to kill you."

"As you did Corinne?" Etienne smiled casually. "I never had the opportunity to tell you what a relief that was. She was so tiresome." He seemed to enjoy the sight of Max's darkening face. "Careful," he murmured. "You'll give me the advantage by letting your emotions get the better of you."

"Let's get this over with," Max said gruffly. They exchanged one last look before turning to take up their weapons. Max pushed away an unwanted memory that hovered entreatingly on the edge of his awareness, a memory of childhood. He wondered if Etienne had given a thought to a fact few people in New Orleans remembered — that once they had been inseparable friends.

CHAPTER
5

Max had often pondered why Sagesse had slept with his wife, and realized the deed had been inevitable. They had been boyhood friends, had sworn to be blood brothers, but even then Etienne had also been Max's greatest rival.

Because they were friends, Etienne struggled to subdue his jealousy. Eventually, however, as they grew into manhood, their friendship was overshadowed by too many arguments and increasing competition, and for a number of years they kept a careful distance from each other.

When Max fell in love and married Corinne Quérand, it had not taken long for the idea of seducing her to take root in Etienne's mind. Once Etienne had succeeded, it became clear Corinne's charm had worn off quickly. Now that Max had repaid the debt by ruining his betrothed, Etienne was determined to settle the score once and for all. He had fancied himself half in love with Lysette Kersaint, and Max would pay for taking that away from him.

★ ★ ★

Lysette walked down the stairs after a sleepless night. The house was still, the hour too early for the twins to have awakened. There was a heavy feeling in her heart, and she could not pretend it was anything other than concern for Max. Just why she should care so much about what happened to him was impossible to explain.

Going to the morning room, she peered through the window and saw that dawn had arrived. Perhaps at this moment Sagesse and Max were dueling, rapiers scissoring and flashing in the pale light.

"By now it is over," she heard Irénée say behind her. The older woman sat at the empty breakfast table. "It seems I have been through a hundred mornings such as this," Irénée continued, looking haggard. "This is hardly the first duel Maximilien has fought. And he is not the only son of mine to have taken up swords. No one understands the grief a woman bears when the life of her child is threatened."

"I do not think he will fail, madame."

"And if he doesn't? How much more will his heart be blackened when he tries to live with Etienne's death on his conscience? Perhaps it would be better for him to . . . to lose this duel than to become so embittered."

"No," Lysette said softly.

The minutes seemed to drag at a fraction

of their usual pace. Surely if Max were all right he would have returned by now. Lysette tried to make conversation, but after a while she fell silent and stared blankly at the cooling liquid in her cup.

"Madame!" she heard Noeline exclaim. Irénée and Lysette both turned with a start. The housekeeper stood in the doorway, her wiry arms bracketing either side of the doorframe. "Retta's boy just ran up to say that Monsieur is coming down the road!"

"He is all right?" Irénée asked unsteadily.

"Just fine!"

Irénée jumped to her feet with surprising alacrity and hurried to the entrance hall. Lysette followed, her heart pounding with some inexplicable emotion.

Abruptly the tension was severed as Max burst through the house, his expression harsh with frustration. He slammed the massive door, scowled at the two women in front of him, and strode to the library. Irénée followed at his heels, while Lysette stood frozen in the hall.

"Max?" she heard Irénée's muffled plea. "Maximilien? What happened?"

There was no reply.

"You won the duel?" Irénée pressed. "Etienne Sagesse is dead?"

"No. Sagesse isn't dead."

"But I don't understand."

Lysette stood in the doorway as Max went

to a bookcase and stared at the colored spines of the leather-bound volumes. "Soon after the duel began, I had Sagesse at my mercy," he said. "His reflexes have gone soft. He couldn't best anyone but the rankest novice."

Max looked down at his right hand as if he still held the rapier. "Child's play," he continued with a curl of his lip. "I gave him a scratch, barely enough to draw blood. Then the seconds conferred and inquired if honor had been satisfied. Sagesse said no, that honor required us to fight to the death. I was about to agree, but then . . ."

Max groaned and swiveled around, clutching his head in his hands. "My God, I don't know what made me do it. I wanted to kill him so badly. It would have been so easy, so *damned* easy."

"You let it end there," Irénée said in disbelief. "You did not kill him."

Max nodded, his face twisting in baffled self-hatred.

"I am pleased," Irénée told him fervently. "You did the right thing, Max."

He made a sound of disgust. "I need a drink." As his gaze moved to the silver tray of decanters, he caught sight of Lysette as she stood in the doorway.

They stared at each other in the highly charged silence. Lysette was at a loss for words. Clearly nothing could be said to soothe him. He was filled with masculine hostility that had been allowed no outlet. Clearly he was furious that he hadn't been able to make himself kill his hated enemy. No doubt he considered that a sign of weakness.

Lysette, on the other hand, recognized the turn of events as evidence that she had been right — Vallerand was not a killer, no matter what the rest of New Orleans chose to believe. "Well," she murmured, "what next, monsieur? Will you be sensible and let the matter rest now? Probably not . . . you'll do your best to find another excuse to duel with Sagesse, and perhaps next time you'll find it in yourself to kill him. Though I doubt it. In any event, I won't be here to see it, thank God."

She gave Irénée an expectant glance. "If you wouldn't mind, madame, I would like to go to the Ursuline convent now. I doubt it will be half so interesting as a stay with the Vallerands . . . but I daresay I wouldn't mind a few days of peace and quiet."

Vallerand pinned her with a surly stare that made her nerves jangle with warning. "You're not going anywhere."

"You have an alternate plan in mind?" she asked crisply.

"You're ruined," he pointed out. "No one in the entire territory would have you now. Everyone believes you to be soiled goods."

"Yes, thanks to you, marriage is no longer a choice for me. But the sisters will have me. So, if you will excuse me, I am going upstairs to pack my few things, and then I expect a carriage to —"

"You're going to marry *me*."

Although Lysette had half expected it, the primitive proposal — or, more accurately, the announcement — caused her heart to stop. In the midst of her alarm, a part of her was able to step back and point out that if she was clever enough, she might be able to get something she had only now realized that she wanted.

"Indeed? How did you come up with such an absurd idea?"

"I have need of a wife."

"Only because of what you did to the first one," she retorted, and turned on her heel.

By the time Max was able to form a reply, she was halfway up the stairs, her legs propelling her to the safety of her room.

Max glanced at his mother with a sardonic smile. Irénée shrugged apologetically. "I do not think she is receptive to the idea," Irénée commented.

Max laughed at the understatement, his fury seeming to abate. He walked over to her and pressed a kiss to her furrowed forehead. "Maman, you must not go around telling my prospective brides that I murdered my first wife. It does little to enhance my appeal."

"Do you think you will be able to persuade her to marry you, Max?"

"Begin making plans for a wedding a week from now."

"Only a week? But how could I possibly prepare . . . No, no, it cannot be done."

"A *small* wedding. I know you, Maman. You could arrange it in a quarter hour if you wished."

"But this haste —"

"Is entirely necessary. I'm afraid my fiancée's reputation could not withstand a lengthier engagement."

"If we could wait just a bit longer, Alexandre and Bernard will be here. Your brothers would want to attend your wedding, Max!"

"I assure you," he said sardonically, "my wedding will lose none of its poignancy for their absence. Now, if you will excuse me, I'll go upstairs to have a private talk with Lysette." He paused meaningfully. "Make certain that we are not disturbed."

The impropriety of his intent was not lost on Irénée. "Max, you will not spend too long with her alone, will you?"

"I might have to. After the confidences you shared with Lysette, it might take strong measures to convince her to marry me."

"What kind of measures?"

A devilish smile crossed his lips. "Don't ask questions, Maman, when you know you don't want to hear the answers."

Lysette leaned against the bed and watched the door intently. The handle was tried, and the lock prevented it from turning.

"Lysette, open the damned door."

"I have not given you permission to use my first name," she said. "And foul language hardly makes your marriage proposal more inviting."

The door rattled more vigorously, the hinges creaking in protest. "Mademoiselle Kersaint, I have no desire to break down the door, since in all likelihood I will have to be the one to repair it. Open it, or —"

Turning the key in the lock, Lysette sent the door swinging open. "Come in." She returned to her position against the bed and folded her arms before her. "I can hardly wait to hear why I should accept your proposal."

Vallerand entered the room and closed the door, his hooded gaze flickering to the bed behind her. Lysette could almost feel the force of his desire. She was actually enjoying this confrontation with the huge, aroused male before her, knowing how badly he wanted her. So he thought he would simply inform her that they would be married, and she would fall gratefully into his arms? Oh, no. If she were to accept him . . . and that was still very much an *if* . . . Max would have to convince her that he was worth the risk she would have to take.

"Mademoiselle —"

"You may use my first name now."

"Lysette." He let out a taut sigh. "I didn't kill my wife," he said baldly. There was no trace of humility in his tone, no sign of vulnerability on his face . . . but the mist of sweat on his forehead betrayed his agitation, and Lysette's heart softened ever so slightly.

"Corinne was dead when I found her. I don't know who did it. I thought Sagesse was guilty at first, but he has many witnesses to confirm that he wasn't with her that night. All the evidence points to me. No one believes that I'm innocent. Not even my own mother. I can't expect you to believe it, either, but I swear —"

"Of course I believe you," Lysette said calmly.

Max looked away swiftly but not before she saw the astonishment on his face. Although his body was rigid, she detected the faint tremor that shook him.

Suddenly understanding the burden he had carried for so long, and the toll it had taken on him, Lysette thought compassionately of how alone he had been for so many years.

"It is obvious that you're no murderer," she continued, giving him time to recover himself. "This morning you couldn't even make yourself kill Etienne Sagesse in a justifiable duel. For all your posturing and snarling, I believe that you are basically harmless. But that is hardly enough to recommend you as a husband."

"*Harmless?*" he repeated, his head jerking up. His face turned dark with a scowl.

"And untrustworthy," she added. "Since the day we met, you have betrayed, manipulated, and lied to me."

"The circumstances were unusual."

"Is that an apology? It doesn't sound like one."

"I apologize," he said through his teeth, approaching her.

"Very well." Lysette gave his disheveled form a boldly appraising glance from head to toe. "Since I am optimistic by nature, I will assume that such behavior isn't usual for you. Now please explain why I should want to marry you."

Max contemplated her for a long time, obviously coming to the realization that bullying would not work with her. His eyes narrowed as he decided to negotiate.

"I'm a wealthy man, by anyone's standards. As my wife, you could have anything that you desired."

How like a man, to think that his wealth was his primary attraction. Lysette showed no reaction to the statement. "What else?" she asked.

He moved closer with the stealth of a

hungry predator. "I would take care of you. You already know that."

The reminder of how he had cared for her during the fever softened Lysette, but she was careful not to let him see it. "What about our age difference?"

"Age difference?" His masculine pride was obviously stung.

She suppressed a smile. "There are at least fifteen years between us."

"That's not uncommon," he pointed out.

That was true. Many Creole men, especially ones from wealthy families, sowed their oats for years before they finally married in their thirties or even forties. Many others lost their first and even second wives to childbirth or disease, and they married again to girls straight from the schoolroom.

"Still," Lysette persisted, "there would be difficulties in store for a couple with so many years between them."

"*Au contraire.* I can guarantee that I would be far more accommodating than a husband your own age. If you marry me, I would allow you a great deal of freedom."

That was his strongest point yet, but Lysette kept her face expressionless. "Is there anything else I should take into consideration?"

He reached for her, fast as a striking panther. "There's this," he muttered, pulling her into his arms.

She inhaled sharply, too stunned to move. His mouth was scorching, his lips searching and pressing with gentle insistence. Lysette pushed at him just a little, and he gripped her wrists and pulled them around his neck. Her slim body was flattened against his from chest to knees, anchored by his large hand at the small of her back. The intimate taste of him, sweet and dark and male, made her feel drunk. Excitement and pleasure flooded her, and she leaned helplessly against his hard body. He tasted her upper lip and then touched the center of the lower one with his tongue, a moist silken stroke that set her nerves on fire. "Open your mouth," he whispered, his hand cupping behind her head. "Open for me, Lysette, yes, yes. . . ."

She was astonished to feel his tongue sliding past her teeth, exploring the inside of her mouth. A moan shivered in her throat. Kissing him was even sweeter and richer than she had imagined — and she could no longer deny to herself that she had imagined it many times. Her sensual awareness of him had begun the moment they had met and had finally expanded into something elemental . . . uncontrollable.

Max claimed her with gently exploring kisses, while his hand urged her hips more tightly against his. He made a cradle of her loins, nudging the hard, unmistakable shape of his erection into the most vulnerable part of her. She gasped at the rising heat that made her want to tear at her own clothes, and his, until they were both naked.

Realizing that she was about to lose all self-control, not to mention her sanity, Lysette tore her mouth from his and drew in huge lungfuls of air. His lips wandered along her throat, licking and nibbling at sensitive places. He murmured in French and English, entreaties that aroused her, promises that astonished her.

"Max . . ." she said breathlessly, "I'm not certain that physical attraction is a good enough reason to marry."

"By God, it is for me," he growled, and fastened his mouth over hers again. The taste of him was addictive. She couldn't stop herself from responding avidly to the deep, languid strokes of his tongue. His free hand coasted over her body, moving up to the curve of her breast. The heat of his hand sank through the soft cotton, and his thumb moved in ever-diminishing circles until it reached the exquisitely hard center. He took the delicate point of her nipple between his fingers, and pleasure shot deep into the pit of her belly. Gripping his hard-muscled back with her hands, she pulled herself against him.

A groan reverberated in Max's chest, and he swung her up suddenly, carrying her to the bed. In the few strides it took him to reach it, Lysette realized what was happening. Although her body demanded that she surrender to him right then and there, her mind recalled the reasons why it was still far too soon.

As soon as he laid her on the bed, Lysette rolled away and sat up. She held out a restraining hand as Max began to crawl over her.

"No," she gasped. "No, don't."

It was amazing, in retrospect, that mere words had the power to stay him, when his gaze devoured her as if he were starved, and his body was clearly primed for conquest. However, he held still and inhaled deeply as he strove to master himself.

"If I were to accept your proposal . . ." Lysette paused to take a deep, steadying breath. "I would require some time to become accustomed to you before I let you into my bed. We are still strangers, after all."

Satisfaction flared in Max's eyes as he realized that the bargain had been struck, and that they were negotiating the fine points.

"From my perspective, *petite,* we are already intimately acquainted."

She knew what he was referring to. "Since I was unconscious for most of that time, it hardly counts."

"Very well. I will allow you some time before we share a bed. However, I reserve the right to try and persuade you *not* to wait."

He reached for her again, but Lysette scooted backward and kept her knees between them. "I should also make it clear that I am not a naturally obedient sort of woman."

A sudden smile lurked at the corners of his mouth. "I knew that from the moment I met you. In return, let me make it clear that I am a man of limited patience. Don't test it too often, *d'accord?*"

"*D'accord,*" she agreed. Glancing down at her knees, she spoke in as diffident a tone as she could manage. "What if I should eventually bear a child? Would that displease you?"

"Not at all," Max said gruffly, his gaze flickering to her stomach in a glance that made her spine tingle. "Although you may wish to wait for a year or so. You'll have quite enough changes in your life to deal with."

"I won't have any choice in the matter, once we begin sleeping together," Lysette said with a frown. "God decides such things."

For some reason he looked amused. "At last, something you don't know," he mocked gently. "There are ways to prevent pregnancy."

"How?"

"It's irrelevant at the moment, isn't it? When you invite me to your bed, I'll enlighten you."

He looked so disreputable and handsome, with his dark hair falling over his forehead and a smile playing on his lips, that Lysette felt a pang of pleasure deep inside. She could hardly believe that this magnificent man was going to be hers. No other woman would ever hold him in her arms or take him to her bed. Lysette intended to enchant him so thoroughly that the thought of straying from her would never occur to him. Of course, she knew that he had absolutely no intention of falling in love with her. He planned to enjoy her body and assume the role of husband without ever endangering his heart. Lysette, however, had very different plans.

Max's eyes turned smoky. "Why are you smiling like that?"

She told him the truth. "I am thinking, Max, that before long, I am going to have you wrapped around my finger."

The statement caused him to laugh. "Lysette," he replied softly, "before long, I am going to be wrapped around your entire body."

The Vallerand clan — not to mention all of New Orleans — reacted with scandalized delight to the news of Maximilien's wedding. Always preoccupied with the subjects of courtship and marriage, the Creoles had already begun to make predictions about the fate of the bride. Some said the wedding would never take place, while others claimed to have heard from a reliable source that the girl was already *enceinte*. One thing was certain: If and when a child was born, there would be an assiduous counting of days to determine when it had been conceived.

Lysette's genealogy was analyzed in every Creole parlor. Little fault could be found with her bloodlines, but that did little to quell the rumors flying around New Orleans. After all, not one member of the bride's family would attend the wedding. Parents held Lysette's situation up to their daughters as an example of the hazards that would most certainly befall a disobedient girl.

Owing to the events leading up to the proposal, there would not be a large wedding at St. Louis Cathedral, but rather a small affair, with only a brief religious ceremony. Still afterward there would be a large banquet at the Vallerand plantation. Everyone in New Orleans begged for invitations, unseemly rumors notwithstanding.

It was expected that the music, food, and wine at the wedding banquet would make the occasion one to be remembered for years to come. In the old days Vallerand hospitality had been known as the finest in the territory. At Irénée's desperate petition, a celebrated old French baker temporarily came out of retirement to bake the many-tiered wedding cake.

The wedding would fall on a Monday, not a bad choice, although Tuesday was currently the most fashionable. It was considered vulgar to marry on Saturday, or Friday, usually the day on which public executions were held. As tradition demanded, Lysette was kept in strict seclusion beforehand, while everyone speculated as to what she looked like. Expectations ran high, as most decided that she must be an extraordinary beauty. *Vraiment,* what other kind of woman would tempt Maximilien Vallerand to marriage, after all these years?

 CHAPTER

6

Irénée walked through the double parlors with a satisfied smile, making certain that the guests would find no flaw in her house, no fingerprints on the glass, no wilted flowers. As Creole tradition dictated, the wedding ceremony would take place in the afternoon.

The house was filled with huge garlands of roses, and the silver and crystal had been polished. The wedding cake was a splendid towering creation adorned with sugar-paste flowers so skillfully tinted that they were nearly impossible to distinguish from real ones. Now, with only a few hours remaining until the wedding, there was little to worry about.

Her smile faded slightly as she heard a minor commotion out in the hall. Certain the twins were up to some mischief, she rushed to the doorway with scolding words on her lips. "Justin! Philippe! *Pas de ce charabia! Pas de ce —*"

She stopped with a gasp as she saw the two tall figures of her younger sons. Alexandre and Bernard were home.

"My sons," she exclaimed in disbelief, "what are you doing here?"

The two tall, dark-haired brothers glanced at each other, and then back at her. Alexandre replied in a quizzical tone. "I was under the impression that we lived here, Maman."

"Yes, but . . . you have returned a bit sooner than I expected."

"We decided we had seen enough of France," Bernard said dryly. "Those Fontaine daughters, Maman . . . *Bon Dieu,* some of our *horses* are more attractive than the choicest of the lot."

"Bernard, how uncharitable! I am certain that you exaggerate."

Alexandre was turning slow circles, gazing at the flower-bedecked house. "What is all this?" he asked in bewilderment. "Has someone died?"

While Lysette was safely tucked away upstairs having her hair arranged, the Vallerands drew together for a family conference in the parlor. Rumpled, dusty, and weary from the long journey, Alexandre and Bernard stared at their mother and older brother in disbelief.

"You are going to be *married?*" Alexandre exclaimed, leaning his hip on the back of the settee and folding his lanky arms across his chest. He snickered and looked at Max, who favored him with a cool stare. "Of all things

I had expected to find on my arrival . . ." For some reason, the sight of his oldest brother clad in wedding finery tickled Alex's fancy. He had always been the most irreverent of Irénée's sons. "*Bien sûr,* he's finally been caught!" He choked with laughter, until even Bernard's sober demeanor cracked with a smile.

"I fail to see what is so amusing," Max said with a scowl.

Alexandre had nearly fallen to the floor by now. "I would like to know what kind of woman managed to drag you to the altar! Did she use a very big club?"

Bernard regarded Max more seriously. "Who is she? Not anyone we know, I would guess. You've never given a second glance to any of the women around here."

Irénée answered for him. "Lysette is a girl of excellent family, from Natchez. *Te souviens de Jeanne Magnier?* Max's bride is Jeanne's daughter."

"A Magnier?" Bernard repeated, looking at Max speculatively. "An attractive family, as I recall. I would wager there was little need for her to carry a club."

Max smiled unexpectedly. "She has many virtues, beauty among them."

"She must be remarkable indeed for you to risk marriage again," Bernard remarked.

They were all quiet for a moment, remembering that other wedding so many years ago.

Irénée broke the spell by speaking briskly. "Lysette will make Max very happy, you will see. Finally the past is behind us."

Lysette's hand shook so badly that Max could hardly slide the gold band onto her finger. Although they both desired to be wed, the ceremony was not an especially joyful occasion. Max was tense and grim-faced, and his hand was strangely cold. Lysette had no doubt that he was remembering his first wedding, and the tragedy that had haunted him ever since. He probably feared the possibility that his second marriage would become a living hell just as the first had.

For her part, Lysette struggled to overcome her own doubts. The words she spoke would chain her forever to the man beside her. Legally Maximilien Vallerand would have the power to punish, abuse, or subject her to any whim, no matter how irrational. In the context of Creole culture, he had what amounted to the power of life or death over her.

She could only hope that her judgment of him had been correct. Perhaps she was mad, to place herself in the possession of a man she knew so little. However, she reminded herself pragmatically that most brides and grooms were virtual strangers, matches being made by parents who rarely asked for their approval.

Incense lent its sweet, pungent scent to the

air as Lysette knelt before the priest and prayed for God's blessing on the marriage. When she was finished, she placed her hands in Max's and allowed him to pull her to her feet.

But while the ceremony had been small, the wedding feast was attended by more guests than Lysette could count. She even lost sight of Max, who was monopolized by crowds of relatives. Lysette stayed by Irénée's side, trying to ignore the snatches of conversation she heard as the woman gossiped over her.

"Not nearly as pretty as I had expected . . ."

"She doesn't *look* ruined, Maman."

"That hair . . ."

"It will not be long before he strays . . ."

". . . Ah, I would not be in her place for any amount of money!"

Irénée drew her to the table where the massive wedding cake, a daunting fortress of sugar and roses, towered in splendor. "It is time to cut the cake, Lysette." Immediately the unmarried maidens gathered around them. According to tradition, each maiden was to receive a slice, which she would take home and put under her pillow along with the names of three eligible men, one of whom might then be moved to propose to her.

Lysette lifted the knife and studied the

towering creation, wondering where to make the first slice. Suddenly she was aware of Max standing behind her. An excited titter ran through the cluster of girls as he placed his hand on Lysette's back and murmured in her ear, "May I help?"

Lysette glanced at him with a half smile. With relief, she saw that his tension had faded, and his face was relaxed and smooth.

"Please do," she invited, turning her full attention to the cake. "I don't think this knife will be sufficient — do you happen to have a hatchet?"

He chuckled. "It is quite an impressive cake, isn't it?" His large hand closed over hers, and he pulled her back lightly against his chest. The guests chuckled and offered encouragement as Max helped his bride cut several slices, his hand engulfing hers as he guided the knife. Lysette was intensely aware of the warmth between their bodies and the way his breath touched her neck whenever he leaned forward.

"You're looking down the front of my dress, aren't you?" she murmured, setting down the frosting-coated knife.

"Certainly not. I am helping you with the cake."

Amusement rose in her chest. "Liar."

She felt him smile against her hair. "If you are going to deprive me of a wedding night, you shouldn't begrudge me a little peek at your breasts. And if you didn't want me to look at them, you shouldn't have worn such a low-cut gown."

"I chose a low-cut gown because I hoped to divert everyone's attention from my hair," she said dryly. "Unfortunately, it doesn't seem to have worked — they're all talking about my hair anyway."

Max touched her chin with his fingertips and nudged her face toward him. While everyone watched, he fingered one of the tiny springing curls that had erupted from the pinned-up mass of her rebellious red hair. The humidity had made it more frizzy than usual, until it appeared as if a fiery halo surrounded her coiffure. "Your hair is one of the things I find most beautiful about you." Leaning closer, he let his mouth drift to the tender edge of her ear. "But even so," he whispered, "I still prefer looking at your breasts."

She laughed and pushed at him. Catching her hand, Max kissed the tip of her thumb, where a patch of frosting had collected. She suppressed a gasp as she felt his tongue remove the dab of sweetness.

"You are wicked," she said, knowing that her blush contrasted violently with her hair.

"Let me visit you tonight. I'll show you how wicked I can be."

"No," she said with a provocative smile. "I am going to hold you to our agreement. I need more time."

"I am sorry to hear that." He flashed her a brief grin and released her hand.

Eventually the dancing began, signaling the time when the bride was to be led to the bedchamber to wait for the "ordeal" yet to come. Traditionally the bride's mother helped her to change into her nightgown, and then explained what would happen when the bridegroom arrived to claim his conjugal rights. Irénée appeared and gave Lysette a motherly smile. "I will take you upstairs now, Lysette. Since your own mother is not here, I will be honored to accompany you to your room."

Max reached Lysette at the same time that Irénée did. His fingers wrapped around Lysette's as he spoke to his mother. "There is no need for you to leave the guests, Maman."

Irénée frowned at her son. "But I must take Lysette upstairs and help her change . . . Max, you know very well that you must wait down here. It is the tradition."

"I intend to break with tradition tonight," he said.

Lysette glanced at him with a perplexed frown but remained silent.

Irénée forced a social smile to her lips, mindful of the guests' attention on them. "*Mon fils,* what will all these people think if you disappear with Lysette like that?"

"They'll think whatever they wish. They always do."

"Maximilien," Irénée persisted, "I will put this to you as plainly as possible. Lysette has not yet been prepared for what is to happen tonight. I have not explained *anything* to her."

Max smiled faintly. "If Lysette has questions, I will be happy to provide the answers. Let us go, Maman."

"Maximilien, this is indecent!"

Ignoring his mother's protest, Max began to lead Lysette from the drawing room. As Irénée had warned, tongues wagged and eyes bulged. A bride and groom departing from the wedding party together was in extremely bad taste, since all the guests were aware of where the couple was headed and what would soon happen between them.

Alexandre stopped them at the door, taking hold of Lysette's shoulders and kissing her heartily on each cheek. His dark eyes twinkled at her. "You are a most welcome addition to the family, little sister. Max should count himself fortunate that I did not meet you first."

Lysette laughed at his outrageous charm, while Max pulled her away from his brother's grasp with a jealous frown. He retained her hand in his as they went upstairs. Neither of them spoke until they reached the master bedroom.

"Now," Lysette said with a quizzical smile, "tell me why you would not let your mother accompany me upstairs. I was quite looking forward to hearing her explanation of what happens between husbands and wives in bed."

Max closed the door and untied his starched white cravat. "That's what I was afraid of. Regardless of whether or not you allow me to make love to you, *doucette,* I don't want you to be misinformed about the marital relationship by my mother."

"After bearing three children, I think your mother must know *something* about it."

"She doesn't believe that sexual intercourse should be practiced unless it's for the procreation of children," he said bluntly. "She's Catholic."

"So are you."

"Yes, but I'm a bad one."

Lysette laughed. "Very well. You may educate me as you wish. Just remember your promise."

"Of course." He removed his coat slowly. Their gazes meshed intimately, and the silence became charged with tension. Despite Lysette's intention to remain composed, she felt her heart beat erratically at the realization that they were now married. He could do anything he liked with her, and no one would interfere. She was fairly certain that he would not betray her trust now, when that betrayal would certainly destroy any faith she might ever have in him. On the other hand

. . . she wouldn't put it past him to test her a little.

Giving him a deliberately offhand smile, she played with the spill of champagne lace that trimmed the elbow-length sleeves of her seafoam-blue silk gown.

After draping his coat and cravat on a chair near the hearth, Max glanced at her with coffee-dark eyes. "Do you know what happens in the marital bed, Lysette?"

"Of course. I have a married sister, remember. And one can't help hearing things here and there."

"Tell me what you know, then."

She adopted an expression of deep concern. "Has it been so long that you've forgotten, Max?"

He grinned at her impudence.

"No, I merely want to hear your version, and perhaps make a correction or two if necessary."

"Very well, I —" She stiffened as he walked toward her. Gently Max took hold of her shoulders and turned her away from him. The brush of his fingers on her back caused her breath to snag. He began to unfasten the buttons of her wedding gown. Lysette found it difficult to speak around the swallow that had lodged in her throat. "What are you doing, Max?"

"Making you more comfortable."

"I am quite comfortable the way I am,

thank you." Her stomach quivered as she felt his fingers moving deftly along the line of tiny silk-covered buttons. "Max, your promise —"

"I agreed not to make love to you," he said, his warm breath falling on the nape of her neck. "You didn't stipulate that I couldn't *look* at you."

"I should think that after seeing me naked for nearly three weeks, that would be enough."

"Since you were unconscious for most of that time, it didn't count."

An unsteady laugh escaped her as she heard her own words being repeated back to her. Finishing the row of buttons, Max leaned closer to nuzzle into the curly upsweep of her hair.

The bodice of her gown slipped down to her elbows, and Lysette gripped the handfuls of silk and lace over her thin chemise. Max stood so close that she could sense the heat and weight of his body, smell the alluring fragrance of his skin, the light hint of bay rum, and the crisp note of starch from his shirt. But he did not touch her.

Inhaling deeply, Lysette moved away from him, heading to the dresser where her nightclothes had been placed. As was the way of most Creole couples, they had agreed to occupy separate bedrooms.

"The marital relationship seems quite

simple," she said, somehow managing to keep her bodice up and simultaneously remove a nightgown from the drawer. As she straightened, she saw Max's reflection in the square Queen Anne mirror on the dresser. He had removed his shoes and was sitting on the bed, thighs spread.

She concentrated on the nightgown in her hands as she continued. "The husband and wife embrace and kiss, until he becomes aroused. Then he puts his . . . his . . . male part inside her, and it is painful. After the first time, it is no longer quite as unpleasant, but it is an obligation that a wife may not often refuse. Unless she has her monthly courses, or some other illness gives her a respite from his attentions."

"A respite," Max repeated in a strange voice. Risking a glance at him, Lysette saw an almost comical mixture of amusement and consternation on his face.

"Well, yes. I can't see that any woman would actually look forward to letting a man do *that* to her. My sister Jacqueline says that it is quite unpleasant."

"Does your sister love her husband?"

"I don't believe so. It was an arranged match, and they don't suit. He is somewhat older than she."

"How old is he?"

"About a hundred and fifty," Lysette said glumly, and Max let out a rich laugh.

"And you were worried about *our* age difference?"

Lysette shrugged and smiled, unable to help contrasting her sister's decrepit husband with the virile creature before her. "I wasn't, really," she admitted. "I was just trying to provoke you."

"You succeeded," he informed her, and she laughed.

Regarding the balled-up gown in her fists, Lysette wondered how to change clothes while preserving her modesty. It didn't seem possible. Wryly she reflected that she had no secrets from him, anyway. Before she let herself think about it too long, she shed her wedding gown and chemise, untied her garters, and unrolled her stockings. The entire process took less than a minute, but she felt her husband's blistering gaze on her, and it seemed an eternity before she finally donned the nightgown.

Her face was vivid red as she glanced at him.

"You're very beautiful," Max said, his voice hoarse.

Lysette knew that she was hardly a raving beauty, but the way he stared at her left no doubt as to his opinion to the contrary. And she was certainly not going to argue. "*Merci*," she murmured. Cautiously she came to the bed and stood beside him, raising her brows expectantly. "Well? Is my version of the marital relationship accurate, or do you wish to modify it?"

Max gestured for her to come to him. Extending one hand, he tugged her up onto the mattress, where she settled with her legs partially curled beneath her.

"There are a few things I want to clarify," he said, lifting a hand to her hair. His fingers smoothed over the ruddy curls and found the pins that anchored her coiffure. With great care, he took down her hair and sifted through the wild mass. She could not suppress the quiver of pure bliss that went down the back of her neck. The tiny aches where the pins had pulled her hair dissolved in a tingle of comfort.

"First," Max said, "it is not an obligation that can only be avoided in the case of illness or monthly courses. You may refuse me at any time, without having to give a reason. Your body is your own, to be shared or withheld at your discretion. I wouldn't find it pleasurable to force myself on an unwilling partner — which leads to a second point. There are things a man can do to make the sexual act pleasant for his partner. It doesn't have to be uncomfortable, after the first time."

Lysette was very still, lulled by his stroking hands in her hair. "Max . . ." Heat blazed over her face, and she felt suffocated by embarrassment. "When we were kissing the

152

other day . . . I *felt* you . . . that is, I felt your . . . and I don't think . . ."

"Yes?" he prompted huskily at her mortified silence.

"There is no possible way that you could make it comfortable," she blurted out.

To her everlasting gratitude, he did not laugh, but replied in a serious manner. "Lysette." He nuzzled the top of her head and worked his way down to her ear. She felt his lips brush the tender lobe. "I think your body will learn to accommodate me," he whispered. "Trust me about that, *d'accord?*"

"All right."

To her surprise, he left the bed. "I have to leave you now, *petite.*"

"But I still have some questions."

"Unfortunately, there are limits to my self-control." His hand descended to her bare ankle and squeezed gently. "Let me go, Lysette, so that I can keep my promise not to ravish you. We'll talk more later, I promise."

"Can't you stay just a little longer?" she asked, reaching out to touch his chest. She felt the play of muscles underneath his shirt, their tension betraying the desire he kept so sternly in check. The soft light of the *veilleuses,* the little lamps on the dresser and bedside table, flirted gently over the firm edges of his cheekbone and jaw.

Wincing visibly, Max removed her hand

from his chest. "Not if you wish to remain a virgin tonight," he said gruffly.

Suddenly Lysette was tempted to invite him to stay. However, she could not allow a single impulsive moment to interfere with her resolve. She could only allow him to make love to her when she was certain that he was truly *in* love with her . . . or at least that he felt something very close to it. And at the moment she knew that the attraction and liking between them had not yet matured into the deeper emotion that could only come with time.

"Then good night," she said, and leaned forward to brush a quick kiss against his mouth.

Max shook his head ruefully. "You don't make it easy to be trustworthy, *chèrie*. You're far too tempting, and I'm not accustomed to denying myself something I want."

He picked up his coat, shrugged into it, and went to the door.

"Max?" Lysette was perturbed by his actions. He would not have put his coat on unless he was planning to go downstairs. But surely he would not return to mingle with the guests — that would be the height of bad taste. Was it possible that he intended to leave the plantation?

He paused and glanced over his shoulder. "Yes?"

"Are you going out this evening?"

A brief but maddening smile touched his lips, as if he knew exactly what she feared — that he might satisfy his desires with his *placée* tonight, since his wife was not available to him.

"Someday, *ma petite,* my whereabouts at night will be entirely your concern." He added with wicked gleam in his eyes, "But not yet."

And with that he left, closing the door gently behind him.

Lysette glared after him, aware for the first time in her life of the acrid taste of jealousy.

Max paused outside the bedroom door, finding it difficult to leave Lysette when every impulse demanded that he return to her. Without conceit, he knew that he had the ability to persuade her to yield to him, and that she would enjoy it as much as he did. However, her trust was too important for him to risk. He would wait as long as she wanted him to, though it was going to be difficult.

Had he wanted Corinne like this? The recollection of his first night with her was little more than a blur, but he did remember that Corinne — the first and only virgin he had ever bedded — had regarded him with resentment and reproach forever afterward. In spite of his efforts to be gentle, it had been a painful and mortifying experience for her.

Corinne had been raised to dread any kind of intimacy with her husband, just as Max had been brought up to think that love for a wife was entirely different than love for a mistress.

Thank God that age and experience had taught him to believe otherwise.

The next day Bernard held a glass of rich red wine between his long fingers as he contemplated his older brother. This was their first opportunity to talk privately since he had returned from France. Max had been gone all day, superintending the repair of a faulty bridge on the property. He had come into the library without changing, intending to have a drink while his bath was being drawn. The filthy condition of Max's clothes attested to his active involvement in the repair of the bridge.

Bernard could not help being amused by his brother's appearance. "That isn't the way I would have expected you to spend the day after your wedding," Bernard said.

"Nor I," Max replied wryly as he sat down and crossed his legs, heedless of the crusts of mud that fell from his boots to the fine Aubusson carpet.

"I see you have not changed in one regard: Nothing is right unless you do it yourself. There is no call for you to wallow in the mud and sweat like a field hand, is there?"

156

Max tightened his mouth with annoyance. Neither Bernard nor Alexandre wanted any of the responsibility of running the plantation. The only times they entered the library were to reach for the liquor decanters on the sideboard or to extend their palms for their monthly allowances.

However, both of them — Bernard in particular — criticized him freely when they did not agree with his decisions concerning the plantation. The irony was, Max didn't even enjoy farming, and had inherited little of his father's fierce love of the land. His interests were directed far more in the areas of business and politics.

Furthermore, his increasing political activities had changed his perspective on more than a few issues. Many of the politicians who visited from the northeast had made no secret of their abolitionist views, and as he debated with them, Max had found it difficult to defend the system of slavery that he had inherited. Many of their points had made him increasingly uncomfortable and even guilt-ridden.

He had heard that President Jefferson himself had mixed views on the issue of slavery, trying to balance questions of ethics with economic concerns. Max's own moral dilemma, combined with his lack of interest in farming, had made the Vallerand plantation a burden that he sorely wished he could discard.

"Since I seem to be the only Vallerand available to run the plantation," Max said sardonically, "I believe I'll do it as I see fit. However, whenever you or Alexandre wish to assume some responsibility, I will yield gladly."

"Our father decided long ago what roles we would assume," Bernard said with a philosophical shrug. "You were to be the paragon, the choicest of all the aristocratic offspring in New Orleans . . . the head of the family. I was to be the prodigal, and Alexandre, the libertine. How dare we step outside the parts we were cast in?"

Max gave him a skeptical glance. "That is a convenient excuse, Bernard. The fact is, Father is gone, and you may do as you choose."

"I suppose," Bernard muttered, studying his boots.

In the uncomfortable silence that ensued, Max considered ways of broaching the subject that had to be discussed. "Were the Fontaine daughters truly that unappealing, Bernard?" he finally asked.

Bernard gave a weary sigh. "No, no . . . but how could I possibly consider marriage when I know that somewhere out there I have a woman and an illegitimate child who need my protection?"

"It's been ten years," Max said flatly. "By now she's probably found a husband."

"And that is supposed to comfort me? That some other man is raising *my* child? My God, every night for the past ten years I've wondered why she left without telling me or her family where she went!"

"I'm sorry, Bernard," Max said quietly. "Back then I might have been able to do something about it, but instead . . ."

He fell silent. At the time he had been too involved in the turmoil of Corinne's murder to give a damn about his younger brother's unfortunate affair with Ryla Curran, the daughter of an American boatman. Bernard and the girl had known that marriage between a Catholic and a Protestant would have meant disaster for one or both of them. When Ryla discovered she was pregnant, she virtually disappeared. In spite of Bernard's efforts to find her and the baby ten years had gone by without a sign of them.

"Bernard," Max said slowly, "you have searched long enough for them. Perhaps now you should let go of the past."

"Is that what *you've* decided to do?" Bernard asked, changing the subject abruptly. "Is that the reason for this precipitous marriage?"

"I married her because I want her," Max said evenly.

"You did not stay the night with her — the entire household knows."

"The household be damned. It's my mar-

159

riage, and I'll conduct it however I wish."

"I know you will," Bernard said lightly. "But I think you're a fool for ignoring tradition. Remember, you should spend at least a week alone with your new bride." He smiled suggestively. "It is your duty as her husband to break her in properly."

Max scowled. "Perhaps someday I'll ask for your opinion. In the meanwhile —"

"Yes, I know." Bernard's dark eyes flickered with humor. "By the way, have you decided to give Mariame up?"

As Max parted his lips to answer, some instinct prompted him to glance toward the doorway. Lysette stood there frozen, having just come in search of him. It was clear from her expression that she had overheard Bernard's question. *Well, hell,* Max thought in exasperation.

Lysette quickly adopted a bright, determined smile as she advanced into the room. "Forgive me for interrupting, *mon mari*," she said lightly. Dressed in a light peach gown that molded her breasts together and draped gently over her slender figure, she looked fresh and vibrant. He wanted to seize her immediately, in spite of his sweat-soaked muddy clothes, and capture her mouth with a lusty kiss. "Your bath has been filled," she told him. "I assume you will want to wash before supper."

Max was at her side at once, feeling his

mood lighten in her presence. She had a remarkable effect on him, reminding him of
the time in his life when he had been young
and idealistic, and had every expectation of
happiness. "Most certainly. We will talk later,
Bernard."

His brother murmured an indistinguishable
reply as they left.

"You are very dirty," Lysette said. "What
have you been doing today, Max?"

Max ignored the question, wondering if
anyone else in the family had speculated on
his possible whereabouts the previous evening. "Did my mother happen to make mention of my departure last night?"

"Oh, yes," she replied with an ironic edge
to her tone. "She counseled me to forgive
you for neglecting me on our wedding night,
and sought to reassure me that in time you
will improve."

He took her elbow as they walked. "Would
you like to know where I went last night?"

"Not particularly," Lysette said, and he
grinned at the obvious lie. "However," she
added, "if you wish to tell me, go right
ahead."

"I went to see my former *placée*." Max's
amusement persisted as Lysette jerked her
elbow away from his grasp. "Shall I tell you
what occurred between us?"

"No," she snapped, and then stopped to
stare at him warily. "Did you say 'former'?"

"Yes, former. And nothing happened, other than that we agreed to end our arrangement for good."

"*Nothing?*" she asked suspiciously.

"Not even a good-bye kiss."

"Oh." Aware of an unexpected wash of relief, Lysette fought to conceal her pleasure. She let him take her arm again, and they walked into his bedroom, where a steaming bath awaited. A cake of expensive hard-milled soap and a pile of folded toweling had been placed on an overturned bucket beside the tub. Max made an appreciative sound at the sight, and stripped off his shirt.

Lysette stopped suddenly, unable to keep from glancing at his body. Max was muscular and sun-bronzed, a healthy male who was fully in his prime. Heavy black hair covered his chest and narrowed into a silkier pelt over the muscled tautness of his abdomen. His bare arms were corded and heavily developed from work on the plantation, not to mention years of fencing. Lysette stopped breathing as she watched him stride to the bed and sit on the edge of it.

Max stared at her with coffee-dark eyes. A smile tipped one corner of his mouth as he noticed her interest. He pulled off his muddy boots with a grunt of exertion, dropped the offending articles to the floor, and brushed the dried clay from his hands. With each movement, muscles flexed beneath his gleaming tanned skin. Lysette noticed a few marks on his torso, including a star-shaped scar on his shoulder.

"Where did those scars come from?" she asked.

"Dueling wounds. My honor, negligible as it may seem, has taken many contests of skill to defend."

The musky, alluring smell of his skin drifted to Lysette's nostrils. It made her want to draw closer and press her face into the salty heat of his neck. She approached him slowly, her gaze returning to the scars. "I suppose some of the young Creoles in town seek to prove their manhood by fighting you," she said. "Like wolves challenging the leader of the pack. Have you ever wounded someone fatally?"

Max shook his head. "Usually honor is satisfied when first blood is drawn. I've always tried to avoid dueling, except for the one with Sagesse. I only fight when they make it impossible not to."

"I understand," Lysette said gently, reaching out to touch the scar on his shoulder. She hadn't been aware of moving closer to his half-naked body, but she was right next to him, her breath stirring the hair on his chest. How many times had Max faced the point of a sword? How close to death had he come? The thought bothered her profoundly. Disconcerted, Lysette turned away from him.

"You must be tired after so much exertion today. No doubt you are looking forward to your bath. I will leave you to —"

Lysette broke off as she heard a rustling sound behind her. He had removed his trousers, she realized. He was completely naked. She was immobilized with indecision, wanting to stay, wanting to go.

She heard the sound of his body plunging into the water. "Why don't you help me bathe, *petite?*"

Lysette turned then, helplessly taking in the resplendent sight of gleaming male skin, the hard curves of his shoulders rising above the wooden rim of the tub. "Do you need help?" Her lungs felt hot and dilated, as if she had inhaled some of the abundant steam around him.

"You said that you wanted to become accustomed to me. I am giving you an opportunity to do that."

"How kind of you."

Max grinned and settled back in the tub, sighing as the scalding water engulfed his strained muscles. He slitted his eyes, looking like a lazy tomcat in the sunshine. "You could at least hand me the soap, *ma petite.*" A smile touched his lips as he added provokingly, "Be brave, will you?"

Lysette was not one to back down from a challenge. And her curiosity far outweighed her apprehension. "Certainly, *mon mari.*" She picked up the cake of soap and sniffed it, detecting the scent of lemongrass.

Max levered himself upward, exposing his broad sinewy back. Again she was reminded of a tomcat, silently demanding to be petted.

Lysette's stomach tightened pleasurably. "Why not? I'll scrub your back, *mon mari*. But you will have to do the rest yourself." She pushed her sleeves above her elbows as she approached the tub. The water was clear beneath the ascending steam, affording her a view of the rampant erection beneath the water. Although she tried not to react to the startling sight, a flush spread upward to her hairline.

Max arched a brow, as if expecting a virginal scream of hysterical surprise. Lysette continued around the tub until she stood behind him. "That looks painful," she commented.

He tilted his head back to look at her upside down. "For me, or for you?"

Lysette couldn't help but smile at the provocative question, while the heat of her blush intensified. "For both of us, I would guess."

Reserving comment, Max leaned forward once more. Lysette immersed her hands in the water and rubbed the soap between them, until the tart scent of lemongrass filled the air. Setting the soap aside, she began to spread the creamy substance over his back, her fingers molding over the hard indentations of muscle and the thick ridge of his spine. Rivulets of water and soap coursed down his tanned skin.

It seemed unspeakably intimate to wash his hair, but she did that as well, her soapy fingers working through the dark wet locks and scrubbing the scalp underneath. Max enjoyed her ministrations unabashedly. Lysette rose to her feet to tip the bucket of fresh water over his head, rinsing the suds away.

Carefully she set the bucket down, while Max raked the wet locks back from his forehead. His water-spiked lashes lifted as he gazed at her. "Why don't you join me in here?"

The suggestion surprised and aroused Lysette. A sweet ache blossomed in her chest, spreading to the tips of her breasts until they tightened into sensitive points. When she managed to speak, her throat felt thick and tingling, as if she had been drinking warm honey.

"There's not enough room for two," she said.

"There is if we sit close enough." When Lysette remained still, Max leaned over to her. His mouth found a vulnerable spot on her throat, and he licked and nibbled gently. She drew in a quick breath, her throat moving against the masculine scrape of his jaw. The world seemed to topple slowly, as if she were inside some vast crystal bowl that rolled languidly on its side.

As Lysette reached out in a bid for balance, one of her hands came to rest on the furry surface of his chest. Her fingers sank into a mat of hot waterlogged curls. Her thumb rested on the silken edge of his nipple . . . She couldn't stop herself from stroking until it contracted into a hard point. Max made a low sound and slid one hand around the back of her head. She let him pull her mouth to his, and he kissed her with lazy hunger.

Pleasure swirled over her, her skin alive to the slightest touch. She opened her mouth dreamily, letting him explore her with slow strokes of his tongue. She did not protest as he took her hand and guided it beneath the water. Hot as the bath was, it was nothing compared to the searing heat of his arousal.

Her fingers were pliable, obedient, curving around the heavy masculine length of him. He felt nothing like she had expected. His skin was like thin satin that had been stretched tightly over the hardness of his shaft. Her hand drifted over the shape of him, exploring delicately beneath the water. Max continued to kiss her, his breath striking hard against her cheek, and the awareness of his growing excitement made her feel dizzy and drunk.

Lysette leaned forward to press closer to him, until the front of her dress was soaked and the rim of the tub dug hard into her middle. It was only that burgeoning pain that recalled her to her senses. She winced and pulled back, panting heavily.

Max's face was at once relaxed and intent, his lashes half lowered over eyes that burned with dark heat. Lysette blinked and rubbed her wet hands over her face.

Max reached out and brushed his thumb over a water droplet that was working its way lazily down her cleavage. "Kiss me again," he murmured.

Lysette laughed shakily and struggled to her feet, while the soaked front of her gown made her shiver. "I think you've had quite enough of me for today, monsieur."

He stood in the tub, water cascading down his aroused body in shimmering streams. "If I'd had enough of you, *ma petite,* I wouldn't look like this."

Lysette whirled away with a gasp. She felt him make a swipe at her, and she eluded him nimbly. A burst of agitated giggles escaped her. "Don't you dare, Max! Don't touch me!"

He climbed from the tub and stalked after her, while she flew to the door. Her hand closed around the painted porcelain knob as it occurred to her that she could not run through the house in this waterlogged condition. Neither could she retreat to her room to change, as the housemaids were probably still occupied with sweeping the carpet and changing the linens. "Now, Max," she said in a reasonable tone, still facing away from him, "enough of this. I'll fetch you a towel and —"

His long, wet arms closed around her, and she felt the water from his chest soak through the back of her gown. Another high-pitched giggle erupted from her lips, and she damned herself for losing all traces of self-possession. "Max, you've made me wet all over!"

His mouth descended to the back of her neck, kissing softly. "Sweet little wife," he whispered. "Let me have just a little more of you. I won't break my promise, I swear. Just let me touch you. Please."

She felt him tug at the back of her gown, and the laces gave way, releasing her confined flesh in an impetuous spill. The bodice of her gown began to slide, and before she could prevent it, the gown dropped to the floor in a wet heap. She was left dressed only in a damp chemise and stockings. Max's hand slid over the tight curve of her bare buttocks, and she jumped at the startling touch.

He crooned wordlessly, his chest working against her back as he breathed in deep gusts. His hand glided over her hip and around to her front, his fingertips brushing across the hollow of her navel. Lysette flattened her palms on the hard wood paneling of the door. "Max," she managed to say shakily, "you shouldn't."

"I'll stop the moment you tell me to." His palm passed lightly over the springy thatch of hair between her thighs. His teeth caught the nape of her neck lightly and then he soothed the nip with gentle strokes of his tongue. "Don't be afraid. I only want to please you. *Dieu*, how sweet you are."

Her traitorous throat closed on a protest, while his nearness caused her body to ache in deep, intimate places. She continued to face away from him, gasping, while he eased the chemise up to her waist. He let the scorching length of his erection press high on her buttocks, the head of the shaft seeming to brand her like heated iron. Reality slid free of Lysette's tenuous grasp, and she let herself push back against his steaming male body.

His fingers wandered through the fiery curls, softly exploring the tender feminine mound. Her lips parted, but she couldn't make herself tell him to stop. It felt too good. He sifted through the springy triangle, until Lysette moaned and spread her legs in an involuntary plea. His mouth touched her ear and wandered to her damp cheek.

Gently his clever fingers parted her swollen lips and entered the tender cleft. "*Petite*, I've dreamed of touching you here . . . like this . . . yes, let me, *ma belle*. . . ." He found the

170

tiny peak of flesh that had begun to throb with sensation, and his wet fingertips nudged, circled, coaxed, until Lysette began to whimper and roll her forehead against the door. Her heart raced out of control, the blood pumping wildly through her veins.

"Max," she said raggedly. "Oh, Max . . ."

His middle finger slipped inside her, gliding easily through the tight opening. She stiffened at the tender invasion, while a hot glow spread through her loins. "Shall I stop now?" he whispered. His finger withdrew, causing her to shudder hungrily. "Tell me, Lysette, tell me what you want, and I'll do it."

She turned to face him, her arms winding around his neck, her nipples pressing into the thick fleece on his chest. All principles had burned to cinders in the white-hot conflagration of desire. "Max, make love to me, now, please, please, *please* —"

"I won't take your virginity yet." His hand coasted down her back in a stroke that was meant to soothe, but caused her to writhe wildly. "Not until I'm certain that you truly want it."

"I do want it," she moaned. "I do."

His hand slid back between her legs, his fingers returning unerringly to the place where she needed them most. "I'll give you ease. I just wanted to make certain that you were willing."

If she were any more willing, she would burst into flames. Her head fell back against his supportive arm while her hips squirmed in constricted circles, responding to his every caress. The sensations flared rapidly, too fast, too hot, and she cried out as her body was suddenly overtaken with rich spasms, her nerves sparking with heat, pleasure inundating every part of her until she was weak and shivering. She sagged against him, burying her face in his shoulder.

"Max . . . take me to bed now."

"No," he muttered stealing a hard kiss from her damp lips. "I don't want to take advantage of you, *petite*."

"I would never think that. Please, Max —"

"Not when you might blame me for it later."

Lysette was amazed that he was going to refuse her, when it was obvious that he wanted to make love to her. Did he care that much about her feelings? Her heart pounded at the thought, and she offered him her mouth again. When their lips parted, she said breathlessly, "If you're implying that I'm not in full possession of my senses —"

"You're not."

"Yes, I am!"

"A good Creole wife never argues with her husband," he informed her.

A reluctant laugh bubbled in Lysette's throat, and she played with the hair on his chest. "Max . . ." She rubbed her cheek against his smooth shoulder. "Do you think the bathwater is still hot?"

"Probably." He lifted her chin and smiled down at her. "Is it my turn to bathe you now?" he asked, and lifted her in his arms before she could reply.

CHAPTER

7

Although Lysette had lived in an almost exclusively female household for much of her life, she now found herself surrounded by men. It did not take long for her to discover that her male in-laws were quite different from her stepfather.

The Vallerands were no less volatile than Gaspard, but even in a temper they were soft-spoken. Unlike Gaspard and his ineffectual rantings, they knew how to wound with a few expertly chosen words, and at times the brothers were merciless with each other. When a woman was present, however, all arguments were restrained, and the conversation was steered into gentler channels.

Lysette was beginning to believe the statement Noeline made one day, that the Vallerand men were born with the knowledge of how to charm women. Since childhood, Lysette had been accustomed to Gaspard's poorly veiled dislike, which was why she found herself so easily disarmed by the Vallerands' attentiveness.

Alexandre often made a great show of

taking her aside to ask her advice on matters of the heart, claiming with a roguish wink that any woman who had managed to catch his brother was certainly a great authority. Bernard regaled her with tales of his travels abroad. Philippe shared his favorite books with her, and Justin accompanied her on rides around the plantation.

They were a literate family, devouring books and newspapers and boxes of periodicals imported from Europe. Lysette quickly came to enjoy the family gatherings in the parlor every evening, when they would read aloud, or play word games, or debate political issues while the twins staged inventive battles with battalions of painted lead soldiers.

Ironically, Lysette saw all the other Vallerands far more than she did her own husband. Max was constantly busy, either occupied with plantation business, his political activities, or his shipping operations. He was in the midst of negotiations to purchase another ship to add to his fleet of six, and he was adding another route to the West Indies and appointing a manager to open an office there.

In addition, he was supervising the construction of more warehouses on the riverfront. These activities occupied him for most of every day, until he returned at suppertime. In the evenings, Max relaxed with the family in the parlor, or shared a bottle of wine with Lysette in the privacy of their room.

Since their passionate interlude two weeks earlier, Max had made no further advances to Lysette. She had been tempted on occasion to ask him to make love to her, but she did not yet feel that the time was right, now more determined than ever to win his affection first. In the meantime, she enjoyed the hours that they talked and argued and flirted. The more she came to know her new husband, the more she was coming to care for him. Max was a strong man who bore his responsibilities without complaint, motivated by duty and a sense of protectiveness toward his family. However, he also possessed a ruthlessness, a dominating strength, that fascinated her. Clearly, if she were a meek and docile wife, she wouldn't have lasted five minutes with him. But instead of being intimidated by his forceful will, she delighted in challenging him, and he knew it.

Even though they did not share a bed, Lysette was aware of Max's comings and goings. About twice a week, he left the house at midnight and did not return until three or four in the morning. She did not believe that he was visiting a mistress. But if he was not with a woman, what in heaven's name was he doing?

Finally Lysette decided to confront him as he returned from one of his mysterious out-ings. Max entered his bedroom in the middle of the night to discover his wife waiting for him, the lamp burning at the bedside. Resting on the pillows propped against the headboard, Lysette greeted him calmly. "*Bon soir,* Max. I wonder, what could you have been doing at such a late hour?"

Max smiled wryly. "Nothing that you need to concern yourself with. Now go back to your own bed, or I'll assume that your presence here means that you've finally decided to fulfill your wifely obligations."

The threat did not deter her in the least. "You can't dismiss me that easily, Max. If this happened on just one or two occasions, I might have overlooked it. But you have made a habit of these midnight excursions, and I want to know what is going on."

Placing his hands on the bed, Max leaned over her until their mouths were nearly touching. "I've been attending to a few matters concerning my shipping operations."

"Why can't such work be done during the day?"

"Some business, my sweet, is better conducted at night."

"You're not doing anything *illegal,* are you?"

He held up his thumb and forefinger an inch apart. "Just a little illegal. Nothing more harmful than a cargo of silk stockings, a few cinnamon bales . . . and several thousand English pounds."

"English pounds? But why?"

"The supply of hard money from Mexico was severed when the Americans took possession of the Louisiana Territory, and no one has confidence in the French and Spanish paper money that is available. I fear Governor Claiborne's plan to distribute American paper will have several false starts, and in the meanwhile . . ."

"But don't you want to support Governor Claiborne's efforts?"

His smile was at once casual and ruthless. "Oh, I'm under no special obligation to Claiborne. I help him when I'm able. I also help myself, when the opportunity arises."

Lysette didn't like the idea of her husband dealing in contraband goods, no matter how minor. "If you're caught —"

"Come, you need to sleep," he interrupted. "You have shadows beneath your eyes."

"I wouldn't, if you stayed home at night," she grumbled, yawning hugely as he pulled her from the bed and slid an arm around her waist.

Max frowned as he walked her back to her room. "You've exhausted yourself the past few days. My mother tells me that you have been doing far too much. I want you to rest more, *petite*, especially in light of the fact that you were quite ill not too long ago."

Lysette waved away his concerns. She had been familiarizing herself with the plantation and looking for ways that she could be of use. There were supplies to be ordered, book-keeping, cooking, baking, cleaning of furniture, rugs, drapes, and linens, and endless laundering and mending. Although Lysette thought Irénée and Noeline did a commendable job in running the Vallerand plantation, she saw a few things that could be improved. However, she feared that the older women might take offense were she to try and alter any of their longstanding habits.

"Max," she said, slipping her hand into his large one, "I would like your opinion about something . . ."

"Yes?"

"Don't you think that some of the ways things are done in this house are rather old-fashioned?"

He stopped in front of her bedroom. "Actually, I hadn't noticed."

"Oh, I suppose it's nothing a man would give much thought to. A hundred little things, really . . ." It would be necessary to train at least two more housemaids to keep the huge mansion as scrupulously clean as it should be. There were sun-faded drapes and carpets in several rooms that needed to be replaced. She had discovered treasure troves of silver that hadn't been polished in years. And from what she had observed, there were never enough fresh linens on hand. That was only the beginning of the list. At Irénée's age, there were things she simply didn't see. But how to address such matters without up-setting Irénée — that was the problem.

"I think I understand," Max said wryly, taking her narrow shoulders in his hands. "Listen to me, *petite* — you have the right to turn the entire house upside down, if you so desire. Noeline will do as you tell her, even if she doesn't agree. As for my mother, it won't be long before she'll appreciate having the leisure that other women her age enjoy. In the meanwhile, I have no doubt about your ability to match her stubbornness. Handle her as you see fit, and I will support you fully."

"But I do not wish to distress her —"

"Oh, I don't think you'll provide her with more distress than she can bear." He grinned suddenly. "Only her grandsons can do that."

"All right. Thank you, Max."

His thumbs caressed the edge of her collar-bone, and he smiled lazily before brushing a kiss against her forehead. "Good night."

She expected him to let go of her then, but he hesitated, his hands flexing on her shoulders. Lysette's heart skipped several beats, and she could not stop the sudden wobble of her knees.

Now it would happen, the thought raced through her mind. Now he would ask to come to bed with her — and she no longer had the excuse of unfamiliarity to hold him at bay. To her surprise, she wanted him so much that it no longer seemed imperative to win his heart first. "Max . . ." she said unsteadily, trying to find the words to encourage him.

"Good night," he said at the same time, kissing her forehead once more. "Get some rest, *doucette*."

He turned and left her to wrestle with a peculiar sense of disappointment.

"Burr will arrive tomorrow, without a doubt," Governor Claiborne said, wiping his perspiring face with a handkerchief. "Damn this heat. And I'm told that the barge he will arrive on was a gift from Wilkinson. *Our* Wilkinson!" He sent a glare out the window as if the governor of the Upper Louisiana Territory were in plain sight.

Max settled comfortably in his chair. Amusement touched his expression. "Ours?" he repeated. "He might be *your* Wilkinson, sir, but I don't care to claim him."

"Blast it, how can you smile? Are you in the least bit concerned about what might happen? The two of them, Burr and Wilkinson, make a powerful pair!"

"I'm concerned, yes. But if Burr's plans are, as we suspect, to seize the Louisiana Territory and Texas —"

"And Mexico!" Claiborne reminded him testily.

"And Mexico," Max continued, "he'll need considerable funds from many sources. Funds he won't be able to get, with or without Wilkinson's influence. The Creoles have a saying, sir: *Il va croquer d'une dent.*"

"Which means?"

"He'll munch with only one tooth."

Claiborne refused to smile at the quip. "There's a possibility that Burr will procure all the money he needs from Britain. He's become damned cozy with the ambassador from Great Britain."

"The British won't finance him."

"They might," Claiborne insisted. "At the moment the United States and Britain are hardly on friendly terms."

"However, Britain's current war with France means they can't afford to back a losing cause — and Burr's tongue is too loose for his plans to prove successful."

"Well." Claiborne was silent for a moment. "That's true enough. His enterprise depends on utter secrecy, and I have been surprised by the rumors of things he has said publicly. It is not like Burr to be quite so foolhardy with his words. Overconfident rascal!" He frowned. "If the British won't finance Burr, he'll turn to Spain."

"How do you know that?"

"I and many others have suspected for some time that Wilkinson is secretly in the Spanish pay."

"Is there any proof?"

"No, but the suspicion is not unjustified."

"And of course," Max said slowly, "His Catholic Majesty would like to take Louisiana back under Spanish protection. Yes, it would be logical for Spain to become a patron of Burr."

"Wilkinson is close to the Spanish high commissioner in New Orleans, Don Carlos, the Marquis de Casa Yrujo," Claiborne remarked. "Burr will probably spend some time with Yrujo during this visit. But none of my people have been able to get any information. At the moment, relations between the Spanish and Americans are too hostile. The quarrel over who is entitled to the Floridas might eventually start a war."

"I am acquainted with Yrujo," Max replied. "I'll see what I can learn from him."

Claiborne mopped his face yet again. "He'll know something. The Spanish talent for intrigue is unmatched. They're probably aware of every move Burr makes. I hope you can get Yrujo to reveal a little of what he knows, Vallerand — for all our sakes."

"I'll do my best," Max said dryly.

"Good Lord, what a tangle. What kind of man could manipulate people and even countries to such an extent? Where does Burr get the ambition?" At Max's silence, Claiborne continued as if to himself. "A close acquaintance of Burr has a theory, that Burr would not be involved in such disreputable schemes had his wife not been taken from him some years ago. She had a cancer of some sort — unfortunately, it was a long death."

Max's fingers began an idle tapping on the arm of his chair. "I can hardly believe that would influence his political ambitions, sir."

"Oh, well, Burr doted on her, and when she was gone . . ." The governor's eyes grew distant as he thought of his own wife, who had passed away so recently. "Losing a woman, a wife, can change everything inside a man . . . although you certainly would know —"

Claiborne stopped abruptly as he met Max's emotionless stare.

There was silence until Max spoke. "There are wives," he said flatly, "and wives. My first was no great loss."

Claiborne nearly shivered at the coldness of the man. What boldness, to admit his dislike of the woman he had purportedly murdered. Every now and then Claiborne was forcibly reminded of what his aides had warned him, that Maximilien Vallerand was acutely intelligent and smoothly charming, but completely ruthless.

"And how do you find your second marriage?" Claiborne could not resist asking.

Max shrugged slightly. "Quite pleasant, thank you."

"I am looking forward to meeting the new

Madame Vallerand."

Max's brow arched at the comment. It was rare that their conversation turned to personal matters. Because their goals and political views were similar, they were on friendly terms, but they did not talk of family, children, or personal sentiments, and each was aware that he would not associate with the other were it not for political necessity.

"I expect it will not be long before I have the opportunity to introduce you," Max replied.

Claiborne seemed to look forward to the prospect. "I must admit, I find Creole women very intriguing. Lovely creatures, and so spirited."

Max frowned impatiently and changed the subject. "Do you plan to welcome Burr when he arrives?"

Claiborne nodded ruefully. "My speech is already written."

"Good," Max said dryly. "You may as well maintain the appearance of having nothing to fear from him."

"I thought we had just agreed there was no reason to be afraid of Burr!"

"But then," Max rejoined wickedly, "I'm not *always* right."

Lysette combed through the tiny kitchen garden at the back of the house, picking herbs to be dried and used for seasoning.

She sighed in frustration as she regarded the shadow her sunbonnet cast on the ground.

It was the tradition that a bride could not go calling or be seen in public for five weeks after the wedding. She was forced to stay at home while everyone else was gone. And although she longed to defy tradition, and doubtless Max would encourage her to do as she pleased, she did not care to alienate half of New Orleans so quickly. She had never been so bored. Bernard and Alexandre had been absent last night and all this morning, in pursuit of amusements that would keep them occupied until much later in the day. As usual, Max was not there. And the twins were busy inside the house with their lessons.

Irénée had left early in the morning with the cook to go to market. It was Irénée's special pleasure to be known as *une plaquemine,* a green persimmon, or tight with her money. All the merchants had considerable respect for her ability to bargain for the cheapest prices. After talking with everyone of note in the marketplace, Irénée would return home with all the latest gossip and repeat several bits of conversation. In the meantime, there was little for Lysette to do but wait.

Her ears caught the sound of muffled whispers and stealthy footsteps approaching from the side of the house. Setting down her shallow basket, she watched as two dark heads came into view. It was Justin and

Philippe, furtively carrying some bulky object in a dripping sack. They each held one end of the huge parcel, rounding the corner and turning toward the grove of cypress trees near the bell tower. As Justin saw Lysette, he stopped abruptly, causing Philippe to bump into him. They nearly dropped the heavy sack.

Justin threw an annoyed glance at his brother. "I thought you said that no one was out here!"

"I didn't see her!" Philippe retorted.

Lysette stared at them quizzically. "What are you carrying?"

The twins looked at each other. Justin scowled. "Now she'll go inside and tell," he grumbled.

Philippe sighed. "What'll we do with her?"

Lysette stared at them suspiciously. "Are you *stealing* something?"

Justin took the heavy object in both arms and gestured to Lysette with a jerk of his head. "Kidnap her," he said brusquely. "If we make her a part of it, she can't tell anyone."

"A part of what?" Lysette asked.

"Shhh . . . do you want us all to get caught?" Cheerfully Philippe grasped her wrists and dragged her along with them.

"You're supposed to be studying," Lysette admonished. "Where are we going? What is in that sack? If you *do* get into trouble, I want it to be clear that I was an unwilling partner. A victim. *Mon Dieu,* why is that dripping?"

"It's from the kitchen," Philippe said in a tantalizing voice.

Immediately Lysette knew what it was. "You didn't," she said. "No, you couldn't have." A huge watermelon shipped from across the lake had been soaking for hours in a tub of cold water in the kitchen. It was intended as a special after-dinner treat for the family that night. Stealing it was a serious crime, indeed. Berté the cook would have an apoplectic stroke when she discovered its disappearance. "You must wait until tonight," Lysette said adamantly. "Stealing it isn't worth the trouble you'll cause."

"Yes, it is," Justin said firmly.

She shook her head. "Take it back now, before they realize it's gone. Right away. Philippe, how could you let Justin talk you into this?"

"It was my idea," Philippe said mildly.

They took cover in the trees and deposited their booty on a large stump. Lysette sat on a fallen tree trunk and watched with dismay as the twins unwrapped the glistening emerald melon. "I'll do the honors," Justin said, and lifted the melon, grunting slightly at its weight.

"I can't look," Lysette groaned, cringing in dread, and Philippe put one of his hands over her eyes as the watermelon was cracked against

188

the tree stump. She heard a juicy splitting sound, and Justin's triumphant chortle.

"We've come too far to turn back now," Philippe commented, enormously pleased. Gingerly Lysette pried his hand away from her face and peered at the splendid sight. Appalled as she was by the crime, she could not stop her mouth from watering at the sight of the cold red fruit.

"You should feel guilty," she said sternly, "for depriving the rest of the family."

"They should have known what would happen to an unguarded watermelon," Justin retorted, pulling an ancient but carefully sharpened knife from the kerchief knotted around his thigh and hacking away at the red and green bounty. "Besides, they've deprived us of *lots* of things. This little watermelon only *begins* to settle the score."

"It's not a little watermelon," Lysette said. "It's a big one. Huge, as a matter of fact."

Justin thrust a dripping wedge toward her. "Try some."

"Are you attempting to buy my silence?" Lysette asked with a severe expression.

"It's not a bribe," Philippe cajoled. "Just a gift."

"It's a bribe," Justin corrected. "And she'll take it. Won't you, Lysette?"

She was torn between principle and desire. "I don't think I could enjoy a stolen watermelon."

"It tastes much better when it's stolen,"

Justin assured her. "Try it."

Reluctantly Lysette arranged her apron over her lap and took the offering. As she bit into it, the sugary juice ran down her chin, and she blotted it with a corner of the apron. The watermelon was sweet and crisp, heavenly on a hot day. She had never tasted anything so delicious. "You're right," she said ruefully. "It is better when it's stolen."

For the next few minutes there was no conversation as they concentrated on the melon. It was only when Lysette was comfortably full and the ground around her feet was littered with crescents of rind that she glanced upward and happened to see a tall form approaching.

"Justin? Philippe?" she said slowly. "Your father is coming this way."

"Run!" Justin said, already on his feet.

"What for?" Philippe countered, watching Maximilien. "He's already seen us."

Deciding to save herself, Lysette jumped to her feet and assumed a stern expression. "Now, you two," she said loudly, "I hope that I've made you see the error of your ways. Because if this happens again —"

Max's arm slid around her front, and his low laugh tickled her ear. "That was a very good try, *petite*. But your sticky cheeks give you away."

She grinned up at him, and he brushed his mouth over hers, savoring the watermelon-sweet taste of her lips.

"Traitor," Justin accused as he glanced at Lysette, but he was laughing with the abandon of a young boy.

Max's warm gaze traveled over the three of them. "It seems we have a conspiracy."

Philippe gazed at his father entreatingly. "You won't tell Berté, will you, Father?"

"Of course not. But I fear you'll give yourselves away by the amount of food you leave untouched on your plates tonight."

"It's still afternoon," Justin said. "We'll be hungry again by supper."

"I have no doubt that my two growing boys will," Max replied, and looked at Lysette speculatively. "I wonder about my small wife, however."

Lysette gave him a sunny smile. "You will have to help me think of something. It is your duty to defend me, *n'est-ce pas?*"

"Indeed it is." Max sat with her on the fallen tree trunk, gesturing for Justin to give him a portion of the melon.

"How did you find us?" Lysette removed her apron and passed it to the boys to wipe their hands and faces with.

"According to Noeline, you were in the herb garden. When I went to look for you, I found your basket and a set of tracks." Max took an appreciative bite of watermelon.

Lysette saw that one of his shirtsleeves was threatening to fall down his forearm. She reached out to roll it more snugly. "And now you're a coconspirator," she told him.

He exchanged a smile with her. "I'm merely trying to help you dispose of the evidence."

Nestled against her husband's side, Lysette enjoyed the next few minutes of lazy conversation, while the boys regaled them with tales of their latest adventures in the bayou. She was touched by the twins' obvious admiration of their father and their desire for his approval. What moved her even more, however, was Max's patience with them, the warm attentiveness of his manner. He was a good father, strong but undeniably loving.

Lysette tried to imagine what it might be like to have a child with Max. Her heart ached a little as she reflected that her children, just like Justin and Philippe, would have to deal with the nasty rumors and dark suspicions that people had about Max's past. However, she would teach her children to ignore the things people might say about their father, and to love him as he deserved to be loved.

As *she* was coming to love him.

Stunned by the thought, Lysette remained very still. Yes, she thought, dumbfounded by the recognition that it was true, she was indeed falling in love with him. A tendril of fear curled through her as she reflected that she must keep such feelings private for a while. It was possible that Max would not want her love, that he would not be ready to accept it for a long time. There were too many shadows from the past. . . . Max could barely bring himself to discuss his first marriage with her, and he grew sullen and irritable whenever she pressed him for information.

Lost in her thoughts, Lysette did not listen to the conversation until she heard Max saying to the boys, "I assume that all lessons have been learned thoroughly, or the two of you would not have time for stealing watermelons."

Neither of the twins met his gaze. "There was only a little left to study," Philippe said.

Max laughed. "Then I suggest you finish it before supper. But first find some way to dispose of this mess."

"What about Berté?" Justin asked. "She will try to kill us when she finds out."

Max sent his son a reassuring smile. "I'll handle Berté," he promised.

"Thank you, Father," the twins said, watching as Max pulled Lysette to her feet.

As they walked toward the house, Lysette remained silent, her sugar-sticky fingers clasped in Max's. He sent her a quizzical smile. "Why have you become so quiet?"

"I was just thinking about what a wonderful father you are. It is obvious that the twins adore you. They are very fortunate to have such a loving parent."

"They are good boys," he said gruffly. "I'm the fortunate one."

"You have every excuse in the world to ignore and deny them," Lysette said, "after the terrible experiences you had with their mother. I have no doubt that you are reminded of her sometimes — Irénée says the twins have Corinne's eyes. But you never seem to let that interfere with your feelings for them."

Max released her hand at the mention of his first wife.

"I don't see anything of her in them." His tone had cooled several degrees.

"Do you ever talk to them about her?"

"No," he said curtly.

"It might be good for them. For Justin, in particular. If you explained to him —"

"I've spent ten years trying to forget Corinne," he said, looking ahead with a grim expression. "And so have they. The last thing any of us needs is to discuss her."

"But she was their mother. You can't ignore the fact that she existed. Perhaps if you —"

"Let the matter rest," he said with a sudden vehemence that startled her. "You don't know what you're talking about."

Lysette withdrew into an offended silence, wondering if she had been wrong to bring up the subject. But if Max refused to share such a significant part of his past, the part that had changed him so drastically, how could she ever truly come to know him? She longed for intimacy with him . . . to have his trust, to talk freely about anything, even when the subject was painful or distasteful. Perhaps it was a mistake for her to want such unusual closeness with him. Most women would be happy merely to have an agreeable relationship with their husbands. Her own expression turned grim as she pondered how to be satisfied with what Max was willing to give and not ask for more than that.

Eventually she brought herself to speak once more. "I am sorry," she said with difficulty. "I did not mean to provoke you."

He gave a single nod, but did not reply.

Max thought he had mastered his emotions by the time he reached the library, but the tightness in his chest refused to go away. He closed the door and downed a brandy, welcoming its fiery smoothness.

For years he had been able to keep himself protected, shutting the past behind doors he had thought would never have to be opened. Feelings, needs, vulnerabilities, all seething behind the barriers he had constructed. And if just one of those doors were unlocked, the rest would follow rapidly, and he would be decimated.

He would not let that happen. But even now he could feel the splintering within himself, impossible to hold back.

Love had cost him everything before. In a way, it had been as fatal to him as it had to Corinne. His old self had died ten years ago — permanently, he had hoped. But it seemed that after all this time there was still something left of his heart, and it ached every moment Lysette was near.

Max left the plantation before supper, without telling anyone where he was going. Confronted by the sight of the empty place where her husband should have been, Lysette was too angry and upset to eat. She pushed her food around her plate while the family talked with forced animation. Living in the same house, they could not help but know that some kind of argument had taken place between Max and his wife.

It was Lysette's misfortune that she overheard the private conversation between Bernard and Alexandre as they enjoyed wine and cigars in one of the double parlors after dinner. Searching for the needlework she had left earlier, she heard their low voices through the half-closed door, and she hesitated as she heard her name.

"I can't help but pity Lysette," Alexandre was saying a trifle nonchalantly. "The problem is, she's too young for Max, and she can't do a damn thing about that."

Bernard's voice was quieter and more thoughtful. "I would not say that is the problem, Alex. For all her youth, she is intelligent and handles him quite well."

"Since when," Alex asked dryly, "is intelligence desirable in a woman? I know *I* never look for it!"

"Well, that explains a great deal about the kind of women I've seen you with."

Alex chuckled. *"Dites-moi, mon frère* . . . what is your opinion of our sweet sister-in-law's inability to keep Maximilien home at night?"

"Very simple. She is not Corinne."

Alexandre sounded startled. "Are you implying that Max still loves Corinne? She was a harlot."

"Yes," Bernard said calmly. "But she was beautiful and charming and irresistible. No man could stop himself from wanting her or falling in love with her. And no woman could ever equal her. In Max's eyes, that is."

"Apparently not in yours, either," Alexandre said slowly. "I never knew she had such an effect on you."

"She did on every man she encountered, little brother. You were just too young to notice."

"Perhaps," came Alexandre's doubtful reply. "But as to this one, do you think there's a chance Max will ever come to love her?"

"Not a chance in hell."

Lysette edged away, the color running high in her cheeks. Hurt feelings battled with anger. Unconsciously she reached a hand up to her hair — the unruly hair that had caused her such misery in her youth. Corinne must have had the smooth, dark hair that Creoles prized so greatly. Corinne must have flirted to perfection with the men who admired her, and hypnotized them with her beauty.

She felt a presence behind her. Whirling, she began to speak, but stuttered into silence when she saw nothing but empty space in the softly lit hall. A ghost, she thought whimsically, and sighed, wondering if some phantom had an eternal claim on Max that Lysette could never hope to break.

Max returned at midnight, ushering in a sheet of rain and a dull crack of thunder from outside as he entered the house. The heavy rain had started early in the evening, breaking the oppressive heat and spreading its cooling touch over the steaming Louisiana marsh and swamps. The downpour had turned the streets and roads into deep sticky mud, almost impossible for horses' hooves to slog through, more difficult yet for carriage wheels.

Max strode through the quiet house, his mouth hardening as he thought of his wife sleeping peacefully upstairs. For him the nights brought no rest, only torment, restless tossing and turning. He made his way to the curving staircase with the overcautious movements of a man who had raised his cup far too many times that evening. He was drunk, having spent his evening at a local tavern swilling strong spirits, not the refined burgundies and ports that Creole gentlemen usually restricted themselves to. Unfortunately, he was not drunk enough.

Water streamed from his hair and clothes to the summer matting on the floor and the carpet on the stairs. It gave Max a petty sense of satisfaction, knowing Noeline would fume tomorrow when she saw the muddy boot marks, but wouldn't dare utter a word. No one dared reprove him for anything he did when his temper was foul. The entire family, including the servants, stayed well out of his way, knowing from experience that it was unwise to cross his path.

"Max," he heard a soft voice as he reached the top of the stairs.

He stopped as he saw Lysette, dressed in a loose nightgown, her heavy braid falling over her shoulder and down to her waist. Her pale face and white gown almost glowed in the darkness.

"You look like a little ghost," he said, taking a step closer to her, then stopping as if encountering an invisible wall.

"I heard you come in. You've been drinking, haven't you?" She came forward and touched his arm. "Let me help you to your room."

"I don't need help."

"I'll reserve opinion on that," she said, and took his arm firmly. "Please, Max."

He complied with a surly grunt, shivering in his cold, wet clothes. They went into his bedroom and Lysette fumbled to light a bedside lamp.

"Don't bother," Max muttered. "I'll be asleep soon. Just need . . . to get out of these clothes." He sat on a chair and removed his muddy boots, while Lysette brought some folded towels. Reaching for his cravat to untie it, Max discovered the damn thing was already loose, hanging limply on either side of his neck. He threw it to the floor and fought his way out of his clammy coat and waistcoat. His dripping shirt was discarded next, and he stood clad only in his breeches as Lysette toweled off his chest and back. She was clean and dainty and dry, whereas he was a clumsy, drunken mess.

"Lysette, you have to leave now," he said irritably.

She paused in her ministrations. "Why?"

"Because I'm too drunk to do anything except the one thing you don't want. So you'd better go to your own bed, or you're going to find yourself heels-up in mine."

A crack of lightning lit the room with blue-white brilliance. During the split second of illumination, Lysette's gaze had fastened on Max with an intensity that caused the hairs on the back of his neck to prickle. He remained motionless, his liquor-dulled brain struggling to understand what that expression had meant.

He felt her small hands slide over his breeches, her fingers prying at the buttons on the front flap. His breath was knocked from his throat, and his cock jerked to life, hardening and swelling irrepressibly. "Lysette . . ." His lungs worked like leaky bellows. "No, don't. Don't. If you touch me, I can't —" He broke off with a sharp gasp as the flap fell open and her warm hand slid over the length of his shaft, up and down. He throbbed violently in response to the deliberate stroking. The other hand cupped his testicles, fondling gently, her palm supporting their weight. "I can't . . ." he managed again, his trembling hands coming to grasp her narrow shoulders.

"You can't what?" Lysette asked, her breath puffing against his nipple. The tip of her tongue flicked at the tiny point. His chest was filled with fire, and the blood roared in his ears until he could barely hear her. "Can't make love to me?" she asked.

He wound her braid around his fist and urged her head back. "Can't stop," he answered raggedly, and seized her mouth with his.

CHAPTER

8

After removing Lysette's nightgown and his own breeches, Max carried her to the bed. "I've wanted you from the first moment I saw you," he said hoarsely. "Even dirty and scratched and with your breasts bound flat, I thought you were beautiful. You were so exhausted you could barely stay on your feet, but you defied me as no one else ever had."

"And you wanted me," she said in pleasure, arching upward as he kissed her throat.

He answered between kisses, each one a slow burst of fire. "So much that I promised myself . . . I would do whatever was necessary to keep you." His breathing turned choppy as he glanced down at her naked body. "Lysette . . . don't change your mind tonight. I'm afraid I won't be able to stop —"

Lysette interrupted him with her mouth, and pulled his hand to her bare breast. "I won't change my mind," she said throatily. "Do anything you want. Do *everything*."

"No, not everything," he said thickly, while his fingertips moved over the small curve of her breast. "You're too innocent for that, *ma petite*."

A delicious shiver coursed down her spine. "Then do as much as you think I can bear."

Max needed no further invitation. His body lowered, and he allowed some of his weight to settle between her thighs, pinning her in place. The length of his sex pressed into the furrow hidden in the triangle of silky-rough curls. Lysette relaxed beneath him, her eyes closing as she felt him take her nipple between his fingers, gently shaping it into a hard peak. His head bent, the soft, wet warmth of his mouth closing around her. He suckled and flicked the delicate tip with his tongue, until she could no longer prevent the helpless moans that surged from her throat. His mouth dragged across her chest, dipping sweetly into the shallow valley in the center, lazily ascending the second gentle curve. His tongue touched her breast in a velvety stroke that made it throb unbearably. She pulled harder at his head, urging him to take her deeper into his mouth, and he complied with a slowness that nearly made her scream. Dimly she began to understand the sensuous game he was playing, that he intended to prolong her torturous desire, and his own, until they could bear it no longer.

With each soft tug of his mouth, Lysette squirmed upward, her hips lifting against the underside of his shaft. The feel of him was so incendiary that she began to concentrate on the motion, her legs spreading, her body rubbing his in a quickening rhythm.

A muffled laugh escaped him, and he rolled away from her.

"No," she panted. "Max, let me —"

"Not yet." His voice was soft and rough with passion. "I'll give you satisfaction, *petite* . . . but not yet."

She climbed over him with feminine determination, crushing her breasts into the thick black fleece on his chest. Her mouth caught at his, and she pressed against his long body in an effort to sabotage his self-control. For a few scorching moments, Max allowed her to make love to him, his large hands sliding over her back and buttocks. Soon, however, he rolled her over and pinned her arms to her sides.

"Let me touch you," Lysette implored, her fingers digging into the mattress.

He ignored her, his thighs wedging between hers.

"Max," she groaned, "I need to touch you. Let go of my hands, please, I have to feel you. . . ."

His mouth wandered from the fine vault of her ribs to her stomach, until the muscles of her abdomen tightened exquisitely. His tongue entered the hollow of her navel with a soft swirl. Her wrists strained against his grasp, and she gasped sharply. He continued to tease and stroke, until she was sweating and rigid beneath him. His mouth drifted lower, moving languidly over her stomach.

She was shocked to feel his lips venture near the triangle between her thighs. "Max," she moaned as his long fingers combed gently through the curls. Catching her salty female scent, he inhaled deeply. Lysette wanted to die at the unbearable intimacy, and her hands went to his head, fingers sliding into his rain-soaked hair. "Don't," she gasped, trying to push him away.

"You said I could do anything." His fingers searched the delicate entrance to her body.

"I didn't know what I was saying. I didn't think . . . Oh, *God*."

He had done the unimaginable, his mouth invading the tender cleft, his tongue thrusting past the sensitive inner lips. She sobbed and clutched at the wet dark head nestled between her thighs. He searched her hungrily, his hands clamping over her hips to hold her still. With each lap and stroke and flick of his tongue, her innocence dissolved like melting sugar. Soon his attentions centered on the erect little peak that throbbed with yearning. He drew her into the soft suction of his mouth, pulling rhythmically at her vulnerable flesh.

Lysette pulled her knees back in a desperate, shameless plea. Taking pity on her, Max flicked her with light, swift strokes of his tongue, while his middle finger found the opening to her body and slid deep inside. She climaxed with a harsh gasp, her knees closing around his head, her body shaking with pleasure. His mouth remained on her for a long time afterward, his tongue nurturing every last quiver of delight, until she was limp and boneless beneath him.

Rising over her, Max positioned himself between her spread legs and entered her in a swift thrust. He filled her completely, stretching her, sliding until he could go no farther. Lysette bit her lip and arched at the painful intrusion of his hard flesh, her hands fisting against his back.

Max stopped immediately. "Does it hurt?" He took her head in his hands, his salt-flavored mouth brushing over hers. "I'm sorry, *ma petite*. I'll try to be careful. I'm so sorry —"

"Don't stop," she moaned, wrapping herself around him.

Max made a rough sound and began to thrust inside her carefully, trying not to hurt her. He kissed her breasts, her mouth, seeming to lose awareness of everything but her. His violent panting contrasted sharply with the easy motion of his hips, and she realized what a tight restraint he had placed on himself. She pressed her face into the damp satiny curve of his neck. "I knew it would be like this," she whispered, caressing his iron-hard back. His skin was slippery with rain and sweat. "I knew how gentle you would be. Don't hold back. I want all of you."

The words seemed to push him over the edge. He groaned and impaled her deeply, his large body jerking against hers. She gasped in delight as his silky-hard flesh throbbed inside her. Strange, that she could feel so vulnerable and yet so strong, with her body filled and weighted and surrounded by the man she loved. Stranger still, that she had finally yielded herself to him without knowing whether he loved her in return. She wanted to give him as much of herself as she could, with no conditions or expectations.

Max rolled to his side and gathered her against his chest. Purring, Lysette insinuated one of her thighs between his, loving the heat and texture of his body. The smell of the storm came in through the partially opened window, mingling headily with the musky spice of damp skin and sex.

Max's hand drifted over her breast. His voice was deep and languid. "It will be better the next time, I promise."

"I hope not." Lysette stroked the side of his waist, her fingers wandering to the line where sun-darkened skin faded into the paler territory of his hip. "I'm not certain that I could survive anything better than that."

A laugh stirred in his chest, and his lips pressed against her hair. "What a passionate little wife you are," he whispered.

"More passionate than your *placée?*"

Max went still at the question. "There is no comparison between you and Mariame, *ma chère*. I have never desired anyone, nor found such pleasure with anyone, as I have with you."

"You do care for Mariame, though, *oui?*"

"Of course. She has been a kind and generous friend. I owe a great deal to her."

"In what way?" Lysette asked, feeling a stab of jealousy.

"After Corinne's death, I thought I would never want a woman again. Every woman in New Orleans was afraid of me, and I . . ." He paused, the words catching in his throat. Surprised that Max had ventured to speak about his mysterious past with her, Lysette waited patiently for him to continue. "In a way I was afraid of myself," Max finally said. "Everything was different. I was accustomed to being liked and admired, and suddenly everyone treated me with scorn, or coldness, or fear. I was celibate for almost two years. Then I heard that Mariame had been abandoned by the man who had been keeping her. I had seen her before and admired her beauty. She needed someone to provide for her and her child . . . and I needed someone like her."

"What is she like?" Lysette asked.

"Comfortable," he said after a moment.

"She has a pleasant nature. I've rarely ever seen her in a temper, and she has never been demanding or impatient."

"Unlike me," Lysette said ruefully.

He rose above her, his broad shoulders blocking the lightning flashes from the storm. "Do you know what I would change about you, *petite?*" he asked softly.

"What?" she asked, half afraid to hear the answer.

"Nothing at all." His head descended to hers, and for a long time he kept her too busy to speak.

CHAPTER

9

Max awakened to the sensation of invisible fiends pounding on his head with mallets. He squinted his eyes open and jerked in painful surprise as a ray of sunshine slanted across his throbbing eyeballs. Cursing in French and English, he rolled to his stomach and rooted beneath his pillow in violent denial of morning.

"Mon mari." He heard Lysette's amused but sympathetic voice. Her gentle hand brushed over his naked back. "Tell me how I can help. What is your usual cure for . . . what do the Americans call it? . . . pickling yourself? Will you take some coffee? Water? Willow-bark tea?"

Max's stomach roiled at the notion of swallowing anything. *"Dieu, non.* Just let me —" He broke off as the touch of her hand recalled memories of the night before. Many of the details were lost in a liquor-soaked fog, but he did remember seeing her when he had arrived home . . . she had helped him to remove his clothes . . . and sometime after that, he had . . .

Throwing the pillow aside, Max sat bolt upright, ignoring the agony that stabbed through his head. "Lysette," he croaked. She sat beside him on the bed, dressed in a white robe with ruffles down the front, her hair hanging in a braid and tied with a strip of lace. Max would have thought she looked angelic . . . except that no angel had kiss-swollen lips and whisker burns all over her throat.

"Relax, *ma cher*," she told him with a smile. "There is no need to look so alarmed."

"Last night . . ." he said unsteadily, his insides turning cold and leaden. "I was with you. I don't remember all of it, but I know that we . . ."

"Yes, we did."

The information shamed and appalled Max. No gentleman would ever take his wife when he was intoxicated . . . much less a virginal wife, who would have required gentleness and self-restraint and skill. He had taken her innocence while he was drunk. The realization was overwhelming. He must have hurt her. Dear God, she would never let him near her again, and he wouldn't blame her. "Lysette . . ." He began to reach for her, then snatched his hands back. "Did I force myself on you?" he asked hoarsely.

Her eyes widened with surprise. "No. Of course you didn't."

"Did I hurt you? Was I rough?"

Her sudden laugh bewildered him. "Don't you remember what happened, *mon mari?* You didn't seem *that* much the worse for wear."

"I remember *my* part of it. But I don't remember yours."

Smiling, Lysette leaned forward and touched his lower lip with her fingertip. "I'll tell you, then. You tortured me, *ma cher,* and made me suffer terribly. And I adored every moment of it."

"I didn't take care of you afterward," Max said in dull horror. "I didn't bring you water, or a cloth, or . . ." A thought occurred to him, and he flipped back the sheets, discovering a small streak of blood on the snowy linen. She had bled, and he had done nothing for her. *"Mon Dieu,"* he muttered.

"You did fall asleep quite suddenly after all your exertions," Lysette admitted with a grin, her fingers trailing over his hair-dusted thigh. "But I didn't mind taking care of myself. It was hardly a problem, *mon mari."*

Max did not understand how she could smile after what he had done to her, debauching her in the middle of the night when he'd been staggering drunk. He tunneled his fingers into his rumpled hair, down to his aching scalp. "Lysette," he said without looking at her, "if you can find some way to forgive me, someday . . . I swear it will never happen again. I'm certain you don't believe that now, but I —"

"I will forgive you on one condition," she said kindly.

"Anything. Anything. Just tell me."

"My condition is . . ." She leaned close to him, her lips touching his bristly cheek. "You have to do it again tonight," she whispered, and left the bed before he could reply.

Gradually realizing that the previous night had not been the catastrophe it could have been, Max leaned back against the headboard. Relief crept through him, and he released a taut sigh.

"A little coffee?" Lysette coaxed. "It might help your head."

He made a gruff sound of assent. Lysette went to the silver tray on the table by the window and poured steaming liquid into a Sevres porcelain cup. Returning to him with a cup and saucer, she helped to lodge a pillow behind his back before handing him the coffee. "*Alors,*" she said conversationally, "now that we've finally slept together, perhaps I will stop finding scraps of red cloth beneath my pillow."

Max paused in the act of raising the cup to his lips. "Red cloth?" he repeated warily.

"*Oui.* Noeline has been hiding them there to attract *le Miché Agoussou.*"

A reluctant grin tugged at his lips. "The Creole demon of love. Well, you can inform her that he's visited us with a vengeance."

Lysette smiled, a blush rising to the

freckled crests of her cheeks. "I don't think there is any need to tell Noeline anything. The entire household seems to be aware of what happened. One of the disadvantages of living with such a big family."

"Does the lack of privacy bother you?" he asked, having never given it a thought before.

She shrugged. "The house is large enough that I have many places to go when I wish to be alone. And I enjoy your family's company, although it would be nice to have more women around. I think we should find wives for your brothers."

"Neither of them sees a need to marry. They live in a well-run house, and they have all the freedom they desire. When they wish for female companionship, there are many women in town willing to accommodate them. Why should either of them want a wife?"

Lysette regarded him with indignation. "What about children?"

Max regarded her sardonically. "It's likely that after living with the twins, my brothers have received a rather negative impression of the joys of fatherhood."

"Not all children are like the twins."

"Thank God for that."

"Besides, if bachelorhood is so wonderful, why did you marry me?"

Max studied her over the rim of the porcelain cup, admiring the shape of her body beneath the cambric robe. "I think I made that clear last night."

"Ah." Lysette stalked over to him, her movements imbued with a new sexual confidence that sent a hum of awareness through him. *God help me,* Max thought wryly. "You married me for my body, then," Lysette said, leaning close enough that he could see down the front of her gown, from the tips of her breasts to the tiny exuberant red curls between her thighs. Max gulped the rest of his coffee, but its scalding heat was nothing in comparison to the rising temperature of his blood.

"Exactly," he said, and she laughed low in her throat.

"Perhaps I married you for yours, *mon mari.*"

"I have no complaint about that," he said, pulling her toward him for a kiss.

However, they were interrupted by a firm knock at the door. Max watched with disgruntlement as Lysette went to answer it. The intruder was Noeline, bearing a heavy-laden breakfast tray. Frowning, Max pulled the covers higher over his bare chest.

Evidently the situation met with the housekeeper's approval. Her expression was as serene as usual, but there was satisfaction in her dark eyes as she set the tray down on a small table by the window. *"Bon matin,"* she said placidly. "It's about time I found madame in here with you, monsieur."

Lysette sat by the tray and picked up a flaky croissant, biting into it with obvious enjoyment.

"Now," Noeline continued, "if it pleases God, there will be babies in the house again. It's been much too long since the twins." Having known Max since his youth, she readily exercised her freedom to say anything she liked to him, no matter how personal.

"Noeline," Max said brusquely, "have a bath readied for me right away I'm going to be late for an appointment in town."

The housekeeper frowned with displeasure. "You are going out today, monsieur? And leaving a pretty wife with no babies?" As far as Creoles were concerned, it was a man's first responsibility to give his wife children. No one in high circles or low would dispute the fact that a new husband should spend every day and night in the effort to impregnate his bride. It was, after all, the entire purpose of the honeymoon.

Max pinned the housekeeper with an ominous stare. "Leave, Noeline."

"*Oui,* monsieur," Noeline replied, unruffled, and muttered to herself as she left, "How she's going to get babies by herself I don't know. . . ."

"When will you come back?" Lysette asked, drizzling honey onto her croissant.

"Early this afternoon, I expect."

"I think I'll go riding around the plantation today," she said. "There are still parts of it I've never seen."

"Take someone with you."

"Oh, but there is no need —"

"Yes, there is. If you should have any difficulty — if the horse loses a shoe, or stumbles — I don't want you to be alone."

"All right." Lysette tilted her head back as she popped a honey-sodden morsel of croissant into her mouth. Her enjoyment of the treat aroused him further, and he turned to his side to watch her.

"Lysette," he said huskily, "bring that honey over here."

"With a croissant?"

"No, just the honey."

Lysette's perplexed gaze met his, and as understanding dawned, she shook her head decisively. "No, you wicked man."

"Now," he insisted, patting the space beside him. "You promised to obey me, *chèrie. Are you breaking your vows already?*"

"I promised no such a thing."

"Yes, you did. During the wedding."

"I crossed my fingers during that part." Seeing his lack of comprehension, she added, "it's what the Americans do when they don't mean what they're saying."

Max threw back the covers, revealing his naked body, and went to retrieve his giggling wife. Picking her up masterfully, he carried her to the bed, and brought the pot of honey along with them. "Do you know what Creoles do to rebellious wives?" he asked, depositing her on the mattress.

"Am I going to find out?" she asked, her face burnished with brilliant pink.

"Oh, yes," he murmured, and joined her on the bed.

As Lysette had expected, she was the object of unusual scrutiny when she joined the Vallerands in the morning room after breakfast. Even Alexandre, who was clearly suffering from a bout of heavy drinking and carousing in town the night before, dragged his bloodshot gaze to her face.

"Good morning," Lysette said cheerfully.

Justin, who lounged in the corner with a sugar-dusted roll, broke the tension with his typical bluntness. "Are we trying to see how she fared the night with Father? She looks well enough to me." It was not said in malice; indeed, there was a twinkle in his blue eyes that was impossible to resist. Lysette smiled at him even as the rest of the family reacted with annoyance, demanding that he leave the room. She touched his shoulder as he departed.

"It's not necessary for you to leave, Justin," she said.

"I was going to, anyway. Philippe and I have a fencing lesson in town."

"I hope it goes well for you."

Justin grinned, raking his fingers through his shaggy black hair. "It always does. I'm the best swordsman in town, after father. *Bon matin, belle-mère,*" he said cheerfully, and went in search of his brother. Although Lysette smiled at his youthful bravado, the other Vallerands did not seem to find it so amusing.

"That boy . . ." Irénée did not finish the complaint, but her irritation was clear.

"Max should have taken a switch to him a long time ago," Alexandre said grimly, taking a tiny sip of coffee and holding his head as if it were about to fall off. "Now the results of Max's spoiling are becoming all too obvious."

"Justin is trying to make himself noticed," Lysette replied, seating herself beside Irénée. "Philippe earns attention through his good behavior. Naturally the only course left to Justin is to be bad. If we treat him with patience and understanding, I have no doubt that he will improve." She turned to her mother-in-law, determined to change the subject. "I thought I might ride around the plantation today."

"Have Elias accompany you," Irénée replied. "He is a good boy, quiet and well mannered."

"Where are you going?" Bernard asked.

She shrugged. "Perhaps toward the east, beyond the cypress grove."

"There is nothing there to see," Bernard replied with a frown. "Except for the ruins of the old overseer's house."

The group fell oddly silent at the mention of the place. Lysette glanced at Irénée, who had suddenly devoted her attention to stirring more sugar into her coffee. Pondering the reasons for such a strange reaction, Lysette realized that the overseer's house must be where Corinne had been murdered.

"I should have thought it would have been torn down," Lysette said.

"It should have been," Irénée agreed. "Unfortunately no one on the plantation, or in New Orleans, has been willing to do it. Superstition, you understand."

Lysette understood. The Creole culture attached great importance to places where murder or death had occurred. Any token of the house — a stick, a chip of brick or molding plaster — carried with it the essence of evil. Such fragments could be used to make a powerful *gris-gris* that would bring death and everlasting grief to a victim. No one would care to bring a curse on himself by desecrating a place riddled with bad spirits.

"Some have foolishly claimed to have seen ghosts there," Irénée said. "Even Justin . . . although I suspect he was merely out to make mischief."

"None of the slaves will go near the place,"

Bernard said. "If you tried to visit it, you wouldn't get within a hundred feet of it before Elias refused to go any farther."

It was not long before Lysette discovered that Bernard had been right. Elias, riding a placid mule behind her dappled mare, stopped short when he saw the broken outline of the overseer's house rising before them. The structure was situated well out of sight of the main house. It was set on the edge of fields that had once been productive, but had been left untouched during the last ten years. The land was overgrown and richly green. Given enough time, the tropical climate would accomplish the destruction of the rickety overseer's house, which had already decayed from mold, dampness, and insects.

"Elias?" Lysette questioned, glancing back and seeing the tense set of the boy's thin frame. He was staring, not at her, but at the house, his eyes wide and nostrils flared.

"You want to go there, madame?" he asked softly.

"Yes, just for a minute or two," she said, urging her horse a few steps. *"Allons."*

The young boy did not move. "We can't, madame. There's ghosts in there."

"I will not ask you to go in with me," Lysette said soothingly. "Just wait outside until I return, *d'accord?"*

But as she met his eyes, she saw that he

was deeply upset. A suspicious brightness had sprung in his eyes, betraying the fact that he was torn between his fear of going near the house and his reluctance to displease her. He remained silent, looking from her to the ominous structure before them.

"Elias, stay right here. I will be back very soon."

"But madame —"

"Nothing will happen to me. I'll only be a few minutes."

Lysette went to the dilapidated house and tethered her horse to the cankered wooden railing of the tiny porch. Absently she untied the ribbon streamers of her glazed straw hat and set it on a sway-backed step. The house was braced a foot or two from the ground in deference to the nearby bayou's occasional wont to flood its banks. Gingerly she set her foot on one of the steps, wondering if it would hold her weight. It creaked loudly but did not break. Cautiously Lysette went to the door, which hung askew, its edges covered with slime. An air of gloom and oppression hung around the place. It was as if the crime that had occurred there had become a part of each board and beam.

She tried to imagine what the house had been like a decade earlier, when Corinne Vallerand had slipped inside for her clandestine meetings with Etienne Sagesse. How could Corinne have betrayed Maximilien in a place so close to the home they shared? It was almost as if she had wanted to be discovered.

Pushing the door to the side, Lysette crept into the house, ducking under a mass of cobwebs. It seemed like a tomb. The room was dank and foul-smelling, its walls shaded with moss. Inches of dust and yellowish matter caked the tiny-paned windows, blocking out most of the sunlight. Spiders scuttled into the corners and cracks of the walls, fleeing from her intrusion.

Driven by curiosity, Lysette picked her way through rubble to the back room. As she looked around, the hairs on her arms stood on end. Although nothing tangible set this room apart from the other, she knew somehow that this was where Corinne had been murdered. A feeling of devastation gripped her, and she froze where she stood.

She heard footsteps, the sounds of someone kicking aside a shard of broken pottery. Her heart leapt in her throat and she turned swiftly.

"Elias?"

"No." It was her husband, coming to the doorway of the small room, his gaze riveted on her.

Max's features seemed to be carved in granite, but his gaze was haunted. He did not ask why she was there. He seemed to find it difficult to speak, his throat working violently. His face was pale, and she saw the remnants of horror in his eyes as memories broke from the dark corners of his mind.

Making her way to him, Lysette lifted a gentle hand to his face. Her compassionate touch seemed to unlock the barricaded words. Max licked his dry lips before speaking in a rusty voice. "I found Corinne over there, in that corner, on the floor. I knew at once what had happened . . . the color of her skin . . . the bruises on her neck. Strangling is a lot of work, I've heard. It takes a great deal of anger, or hatred, to kill someone that way."

Lysette stood very close to him, stroking his chest with the flats of her hands. "I know that you didn't do it," she said quietly.

"I could have, though," Max whispered. "I wanted to. Corinne did and said unimaginable things. . . . She made me feel poisoned. It wasn't hard to hate her. I don't know what I would have become, had I lived with her any longer."

"Why was she like that?" Lysette asked softly.

"I don't know." His eyes were those of a drowning man. "I think there was something wrong with her, inside. There were rumors of madness in her family, but the Quérands always denied it." His gaze arrowed to the rubble-filled corner. "When I realized that Corinne was dead, I was stunned. Sorry for

her. But at the same time, part of me felt
. . . relieved. The thought that I was rid of
her, that she was gone for good . . ." Max
stopped, his face flushing, his jaw shaking. "I
was so damned glad she was dead," he said
in a raw whisper. "Feeling that way made me
just as guilty as her murderer, don't you
think?"

Overwhelmed with sympathy, Lysette
hugged herself against his rigid body. "No,
that is nonsense. Is that one of the burdens
you've carried for so long? Feelings are not
the same as actions. You didn't harm her.
You have no reason to feel guilty." Although
Max did not respond to her touch, Lysette
pressed her head to his chest. "How did you
know that I was here?" she asked against his
pounding heart.

Max strove to steady his voice. "My meeting in town was canceled, as Claiborne had
more pressing business elsewhere. When I returned to the plantation a few minutes ago, I
saw Elias, riding home as fast as that sorry
mule could take him. He told me where you
were."

"I'm sorry," she said sincerely. "I didn't
mean to distress him. Or you. I was just curious."

"Of course you were. I knew it was only a
matter of time before you found this place.
I'm going to have it torn down, if I have to
do it with my own hands."

Lysette glanced around the room, suddenly anxious to leave the ramshackle house and the ugly memories it held for her husband. "Max, take me home. Please."

Max didn't seem even to have heard her. "Come," she urged, beginning to step away from him. Suddenly he startled her by seizing her, burying his face in her hair, pulling her close until her toes left the ground. A shudder wracked his body. "Why aren't you afraid of me?" he asked raggedly. "You *have* to have doubts. . . . I'm still a stranger to you. You can't be certain that I'm innocent. Sometimes *I* don't even believe —"

"Hush, not another word," she whispered, turning her mouth to his. "I know you. I know exactly what kind of man you are."

Max let her kiss him for just a moment, then pulled back, clearly not wanting to share an intimate moment with her in this place. "Let's leave," he muttered, taking her arm.

Seeing how troubled and quiet Max was for the rest of the day, Lysette regretted her visit to the overseer's house. She would never have intentionally caused him such distress. Although Max kept to himself, working in the library for the rest of the afternoon, his dark mood seemed to have infiltrated the rest of the house, the atmosphere becoming quiet and uneasy. However, no one mentioned a word to Lysette . . . until Bernard cornered her after dinner. They happened to pass in the hallway, as Bernard headed to the small guest house where he resided. Glancing from left to right to make certain they would not be overheard, Bernard spoke to her in a cutting voice.

"I'll say this once, Lysette, not only for your sake but for Max's. Rid yourself of this curiosity you have about Corinne. It is dangerous, do you understand? Leave the past alone — or it will come back to ruin you."

She was too astonished to reply.

After staring at her with dark eyes that for the first time held an expression of dislike, Bernard strode away.

CHAPTER
10

"Another letter to your mother?" Max inquired, coming to the tiny satinwood table where Lysette sat.

"I can't find the right words," Lysette grumbled, indicating several crumpled sheets of parchment.

Max smiled as he noted that her personal writing table and matching clawfoot chair had been mysteriously moved from her bedchamber to his. It was yet another sign of the feminine invasion that seemed to be taking place.

Wryly he supposed he should be grateful for the considerable size of his room. Despite their agreement to keep separate bedrooms, Lysette had moved more and more of her possessions into his territory. Every day he discovered new articles strewn over his dresser and bedside table. There were bottles of scent and boxes of powder, fans and gloves and flowered hair ornaments, pins and combs, stockings, garters, and laces.

When Max retired in the evenings, he found Lysette in his bed, contrary to the

Creole custom that a wife should remain in her own bed and allow the husband the choice of visiting her. He didn't dare say a word to her about it, however. Not only did he want to avoid hurting her feelings, but in a strange way, he liked the situation.

After years of isolation and loneliness, he found himself enjoying the companionship that Lysette offered him, and the attention she lavished on him. He would have expected the sudden lack of privacy to be difficult, but it did not annoy him. And there were distinct benefits to having Lysette so close at hand. He had an unlimited view of her bathing, tending her hair, dressing . . . and undressing. He enjoyed watching the rituals of a wife's toilette, the sight of Lysette trying on earrings, braiding her hair, unrolling her stockings, applying perfume behind her ears.

Returning his attention to the matter at hand, Max braced his arms on either side of her and leaned over the table, reading the unfinished letter.

"Neither Maman nor Jacqueline answered the first letters that I wrote," Lysette told him. "Perhaps Gaspard won't let Maman write to me. Perhaps he won't even allow her to *receive* anything from me . . . but I did expect some sort of a reply from Jacqueline!"

Max brushed his lips over the top of her head. "Give them time. It has been merely a month since the wedding. And you did marry one of the more notable scoundrels of New Orleans."

"You're too modest, *mon mari*. As a scoundrel, you have no peer."

He grinned and tilted her chair back in revenge, causing her to gasp with surprised laughter. She clutched at his arms. "Max!"

"Relax, sweet . . . I wouldn't let you fall."

"Max, behave yourself!"

Slowly the chair was raised to its original position, and she jumped to her feet with a wary smile.

Holding her gaze, Max advanced to the desk and crumpled her letter in one hand.

Lysette's mouth fell open. "Why did you do that?"

"Because I didn't like it," he said without remorse. "I won't have you begging and pleading for their favor."

She glared at him wrathfully. "I'll write whatever I wish to my mother."

Max scowled back at her, and then looked away, taking a deep breath. "I'm sorry," he finally said. "I didn't mean to be arrogant. But I don't want anyone to hurt your feelings. Especially your own family."

Lysette's anger faded. "Max," she said in a softer tone, "you can't protect me from everything."

"I can try, though."

She laughed and shook her head. "I suppose this is what I deserve for marrying a Creole."

"Do you plan to begin another letter this very moment?" he asked.

"Probably not. *Pourquoi?*"

"Because I would enjoy it if you would accompany me to town. An important visitor arrived this morning, and I expect to hear some interesting speechmaking at the Place D'Armes."

"Oh, I would enjoy leaving the plantation," Lysette exclaimed. "I haven't set foot off it even once since I first came here. But it will be another week before I can properly be seen in public, and I don't wish to start all of New Orleans gossiping —"

"We'll stay in the carriage," Max interrupted, amused by her excitement. "We would have to in any case — it will be too crowded for us to move about freely. Cannon fire, parades, music. All to celebrate the arrival of one Aaron Burr."

"Who is he? Oh, yes, that man you and Governor Claiborne don't like." Flying to the dresser, Lysette rummaged through his top drawer for her gloves.

The Place D'Armes, the town square built to face the river, was filled with a noisy crowd that had gathered from miles around to see and hear the notorious Colonel Burr. This morning, the twenty-fifth of June, he had arrived in New Orleans after a long western tour through Ohio, Kentucky, Tennessee, and Natchez, paying visits to powerful allies and making speeches to approving crowds.

Burr had been received everywhere with hospitality and acclaim, for he stated that he had the interests of the West at heart, and that he only wanted to help the territory grow and flourish. Few people suspected the more sinister purpose behind his journey.

It was remarkable that in the upheaval of the festivities, the distinctive black and gold Vallerand carriage drew almost as much attention as the sight of Aaron Burr himself. The rumor that Maximilien Vallerand's new wife was there spread quickly and soon there were swarms of people surrounding the vehicle, both American and Creole, craning their necks to see inside. Even Max had not expected the attention Lysette's presence would attract.

Lysette stayed away from the windows of the carriage, concealing herself from view, but she could still hear the excited voices outside, referring to her as *la mariée du diable* . . . the devil's bride. She looked at Max in amazement. "Why do they call me that?"

"I warned you what to expect," he said. "You're married to me, which is reason enough. And no doubt your red hair causes people to assume that you have a volatile temperament."

"Volatile? I have the mildest disposition

imaginable," she said, and frowned at his sudden snort. Before they could debate the issue, however, Governor Claiborne began to make his welcoming speech. Lysette leaned forward in the carriage seat, wishing she could be outside.

There was a world of alien sights, sounds, and smells just beyond the walls of the carriage: abrasive calls of vendors selling fruit and bread, the barking of dogs, the cries of chanticleer roosters and dunghill fowls.

Occasionally she caught a whiff of strong French perfume as fine ladies passed by, and the smells of salt, fish, and refuse carried on the breeze from the riverfront. Boatmen strolled by chattering in languages she had never heard before. And as always, whenever Creoles and Americans were in the same vicinity, there were scuffles, arguments, and swift challenges to duel.

Above the melee, Governor Claiborne struggled to be heard. As the speech progressed, Lysette accepted a glass of wine from her husband, and rested her foot on his lap as he removed her shoes and massaged her soles. His hands were strong and thorough, making her squirm in pleasure as he worked the soreness out of her feet.

Lulled by the wine and the gentle manipulation of her feet, Lysette let her mind wander as the governor detailed many of Burr's past achievements. "He's rather long-winded," she remarked, and Max chuckled.

"That's the kindest description of a lawyer I've ever heard," he replied.

"It sounds as though Governor Claiborne admires Colonel Burr very much," Lysette said.

"He despises Burr," Max replied with a grin.

"Then why —"

"Politicians, sweet, often find themselves required to pay homage to their enemies."

"I don't understand —" Lysette said, and stopped as she heard a dull roar that began on the edge of the crowd and grew until it became a great wave of sound. Her eyes widened. "What is it?"

"Burr must have stepped into view," Max said. "Thank God. Claiborne will have to end his speech now." He moved to the door and opened it. "I'm going to stand outside to listen."

"Max, may I —"

"You'd better stay in here." He threw her an apologetic glance. "Sorry."

Lysette folded her arms resentfully as he left the carriage. "Well," she muttered to herself, "what good is leaving the plantation when I have to stay in here the whole time?"

The tumult outside increased, and she sidled to the window, sticking her head outside in an effort to see past the mass of people, carriages, and horses. She heard a new voice in the distance, a strong and forceful one that cut through the hubbub, greeting the crowd first in French, then Spanish and English. The congregation erupted in hearty applause, shouts, and whistles.

The cheering lasted through the speech's prelude, but gradually Lysette could hear Aaron Burr's voice again.

Lysette strained farther out of the window. Women scolded their husbands for staring at the flame-haired girl, youths abandoned their quarreling and watched her closely, old women gossiped while old men wished aloud that they were but a decade or two younger.

Standing a few feet away, Max became aware of the growing disturbance, and followed the gazes of those next to him. He sighed ruefully as he saw his wife leaning halfway out of the carriage in an effort to get a better view of Aaron Burr. Sensing her husband's gaze, Lysette glanced over at him guiltily and disappeared like a turtle retreating into its shell.

Smothering a laugh, Max went to the carriage, opened the door, and reached inside. "Come here," he said, hooking an arm around her waist and swinging her to the ground. "Just don't complain when everyone stares at you.

"Mon Dieu," Max continued beneath his breath as he heard Burr's inflammatory words. "He's treading on the edge of treason.

He can't think that Jefferson will turn a deaf ear to such statements."

Lysette stood on her toes. "I can't see anything," she said. "What does he look like?"

"You'll meet him later," Max promised. "We'll be attending a ball held in his honor next week."

"We are?" She frowned at him. "When were you going to tell me?"

"I just did."

They listened until the crowd showed signs of becoming unmanageable. Tempers always ran hot under the Louisiana sun, and inhibitions were weakened from the drinking and feasting that had already begun. And the sight of Lysette was attracting too much attention. People were staring and pointing openly, eager young men were gathering in groups, and boys were overheard daring each other to run up and touch a lock of her fiery hair.

"It's time to leave," Max said wryly, drawing his wife to the carriage. "Or in another few minutes I'll be forced into a score of duels over you."

Partly for his own reasons, partly as a favor to Claiborne, Max arranged a private meeting with the Spanish minister in New Orleans, Don Carlos, the Marquis de Casa Yrujo. Since Aaron Burr's arrival in town yesterday, there had been many comings and goings between the Spanish officials residing in New

Orleans. Max hoped he could persuade Yrujo to reveal some pertinent bit of information about Burr's coconspirator, General Wilkinson.

Yrujo was an experienced diplomat. His sharp brown eyes, set deeply in his lean, olive-skinned face, gave nothing away. Despite the half hour of verbal fencing that had taken place, Yrujo had not said anything that exposed Governor Wilkinson as a Spanish agent, nor revealed what he knew of Burr's treasonous conspiracy. However, there was no doubt in Max's mind that Yrujo knew a great deal.

"To me it is an interesting puzzle, how Claiborne managed to enlist your support, Vallerand," Yrujo remarked in a congenial way as the two men talked over drinks and thin black cigars. The conversation was coming to a conclusion as both realized that neither was going to learn anything from the other. "I have never believed you to be a fool," the Spaniard continued. "Why, then, do you ally yourself with a man whose control over the territory is about to be stripped from him? You have much to lose."

"Stripped away by whom?" Max countered, exhaling a channel of smoke to the side.

"My question first, *por favor.*"

Max's smile did not reach his eyes. "Claiborne has been underestimated," he said casually.

Yrujo laughed, openly scoffing at the answer. "You will have to do better than that, Vallerand! What has he promised you? I suppose the retention of land grants that should have been abolished when the Americans took possession. Or perhaps you are merely hoping to store up political influence. Do you think it wise to bet that the Americans will be able to prevent the secession of Louisiana?"

"My question now," Max said. "Whom do you think is going to strip away Claiborne's control over the territory?"

"Colonel Burr, of course. The fact that he is hoping for disunion is no secret."

"Yes. But Burr is doing more than merely *hoping*." Max watched closely for Yrujo's reaction.

The Spaniard's expression gave nothing away. "That, my friend, is something no one knows for certain. Not even I."

Max knew that was a lie. If Wilkinson was conspiring with Burr *and* remaining secretly in the Spanish pay, Yrujo had definite knowledge of Burr's intentions.

Leaning forward in his chair, Max renewed the verbal assault. "Recently, Don Carlos, you refused to give Colonel Burr a passport to Mexico. Obviously you had misgivings about allowing him inside Spanish territory. What made you suddenly so suspicious of Burr?"

"I have always exercised caution in my

dealings with the man," Yrujo said abruptly.

"Not so. You once granted him permission to enter the Floridas."

The Spanish minister laughed heartily, but there was little amusement in his eyes. "Your sources, Vallerand, are better than I suspected."

Silently Max drew again on his cigar, wondering how much Yrujo really knew. Burr and Wilkinson intended to secure the Floridas for themselves and were undoubtedly trying to keep their true purposes from the Spaniards, who would never voluntarily relinquish the territory. If it were taken from Spain, Yrujo would be held responsible. That prospect had to alarm him.

"Don Carlos," Max said quietly, "I hope you won't be deceived by any claims Burr might make that he is trying to serve Spain's interests."

They exchanged a glance of sharp understanding. "We are perfectly aware," Yrujo continued after a deliberate pause, "that the only interests the colonel serves are his own."

Max decided to take another tack. "Then perhaps you can see your way clear to tell me what you know about the letter of introduction Burr has given to one of the Spanish boundary commissioners here in New Orleans, the Marquis de Casa Calvo."

"I know nothing about a letter."

"It is suspected that several such letters

have been delivered to those who might be sympathetic to Burr's cause." Max studied the tip of his boot as he added, "Including Casa Calvo." Then his golden eyes surveyed the implacable Spaniard once more.

"I am certain I would have heard of it, had Casa Calvo received one. *Lo siento.*"

The finality in Yrujo's voice left no room for deeper prying. Max stubbed out his cigar, annoyed even though he had expected nothing more than what he had gotten. He would dearly love to know what was in that letter, to have some written proof as to Burr's intentions.

Twilight was fast approaching as Max rode home to the Vallerand plantation. He slowed his black stallion from an easy canter to a trot when he saw an enclosed carriage stopped at the side of the road. One of the carriage wheels was broken, and only one horse was harnessed to the vehicle. There was no driver in sight. Stopping by the side of the carriage, Max saw a movement inside. He lightly fingered one of the brace of pistols he always wore when traveling.

"May I be of assistance?" he asked, reining in the stallion as it fidgeted.

A woman's face appeared. She was young and reasonably pretty, and most definitely French, although Max did not recall having met her before. Evidently judging from his appearance that he was a gentleman and not a highwayman, she rested her forearm on the edge of the window and smiled. *"Merci, monsieur . . .* but there is nothing we require. Our coachman will return at any moment with help."

"Do not speak to him, Serina," came a voice from inside the carriage, a strident feminine voice filled with rebuke. "Don't you know who he is?" A second face appeared at the window.

Max stared at the woman with a slight frown, knowing he had met her before, though he was unable to remember her name. She was at least his age, perhaps a little older, her dry white skin stretched over prominent cheekbones. Her pale green eyes were venomous, and her lips turned down at the corners as if they were anchored by invisible threads.

"Don't you recognize me?" she hissed. "No, I suppose you would not. Vallerands have short memories."

"Aimée," the younger woman protested softly.

With a shock, Max realized the woman was Aimée Langlois. He had known her when they had both been in their teens. He had even courted her for a time, before he had met Corinne. Back then Aimée had been lovely. He remembered having teased her, drawing elusive smiles from her, even stealing a kiss or two when her nearsighted aunt had been less than vigilant.

"Mademoiselle Langlois," Max said with unsmiling courtesy, remembering that Irénée had once mentioned that Aimée had remained unmarried. Now, glancing at those pinched-in lips, he knew why. No man would ever have the courage — or the incentive — to kiss her. But what had wrought such a change in her? What had made her so bitter?

Still staring at him coldly, Aimée spoke to the young woman beside her. "This is Maximilien Vallerand, Serina. The man who murdered his wife. You've heard the stories, haven't you?"

Embarrassed, the girl clutched at Aimée's forearm to quiet her. "I apologize for my sister-in-law, monsieur. It has been such an exhausting day, and we —"

"Don't you dare offer excuses for me!" Aimée snapped, and glared back at Max. "Leave us this moment!"

Max would have liked nothing better, but they were alone and unprotected, and no gentleman would leave them in such a situation. "Permit me to wait nearby until your coachman returns," he said. "Night is falling, and it is dangerous to —"

"*You* present the only danger to us," Aimée interrupted. "Therefore, I would appreciate your immediate departure!"

Max gave her a curt nod. "Good evening,

ladies," he murmured, and urged the stallion away from the carriage.

Max went a bit farther along the road, and watched the vehicle until another carriage arrived for the two women. Disturbed by the encounter, he tried to force thoughts of the past from his mind, but they kept returning. He remembered the innocent days of his boyhood, the happiness he had taken for granted, the stern but comforting presence of his father, his reckless adventures with his friends, his careless assurance that he could have any girl he wanted.

Aimée's reticence had been an engrossing challenge, until he had been introduced to Corinne — and then he had forgotten everyone but her. Corinne had dazzled him, aroused him, made him crazy with the need to possess her.

However, soon after their marriage, the mercurial moods that Max had found so charming became much worse, and he had been at a loss to know how to deal with her. One day Corinne was vivacious, the next sullen and quiet. She might explode in fury because Max did not pay her enough attention, or she might scream at him to stop hovering about her.

Max had naively assumed that Corinne's behavior would improve in time. Unfortunately, it deteriorated even further, until she would throw violent tantrums for no reason.

When she became pregnant, she began to treat Max with active hatred.

Giving birth to the twins had nearly killed her, and she had held him responsible for it. Bewildered and hurt, he had begged her to forgive him for whatever it was he had done. Each time he approached her, she had thrown his love back in his face, until the weight of her contempt crushed him utterly. It was the last time Max had ever asked a woman for anything . . . until Lysette.

The thought of Lysette calmed him and eased the pain of remembering. He needed her, needed to drown himself in the pleasure of her body. As great as the physical satisfaction Lysette offered was, however, it was nothing compared to the healing power of her faith in him. She was the only person in the world who did not believe the worst of him. If anything ever happened to make Lysette doubt him, Max knew that he would not be able to bear it. He hated depending on her so greatly, but he seemed to have no choice about it.

As soon as Max reached the house and walked in the front door, Alexandre attempted to corner him. "Max, I have been waiting for you. There is a matter I would like to take up with —"

"It's been a long day," Max said brusquely, shedding his coat.

"*Oui,* but —"

"We'll talk tomorrow."

"*Oui,* but . . . I have run into a few extra expenses this month. . . ."

"Gambling debts?" Max strode to the curving staircase while Alex followed at his heels.

"I have left an accounting on your desk."

"Perhaps you could find a less expensive habit to amuse yourself with?"

"I could," Alex agreed readily. "In the meantime, however, will you take care of this for me?"

"*Bien sûr,*" Max assured him shortly, leaving him at the foot of the stairs. He wanted to see Lysette so badly that he was unwilling to wait for even a minute.

Alex relaxed, a relieved grin spreading across his face as he watched Max ascend the steps. "*Merci,* Max. Not long ago you would have lectured me for an hour."

"I would now, if I thought it would make an impression."

"I rather think that something — or someone — has done much to sweeten your temper, *mon frère.*"

Max did not pause to reply, even when Irénée's voice floated up to his ears. "Is that Max's voice I hear, Alex? Has he had supper? Well, why didn't you ask? Did he look hungry?"

Striding into his bedroom, Max closed the door with his foot and dropped his coat on the floor. Lysette emerged from the adjoining garderobe, a small room used for dressing and sometimes bathing. Her eyes glowed at the sight of him.

"You have been gone for a long time, *mon mari.*" The sound of her voice dispelled his gloom immediately. It seemed that Lysette had been trying on some new gowns, for garments of silk and lace were strewn about the room, and brocaded slippers were piled in a glittering heap beside the bed. She was dressed in an ice-blue ball gown, the bodice trimmed with swaths of matching gauze. The gown was very low-cut, molding her breasts together and upward, her cleavage covered with a translucent bit of gauze that served to enhance rather than conceal the tempting little valley. She looked slim and feline, the blue silk emphasizing her eyes and making her hair gleam like living flame.

As Lysette walked to him, clearly intending to welcome him with a kiss, Max lifted his hands in a gesture for her to stay back.

"*Petite,* wait. I am dusty from the ride, and I smell of horses," he said, smiling. "Let me see what you're wearing."

Lysette turned for his benefit, glancing flirtatiously over her shoulder. The gown was partially unfastened in the back, and Max let his gaze linger on the vulnerable curve of her spine. He wanted to devour her.

"Very beautiful," he said.

"I am going to wear this to the ball, when

I meet Colonel Burr. Have you realized that it will be my first appearance as your wife?"

Max displayed no reaction, but inwardly he was troubled. Lysette couldn't possibly be prepared for the pointed questions, the razor-sharp curiosity she was likely to encounter at the gathering. He was used to it by now, but for someone as sheltered as she had been, the experience might prove distressing.

"You should be warned about what will happen, Lysette. Yesterday was nothing compared to what the ball will be like. My fall from grace was infamous, and memories here are nothing if not long. As you know, some believe you're married to the devil incarnate."

Lysette considered him thoughtfully. Then she came to him, placing her slender hand on the side of his lean face. "But you are a devil. I already know that."

Max bent and nuzzled her throat, unable to stop himself. "I don't think I like having so much of my wife exposed to other men's gazes," he said, his fingertips measuring the amount of skin left uncovered by the deep neckline.

"Oh, but it is a *modest* gown. Many other women will be wearing styles far more daring."

"Perhaps, but I'm not married to them."

"I was not aware you had such a jealous nature," Lysette said, clearly pleased by his possessiveness.

She was so clean and sweet and adorable that Max picked her up and tossed her onto the bed.

"Then let me remove all doubt," he said climbing over her, boots and all. His body crushed the shimmering material of her skirt between them. Lysette giggled at his on-slaught of ardor, and wrestled with him. He subdued her easily, yanking up the hem of her gown and settling between her flailing thighs.

"Max," she protested, breathless with laughter, "my gown, you'll ruin it!"

"I'll buy you another. A dozen more. Now let me have my way with you." His teeth closed over the silk-covered peak of her breast, and Lysette stopped struggling. She was not wearing a chemise, and as he wet the thin slippery fabric with his tongue, the textured crest rose against his tongue. He rubbed his mouth over the tender point, flicked at it, nibbled, until she lay gasping beneath him.

Reaching between their bodies, he found the soft heat of her cleft and teased his finger inside her. She was wet and pliant, her body accepting him eagerly. Sliding a second finger inside, he covered her mouth with his. Lysette moaned and struggled to press closer to him, her hips arching into the warmth of his palm.

He kissed and teased her, loving the small

sounds she made in her throat, the urgent writhing of her body. When he felt her tensing at the approach of a climax, he withdrew his fingers and unfastened his breeches.

Greedily Lysette reached for his cock and guided him into place. Her body clasped him with a delicate, snug fit, sheathing him sweetly. She whimpered in pleasure as he circled and ground himself against her, burying his cock in deep slick thrusts, bringing her to a shuddering release. Obeying his gravelly murmur, she wrapped her legs around his waist, and he made love to her until his passion was spent in an explosion of bliss.

On the night of the ball, Max and Alexandre occupied themselves with drinks in the library while Irénée and Lysette remained busy upstairs. "Women," Alex grumbled, "and their primping."

Max smiled leisurely and lifted a glass of burgundy to his lips. "Why are you so eager to arrive at the ball on time, Alex? I do not believe it is to catch a glimpse of Aaron Burr."

"Perhaps I've taken an interest in politics," Alexandre replied, and Max snorted in skeptical amusement.

He refilled Alexandre's drink and rested his elbow on the marble mantel. "You realize, Alex, that as an unattached man, you'll be occupied the entire evening with mothers and *tantes* parading their young charges before you. Usually you can't abide such evenings."

"Ah, well, I will bear it for one night."

Max grinned, suspecting that some girl had caught his younger brother's roving eye. "Who is she?" he asked.

Alex smiled sheepishly. "Henriette Clement."

"Jacques' youngest sister?" Max inquired with surprise, remembering the last time he had seen the girl outside the milliner's shop with her older brother. "Hmm . . . an attractive girl, as I recall."

"*Sang de Dieu,* I haven't even *danced* with her yet! Just because you've plunged into marriage doesn't mean the idea holds appeal for *me.*"

Max smiled at him. "I said nothing about marriage."

Flustered, Alex cast his mind in search of a reply, and was saved by the sound of the women's voices. "*Bien,* they're ready now," he said, hurriedly setting down his glass.

Following his brother to the entrance hall, Max stopped at the doorway, still holding his drink. At first he did not see Lysette, who was standing beyond Irénée and Noeline, but then the pair moved to the mirror to inspect a coil of Irénée's hair. He stared at his wife with open pride. Lysette was striking in an exquisitely simple amber gown, the warm color flattering her skin and vibrant hair. The low scooped bodice and high waist displayed her slender body beautifully.

Lysette possessed an astonishing composure for a girl her age, seeming calm and relaxed, her blue eyes bright with the intelligence that attracted him so strongly. Max was not ordinarily a humble man, but as he watched her come down the stairs to him, he was aware of a deep gratitude and sense of wonder. Fate had so often been unkind, but having Lysette for his wife made up for everything.

Her gaze traveled over his ruffled white shirt and starched cravat. "How handsome you are," she said, picking a thread from the lapel of his black coat.

Max's dark head bent, and he kissed the side of her neck. "You'll have no equal tonight, Madame Vallerand. I've never seen you look so beautiful. Here, I want to give you something." She went with him willingly as he drew her to the parlor, away from the others' view.

He withdrew a black velvet pouch from his pocket and gave it to her. "In honor of your first ball."

Lysette flashed him a smile. "I wasn't expecting a gift, Max." Unlacing the pouch, she tilted the contents into her hand. It was a set of earrings and a matching bracelet, made of diamonds set in a flower pattern. The centers of the ten blossoms were set with rose-cut diamonds, each two carats in size.

Lysette shook her head, apparently at a loss for words.

"Do you like them?" he asked.

"Oh, Max, you're too generous. How utterly magnificent!" She slipped the glittering bracelet on her gloved wrist, and held still as Max fastened the earrings to her ears. The rich gleam of the jewels paled in comparison to her smile. She shook her head to set the dangling earrings swinging. "How can I thank you for such a beautiful gift, *mon mari?*"

"A kiss, to start with." He smiled as Lysette twined her arms around his neck and pressed her lips against his ardently. "Later," he murmured, "I'll tell you what you can do to earn the matching necklace."

She blushed and laughed, and walked back with him to the entrance hall.

"Ah, let me see!" Irénée exclaimed, immediately catching sight of the finery. She took Lysette's wrist and turned it from one side to the other, appraising the bracelet with the analytical expertise of a jeweler. "Quite exquisite, *mon fils,*" she said to Max. "The stones are of excellent quality."

Alex cleared his throat noisily, alerting them to the fact that it was time to leave. "We don't wish to be late, do we?"

Lysette took Max's arm and murmured sotto voce, "Isn't Bernard coming?"

Max shook his head, suddenly grim. "Bernard doesn't usually care for these events. And he wants to avoid me this evening, as we had an argument earlier."

"About what?"

"I'll explain later."

The ball was being hosted at Seraphiné, one of the plantations lining the river road. Lysette thought the main house was magnificent, with wide galleries and rows of dormer windows built out from the sloping green tile roof. The inside of the house was just as impressive, furnished with venetian chandeliers, richly colored rugs, and massive portraits of prominent Seraphiné ancestors.

Along the sides of the great dance hall, ladies fatigued by the dancing rested their feet, and the chaperones of eligible Creole girls sat to monitor their charges. Groups of young men positioned themselves nearby, most of them wearing *colchemardes,* small but deadly sword-canes. Hot-tempered youths were wont to quarrel at such affairs, and duels were the natural result of even insignificant disputes.

Alexandre amused Lysette by relating an account of the last ball he had attended, at which a duel had exploded in the middle of the room, instead of being conducted outside. Men had chosen sides, benches and chairs had been thrown, women had fainted, and the military guard had been forced to storm inside to quell the riot.

"What caused the duel?" Lysette asked.

Alexandre grinned. "One of the young men happened to tread on another's toes. It was taken to be a deliberate insult, *et ainsi de suite . . .* a duel."

"Creole men are dreadful," Lysette said with a laugh, placing her hand on her husband's arm. "Why do you not wear a *colchemarde*, Max? Don't you intend to defend your toes if the need arises?"

"You defend them for me," he replied, his gaze warm.

There was a ripple of murmurs and speculation as the Vallerands ventured farther into the ballroom.

Reminding herself that she had nothing to be afraid of, Lysette forced a smile to her lips. Suddenly a pair of intense, jet-black eyes stared into hers. They belonged to a small, delicate-featured man standing across the room, surrounded by a large entourage. He continued to stare at her steadily, causing a light blush to steal over her face.

"It appears," she heard Max mutter, "that you've attracted Colonel Burr's notice."

"*That* is him?" Lysette exclaimed in a whisper. "But it can't be. I expected him to be . . ."

"What?" Max asked, now sounding amused.

"Taller," she blurted out, and he laughed quietly. In the distance, Burr murmured to one of his companions. "And now," Max said under his breath, "he is asking who you are. And if he pays too much attention to you, he's going to have a duel on his hands. Let us hope one of his aides warns him that I'm a much better marksman than Alexander Hamilton."

Lysette blanched, recalling that Colonel Burr had reportedly forced Hamilton, a patriot who had helped write the new constitution, into a duel that Burr had been certain to win. Many had called it cold-blooded murder, for it had been known by all that Burr's dueling skills were far superior to Hamilton's. It was rumored that Burr had shown not one sign of compassion or regret for Hamilton's death.

"Let's have no more talk of duels," she said hastily.

Before Max could reply, the mayor of New Orleans, Mr. John Watkins, appeared at his elbow. After greeting them effusively, the mayor informed them that Colonel Burr desired to make their acquaintance.

"We are honored," Max said perfunctorily, following the mayor with Lysette on his arm.

Colonel Burr was dressed with the exquisite care of a dandy. Lysette liked the fact that although he had lost much of his hair at the front and crown, he did not wear a wig. Max had told her that Burr was at least forty-eight, but the colonel appeared much younger. His face was deeply tanned, and his smile was quick and self-assured. And those jet-black eyes were even more remarkable up close, filled with snapping energy and vitality.

Although a man of Burr's size was physically dwarfed by Max's superior height, the former vice president had a magnetic presence that held its own. He made a great show of kissing Irénée's and Lysette's hands, then looked up at Max.

"Monsieur Vallerand," Burr said in English, "at last we meet." He regarded Lysette with twinkling eyes as he continued. "My congratulations on your marriage, sir. Now, having seen your lovely bride, I consider you the most fortunate of men."

Before Max could reply, Lysette answered Burr in his own language. "Your facility with words, monsieur, is quite impressive. But of course that is no surprise."

Burr looked at Lysette with warming interest. As most Creole women spoke nothing but French, he had not expected her to understand what he had said. "May I offer my compliments on your English, madame? You speak it quite well."

Lysette gave him a nod of thanks. "That is my good fortune, Colonel, as I was able to listen to your speech at the Place D'Armes last week without requiring translation."

"Did you enjoy it, madame?"

"Oh, yes," she replied without hesitation.

"You are a gifted speaker, and the speech was quite rousing. I was even tempted to clap at the parts that I didn't agree with."

Burr laughed so heartily that half the room strained to pay keen attention to them. "I must know, madame, what parts you did not agree with."

Lysette responded with a provocative smile. "My opinions are insignificant, Colonel Burr. My husband's views are the ones you should take note of."

"And so I shall," Burr said with a chuckle. His gaze focused on Max's expressionless face. "Your wife is not only lovely and accomplished, but also clever. You are a fortunate man, Monsieur Vallerand."

Although Max did not respond to the comment, Lysette sensed his jealous bristling. He changed the subject abruptly. "How do you find the climate in New Orleans, Colonel?"

The question caused Burr to smile. "I believe you are referring to the political climate, are you not? I find it very pleasant, Monsieur Vallerand. We had quite an agreeable journey down here, as we encountered many unexpected friends."

"So I've heard."

"Is it true that you own a shipping business, monsieur? That is rare for a man of your background, I believe. Don't Creoles as a rule consider anything mercantile to be beneath them?"

"As a rule, yes. But I seldom follow the rules."

"Neither do I," Burr said agreeably, and gave Max a speculative stare. "I have been meeting many gentlemen in the community, monsieur, most of whom belong to the Mexican Association. Do you happen to subscribe to it?"

Lysette recalled what Max had told her of the Mexican Association, a group of prominent citizens who desired the liberation of Mexico, and all the attendant trade benefits it would give to the merchants of New Orleans. Anyone who belonged to the group was certain to sympathize with Burr's cause.

"No, I do not," Max replied. "I have found that belonging to organizations of any kind invariably results in unwanted obligations."

"Interesting," Burr commented, his eyes alight with the enjoyment of a challenge. "I would like to have an opportunity to try and persuade you otherwise, monsieur. Shall we talk at a later date?"

"That might be arranged."

Soon Colonel Burr's attention was claimed by others who wished to be introduced, and Max drew Lysette away.

"What is your impression of him?" he asked.

"Dangerous," came Lysette's blunt reply. "I don't think Colonel Burr would be so confident if he didn't have good reason. It is likely that he has persuaded many men to join his cause, Max."

"I think so, too," he said ruefully.

Alexandre approached them after having delivered Irénée to her friends, who were clustered at the side of the room gossiping. "My lovely sister-in-law," he said to Lysette, "dance with me, *s'il vous plait.*"

Lysette took his arm. "Do you have any objections, Max?"

Her husband shook his head, but gave his younger brother an ominous frown. "Do *not* leave my wife unattended."

"I hope that I have better manners than that, *mon frère,*" Alexandre said indignantly. He pulled Lysette along with him, and stopped at the edge of the crowd. "Do you see the girl in the green gown?" he asked her. "The one with the dark hair?"

"No, I do not see —"

"She is tall. There are yellow ribbons in her hair. The blond man dancing with her is her cousin. See her? That is Henriette Clement. I want to attract her attention. Make certain you look as if you are enjoying yourself. Laugh as if I am saying something witty."

"I'll do my best." Lysette smiled and placed her hand in his. "Do you intend to court her, Alexandre?"

Alex looked over her shoulder and scowled. "I want to," he admitted. "Very much. But

259

her family doesn't approve of me."

"Does Mademoiselle Clement have an interest in you?"

"I'm not certain. If only I could spend some time with her . . . but every time I am within ten yards of Henriette, the entire Clement family descends on me like a pack of bloodhounds."

"If you are to talk to Mademoiselle Clement, you will have to enlist the help of her *tante*."

"Her *tante* is a dragon," Alexandre said morosely.

"Well, you'll have to put some work into charming her. If you make the *tante* like you and plead your case well enough, she may be persuaded to help you meet with Mademoiselle Clement. *Alors*, go find the *tante* and be nice to her."

"Now?" Alexandre asked blankly. "But you are not to be left alone. Max will turn me inside out if I don't stay with you."

"Irénée is right over there, not twenty feet away. I will go to her."

"What about our dance?"

"We will dance later," Lysette promised with a laugh. "At the moment, this is more important."

"All right," Alexandre muttered, squaring his shoulders. "I suppose I have nothing to lose, *n'est-ce pas?*"

Smiling, Lysette headed toward Irénée and

the gaggle of gray-haired women around her. She could not help but be aware of the indiscreet stares that followed her. One group of young bucks stopped their conversation altogether, watching her every move. Lysette became absurdly self-conscious, and by the time she reached her destination, she felt a blush climbing up her cheeks. Irénée welcomed her warmly.

"Belle-mère," Lysette said, "Are you enjoying yourself?"

"Of course I am!" Irénée replied matter-of-factly. "And from all accounts, you are a great success, my dear. Why, Diron Clement, the old gentleman over there, was overheard to say that in his opinion you are a great beauty!"

Lysette laughed. "Someone should clean his spectacles."

"He would not have said it if it were not true." Irénée nudged a stout, flower-bedecked matron nearby. "Tell her it is so, Yvonne, tell her!"

Yvonne, an older cousin on Irénée's side of the family, gave Lysette a plump-cheeked smile. "You are a very attractive girl, Lysette. I remember it was the same with your mother when she was young. How lovely and full of life she was, and how they all stared when she entered a room!"

Lysette reflected wistfully that no one would consider her mother a beauty now, after the ravages of her marriage to Gaspard.

Seeing the trace of sadness in her expression, Yvonne sought to change the subject. "What splendid diamonds, Lysette! Irénée told me they were a gift from Maximilien."

Lysette smiled, glancing down at the glittering bracelet. "My husband is quite generous."

The older woman leaned forward and spoke in a confidential tone. "I'm certain he is, my dear. But mark my words, your husband will be even *more* generous once you bear him children. You must conceive as soon as possible."

Amused by the Creole preoccupation with producing babies, Lysette tried to appear suitably impressed. "*Oui*, madame."

"As the wife of a Vallerand," Yvonne continued with increasing enthusiasm, "you will have to set the standard for all the young Creole matrons. We have need of such good examples, with all these brazen American women moving to New Orleans!" She clucked her tongue in displeasure. "Shameless creatures — no modesty or delicacy. Why, they think nothing of walking anywhere unescorted, and interrupting their husbands freely! Bah! It is the responsibility of young Creole women to cling fast to the old values. But until you produce children, you will have no real authority."

"Yes, that is very true," Irénée agreed meaningfully.

Lysette nodded gravely, while inside she wanted to laugh, fearing that she was far more like the brazen American women than the proper Creole ones. "I will pray to be blessed with children soon, madame."

"*Bien sûr,*" Yvonne replied, satisfied that her admonition had been heeded.

They continued to chat until a flutter of excitement ran through the group of ladies and Lysette half turned to find the dark figure of her husband beside her. Max greeted the women politely and extended his gloved hand to Lysette. "I am stealing you for a dance," he informed her.

Lysette went with him gladly, lured by the buoyant melody of a quadrille.

"I haven't danced in a long time," Max told her. "I am somewhat out of practice, *petite.*"

"Don't you like to dance, Max?"

"Yes, I do. But it hasn't always been easy for me to find partners. My wicked reputation, remember."

"You have a partner now," Lysette said as they took their places in the quadrille. "A most willing one." After they danced several sets, they stopped as the musicians took a brief respite from playing. Max drew Lysette to the side of the drawing room, next to a row of French doors that opened to the outside gallery.

As a servant passed bearing a tray of

263

champagne, Max took two glasses of the sparkling vintage and gave one to Lysette. She accepted it without hesitation and drank thirstily, heedless of the disapproving stares from nearby matrons. It was not proper for a young woman to drink in public, even a married one. Max, however, seemed amused, as if he were being entertained by the antics of a playful kitten.

"Mmmm . . . I feel a bit dizzy," Lysette said breathlessly when she finished the champagne. Smiling, Max gave their empty glasses to another passing servant.

"Some fresh air will clear your head," he said. "Would you like to go outside?"

She gave him a suspicious glance. "Are you going to make advances on me if I do?"

"Of course," he replied without hesitation.

"In that case, yes."

Adeptly Max slipped her past the French doors. Lysette laughed under her breath as he pulled her into the rustling garden, past tall yew hedges and rosemary-covered walls. She felt wicked and giddy, as if she were having a clandestine meeting with a lover. Max lifted her off her feet and whirled her around, making her giggle. Throwing her arms around his neck, she leaned against him, while a sobering thought occurred to her.

"Max . . . what if we had met this evening for the very first time, and I were Etienne Sagesse's wife?" Lysette tightened her arms a little. "I could so easily have been his bride instead of yours. If I hadn't run away, or if Justin and Philippe hadn't found me . . . or if you had decided to give me back to the Sagesses —"

"I would never have given you back. And if you had married Sagesse, I would have taken you away from him. No matter how I had to do it."

From any other man, it would have sounded like an empty boast. From Max, however, it was entirely believable. Lysette gazed at him in wonder, his face shadowed and his head silhouetted against the hazy starlit sky. *"Mon mari,"* she said softly, "sometimes you almost frighten me."

Max stroked her throat and let his fingers drift to the perspiration-dampened valley of her cleavage. "Why?"

Lysette's eyes half closed as his fingers slipped inside her bodice to touch her nipple. "You are so ruthless when it comes to getting what you want. It makes me wonder if anything could ever stop you."

"You could." Max played gently with the soft peak of her breast until it budded against his fingers. "You know that."

His mouth descended to her neck, and she sighed in pleasure. "Then if I ever asked you to do something against your will . . . you would?"

"Of course."

Her breathing hastened as she felt the warm slide of his lips over her throat. Slipping her hand behind his neck, she nuzzled into his thick hair. "Max . . . I must tell you how much I —"

She broke off, startled as a shadow disentangled itself from the tall yew shrubs. Her first thought was that it was some kind of animal, but quickly the shadow assumed the shape of a man strolling toward them. Max turned and automatically jerked Lysette behind him as he faced the approaching figure.

Lysette felt an unpleasant shock, rather like the all-over stinging sensation of barely saving oneself from a fall, when she heard the voice of Etienne Sagesse.

"Ah, Lysette," he drawled, coming closer. It was obvious that he was drunk, his words slurred, his face puffy and florid. "You seem to be enjoying yourself, *ma chère*. But I pity you. Someday you'll realize how much wiser you would have been to stay with me. And I'm afraid that poor Corinne would most definitely agree."

CHAPTER

11

Lysette had known it was inevitable that she would someday come vis-à-vis Etienne Sagesse. However, no amount of expectation could have prepared her for it. She remembered in a flash the loathing she had felt for him, the fear and desperation that had driven her to take the foolish risk of traveling through the bayou alone. She did not doubt for one moment that her opinion of him had been well founded. If she had married Sagesse, he would have insulted her, condescended to her, debased her in a hundred ways. Blindly searching for Max's hand, Lysette felt his fingers close reassuringly over hers.

"What do you want?" Max asked Sagesse curtly.

"Why to congratulate you. Since I was not invited to the wedding, I didn't have the opportunity before now." Sagesse's smile was reptilian as he regarded Lysette's flushed face. "You seem to be content as a Vallerand, Lysette. But as I recall, so did Corinne . . . at first."

"If you want another duel," Max growled,

"you'll have it. And this time I'll finish it."

"Is that a challenge?"

"No," Lysette said quickly. "Max —"

"Not a challenge, but a warning," Max said, ignoring Lysette's outburst. His hand tightened to silence her, and she flinched as her fingers were squeezed together.

"You think you've won," Etienne said to Max. "You have everything you want, don't you? But it is only a matter of time before you lose it all — and it will be my pleasure to watch your downfall."

He nearly tripped over his own feet as he wandered away, weaving drunkenly across the lawn.

Lysette and Max watched in silence until he disappeared. "I hope that his family takes him home before he makes a public scene," Lysette said. "He seems to want to ruin himself. It is strange, but as much as I hate him . . . just now I actually pitied him."

Max regarded her with a sardonic expression.

"Didn't you?" she asked.

"No."

"I think you did." Lysette pressed against his shirtfront, breathing in his familiar scent. "We won't let Sagesse spoil our evening, Max. Take me back inside — I want to dance again."

Unfortunately, despite Lysette's determined efforts to enjoy herself, Sagesse's presence cast a pall over the evening. He remained in the corner of the drawing room, staring at her, while the other Sagesses endeavored to keep him quiet. The guests at the ball kept glancing between the Sagesses and the Vallerands, until finally Lysette gave in and ruefully asked Max to take her home.

Max said little on the way back to the Vallerand plantation. Lysette made desultory conversation with Irénée and Alexandre, exchanging observations and bits of gossip. "How was your evening?" she asked Alexandre. "Did you approach Henriette Clement's *tante?*"

"Oh, yes," Alex said gloomily. "I hovered around her for at least a quarter hour, feeling like a complete fool. She seems to believe that no innocent young woman would be safe in the company of a Vallerand, even with ten chaperones present."

"I can't imagine why," Lysette said dryly, and glanced at Max with a smile. *"Quest-ce que c'est?"* she asked softly, while Irénée and Alexandre became involved in a discussion of the Clements. "Still thinking about Etienne Sagesse?"

Max shook his head, staring at the scenery outside as the carriage sluggishly traveled the muddy road. "No . . . it has nothing to do with him, but I have a bad feeling. I'm not certain why. But I will be glad when we reach home."

Unfortunately, Max's premonition was

proven right. As soon as they entered the house, Noeline greeted them, her usually imperturbable face set with worry. Philippe sat on one of the narrow benches in the entranceway, looking haggard.

"Monsieur, Justin has been gone all day," Noeline told them tersely. "He did not come home to eat tonight."

Max turned to Philippe. "Where is he?"

Philippe stood to face him with a troubled expression. "I don't know, Father. The pirogue is gone — Justin has taken it somewhere."

"When did you last see him?"

"This morning. Justin was boasting that he sneaked out last night after bedtime. He said he had met some of the crew of a flatboat on Tchoupitoulas Street and planned to go with them tonight. But I didn't think he would actually do it."

"Oh, my poor Justin!" Irénée cried in distress.

Max cursed quietly. Flatboat men lived, ate, and slept on the deck of their boats with no protection against the outdoors. Their idea of entertainment was to swill rye whiskey, brawl, and wallow in unsavory flesh houses where disease and violence were rampant. When they fought, they bit, kicked, and gouged eyes out, mutilating an opponent without mercy. By now they might have made short work of Justin.

"Which crew?" Max demanded. "Which boat?"

Philippe shook his head helplessly.

Max turned to the door, where Alexandre stood with his mouth open. "We have to find him."

Alex backed away a step. "Oh, no. I make every effort to steer clear of such fellows. I won't risk my neck merely to rescue your fool of a son, who doesn't want to be found in the first place. Just go to sleep. He'll probably be back by morning."

"Or end up in the river with his throat cut." Max brushed past his brother and headed outside.

"You won't find him," Alexandre warned.

"Oh, yes, I will. And after I make certain he's all right, I'm going to tear him limb from limb."

Hastily, Lysette ran after him. "Max, be careful." He acknowledged her with a brief gesture of his hand, not bothering to look back. She bit her lip, wanting to call after him again, knowing how terrified he was for his son. Whirling around, she went back to Alexandre, gripping his arm and tugging hard. "You must go with him. You must help him."

"I'll be damned if I do."

"Max needs your help," she persisted impatiently. "Oh, be of use for once, Alexandre!"

Irénée took up the fight, helping Lysette to

urge Alexandre toward the door. "Yes, you must accompany Max, *mon fils*."

"I am tired," he said with a scowl.

"Think of Justin!" Irénée commanded, pulling at his other arm. "He may be in trouble this very moment. He may be suffering!"

"If there is any justice he is," Alex muttered, shaking off their hands as he hurried after his older brother.

They closed the door immediately, half afraid he would try to come back in.

"That Justin," Irénée said sorrowfully, "will no doubt be the death of me." She glanced at Philippe. "Why can't he be more like you?"

Suddenly Philippe exploded. "Why does everyone have to ask that? I am not the good one. Justin is not the bad one."

Irénée sighed, her face creased with exhaustion. "I am too exhausted to discuss this now. Noeline, help me upstairs."

All were silent as the two women left and headed to the curving staircase. Philippe buried his face in his hands, digging his knuckles into his eyes. Filled with sympathy, Lysette sat beside him.

"Justin is different from me," Philippe said in a muffled voice. "Things are too slow and dull for him here. He has always wanted to run away. Most of the time he feels as if he's living in a cage."

"Is it because of what happened to your mother?" Lysette asked. "Because people think that Max killed her?"

"Yes, partly," Philippe admitted with a heavy sigh. "It's not easy being a Vallerand. Justin and I know what people think of us. We've heard what they say about our mother — that she was mad, or a slut, or both. And everyone in New Orleans believes that her blood is on Father's hands."

"I don't believe it," Lysette said firmly. "And neither should you."

"Most of the time I don't." His haunted gaze met hers. "But Justin does, and that makes things very hard for him."

Max and Alexandre were gone all night, returning early the next afternoon without Justin. Max was more agitated than Lysette had ever seen him. His thoughts seemed to race faster than conversation would allow.

"No sign of him," he said hoarsely, downing half a cup of coffee in one swallow. "We found a boatman who claimed to have seen a boy matching Justin's description on the waterfront. God knows if he was lying. Justin might have signed on with a crew, but I don't think he would be so damned foolish."

"I'm going to bed," Alex mumbled, his face pasty and eyes bloodshot.

Lysette came to stand behind her husband, her hands drifting soothingly over his taut shoulders. "Max, you need to rest also."

He motioned for Noeline to pour more coffee. "I am leaving again in a few minutes. Bernard will go with me. I'm going to ask Jacques Clement and one or two others to help in the search."

Lysette wished that she knew how to comfort him. "I don't think Justin has run away," she said, sitting beside him. "I think this is another bid for attention. He is staying away deliberately, waiting until he is certain of an uproar before he returns."

Max held the coffee cup in fingers that trembled slightly. "When I get hold of him, he'll have more attention than he ever bargained for."

She took his free hand in both of hers, clasping it tightly. "I know that you're angry with him, but I think that you are mostly afraid for him. Perhaps you should let Justin know that, when you find him."

Max rested his elbows on the table and massaged his temples. "Justin is too hardheaded to listen to anything I say."

"I believe," she said wryly, "that he has made the same remark about you on occasion."

Max smiled faintly. "Sometimes I see myself in him," he admitted. "But at his age I was not half so stubborn."

"I'll ask Irénée about that," Lysette said, gently teasing. "I suspect she might not agree."

Max brought her hand to his bristled face and pressed his lips against the back of it. "If I don't find him, Lysette . . ."

"You will."

The search continued for another day and night. Max enjoined most of the workers on his own trade vessels to find out what they could. A few boatmen admitted that Justin, or a boy remarkably like him, had been in their company. After a few hours of drinking and gaming, they said, he had left with a waterfront prostitute and had not been seen again. "How splendid," Bernard had commented upon hearing this bit of information. "Now it seems we must worry about him developing a case of the clap."

"If only that were the worst to fear," Max had replied grimly.

After questioning dozens of men and combing through every keelboat, kentucky flat, barge, and raft in sight, the searchers were forced to temporarily disband with the agreement that they would resume the next morning. For two days and nights Max had barely paused to rest his feet, and the strain was telling. Looking very much like the unkempt, unshaven boatmen he had associated with for the past forty-eight hours, he made his way into the house with overcautious movements, blinking hard to stay awake.

It was past three in the morning, but

Lysette was waiting for him. It tore at her heart to see him so careworn and defeated. She tried to guide him upstairs, but Max refused to go to his bedroom, afraid that he might sleep too soundly. He had time for only a few hours of rest. Together Lysette and Philippe helped him to the parlor and removed his boots. He unfolded his long frame onto a settee, dropped his head in Lysette's lap, and closed his eyes. Philippe left them, anxiously glancing back over his shoulder.

"He's gone," Max mumbled, turning his face against the soft line of Lysette's thigh. "As if he's vanished from the face of the earth."

Lysette stroked his forehead gently. "Sleep now. It's not long until daybreak."

"I keep remembering when Justin was a baby. Sometimes I held him when he slept. I wanted to keep him safe and happy for the rest of his life. But I can't keep him safe from anything."

"Rest now. You'll find him tomorrow, *bien-aimé*."

As Max fell asleep, Lysette watched him for a long time. She was surprised to realize how much she had come to care for Justin and Philippe in such a short time. She shared Max's concern for the twins, and she wanted desperately to help them find peace. How unfair life could be, laying such burdens

276

on the shoulders of the innocent, and letting them suffer the consequences of others' mistakes.

Curling up beside Max, Lysette dozed lightly. The sky outside changed, darkness lightening to lavender-gray. Watching the dawn arrive, Lysette rubbed her eyes, careful not to disturb her sleeping husband.

Alertness came in a flash as she heard a scraping sound in the entrance hall. It was the front door opening. Stealthily the intruder crept into the house and paused at the parlor doorway.

It was Justin, dirty and disheveled, but looking a good deal better than Max. Silently he looked at Lysette and his father's long, sprawling form on the settee. Lysette thought of motioning him upstairs and allowing Max to sleep, but Max would want to know about his son's return right away. He would be furious if he did not have the opportunity to confront Justin the moment he entered the house.

"Come in," Lysette said quietly.

At the sound of her voice, Max stirred, and she bent over his dark head. "Wake up," she whispered. "It is over now, *bien-aimé*. He is home."

Blindly Max twisted and sat up, shaking his head to clear away the mist of sleep. "Justin? Where have you been?"

"With friends."

"Are you all right?" Lysette asked. "You have not been hurt?"

"Or course I am all right. Why wouldn't I be?"

Lysette winced, knowing that even a touch of humility or repentance on the boy's part would have kept Max from going off the edge. As it was, Max turned white with frustration.

"The next time you decide to leave," he said through clenched teeth, "without letting anyone know where you're going or when you plan to return, don't come back."

"I don't have to live under your roof!" Justin exploded. "I don't have to depend on you for anything! You want me to go? Then I will, and I'll never look back!" He spun around and darted out the way he had come.

"Justin, no!" Lysette scrambled up from the sofa. Max did not move. She stared at him with wide eyes. "Aren't you going to go after him?"

Clearly he was too furious to think clearly. "Let him leave."

Lysette scowled at him. "Between the two of you I don't know who is more stubborn!" She hurried after Justin, while Max swore violently.

Lysette winced as she stubbed her toe on the front steps. "Ouch!" Painstakingly, she hopped to the ground. "Justin, stop this very second! Stop!"

Surprisingly, he did. He stood with his back facing her, his hands clenched at his sides. Lysette hobbled partway along the drive. "Max has been desperate to find you," she said. "He's had people out looking for you. He hasn't eaten. He hasn't slept, aside from three or four hours on the settee last night."

"If you're trying to make me say I'm sorry, I won't!"

"I am trying to make you understand how worried he has been. He was terrified that something had happened to you."

Justin snorted sardonically. "He didn't look so terrified to me."

"You're not fair to him."

"He's not fair to me! He has to have everyone and everything under his control."

Lysette closed her eyes and breathed a quick prayer for patience. "Justin," she said, keeping her voice even, "please turn around. I cannot talk to your back."

The boy swiveled to face her, his blue eyes radiant with anger.

But Lysette did not retreat. "You don't realize how much he loves you."

"He's not capable of loving anyone," Justin said roughly. "Not even you."

Even though Lysette knew that Justin didn't mean it, the words shocked her. "That's not true!"

"And you're a fool for believing in someone who murdered his wife." The boy stared at the ground, his entire body trembling.

"Justin," she said softly. "You know in your heart that your father never could have done it."

"I *don't* know that." Justin inhaled deeply, his gaze still fixed on the ground. "He could have. Anyone could be driven to murder."

"No, Justin." Cautiously she approached him. "Come inside with me." She took hold of his wrist.

Justin wrenched his arm away. "He doesn't want me to."

"I suppose that is why he has exhausted himself searching for you." She refrained from touching him again. "Justin, did you stay away because you knew it would upset him?"

"No . . . it was . . . I had to get away."

"From what?"

"From everything. I can't do what they want. They want me to be a good boy like Philippe, and not ask questions that make them uncomfortable, and not remind them of my mother." Justin's eyes glistened, and he clenched his fists, struggling to master the traitorous tears. "But I am like her. I know I am."

Lysette had to repress the urge to put her arms around him and comfort him as she would an unhappy child. She did not argue with him, knowing that he was too tired and emotional to think clearly. "Come with me," she murmured. "Your family has worried enough. And you need to rest." She turned back to the house, holding her breath until she heard his slow footsteps behind her.

Fearing what he might say to Justin before his anger cooled, Max avoided him for the next day. Gently Lysette pressed him to have a talk with the boy, and he agreed reluctantly that he would, immediately after his meeting with Colonel Burr.

It was nearly midnight when Max welcomed Burr into his library, knowing that Burr was expecting to win yet another wealthy patron to his side. Daniel Clark, a New Orleans merchant with a large fleet of commercial ships and warehouses, had reportedly given Burr at least twenty-five thousand dollars in cash, and several others had matched that sum. Max did not intend to contribute a penny, but he was interested to hear what the ambitious colonel had to say.

Burr had charmed almost everyone in New Orleans — even the Ursuline nuns. He had been received everywhere with elaborate hospitality. The Catholic authorities and the Mexican Association, which had long agitated for the conquest of Mexico, had granted him their support. It was generally thought that Burr was planning an attack on the Spaniards, and that he had gained the secret support of Jefferson's government. However, Max had heard enough confidential information from varying sources to know better. Burr was certainly not in league with Jefferson; he was forming a conspiracy for his own gain.

With deliberate bluntness, he asked Burr why he desired this private, highly confidential meeting, when Burr had nearly every man of importance in his pocket. "After all," Max pointed out, "one more or less won't make a difference to your plans — whatever they may be."

"You are known as a most enterprising man, Monsieur Vallerand. I would value your political support. And frankly, you are so wealthy that I could not afford to overlook you."

Max smiled, actually liking the man's bluntness. "Perhaps you haven't taken my rather blemished reputation into account, Colonel. That could be a great liability to any politician who chooses to associate with me."

Burr shrugged negligently. "I've heard the rumors about you, but I do not believe they would interfere with my plans."

"Which are?" The two words seemed to charge the air with tension. For a moment there was silence.

"I think," Burr finally said, "that you already have an idea about that."

"Not really," Max lied smoothly.

Refusing a drink, Burr sat in a deep leather chair and pursued a seemingly idle line of conversation. Looking handsome and mysterious, sitting outside the direct pool of light cast by a lamp, he lazily plied Max with questions about New Orleans, his family, his politics.

Max understood Burr's dilemma perfectly. Burr had to risk revealing enough information to gain Max's support, but not give away enough to endanger his plans. The former vice president explained that he intended to use New Orleans as a base from which to conquer Mexico and wrest the Floridas away from the Spanish — if, of course, war happened to break out between the United States and Spain.

After Burr had finished talking, Max smiled with maddening indifference. "And this will be done for whose benefit?"

As Max had expected, Burr refrained from confessing that he planned to be the sole ruler over his new empire. "Let us say that the entire Louisiana Territory will profit."

"And your fortunes will improve as well, *n'est-ce pas?*"

"So will yours," Burr replied, "if I can count you among our group."

Max let the moment draw out to its fullest before replying. "I find it impossible to pledge support to a cause with such nebulous outlines. Unless you can provide more details . . ."

Burr frowned, clearly surprised at Max's lack of enthusiasm. "I have provided all the information I can for now. In my view, you have little reason *not* to join me."

Max spread his hands slightly, palms up. "I have certain loyalties, Colonel."

"Loyalties to Claiborne?"

"To the United States as well."

"I'm afraid, Vallerand, that I don't understand your allegiance to a country that has refused to grant your people citizenship. You should consider the interests of the territory — and those of your family — more carefully. It is clear that your loyalties are misplaced."

"That may be proven in time. However, for now I will keep to the course I've already chosen. I have enjoyed our talk, Colonel, but I think it is time for you to leave."

Burr replied with barely controlled fury. "There will come a day when you will regret aligning yourself with my opponents, Vallerand."

After Burr left, Max released a slow sigh. He reflected that it was possible Burr would accomplish all he planned, and New Orleans would someday be part of a new empire separate from the United States. If Max had chosen unwisely, he could lose a large portion of his wealth and property. Burr was known to be a vindictive opponent.

"He's not very convincing, in my opinion. He doesn't give a damn about the territory or his so-called friends. He wants power for himself."

Hearing Lysette's voice, Max turned with a questioning look. She stood a few feet away, wearing a lacy white pelisse that was buttoned from the neck to the floor.

"You listened," he said wryly.

She didn't bother to deny it. "Voices carry very easily from this room, even with the door closed. If you desire privacy, you should try the other parlor."

Max laughed shortly. "I'll remember that."

Lysette frowned. "Is it possible that the colonel will succeed? Could he actually create his own empire, and make New Orleans part of it?"

"I may be underestimating him," Max admitted. "I don't think anyone could have anticipated his popularity, after his journey through the West. Recently Burr was heard to say that he expects that a king will someday sit on the throne of the United States. No doubt he's already had his head measured for a crown."

"A king? Doesn't he believe in democracy, then?"

"No, *petite*."

"Do you, Max?" she asked, knowing that many Creoles had grave doubts about the American system of government.

Max grinned and reached for her, swinging her slight body up into his arms. "Everywhere but at home."

She persisted in questioning him as he carried her upstairs. "Do you think you may come to regret not siding with Monsieur Burr?"

"I suppose I might, if he succeeds in taking over Louisiana."

Lysette wondered why Max didn't seem more concerned. "If he does, you could stand to lose a great deal, couldn't you?"

"I've made provisions for any circumstance," he said, giving her a comforting squeeze. "Don't forget, the territory has changed hands many times before, and the Vallerands have weathered it quite well. Do you doubt my ability to take care of you?"

"No, of course not." Lysette curved her hand around his shoulder, and with her fingertip traced a line from his ear down the side of his neck. "Max . . . you never told me what you and Bernard argued about, the day of the Seraphiné ball."

He sighed tautly. "It's too much to explain right now. I'm tired, my sweet. Tomorrow —"

"Tell me just a little bit," Lysette coaxed.

He scowled but complied reluctantly. "Very well. After all the comments I've made to Bernard about assuming some responsibility around here, Bernard finally did. Much to my regret."

"He did something wrong?"

"Worse than wrong. Something abhorrent, not to mention cruel and senseless. You've met the overseer, Newland? The other day Bernard ordered him to whip a slave for not working hard enough. The slave had been ill with fever last week and was in no condition to be out in the field in the first place. So Newland disregarded the orders, and Bernard had him whipped instead. To my eternal regret, I was in town at the time — I wish to God I had been here to stop it."

"Oh, Max," she murmured, feeling ill.

They had reached the bedroom; Max set her on the bed. "When I found out, it was all I could do to keep from skinning Bernard alive. He sees nothing wrong in what he did. It's clear that I can never allow him to be in charge of the plantation — and he has no real interest in it. Neither does Alex. As long as I supply my brothers with their monthly allowances, they are content to spend most of their time in town. For that matter, I've made no secret of my own dislike of farming."

"I know," Lysette said, reaching out to untie his cravat. "It's a duty to you."

Max sighed heavily. "My father took enormous pleasure in the sight of crops growing. He was a man of the earth — he loved plantation life in a way that I never will. Perhaps it is fortunate that he didn't live to see that none of his sons inherited his passion for this place. I've entertained thoughts long before this incident with Newland and Bernard . . . thoughts of selling the plantation, or at least reducing its size. But those ideas seem like a betrayal of my father and all that he worked so hard to achieve."

"And the plantation is a way of life for all the Vallerands," Lysette commented, drawing the cravat from his neck. "If you reject it, there will be consequences. Your friends and acquaintances may feel betrayed."

"Oh, they will," Max assured her grimly. "Fortunately, I've been used to public disapproval for so long that their opinions don't matter." He was very still, his eyes dark and troubled as his gaze searched hers. "But you haven't."

"I am strong enough to deal with any controversy," Lysette murmured with a faint smile. "I have already become accustomed to being known as *la mariée du diable*."

His gaze caressed her as he reached out to twine a gleaming red curl around his finger.

"You are not trapped, you know," Lysette told him. "You don't have to maintain this place. Do whatever you like with it. Whatever the consequences may be, I will face them with you."

"My little rebel," Max murmured with a swift grin, his hand playing in her hair. "I should have known that you would encourage me to make the unconventional choice. Very well, I'll tell you the truth — I hate this damned place, for all the work it requires, the memories that it holds, and for the moral compromises it demands."

"Are you going to sell it, then?"

"Not entirely. I've considered selling half of it to our neighbors, the Archambaults. They would pay any price I would name."

"What about the slaves?"

"I don't want to own slaves. I'm tired of clouding the issue with questions of economics and traditions and politics." A frown scored across his forehead as he continued. "I've been on the wrong side of the argument for too long — I can't defend it with any conviction. I don't want this way of life for myself, and I don't want it for my children, either. God knows why I can't share my father's beliefs, or those of my family and friends, but . . ." His mouth twisted impatiently. "What I am trying to say is that I want to free the Vallerand slaves."

"All of them?"

"Yes, all. And hire the ones who decide to stay on as freemen." Seeing Lysette's stunned expression, he smiled wryly. "It's been done before, actually. There is a New Orleans sugar planter of mixed race, Maurice Manville, who has freed his slaves and now pays them wages — and he makes a profit, admittedly a modest one. If I follow suit, and reduce the plantation by half, I would have far more time to give to our cypress mill and the shipping business."

Lysette tried to absorb everything he had proposed. "It's very difficult to predict what will happen, *n'est-ce pas?*" She reached out to stroke the indentations between his brows. "Will there be financial repercussions, Max?"

"Are you asking if we'll lose money? Yes, at first. But the shipping business is growing. You'll have to trust me to make it a success."

Lysette smiled and applied herself to loosening his cravat. "That will be no problem, *ma cher.*"

"But about your children's inheritance, and Justin and Philippe's —"

"There are far more important things you can leave them than a parcel of land. And they will still be Vallerands, with or without a great plantation." Removing the starched linen from his neck, Lysette pressed her face into his warm throat. "Mmmn . . . how good you smell." She kissed the pulse that beat in the triangular hollow. "Do what you feel is right, Max."

Drawing back slightly, Max cradled her cheeks in his hand. His gaze was dark and tender. "This is one of the advantages of having a young wife," he said with a sudden grin. "You obviously don't know enough to dissuade me."

"There are other advantages of having a young wife." Busily she tugged the hem of his shirt from his breeches.

"Show me," he said softly, and she did.

It did not seem too much to ask that the Vallerand family be granted some peace for a while, but apparently that was not possible. The trouble was started unintentionally by Philippe, who was on his way to a fencing lesson.

As Philippe dismounted his horse and walked to the establishment of the fencing master Navarre, he was only half aware of the sound of voices nearby. As usual, his blue eyes were fixed on the ground, his thoughts far removed from the practical day-to-day routine of living. As Justin so often mockingly pointed out, Philippe was a dreamer, not a realist.

Suddenly Philippe was jolted out of his imaginings when a hard shoulder slammed into his, knocking him off balance. Staggering back a few steps, he looked up in bewilderment. He faced a group of three boys who had just finished their fencing session with Navarre. Excited by their exertions, filled with vigor, they were clearly spoiling for a fight. The bump had been no accident. The leader of the group, Louis Picotte, had clashed with Justin before — it was well known that they hated each other.

Philippe, however, had no quarrel with anyone, and he preferred to keep it that way. He apologized instantly, something his brother would never have done. "*Pardonnez-moi* — I was not looking."

"It *would* be a Vallerand, of course," Louis sneered. He was a large, husky boy, with a shock of white-blond hair. "They think they own every street in town."

Philippe felt his heart sink. "I am late," he muttered, taking a few steps away, but the three blocked his path.

"Your apology wasn't good enough," Louis said, a smirk appearing on his lips.

Philippe raised troubled blue eyes to his. "I'm sorry for bumping into you. Now let me pass."

Louis pointed to the ground, smiling nastily. "Get on your knees and say it."

Philippe flushed, wanting to turn and run, but knowing that if he did, Louis would torment him forever. Looking from one face to another, Philippe saw nothing but hatred, the kind of hatred he and Justin had come to expect after years of being known as the sons of Maximilien Vallerand.

"I won't," he said, staring steadily at Louis.

"Then let's take the matter somewhere private," Louis said, jerking his thumb in the direction of a small lot where hasty duels were sometimes conducted. It was concealed by trees and buildings, and they would not be seen by passersby. His hand settled on the hilt of the sword at his waist.

Startled, Philippe realized the boy wanted something more than mere fisticuffs. Philippe had resigned himself to being bruised and beaten. After all, Justin had survived it often enough. But swords — it was too dangerous. "No," he said, and nodded in the direction of the fencing master's place. "We'll settle it there." The master often supervised such bouts between his students. Navarre had forbidden them to settle their disputes outside of the school, unless it was with mere fists, not swords.

"Are you afraid?" Louis demanded.

"No, I just —"

"You are. It's what everyone says. You're a coward. If I were you. I wouldn't be so proud of your dirty Vallerand name." Louis spat on the ground. "Your father is a murderer, your brother is a blustering bully . . . and you are a little coward."

Philippe quivered with sudden rage.

"Ah, look at him tremble," Louis jeered. "Look at him —" Suddenly he stopped, wincing as he felt a tiny, sharp blow to the back of his head. He clasped the spot and swung around. "What —" Another thud, this time on his chest. Louis stared in disbelief at the sight of Justin, who was lounging behind them and calmly aiming pebbles at him. Justin intently examined a small stone pinched between his thumb and forefinger. "What is it I heard him say, Philippe?"

Philippe gulped with relief and apprehension. "Nothing. Justin, we're late for —"

"I thought I heard him call you a coward." Justin dropped the stone to the ground and selected another from the handful he held. "We know that isn't true. And I also thought I heard him say I was a bully. I don't agree with that, either."

"Don't forget," Louis sneered, "I also said your father was a murderer."

Abruptly the handful of pebbles was released to scatter at Louis's feet. Justin smiled, his blue eyes so dark they were almost black. "Philippe, give me your sword."

"No," Philippe said, striding rapidly to his brother. "Justin, not with swords." They understood each other's thoughts clearly. "It should be me," Philippe told him.

"He doesn't want to fight you," Justin said. "He went after you in order to get me."

"Not with swords," Philippe repeated.

Louis called to them tauntingly, "Are you going to let your brother make a coward of you, too, Justin?"

Justin drew in his breath angrily. His eyes met Philippe's, and he vowed, "I'll carve him to pieces before he has time to blink!"

"He has practiced today, and you haven't," Philippe said, abandoning moral arguments in favor of practical ones. "He'll be far more limber than you, Justin."

Louis interrupted them impatiently. "Let's get on with it, Justin."

"Philippe," Justin growled, "give the damn thing to me!"

"Not unless you promise to stop at first blood."

"I can't —"

"Promise!"

They glared at each other, and then Justin nodded. "Damn you, all right." He reached for the sword. Turning pale, Philippe gave it to him.

The small group made its way to the lot. By tacit consent, they were furtive and quiet, knowing the duel would be forbidden if anyone else learned of it. Boys their age did not usually settle their differences in such a manner — it would not be appropriate for another two years or so.

Keeping to the rules they had learned at Navarre's, seconds were appointed. Louis removed his coat slowly, glancing over his shoulder at the twins. Philippe was standing with his fists clenched, his tense posture revealing his anxiety. Justin was waiting with unnatural patience.

Louis almost began to regret challenging the Vallerands. Philippe's gaze had been mild and frightened, but Justin's hard blue eyes promised far more to contend with. Justin's swordsmanship was also quite good, Louis reflected, almost equal to his own. He had watched Justin practice at Navarre's, and as the fencing master said, Justin would be superb but for a lack of discipline. Walking forward until they were separated by only a few feet, Louis assumed the proper stance.

The group was quiet as they saluted each other and began the match with a click of steel against steel. They tried a few elementary combinations, each searching out what he needed to know in order to best his opponent. Double feint, lunge, parry, followed by a quick riposte. Both moved with fine coordination and equal skill. One of Louis's companions couldn't help murmuring to the other that he wished Navarre could see this. It was an impressive exchange.

Then the contest began in earnest, and the balance tipped. Louis sweated profusely as he tried to maintain his concentration. Justin fought with a cold, technical aggression that he had never displayed at school. Philippe was the only one who understood the reckless edge that made his brother so proficient. Justin did not care what happened to himself, and the more time went by, the less anything mattered to him. He was not afraid of pain or solitude, perhaps not even of dying . . . and that frightened Philippe.

Louis jerked back in surprise as he felt the point of Justin's sword touch his shoulder. In disbelief he looked down at the dot of blood on his shirt. Exclamations broke from the boys, and Philippe rushed over to Louis's second.

"Honor is satisfied," Philippe said breathlessly, wiping at the sweat dotted on his forehead.

Louis felt sick with humiliation. He saw Justin through a haze of fury, sickened at the thought that such a minor mistake, one tiny opening of his guard, had led to defeat. His friends would snicker. Even more enraging was Justin's surprising quietness. Louis would have expected a Vallerand to gloat. Instead Justin wore a serious expression as he watched the seconds confer . . . and for some reason, that seemed more contemptuous to Louis than open ridicule.

"It's over," Philippe said, making no effort to suppress the gladness in his voice. He smiled slightly as he saw the relief in Justin's eyes.

"It's *not* over!" Louis snarled, but they paid him no attention.

Justin started toward Philippe, intending to give back the sword, then stopped as he saw the flash of horror on his brother's face.

"No!" was all Philippe had time to cry before Justin turned swiftly and saw Louis lunging at him.

Startled, Justin felt a flare of heat in his side, looked down, and saw the thin blade of steel withdraw. There was a glow of pain.

Awkwardly he fell to his knees, staring dumbly at the blossoming stain on his shirt. He pressed his hand to the crimson smear and collapsed to the ground as his head swam. Breathing hard, he caught the salty, rich scent of his own blood, and he clutched harder at his waist.

"Oh, Justin," Philippe gasped, falling beside him. "Oh, Justin."

Louis was slow to realize what he had done. His friends were staring at him with amazement and disgust. "I didn't mean . . ." Louis began, and his voice trailed off into ashamed silence. He had done something too dishonorable, too unmanly, for words. Backing away, he turned and fled.

Justin stirred at the sound of Philippe's anxious entreaties, and his dazed blue eyes opened. He turned his face away from the cool grass and looked up at his brother, managing to find his old tone of annoyance. "It's only a scratch."

Philippe gave a choking laugh. "You're *bleeding*, Justin."

"Where is Louis . . . the sneaky, goddamned, cowardly bastard!"

"He's gone," Philippe said, some of his initial fright dissolving. "I think he was as surprised as the rest of us."

Justin struggled clumsily to get up. "Surprised? I'll kill him! I'll —" He broke off and gasped, his side aching. Under his fingers there was a new surge of hot fluid.

"Stop!" Philippe cried, catching him behind the shoulders. "The blood . . . we need a doctor . . . I'll leave you for just a minute and —"

"No. I'm going home, where Father will probably finish me off."

"But —"

"Get me home," Justin whispered with an intensity that silenced his brother.

Philippe tried to stanch the flow of blood with the pressure of his hand, causing a new round of curses from Justin. He did not notice the two other boys standing above them until one of them handed down his wadded-up vest. "Thank you," Philippe said breathlessly, taking the garment and pushing it inside Justin's shirt, over the wound.

"Louis shouldn't have done it," the donator of the vest commented. "I'll never act as his second again."

"There shouldn't have been a duel in the first place!" Philippe said angrily. There was no sound from Justin, who had closed his eyes. His bloody hands were palms-up on the ground.

The boy regarded Justin's long, sprawled-out form admiringly. "He's got courage."

"And the brains of an ox," Philippe muttered.

"He'll win a lot of duels before he's through."

"He'll die before he's twenty," Philippe said under his breath.

Justin's eyes flickered open. They were dark and luminous violet, devoid of their usual snapping energy. Painstakingly he reached up to grasp Philippe's collar, smearing it with blood. "Let's go."

Philippe did not bother to ask how Justin had gotten to town. One of Louis's friends brought Philippe's horse, and the three of them pushed and shoved Justin into the saddle. Philippe swung up behind him, checking to make certain Justin was holding the pad over his wound.

"I've got it," Justin said hoarsely, drooping low over the horse's neck. "Go, before I fall off."

The ride home was torturous, Philippe suffering every bit as much as Justin. He was terrified that Justin would die.

"Why did you want to fight Louis?" Philippe asked in bewilderment when they were halfway home. "Do you hate him that much?"

Now that the bleeding had stopped, Justin was feeling more clear-headed. "I just wanted to fight," he said, his voice weak. "It feels so good. I want to fight all the time."

"Why?"

"It satisfies something inside me — I don't know what it is."

"Something inside that wants you to de-

300

stroy yourself," Philippe said. "But I won't let you, Justin. I can't lose you."

Justin knew that Philippe said more to him, but suddenly the words became indistinguishable sounds, and he felt his eyes begin to roll back in his head. He drifted in and out of a strange dream. They were at the house and hands were reaching up to him, and he was falling into a deep purple sea, being carried away on the crest of a wave. His head ached, his side hurt. He felt like a little boy again. Gently he was lowered to his bed, his head dropping to the pillow, and he rested for what seemed to be hours until he was awakened by a terrible sense of aloneness.

"*Mon père,*" he whispered, moving his hand restlessly until it was enfolded in a large, strong one. The vital force of that grip seemed to bring him back to his senses. He saw his father's tense face, and the tenderness in his eyes. It made no sense, but it seemed that as long as his father held his hand, he would be safe. Sensing Justin's need, Max did not let go of him, not even in the presence of the doctor.

Justin writhed in pain as the wound was being cleaned, but he kept silent, sweat dripping off his face. It felt as if a burning poker were twisting in his side. "Aren't you finished yet?" he asked when he could stand no more. His father held and soothed him while the doctor finished. They gave Justin a foul-tasting medicine after he was bandaged, and he insisted on taking the glass in his own hand. His father slid an arm behind his neck and lifted his head up, helping him to drink. Justin found it utterly humiliating.

"Aren't you going to shout and give me hell?" he croaked when the last of the bitter medicine was gone.

"Hell will arrive tomorrow," Max said, carefully rearranging the covers over him. "Right now I'm just relieved that you're all right."

Justin yawned widely, the medicine making him sleepy. His eyes flew open as he felt Max's weight shift. "Are you leaving?"

"No, *mon fils.*"

"You can if you want," Justin muttered, even though he yearned for him to stay.

"I wouldn't leave you for any reason," came his father's quiet reply, and Justin relaxed in relief. He reached out for his father's hand once more, and fell asleep holding it.

CHAPTER

12

"How is he?" Alexandre asked, starting to pour Max a drink. Max gestured for him to put the bottle down.

"He'll be fine." Max had just come from upstairs, where Justin was sleeping comfortably, to join his brothers in the library. Lysette and Noeline were busy helping the distraught Irénée into bed, giving her liberal doses of brandy-laced coffee. "The wound isn't bad, thank God." He shook his head, his face pale and strained. "I can't believe this happened to my son."

"This was a *surprise* to you?" Bernard asked. "I am only surprised it hasn't happened before now."

"Justin is following in his father's footsteps, isn't he?" Alexandre added.

Max sent them both a cold glare.

"Well, it is true," Bernard said. "Max, you know what the boy is like. You cannot say you weren't expecting this. And you are a fool if you don't expect it again."

Before Max could vent his fury, Lysette's calm voice interceded.

"Max," she said, coming into the room and taking his arm, "I do not wish to deprive you of such brotherly compassion and sympathy, but Berté has warmed some food for our supper. Come, have something to eat."

"I'm not hungry —"

"Just a little something, *bien-aimé*," Lysette entreated in a winsome manner. "You would not have me eat alone, would you? Please . . . for my sake."

With a low grumble, Max turned to accompany her, the quarrel discarded for the moment. As they reached the doorway, Lysette looked back over her shoulder and gave the brothers a quick, shaming glance before serenely following her husband from the room. The glare was such a contrast to the sweet expression she had used with Max that Alexandre couldn't help chuckling.

"In her own soft little way," he commented with a smile, "she's rather a despot."

"It is not amusing," Bernard said.

"Why not? Lysette is obviously good for Max."

"I wouldn't say so." Bernard took a long drink, staring at the empty doorway.

Alexandre tilted his head thoughtfully. "You don't like her, do you? I never realized that before now."

Bernard's voice was flat and cold. "No, I don't. I don't like the effect she has on Max, or the trouble she stirs up in the family.

Things were better before she came."

When Justin awakened the morning after his duel, he found his room invaded by his brother, father, and stepmother. Lysette fussed over him like a mother hen, arranging his breakfast tray and tying a napkin around his neck as if he were five instead of fifteen. He was grateful for her presence, for their unspoken understanding that Lysette would use her influence with his father on his behalf. Justin wasn't certain when or how Lysette had become his ally, but as he stared into her steady blue eyes, he felt a rush of adoration.

His father, of course, started the morning by demanding a full explanation of the previous day's events.

"Tell me your part of it, Philippe," Max said from the side of the bed, where he sat in a mahogany chair with a curved back.

As always, Philippe chose his words carefully. "I was having a confrontation with three boys, one of whom wished to provoke me into a duel. I refused, and that was when Justin appeared —"

"And eagerly picked up the gauntlet," Max said ruefully.

Justin scowled. "They called him a coward," he said defensively. "No one insults a Vallerand and gets away with it."

"Was that all that was said?"

"No." Justin's gaze fell to the counterpane over his lap. "They called me a bully, and you —" He stopped suddenly, while a tide of red swept over his face.

"And me what?" Max asked gently, although it was clear that he already knew.

The heat spread to Justin's neck and ears. "The same thing," he said tightly, "that you've always been called."

"And what is that?"

"Why ask? You already know!"

"I want to hear you say it."

Justin dragged his hands through his hair several times, feeling as agitated as a caged animal.

"Say it, *mon fils*," Max prompted quietly. "Please."

Lysette and Philippe might not have even been in the room. The tension gathered until none of the four of them dared to move or breathe.

Suddenly tears shimmered in Justin's blue eyes, and he gritted his teeth in humiliation and anger. "They called you a murderer. It's what they've always said. Everyone. And you ask why I fight? I've never known what it is to have a friend. Neither has Philippe." He turned his head to glare at his brother. "Tell him!"

Max moved to the bed and sat beside him. "Listen to me, Justin. I understand every-thing —"

"No —"

"By God, don't interrupt me! You'll never be able to change what they say. You'll never be able to stop them. The rumors will go on, and you can't crush them, you can't silence them. You can even kill a man, Justin, dozens of them, but the past will not change, and you'll still be my son. Curse that fact if you wish, but you can't change it. You'll die trying . . . and that would break me as nothing else could, Justin."

"What happened to my mother?" Justin demanded, the tears sliding down his tanned cheeks.

"There isn't much I can tell you," Max replied gruffly. "I married your mother because I loved her. But the marriage turned sour, and not long after you were born, I realized that Corinne was having an affair with another man."

"Who?" Justin demanded.

"That doesn't matter —"

"Was it Etienne Sagesse?"

"Yes."

"Why?" Philippe asked from several feet away. "Why would she do that?"

"I believe she thought that she was in love with him," Max said with outward calm. Only Lysette knew of the effort it took for him to speak of the past. "I was not able to make Corinne happy. That, in part, drove her to someone else."

"There is no need to make excuses for

her," Justin said. "I'm glad she's dead."

"No, Justin. Pity her, but don't hate her."

"Did Etienne Sagesse kill her?" the boy demanded.

"No, I don't believe he did."

Justin's chin trembled. "Then you did?" he asked, his voice cracking.

Max seemed to find it difficult to speak. "No. I found her, already dead. I don't know what happened to her."

A mixture of anger and disbelief crossed Justin's face. "But you have to! You *must* know."

"I wish I did," Max said. "And most of all, I wish you had not grown up in the shadow of all this. I would do anything to change that, Justin. I want your happiness above all else."

Justin closed his eyes and leaned his head back against the pillow. "Isn't there anyone you suspected? Isn't there anyone who might have wanted her dead?"

"Years ago I talked to Etienne Sagesse, thinking that he might be able to reveal something."

"And?"

"He believes that I killed Corinne out of jealousy."

"You should have finished him off in that duel," Justin muttered.

"Look at me." Max waited until Justin's eyes opened. "You must choose your fights carefully. I would rather you be branded a coward than have you jump every time some little bantam throws a challenge at your feet. The more fearsome your reputation, the more others will try to provoke you — and the more you use your sword, the more you'll *have* to. I don't want that for you, or your brother. You mean too much to me, Justin. You must walk away the next time . . . for me. Please."

Justin swallowed hard and lifted himself away from the pillows, leaning toward him. "*Je t'aime, mon père,*" he said in a muffled voice. Max put his arms around him carefully, ruffling Justin's hair, murmuring softly to him. Lysette noticed Philippe taking a halting step forward, then stopping as he realized the moment belonged to Justin and his father. How unselfish Philippe was, she thought, and reached out to take his hand, her fingers curling around his palm. The boy looked down at her, his frown disappearing as she stretched up to kiss his cheek.

Having accomplished all that he intended in New Orleans, Aaron Burr headed back to St. Louis to plot with General Wilkinson. His journey began overland toward Natchez, on horses furnished by Daniel Clark, the most influential and well-established merchant in the territory. Burr's trip westward had been tremendously successful. By his reckoning, it would not be difficult at all to lead the populace against the Spaniards in order to secure west Florida and Mexico.

Burr was certain he had blinded the Spanish officials, especially Yrujo, as to his true intentions, and had successfully reassured them he had no designs on their lands. In less than a year, Burr reasoned, he would be able to launch an expedition and bring all his ambitions to fruition. And those who had tried to impede his plan — Maximilien Vallerand, for example — would beg to be in favor.

The messenger departed from the residence of Don Carlos, the Marquis de Casa Yrujo, early in the morning. As he headed southward out of the city at a circumspect pace, he was forced to rein in his horse suddenly. Two men on horseback, armed with pistols, were blocking his way. Turning pale with fright, the messenger began to splutter in Spanish. Certain they meant to rob him, he protested that he had no money, nothing to offer them. One of them, a large, dark-haired man, gestured for him to dismount.

"Give me the letters you're carrying," the dark-haired man said, his Spanish rough but serviceable.

"*N-no puedo,*" the messenger stammered, shaking his head emphatically. "They are private, highly confidential . . . I — I have staked my life on delivering them without —"

"Your life," came the gentle reply, "is precisely what is at stake. Hand over the letters if you wish to preserve it."

Fumbling in the inside of his coat, the messenger withdrew a half dozen letters, all bearing the official seal used by Yrujo. He wiped his sweating brow with his sleeve as the man leafed through them. One of them seemed to catch the man's interest, and he kept it while handing the others back.

Max looked at Jacques Clement with an ironic half smile. "It's addressed to a Spanish boundary commissioner who has lingered in New Orleans for unexplained reasons."

"Perhaps he likes it here," Clement remarked diffidently.

Max opened the letter, ignoring the faint cry of protest from the messenger. He scanned the contents, his smile fading quickly, then looked at Clement. The golden eyes gleamed with satisfaction. "I love the way the Spanish officials have of wishing a friend a fond farewell, and then — ever so politely — knifing him in the back."

Not understanding their conversation, the messenger watched them anxiously, then dared to interrupt. "Señor, I cannot deliver the letter with a broken seal! What am I to do? What —"

"You're not going to deliver the letter," Max replied, "because I am going to keep it."

A stream of volatile Spanish greeted this statement. It was too fast for Max to follow, but the man's unhappiness was clear.

"He'll probably be imprisoned when they find out," Jacques commented. "They won't pardon him for letting the letter be stolen."

Max tossed a small bag to the messenger, who paused in his barrage long enough to catch it. It landed with a heavy clink in his palm. "That's enough to allow you to disappear and live in comfort for a long time."

Another rapid speech followed. Max glanced questioningly at Jacques, whose Spanish was more proficient than his. "What is he saying?"

"He needs more, for his wife and children."

Max smiled wryly. "Give him what you have," he told Jacques. "I'll reimburse you later."

"Is the letter worth that much?" Clement asked incredulously.

Max tucked the letter in his own coat with great satisfaction. "Oh, yes."

Max enjoyed Claiborne's astonishment as he read and reread the letter. "Are the Spaniards aware that we have this?" Claiborne finally asked.

Max shrugged. "It doesn't matter. It won't change their plans."

"This is quite a piece of news," Claiborne

said slowly. "Not only do they not trust Burr, they're starting a backlash against him. If this letter is accurate, they'll discredit him completely!" He looked back over the letter. "And the clever bastards are using an American to do it! Have you met Stephen Minor before?"

"Briefly."

"Did you know before you read the letter that he was in the Spanish pay?"

"No." Max smiled casually. "But I can't be expected to keep track of *all* the Americans in the Spanish pay."

"Insolent Creole," Claiborne retorted, beaming at him. "Are you implying that Americans are easily bought?"

"It does rather seem that way, sir."

Claiborne contained his jubilation and assumed a more statesmanlike expression. "For now all we need do is wait. If this information is accurate, Minor will spread rumors throughout the territory that Burr is planning to separate the West from the rest of the nation, unite it with Spanish possessions, and claim it as his own empire. That should set the country ablaze all the way up to the Northeast."

"The rumors should reach St. Louis at the same time Burr does," Max agreed.

"I would give a fortune to see General Wilkinson's face. It shouldn't take long for him to disassociate himself from Burr completely."

Max stood up and extended his hand. "I must be leaving now. If you require me for anything else . . ."

"Yes, yes." Claiborne stood up and shook his hand, gripping it more warmly than usual. "Vallerand, you have proved your loyalty this day."

Max arched a brow. "Was it in question?"

"I did wonder what you may have omitted when you described your meeting with Burr," Claiborne admitted. "He is a persuasive man. You might have shared part of his glory by siding with him."

"I have no desire for glory. I only want to keep what is mine," Max said seriously. "Good day, your excellency."

In an unexpected move, Max appointed Justin to supervise the destruction of the old overseer's house. Lysette was pleased by the news, understanding its significance. The past was losing its terrible hold over Max and his sons. Justin took great pride in the responsibility, organizing a crew to help him pull the ramshackle structure to the ground and burn the rubble. Philippe preferred to apply himself to his studies, perfectly happy in his world of books.

Lysette found herself also facing challenges of a different nature. Although she and Irénée were undeniably fond of each other, there were the inevitable points of contention between a daughter- and mother-in-law. Irénée was firmly attached to the old Creole ways while Lysette embraced the changing attitudes of their small society. Irénée had never been so horrified as she was the first time Lysette invited some of the young American matrons of New Orleans to visit the plantation.

"They are nice, well-bred women," Lysette had told her gently.

"They are *American* women! What will my friends think when they hear of this?"

"Americans are part of New Orleans now, just as much as Creoles. We share many of the same concerns."

Irénée stared at her, scandalized. "Next you will be saying it is acceptable for Creoles and Americans to intermarry."

"Oh, *never* that," Lysette said dryly.

Irénée's eyes narrowed in suspicion. "Does Maximilien know about this?"

Lysette smiled, knowing the older woman was planning to go to Max behind her back. "He approves of it wholeheartedly Maman."

Irénée sighed in disgust, silently vowing to speak to her son about the matter that very night.

But Max paid no attention to Irénée's complaints, saying that he did not see what harm would befall them if Lysette had friendships with a few American women.

Irénée was also troubled by the way Max

was indulging Lysette's every whim, encouraging her outspokenness, talking to her about worldly subjects that Creole gentlemen never mentioned to their wives. Worse, Max seemed to expect the entire family to pay attention to Lysette's opinions.

Not long ago, no one would have believed that any woman would be able to manage the infamous head of the Vallerand family with such adroitness. The fact that a young, inexperienced, and fairly average-looking girl could manage such a feat was no less than astonishing.

Torn between pleasure at her son's obvious happiness and discomfort at Lysette's unconventional ways, Irénée wrestled with the issue before finally deciding to approach Max.

"If Lysette were a child," she said to Max in private, "I would say that she was being spoiled. You are encouraging her to believe that she can do, say, or have anything she wants."

"But she can," he said evenly.

"Lysette feels free to contradict anyone she does not agree with, regardless of age or authority. A young Creole matron would *never* think of telling any man what to do. And this very morning Lysette was trying to force her opinions on poor Bernard, telling him he should work more and drink less!"

That provoked a laugh from Max. "In that case I'm afraid she was repeating *my* opinion.

And you know that you agree with her."

"That is beside the point!"

"What *is* the point, Maman?"

"For lack of a better expression, you must tighten the reins, Max. For Lysette's sake as well as everyone else's. It isn't good for her to be allowed so much freedom."

His mouth hardened, and he gave her a perplexed stare, as if she did not understand something that should have been obvious. "Tighten the reins? I'll do my damnedest to make her as assertive as possible. Lysette should be terrified of me, yet she somehow has the courage to face me as an equal. I don't deserve such a gift. God knows I won't be fool enough to throw that away. I would slit my throat before asking that she pander to the rules of our quaint little society."

"You seem to forget, Maximilien, that your family and friends are all part of this so-called quaint society!"

"A society that deemed me an outcast ten years ago." He paused as he saw her expression. "I'm sorry," he said in a gentler tone. "I don't blame anyone, not anymore. But you can't deny that the shadow I cast falls on everyone I care for, including Lysette. Especially her."

"That is nonsense!" Irénée exclaimed. "You have many friends."

"Business partners, you mean. Jacques Clement is the only man in New Orleans who calls himself my friend for reasons other than financial profit. You yourself have seen the way people cross the street to avoid acknowledging me."

"People pay calls —"

"To you. Not to me."

"You are invited to social gatherings —"

"Yes, by out-of-pocket relatives with an eye on our money, or by those who feel they owe it to the memory of my father. When I attend such gatherings, I'm surrounded by stiff conversation and frozen smiles. You know that if I were anyone but a Vallerand, I would have been forced to leave New Orleans long ago. The gossip lingers like some slow-acting poison. And now Lysette will have to suffer for a past she had nothing to do with."

Max fell silent for a moment, knowing that his mother did not fully understand the dread that knifed through his heart whenever he pondered this subject. The hatred and suspicions of others, formerly directed only at him, might be turned against his wife. It agonized him to know that there were possible slights in store for Lysette because she had taken his name. "It isn't easy for Lysette, being my wife, although she's never uttered a word of complaint."

"Max, I think you overestimate the difficulty —"

"If anything, I'm underestimating it."

"You must put a stop to Lysette's unruliness now, or she will soon become unmanageable," Irénée warned. "You don't want her to become like Corinne, do you?"

Max lost his temper then, responding with such scathing anger that Irénée did not speak to him for days. . . . Irénée at last realized she would no longer be able to influence Max as she once had. He would never take anyone's part against Lysette. And the rest of the family was forced to acknowledge that if anyone dared to criticize Lysette, they would face Max's certain wrath.

Utterly frustrated by Max's behavior at one of the Vallerands' Sunday evening soirees, Lysette took it upon herself to upbraid him in private. Max had been rude to a guest one of his cousins had brought, a visitor who was unfortunately quite voluble about his hostility toward Governor Claiborne and the Americans. Although Lysette knew that such remarks would send Max's temper through the roof, she had sent him a beseeching glance in the hope that he would hold his tongue.

Ignoring her silent plea, Max had responded so sharply that the evening had become uncomfortable for everyone. Usually, at Creole soirees, there was music, conversation, and a little dancing, followed by refreshments at eleven o'clock, with the gathering dispersing around midnight. This one ended at ten, before refreshments were even brought out.

Determined, Lysette approached her husband in the library, where he had gone with Bernard for a drink after the guests departed. Before she could say a word, Max turned and faced her without surprise. "I'm in a bad humor," he warned.

"So am I," she replied shortly.

Realizing that a storm was brewing, Bernard set his drink down. "I'm exhausted," he said uncomfortably. "Good night."

Neither of them noticed his departure.

"There was no need to be so unpleasant to Monsieur Gregoire just because of a few remarks he made about the governor," Lysette said in annoyance. "I've heard you yourself say much worse about Claiborne!"

"When I criticize Claiborne, at least I know what I'm talking about. Gregoire is an idiot."

"Your opinion isn't the only correct one, Max. And a man is not an idiot just because he happens to disagree with you."

"In this case he was," Max said obstinately.

Annoyed as she was, Lysette felt her mouth quiver with sudden amusement, and she clamped her lips together. She took another tack. "Part of being a good host is being gracious enough to overlook the ignorance of a guest so that everyone else can enjoy themselves!"

320

"Whose rule is that?" he asked, arching one brow.

"Mine."

Max gave her his most authoritative scowl. "I'm master of the household, and I can do or say whatever I wish."

Unimpressed by the display, Lysette rested her hands on her hips. "That was a good try," she said dryly. "But you'll have to win the argument some other way."

Max rose from his chair, looking even larger and more towering than usual in his formal wear, his muscular legs outlined by snug pearl-gray pantaloons, his broad shoulders sharply defined in his black coat. "Are you challenging my authority?"

Lysette became aware of a change in the atmosphere, the challenge between them turning sexual in some indefinable away. Her heartbeat was suddenly spurred to a reckless pace, and she felt a ripple of pure lust as their gazes locked together. "What if I am?" she asked, her voice even softer than his. Recognizing the predatory gleam of enjoyment in his eyes, she took a strategic route to the round mahogany table in the center of the library, keeping it between them.

Max followed her without haste. "Then, as a Creole husband and head of the household, I would have to demonstrate who makes the rules . . . and who follows them."

Lysette smiled provokingly as they circled

the table. "*Mon mari* . . . you are actually quite adorable, in your own arrogant and domineering way."

"Adorable," he mused, moving in slow pursuit of her. "I don't believe anyone has called me that before."

"That is because no one else knows how to manage you."

She heard the quick catch of laughter in his throat. "But you do?"

"Of course."

Now there was no mistaking the heat of desire in his gaze, or the growing arousal of his body "*Ma femme,* you need to learn a lesson," he murmured in such a deliciously threatening manner that Lysette felt the tips of her breasts hardening in response. His gaze dropped to the silk panels of her bodice, and he noted the distinct peaks beneath the shimmering fabric. "You had better pray that I don't catch you before you reach that door."

They faced each other with the table between them. Flattening her palms on the gleaming surface, Lysette leaned toward him and gazed at him steadily. "And the lesson you are referring to is that even when you are horrid, arrogant, and rude, I must tolerate it because you are the husband and therefore all-powerful?"

His eyes sparkled with dark mischief. "Yes, that one."

"I don't think so, *mon mari*. Since I am faster than you, I am going to make it through the door and up to my room before you have any chance of catching me. When you finally reach my door, it will be locked. And then you can spend the rest of the night in your own company. That will give you some time to contemplate your bad behavior at supper."

His smile was distinctly wolfish. "Try," he invited.

Lysette was gone in an instant, heading for the door in quicksilver strides. However, there were two things she hadn't counted on . . . not only was she hampered by the skirts of her gown, but Max's legs were twice as long as hers. Despite her head start, he reached the library door just as she did, and shoved it closed to prevent her escape. Gasping with laughter, Lysette let him turn her around and haul her against his body.

"It wasn't fair," she said breathlessly. "I'm wearing skirts."

"You won't be for long," Max panted, crushing his mouth over hers. Lysette clutched the back of his head and urged him to kiss her harder, her lips opening eagerly. His weight pressed her against the door, and she moaned at the exciting imprint of his body, the hard chest and stomach, the stiff masculine ridge that was discernible even through the layers of her gown. Kissing her ravenously, Max fumbled at the door and turned the key in the lock. He gripped Lysette's buttocks to pull her higher and tighter against his hips. She wanted to devour him, bite, lick, kiss him, pull him completely inside herself. He was hers, every obstinate, exciting, masculine inch of him.

His mouth broke free of hers, and he pulled her toward the table like some predator dragging its vanquished prey. Lysette emerged from the hot, swirling fog of desire long enough to gasp, "Not here. Someone will interrupt."

Max lifted her and sat her on the table, pulling up huge handfuls of her skirts. "The door's locked."

"They'll still know," she protested, pushing at his busy hands.

Too inflamed to care, Max found the ribbons of her garters, and followed the line of her bare thighs. The rasp of his callused fingers on her tender skin made her quiver with pleasure, and her thighs parted despite her will to deny him.

"Max, upstairs," she whimpered, as he reached the tuft of cinnamon hair and parted the damp curls.

"I can't wait," he muttered, circling the slick nub that swelled at his light touch. His fingertip rubbed gently over the rosy peak, and Lysette writhed in sudden desperation. She plunged her hands inside his evening coat, clawing frantically over his shirt, wild to touch his warm male skin.

Max's mouth caught hers in another rough kiss, while he used his foot to hook a nearby chair and drag it closer. Pulling Lysette to the edge of the table, he sat and buried his mouth in the delicate folds of her cleft, his tongue searching hungrily for her intimate flavor. She bit her lip to restrain an involuntary cry, her body jerking upward into the devastating heat of his mouth. Helplessly she ran her fingers through the thick black locks of his hair, gasping as his tongue slid inside her.

"Max? Are you in there? Why is the door locked?" Alexandre's muffled voice came through the door, and the handle clicked and rattled. Freezing, Lysette shot a horrified glance toward the sound. When it became clear that Max did not intend to respond, she tugged his head upward.

Although Max's breathing was no less rapid than her own, he answered his brother in a voice that sounded remarkably normal. "Go away, Alex."

"I want a drink."

Max slid two fingers into the intimate channel of Lysette's body, and she flushed deeply.

"Get your liquor from the kitchen," he told his brother tersely.

"But my special brandy is in there,"

Alexandre complained. "If you just let me in for a moment, I'll get it and leave —"

"Alex, my wife and I are having a dispute. She's about to start throwing things." Max's long fingers twisted gently, causing Lysette to gasp in pleasure. "Trust me, you don't want to be in the line of fire." Lowering his head, he drew his tongue over the rosy peak of her sex in strokes that corresponded to the thrusts of his fingers. Lysette covered her mouth with her hand to hold in her moans. His rhythm quickened, his mouth tender and demanding, his fingers reaching unbelievably deep inside her.

She barely heard Alex's final words. "Lysette, if you're arguing with my brother concerning his remarks to Gregoire at supper, I am completely on your side."

"Th-thank you," she managed to say, her stomach tightening.

"*Bon soir,*" he said glumly, and left.

Max added a third finger to the ones already inside her, and began to suckle her aching flesh with quick, smooth tugs. Lysette sobbed as a climax rolled through her, blinding and dark and fiery-sweet, pulsing through her in relentless waves. As she shivered in the aftermath, Max pressed her flat on the table, keeping her legs spread on either side of his hips. His face was gleaming with perspiration, his eyes smoldering. He pushed inside her slowly, gently courting her swollen flesh until she had engulfed every inch of him. He gripped her bare hips and manipulated her in a rhythm that dragged her back and forth across the table, her silk gown sliding easily over the polished wood. Lysette wouldn't have thought it possible, but the pleasure rose again, building with each plunge of his hard shaft. She convulsed in a second climax, and he followed her with a muted groan, his big body shuddering over hers.

Lysette gradually came to her senses, finding herself pinned between the hard table and the weight of her husband's head on her chest. His breath came in swift rushes that teased her nipple. Completely drained of strength, her body replete with luxurious sensation, she lifted her hand to stroke his hair.

"Who won the argument?" she asked languidly.

She felt Max smile against her breast. "Oh, yes, the argument." He nuzzled her flushed skin and traced his tongue from one golden freckle to another. "Shall we call this one an even match?"

Purring her approval, she wrapped her arms around his neck.

Max was occasionally a difficult man to live with, but Lysette never doubted her ability to match him. He had become everything to her: friend, lover, protector, a source of excitement, a comforting sanctuary. There were times when Lysette felt the only safe place in the world was in his arms. And there were other times when Max would dispel any illusion of safety. He could be devilishly patient, taking hours to coax her into a state of sensual madness . . . or he could be reckless and wild, setting every nerve on fire and consuming her in the blaze.

To Lysette's delight, Max showed no hesitation in taking her everywhere with him, even when he was conducting business. Taking an interest in his shipping business, she frequently accompanied him to the New Orleans waterfront, where the keelboats and barges were so numerous that one could walk a mile across their decks. When one of the Vallerand ocean trading vessels came into port, laden with goods from Europe and the tropics, she went aboard with him while the cargo was being inspected and unloaded.

Max left Lysette in the care of an officer while he went below with the captain to examine some water-damaged goods. While she stood at the rail of the high-sided frigate, watching the crew of a nearby flatboat unloading the boxes and supplies of a theatrical troupe, many of the frigate's crew gathered around her at a respectful distance. Sensing their gazes, she turned and stared curiously at the swarthy group. They were a dirty, brawny lot, dressed in strange, loose clothing, their shirts fastened by pegs of wood thrust

328

through the buttonholes. The tops of their shoes had been cut off, leaving only two or three lace holes.

"Don't be afraid, ma'am," the first officer said. "They just want to look at you."

"Whatever for?"

"Oh, they ain't seen a woman for well nigh a month."

Lysette gave them an uncertain smile, which caused the crew to murmur appreciatively. Gesturing to their feet curiously, she asked in English what had happened to their shoes, as the tops had been removed and the lace holes stitched together.

"These here is pumps," one of the sailors explained. "When the mate bawls, 'all hands reef top-sails,' there ain't time fer lace-up shoes."

Intrigued, Lysette asked a few more questions, and then they began to compete for her attention, singing ribald sea chanteys, showing her a set of brass knuckles, making her laugh by claiming she was a mermaid who had stowed away during their journey.

Coming up from the ship's hold, Max stopped at the sight of his wife smiling at the sailors' antics. A breeze molded the yellow fabric of her gown against the slim shape of her body, while her hair was flame-colored against the deep blue of the sky. He was suddenly overwhelmed with possessive pride.

"Well, now," said Captain Tierney, stopping

beside him to admire the picture. "Forgive me, Mr. Vallerand, but I don't envy a man with a wife so comely. If she were mine, I'd keep her locked away out of sight."

"It's a tempting idea," Max said, and laughed. "But I prefer having her with me."

"I can understand why," Tierney said fervently.

When Max discovered Lysette's enjoyment of the theater, he began taking her to the St. Pierre, where the prominent members of the community gathered on Tuesdays and Saturdays to enjoy music, drama, and opera. Between acts, people moved around the theater to socialize and gossip.

Gradually it became the habit of many couples to stop by the Vallerands' box and chat idly, for it was noticed that since his marriage, Maximilien had undergone a marked change in character. Although he still possessed a certain reserve, he was far more amiable and relaxed, reminding many of the charming boy he had been in the years before he had married Corinne Quérand. The old rumors lost some of their power as Creoles and Americans alike saw that Maximilien's new wife regarded him with an obvious lack of fear. Perhaps, it was whispered, he wasn't a devil after all. No man who doted on his wife so openly could be entirely bad.

"Maman," Lysette said lightly, laying her

hand on Irénée's shoulder as the older woman bent over needlework in the parlor, "I have something to ask you."

"*Oui?*"

"Would you have any objections if I went through some of the things in the attic?"

Irénée's head remained bent. Her fingers stopped moving. It was clear she was startled. "Why would you want to do that?"

Lysette shrugged diffidently. "No particular reason. Justin mentioned that there are some interesting things stored away up there — portraits and clothes, old toys. One of these days, perhaps there will be a need to refurbish the nursery, and —"

"Nursery?" Irénée repeated alertly. "Do you suspect you might be with child, Lysette?"

"No."

"Incomprehensible," Irénée murmured under her breath. At first she had been mildly amused by her son's voracious appetite for his new bride. Now she was beginning to find it vaguely appalling. Noeline had smugly attributed it to the voodoo charms she had hidden under Lysette's pillow the first few weeks of the marriage.

Lysette smiled idly. "Now that I've spoken to you about it, I'll put on an apron and see what I can find up there."

"Wait," Irénée said with an edge in her voice that Lysette had never heard before.

"You are going up there to search through *her* things, are you not?"

"Yes," Lysette admitted, her blue eyes unblinking.

"What do you hope to find?"

"I don't know. I'm certain that it won't harm anyone if I look through a few old trunks and boxes."

"Does Max know?"

"Not yet. I will tell him tonight, when he returns home."

Irénée held back her advice to wait and ask Max first. She hoped Max would be furious when Lysette told him what she had done. Perhaps then he would set the girl back on her heels, and Lysette would no longer be given free rein. Max needed to see that he was allowing the girl too much freedom. "Very well," Irénée said evenly. "Ask Noeline for the keys to the trunks."

Lysette and Justin had climbed up into the attic and cleared a place among piles of oddities. There was a set of bronze lamps and an old bayonet in the corner. Behind the trunks were a disassembled tester bed, a rocking cradle, and a wooden tub.

Lysette sneezed repeatedly, waving at a cloud of dust as she struggled with the massive lid of a trunk. As she opened it, its rusted hinges squealed. There was a protesting noise from Justin, who was rattling a key in the lock of another trunk nearby. "*Sang de Dieu,* don't do that again," he exclaimed. "I hate that sound. Worse than fingernails on a slate!"

"I had no idea your nerves were so fragile, Justin." Lysette laughed as she pulled out a folded quilt, a sumptuous trapunto design of delicate rococo swirls, vines, and flowers. Thousands of tiny stitches and much painstaking work had contributed to its exquisite texture. "What did Philippe say when you told him what we were doing?" she asked.

"He is glad that I am with you. Someone needs to protect you if Maman's ghost jumps out of one of these trunks."

Lysette frowned. "Justin, don't!"

He grinned. "Are you scared?"

"I will be if you keep talking about ghosts!" She smiled at him ruefully. Dust motes drifted in and out of the light that came through the attic window. "Justin, will it upset you if I look at these things?"

"No, I'm as curious as you are. You're hoping to find some clue about who might have killed her, *n'est-ce pas?* You'll do better with my help. I might be able to recognize something you —"

The boy stopped speaking as he looked at the quilt she held, his eyes wide. "I remember that!"

Lysette looked down at the quilt, her hand smoothing over the intricate swirls. "You do?"

"It was on Maman's bed. There should be a stain on one of the edges. I jumped on her bed once and made her spill her coffee." Justin had a faraway look on his face. "She was so angry. *Dieu,* what a temper she had."

"Were you afraid of her?"

Justin stared at the quilt with dark sapphire eyes, still remembering. "Sometimes she was so beautiful and soft. But when she was in one of her rages . . . *oui,* I was afraid of her. It's strange to love someone and at the same time fear that she might kill you."

"Justin, you do not have to stay up here with me. If it is painful for you —"

"It was odd, the way it happened," he continued absently. "Maman was there one day, and then the next, she was gone. Completely gone. Father made certain that every trace of her was removed from sight. *Grand-mère* told me that she had gone away for a long visit. Then Father left for several days. When he returned, he didn't look the same at all. He was hard and cold . . . he looked like the picture of the devil in one of my books — I thought he *was* the devil. I thought he had taken Maman away."

Lysette's heart ached for Max and his sons. She lay the quilt aside and delved back into the trunk, coming up with an armful of tiny baby clothes and bonnets. "It's not difficult to guess who these belonged to," she said. "Everything is in twos."

Justin reached out and took one of the miniature gowns in his long, callused fingers. "You can tell them apart. Everything I wore has a rip or a stain. Everything Philippe wore is immaculate."

Lysette laughed. As she searched the trunk, she discovered piles of lace collars, embroidered gloves, delicate painted fans. All of them must have belonged to Corinne. She picked up a pair of silk lace gloves and put them down hastily, feeling guilty at sorting through a dead woman's possessions. To her discomfort, she was also aware of a sting of jealousy. Seeing these personal belongings made it seem real, that there had been another woman Max had loved enough to marry. He had made love to her, and she had borne him two children.

Searching through more trunks, Lysette found elaborately beaded and festooned garments, lavish gowns, dainty undergarments. The clothes were made for a tall, slender woman. Lysette's sense of being an intruder grew stronger with each revelation. She discovered a tiny bronze box containing two dried cakes of red face paint, and an ornate comb, decorated with pearls and an egret feather. Two or three long, dark hairs were caught in the teeth of the comb. Corinne's hair, she thought, and a cold feeling went down her spine.

"Justin," she asked reluctantly, "are there

any portraits of your mother up here?" She had to see what Corinne had looked like. Her curiosity was nearly unbearable.

"I suppose." Justin climbed over an armoire on its side to a stack of frames covered by a canvas tied with cords. Pulling out his knife, he cut the cords and tugged at the dust-caked cloth. Lysette scrambled to her feet, sore from having been on her knees so long. She made her way to him and looked over his shoulder at one portrait after another. One was of a very attractive woman.

"Is that her?" Lysette asked hopefully.

"No, it is *Grand-mère*. Can't you see?"

"Oh, yes." She recognized Irénée's dark eyes in the woman's young, solemn face.

"Here is Maman," Justin said, pulling the portrait aside to display the next one.

Lysette went still at the sight, amazed by the lavish beauty of the young woman. Her sultry violet-blue eyes — Justin's eyes — were exotic and heavily lashed. Sable curls framed her face, one dangling artlessly against her long white throat. Her lips were red and perfectly bow-shaped, touched with a flirtatious quirk. For all her dazzling beauty, however, Corinne had possessed a soft, vulnerable quality. No wonder Max had succumbed to her heartbreaking beauty.

"Did she really look like that?" Lysette asked, and Justin smiled at the plaintive note in her voice.

"Yes, *belle-mère*. But you are just as pretty."

Lysette smiled ruefully and sat on a trunk. A cloud of dust wafted upward and swirled around her. She heard Justin snicker.

"What is it?" she asked.

"Your hair is all gray. So is your face."

She returned Justin's smile, observing that his black hair was covered with dust and spiderwebs, and his face was streaked with filth. "So is yours."

He grinned crookedly. "Have we seen enough for today, *belle-mère?*"

"Yes," she said fervently. "*Allons,* Justin. I am ready to leave now."

She began to climb down from the attic through a square opening framed with beams, to a ladder propped against the wall below. Justin cautioned her to mind her balance, as it was a long distance to the cypress floor below. "Careful," he said, watching her descend the first few steps. "There used to be a railing, but it was broken."

"Why doesn't someone fix it?"

"Because no one ever comes up here."

Lysette made no reply as she concentrated on placing her feet securely. Suddenly the silence was broken by a startling shout.

"What are you doing up there?"

Her entire body jumped at the unexpected noise. Terrified, Lysette felt herself lose her balance and sway backward. With a sharp cry, she reached out frantically to save herself, but her fingers clutched empty air. Swiftly Justin leaned over the attic opening and grabbed for her, crushing her wrist in a brutal grip. She gasped as she felt herself dangling in midair, suspended only by Justin's hand wrapped around her arm.

Glancing downward, she saw a man with dark hair below them. "M-Max!"

But it wasn't Max. It was Bernard, who repeated his furious shout.

Lysette reached for Justin's arm with her free hand. "I have you," the boy said roughly. "You're not going to fall. Can you reach the ladder with your feet?"

She strained, but could not touch it.

"Uncle Bernard . . . help . . ." Justin gasped, but a searing pain in his side prevented him from speaking further.

Bernard was strangely slow to move.

Lysette felt the grip around her arm slip a little. "Justin!"

"I'll help," Bernard murmured, moving beneath Lysette.

However, Justin had used every ounce of his remaining strength to pull Lysette up to the opening of the attic. Her stomach slammed against the exposed beam, and she lost her breath. Justin kept pulling until she was halfway across his lap. She lay without moving while Justin pried her fingers away from his trembling arm and dragged his sleeve across his face. He blinked rapidly and shook his head, as if he couldn't quite focus properly.

Bernard appeared at the top of the steps. His face was dark with rage. "You could have waited for me to assist you."

Justin moistened his lips and spoke with an effort, his young face gray with pain. "You *wanted* her to fall, Bernard."

"What kind of insane accusation is that? I was coming to help!"

"You took your damned time about it," Justin said hoarsely.

"Explain what you two were doing up there," Bernard demanded.

Ignoring him, Justin bent over Lysette and urged her to sit upright. Dazed, she held her stomach and breathed deeply. "Justin," she said, realizing what he had done, "are you hurt? Your wound — is it bleeding?"

He shook his head impatiently.

"You were searching through Corinne's belongings, weren't you?" Bernard shouted. "You have no right to do such a thing. I forbid it!"

Justin began to retort hotly, but Lysette silenced him with a touch on his shoulder. She stared coldly at Bernard.

"You *forbid?*" she repeated. "I was not aware, Bernard, that you were in a position to forbid me anything."

"Or me!" Justin added, unable to keep quiet.

"It's not decent," Bernard said savagely. "Pawing through her possessions just to satisfy your petty jealousies, prying and staring. By God, I hope she curses you from the grave!"

His words lashed through the silence. Until now Lysette had never seen evidence of Bernard's temper. She found it curious that his wrath had been aroused on behalf of his dead sister-in-law.

She kept her voice very soft. "Why are you so upset, Bernard?"

He ignored the question. "I'm going to tell Max about what you've done as soon as he arrives home. By the time I'm through, he'll beat you — as he should have a long time ago."

"We'll see," Lysette said. "Now please leave so Justin and I may descend without further mishap."

Bernard's face purpled, and he went down the steps. Unfortunately, Justin's temper was still smoldering, and he leaned over the edge of the stairwell to call after Bernard.

"Who appointed you guardian over her belongings, Uncle? She was *my* mother. What was she to you?"

Bernard swung around as if he had been struck, looking up at Justin with a flash of pure hatred. Uncomprehending, Justin stared at his uncle, his blue eyes bewildered.

Had Lysette wanted, she could have been the first to rush to Max when he arrived, to

340

tell him her side of the story before Bernard or Irénée spoke to him. She chose not to. Opening the bedchamber door, she looked down as Max came into the entrance hall. Immediately Bernard and Irénée besieged him, one angry, the other merely concerned, while Max stared at them both in dumbfounded silence. It was impossible for Lysette to hear what they said, but the tone of their complaints was clear.

Sighing, Lysette closed the door. She went to the large chair by the hearth and rubbed her temples to soothe a throbbing ache. Several minutes passed, but she did not move until she heard Max come into the room.

"*Bon soir,*" she murmured with a weary smile, knowing that he was undoubtedly furious with her. But she was too tired to argue, or win him over, or try any of her usual tactics to divert him. "Tell me right away, *mon mari* . . . how much trouble am I in?"

CHAPTER

13

Max's gaze swept over her, and his stern face softened as he crossed the room. Lysette gave a sigh of relief as he gathered her in his arms. The tightness in her chest eased. The familiar scent of him was soothing and pleasant, and the strength of his body elicited a shiver of comfort from the very marrow of her bones.

His lips brushed over hers, and he sat down in the chair, pulling her onto his lap. "Madame, would you care to tell me what happened today?"

Lysette snuggled against his chest. "I did not expect one little visit to the attic to stir up such trouble. Besides, you've told me before that I may do whatever I please in this house."

"Of course you may."

"Justin was with me."

"Yes, I heard."

"All we did was open a few boxes and trunks."

His warm hand moved over her back in an idle pattern. "Did you find what you were looking for?"

"I wasn't looking for anything. I was just *looking.* And Bernard behaved very strangely, Max." Lifting her head from his shoulder, she gazed at him earnestly. "From the way he behaved, one would think that Corinne had been *his* wife. He was absolutely furious."

"I understand. Bernard can be high-handed at times."

"This was more than high-handed!"

"Let me explain my brother to you, *petite,*" Max said gently. "You've always known him to keep his emotions to himself. But occasionally they do surface, and when that happens they do so with an explosion. Today Bernard had a rare burst of temper. Tomorrow he'll be his usual glum self. *C'est ça.* He's always been like that."

"But when he spoke about Corinne —"

"Her death, and the circumstances surrounding it, affected us all. I'm certain Bernard has done his share of wondering what happened to Corinne, and whether he could have done something to prevent it. Perhaps that is why he is so protective of her possessions now."

Lysette pondered his explanation. In that light, the episode seemed far more reasonable than it had this afternoon. But there was a question in her mind that refused to go away, and she had to ask it, even at the risk of making him angry.

"Max, are you certain that Bernard's feelings for Corinne were not something more than brotherly affection? Whenever Corinne's name is mentioned, he reacts in what I consider to be an odd manner. This afternoon wasn't the first time he and I have exchanged words about her. After I went to the old overseer's cottage — you remember that day? — he told me not to pry into the past anymore, or it would come back to ruin me."

Max was still, but she sensed a new tension in his limbs. "Why didn't you tell me about that before?"

"I didn't know you well enough," Lysette replied in a subdued tone. "I was afraid it would upset you." She peered into his face, trying to read his thoughts. "You haven't answered my question about his feelings for Corinne."

"As far as I know, there is only one woman Bernard has ever loved. Ryla Curran, the daughter of an American who settled his family in New Orleans after years of running a flatboat up and down the river. The match was an impossible one . . . she was from a Protestant family. But eventually they had an affair, and she became pregnant with his child. She disappeared without a word to her friends or family about where she was going. Bernard has searched for years, but he has never been able to find her."

"When did all of this happen?"

"At the same time Corinne was murdered.

No, there was nothing between Bernard and Corinne. He was completely involved with this girl. Losing her affected him so deeply that he had never wanted to marry anyone else."

"I didn't know." Lysette actually found herself feeling sorry for Bernard. *"Bien-aimé,"* she said tentatively, reaching up to stroke his bristled cheek, "are you unhappy about what I did this afternoon?"

He rubbed his cheek against her soft palm. "Actually, I was expecting it, my curious little cat."

"I saw Corinne's portrait," she said soberly. "She was very beautiful."

"Yes." He brushed a wisp of hair off her forehead. "But she didn't have hair the color of a sunset." His thumb glided over her lips. "Or a mouth I wanted to kiss every time I saw it." His lips moved to her ear. "She certainly didn't have a smile that stopped my heart."

Lysette's eyes half closed, and she shifted closer to him. As she slid her arms around his neck, her wrist bumped against the back of the chair. She winced at the unexpected pain.

Max looked at her sharply. "What is it? Are you hurt?"

"Oh, it's nothing." Lysette groaned inwardly as she realized that the sight of her bruised wrist was going to bring up more questions about today, when she was now willing to forget the entire matter.

Ignoring her protests, Max unwrapped her arms from around his neck, his gaze raking over her. "Why did you flinch like that?"

"It's only a little —"

He drew in his breath sharply at the sight of her swollen, discolored wrist. Black finger marks showed against her pale skin. Suddenly there was a look in his eyes that made her uneasy. "What happened?"

"Just a little accident. I was coming down from the attic — the steps are so narrow, and there is no railing — and I lost my balance. Justin was quick enough to catch my wrist and pull me back. Everything is fine now. In a day or two my wrist will be perfectly —"

"Did this happen before or after Bernard appeared?"

"Er . . . during, actually. Bernard shouted and startled me, and that was when I fell." Lysette did not tell him how slow his brother had been to offer help. Her perception of things might have been more than a little awry. And Bernard had probably been too stunned to move. Some people were quick to act in such situations, like Justin, while others froze.

"Why didn't Bernard mention it to me?"

"I have no idea."

He lifted her out of his lap and set her on her feet.

"What are you doing?" she asked warily.

"I'm going to get an explanation out of him."

"There's no need." She tried in vain to make peace, reluctant to cause further trouble between the brothers. "It is all over now, and I —"

"Hush." Gently he took her arm, holding it in order to inspect her wrist. He uttered a curse that made her ears burn. "I want you to go to Noeline. She has a salve for bruises."

"But it is nasty," she protested. "I was there once when she was putting it on Justin. The smell of it made me ill."

"Go to her *now*. Or I'll see that you do later." He paused meaningfully. "Believe me, you would prefer to do it now."

A few minutes later Lysette sat glumly in the kitchen with Noeline, focusing her attention on the kettles bubbling merrily in the fireplace while the housekeeper tended to her wrist. A housemaid stood at the huge wooden table, cleaning the iron chandelier. Deftly Noeline smeared the mustard-green salve on Lysette's arm. The noxious odor caused Lysette to jerk her head back. "How long must I keep this on?" she asked in disgust.

"Until tomorrow." Noeline smiled a little. "You're not going to make babies with monsieur tonight, I think."

Lysette raised her eyes heavenward. *"Bon*

Dieu, I'll be fortunate if he ever comes near me again!"

Justin appeared at the doorway of the kitchen. Keeping his hands in his pockets, he wandered over to them. "What is that smell?" he asked, and clutched his throat, pretending to gag.

Silently Lysette vowed to wash her wrist as soon as she escaped from Noeline.

Justin grinned at her consolingly. "It smells like the devil, *sans doute*. But it does work, *Belle-mère*."

"He knows for certain," Noeline said, wrapping a length of cloth around the arm.

"I know what you put in your salve, Noeline," Justin said. He squatted on his haunches and murmured confidentially to Lysette, "Snakes' tongues, bats' blood, toad hairs . . ."

Lysette scowled at his teasing. "Why don't you go find Philippe? He can help you with some of the Latin lessons you've missed."

Justin grinned. "There is no need to bring Latin into this. I will leave. But . . ." He glanced at her bandage. He was silent, as if he wanted to say something but was uncertain of the right words. Raking his hand through his black hair until it stood on end, he looked at the floor, the ceiling, and then his gaze met hers.

"What is it?" Lysette murmured, surprised by his sudden shyness.

Noeline went to check one of the pots over the fire.

"I didn't mean to hurt you, *belle-mère*," Justin muttered, gesturing to her wrist. "I'm sorry."

"You helped me, Justin," Lysette said gently. "I am very grateful for what you did. I might have been badly injured otherwise."

Seeming relieved, Justin stood and dusted his breeches unnecessarily. "Did you tell Father what happened?"

"About your saving me from falling? Yes, I —"

"No, about Uncle Bernard, and how strange he was this afternoon."

"*Oui*." Lysette smiled wryly. "Your father seemed to think it was not unusual. He told me your uncle has always been a bit peculiar."

"*Bien sûr*, that's true enough." Justin shrugged. "I'll go now."

Lysette watched him as he left, thinking that the boy had changed since the duel and his confrontation with Max. He was friendlier, less sullen, as if his dark nature had been tempered by new understanding. Noeline sat down beside her again, shaking her head with a smile. "That boy was born for trouble."

"And what is their complaint?" Bernard asked, looking wounded and upset. "That I did not move quickly enough? I was startled, Max. By the time I recovered my wits, Justin had already pulled her to safety!"

Max's frown did not ease. "Your manner seems to have been rather belligerent. Why is that?"

Bernard hung his head with an ashamed expression. "I didn't intend to lose my temper, but all I could think of was how it would upset you, knowing they had been combing through relics of the past. You're my brother, Max. I don't want you to be troubled with reminders of that horrible time. I tried to tell them that it was better to let things be. I suppose I expressed myself far too strongly."

"Corinne was Justin's mother," Max said. "He has a right to look through her belongings anytime he wishes."

"Yes, of course," Bernard replied contritely. "But Lysette —"

"Lysette is my concern. The next time you object to something she does, take the matter up with me. Bear in mind that she is the mistress of this house, and more of a wife to me than Corinne ever was. And . . ." Max paused to give his next words emphasis, staring hard at his brother. "If you ever raise your voice to my wife again . . . you'll take up residence somewhere else."

Bernard's cheeks flushed with suppressed emotion, but he managed to nod.

Early in the morning, Max strode down the long curved staircase, having been sent out of the bedroom with Lysette's adamant refusal to ride around the plantation with him. After the previous night's vigorous lovemaking, she had decided that it would be too uncomfortable for her to manage the high-spirited Arabian he had recently purchased for her.

As he headed to the front door, his attention was caught by the sound of a groan from one of the double parlors. Investigating the sound, he saw Alexandre's long body stretched out on the parlor settee, one booted foot braced on the gilded rococo arm, the other resting on the floor. His hair was wild, his face unshaven, and his clothes were disheveled. There was a sour alcoholic smell in the air.

"What a pretty sight," Max remarked sardonically. "A Vallerand after a night of self-indulgence." He jerked the drapes away from the windows, letting in a flood of brilliant sunshine.

Alex groaned as if he had just been stabbed. "Oh, you evil bastard."

"Fourth night this week?" Max said casually. "Even for you, that is an excess."

Alex tried to burrow into the settee, like a wounded animal seeking refuge. "Go to hell."

"Not until I find out what is bothering

you. At this rate you'll kill yourself by the end of the week."

Alex made a smacking noise and caught the scent of his own breath. His face crumpled in disgust. He squinted at Max and raised an unsteady finger to point at him. "You . . ." he said heavily, "tipped your wife this morning, didn't you?"

Max smiled pleasantly.

"I can always tell by the disgusting smirk on your face. Tell me . . . married life suit you? Good. Too bad you ruined it for the rest of us."

"Oh?"

"Don't look at me like that. Did you ever think *I* might like to have a wife . . . a woman to cover whenever *I* felt like it . . . maybe even have children someday?"

"Why don't you?"

"*Why?*" Alex wobbled to a sitting position, holding his head as if he feared it would topple from his shoulders. "After you ruined the Vallerand name, do you think a decent family would give their daughter to a brother of yours? All fine and good for you now . . . you've got Lysette . . . but me . . ."

"Alex, *tais-toi*," Max said, his amusement replaced by compassion. He sat in a nearby chair. "Hush." He had never seen his youngest brother so miserable. "I should wait until you're sober before attempting this, but we're going to try talking about it anyway."

"All right," Alexandre said gamely.

"Now, this is about Henriette Clement, isn't it?"

"Yes."

"You're in love with her? You desire permission to court her?"

"Yes."

"But you don't believe her father will give his consent?"

"I *know* he won't. I've already tried."

Max frowned. "You've asked for Clement's leave to court Henriette, and he refused?"

"Yes!" Alexandre began to nod, and stopped with a wince. "And she loves me . . . I think."

Leaning forward, Max spoke slowly. "I will take care of it. For your part, I want you to — Alexandre, are you listening? Stay here and rest today. And tonight. No more drinking, do you understand?"

"No more," Alex repeated obediently.

"I'm going to tell Noeline to bring you her special remedy."

"*Bon Dieu,* no."

"You'll do it," Max said evenly, "if you want Henriette. By tomorrow morning I want you looking like a fresh-faced boy."

"I can do it," Alex said after a moment's painful thought.

"Good." Max smiled and stood up. "You should have talked to me about this before, instead of drinking yourself into a stupor."

"I didn't think you could do anything." Alex paused. "Still don't, really."

"People can be managed," Max assured him.

Alex looked up at him quizzically. "Are you going to threaten a duel?"

"No," Max said with a laugh. "I think the Vallerands have had enough of dueling."

"Max . . . if you persuade Clement to say yes . . . I . . . . I'll kiss your feet."

"That won't be necessary," Max said dryly.

Jacques Clement greeted Max in the hallway with wry amusement. "I expected you would be here today, Vallerand. Here on your brother's behalf, *oui?* Father is having *café* in the breakfast room."

Max leaned against one of the elaborately carved columns framing the wall. He was in no hurry to confront Jacques' father, Diron Clement, who was a venerable lion of a man, and in a perpetually bad temper. Descended from the first French settlers in the Louisiana Territory, Creole in every drop of his blood, Diron had no tolerance for those who wished Louisiana to become part of the United States. Or for those who were on friendly terms with the American governor.

The old man was experienced and clever, and had proven himself to be a survivor. Along with Victor Vallerand, Diron had been richly rewarded by the Spaniards for using his influence to soothe the discontent in the city when they took possession of it from the French forty years earlier. Now Diron was wealthy and influential enough so that he never had to do anything he didn't wish.

Victor and Diron had been good friends. Unfortunately, Diron's warm feelings for Victor had never extended to Max. For one thing, their political beliefs were too sharply opposed. For another, Corinne's death had widened the gulf between them, as Diron hated scandals.

Max glanced upstairs. "Jacques," he said speculatively, "has your sister indicated that she feels any sort of affection for Alexandre?"

"Henriette is a little goose," Jacques said. "She always has been. Tell your brother he could find another girl just like her for far less trouble."

"Does that mean she would not welcome his suit?"

"She fancies herself madly in love with him. And this scenario of star-crossed love —"

"Only makes it worse," Max finished for him. "How does your father regard the matter?"

"He disapproves, of course."

"Truthfully, it wouldn't be a bad match, Jacques."

Jacques shrugged. "My friend, I know what Alexandre is like. You will never make me believe that he will stay faithful to Henriette. This so-called love will last a year at most, and then he will take a mistress, and Henriette will be devastated. Better for her to marry without the illusion of love. With a well-arranged match, she will know exactly what to expect."

"On the other hand, perhaps a year of illusion is better than no love at all."

Jacques laughed. "What an American notion. Love before marriage is *their* way — Creoles will never take to it. And I warn you, don't try to convince that crusty old man upstairs otherwise, or he'll have your head."

"My thanks for the warning. I'll go see him now."

"Would you like me to accompany you?"

Max shook his head. "I know the way."

The Clement home was designed with simplicity and elegance. The red pine floors were polished to a ruby gleam, the rooms filled with dark oak and fine hand-knotted carpets. As Max walked up the staircase, he ran his fingers lightly over the balustrade, remembering sliding down it when he and Jacques were boys.

He stopped in the hallway upstairs, sensing someone's gaze upon him. Looking over his shoulder, he saw that one of the paneled doors was partially ajar. Henriette stared at him through the narrow crack, her eyes filled with pleading. Max guessed that some watchful *tante* was nearby and Henriette did not dare say a word for fear of detection. He

356

gave her a short, reassuring nod. Throwing aside caution, Henriette opened the door wider, and suddenly there was a burst of chatter from inside the room, a woman's voice scolding the wayward girl. The door closed immediately.

Max grinned ruefully. He hated the feeling of being the distraught lovers' last hope. He made his way to the breakfast room, hoping to hell that he'd know what to say to Clement.

Diron Clement greeted him with a glare. A ruff of white hair haloed the top of his head. When he spoke, the edge of a sharp jaw showed through his sagging jowls. Iron-gray eyes bore through Max's, and he gestured to a chair.

"Sit down, boy. We have not talked for a long time."

"The wedding, sir," Max reminded him.

"*Non.* We exchanged four words, perhaps. You were too busy staring at your flamboyant little bride to pay me any attention."

Max sternly held back a smile, remembering that most frustrating of evenings. He had not been able to tear his gaze from Lysette, dying to have her, but knowing it was too soon to have her. "I regret that, sir."

"Do you?" Diron harrumphed. "Yes, I suppose you do, now that you desire my good favor. What about the marriage? Do you have regrets about that as well?"

"Not in the least," Max replied without hesitation. "My wife pleases me very well."

"And now you've come to plead your brother's case, eh?"

"Actually, my own," Max said. "Since that seems to be your main objection to Alexandre's suit."

"Untrue. Is that what he told you?"

"He has the impression, sir, that were it not for the damage I have wrought on the Vallerand name in the past, his intentions toward your daughter would be welcomed."

"Ah. You are referring to that business about your first wife."

Max met his piercing gaze and nodded briefly.

"That was bad," Diron said emphatically. "But my objection to the match has to do with your brother's character, not yours. Foppish, weak-willed, lazy — he is unsatisfactory in all respects."

"Alexandre is no worse than any other young man his age. And he will be able to provide well for her."

"How is that? I would wager he has run through most of his inheritance by now."

"My father charged me with the responsibility of overseeing the family's finances. I assure you, Alexandre has the means to support a family in a suitable manner."

Diron was quiet, glaring at him from beneath massive gray brows.

"Monsieur Clement," Max said slowly, "you know the Vallerands are a family of good blood. I believe your daughter would be content as Alexandre's wife. Discarding all sentimental notions, the pairing is both practical and suitable."

"But we *cannot* discard these sentimental notions, can we?" the old man shot back. "This entire situation *reeks* of mawkish sentiment. Is this the foundation for a good marriage? *Non!* These impetuous propositions, these demonstrations and histrionics, this gnashing of teeth and beating of breasts — this is not love. I distrust all of it."

All at once Max understood what the old man's objection truly was. It would damage Diron's pride to allow his daughter to marry for love. It was not the continental way. People would make jest of the old man's decision, and say his iron will was softening. Perhaps they might even dare to say he was influenced by the new American values that were infiltrating the territory. Quite simply, a love match would embarrass Diron.

"I agree," Max said, thinking rapidly. "You realize if we keep them apart, all this overwrought emotion will continue. So, that is why I favor the idea of a long courtship — with strict supervision, *naturellement*. We'll allow them enough time to fall *out* of love."

"Eh? What?"

"It will only take a little time, not even a

year. You know how fickle the young are."

Diron frowned. "Yes, indeed."

"And then, when all this violent love has faded into indifference, we will marry them to each other. Henriette will probably object to the match by then. It would be a lesson for both of them. Then, through the years, Alexandre and Henriette will slowly develop the sensible kind of affection for each other that my parents did . . . as you and your wife did."

"Hmmm." Diron stroked his chin. Max nearly held his breath, waiting for the answer. "There is something to the idea."

"It makes sense to me," Max said blandly, sensing the old man was secretly relieved to be handed a solution to the dilemma. This way Henriette would have the husband she desired, and Diron's pride would be preserved.

"Hmmm. Yes, that is what we will do."

"*Bien.*" Max adopted a matter-of-fact expression. "Now, about the dowry —"

"We will discuss *that* at a more appropriate time," Diron interrupted grumpily. "Already thinking of the dowry . . . how like a Vallerand."

"Pretend *not* to love her?" Alex exclaimed. "I do not understand."

"Trust me," Max said, catching Lysette around the waist as she passed him. He pulled her onto his lap. "The sooner you and Henriette convince everyone that you are indifferent to each other, the sooner you can marry."

"Only you could come up with such a convoluted scheme," Alex said sourly.

"You want her," Max said flatly. "That is how you can have her."

Lysette cuddled against her husband, stroking his hair. "It was very clever of you, Max."

"Not at all," he said modestly, enjoying her praise.

Her voice lowered. "It will be a happy ending, all thanks to your romantic nature," she said, and he exchanged a slow grin with her.

Alexandre made a sound of disgust and stood up to leave. "Imagine, Max having a romantic nature," he muttered. "*I* must be having a nightmare."

In the weeks to come, Alexandre's romance with Henriette Clement continued on its precarious way. On countless evenings he sat with her in the parlor, the entire Clement family in attendance. When he took her on sedate carriage drives, her mother and aunt accompanied them. He never dared meet Henriette's eyes in church or at the balls they attended. The nearness of Henriette, and the rigorously imposed distance between them, caused Alexandre's feelings to ascend to new heights of longing.

The tiniest signs from Henriette were significant — the way her footsteps slowed when she had to leave him, the flash of her gaze when she allowed herself to look at him. It was any young man's idea of a perfect hell.

To Alexandre's own surprise, he found he had no desire for any other girl. It was with genuine indignation that he reacted to Max's suggestion that he visit some of his former haunts with Bernard.

"Rumors of your new celibate ways are reaching Diron's ears," Max informed him calmly. "It is clear to him and everyone else that you're smitten with Henriette. It's time to give the appearance that you are losing interest in her."

"And therefore you wish me to visit some harlot?"

"You've done it before," Max pointed out.

"Yes, but that was a long time ago. At least two months!"

Max laughed and suggested that he find some other way of appearing bored with his pursuit of Henriette. Miserably Alexandre began to ration his visits to the Clement household, making them more and more infrequent, while Henriette strove to appear indifferent to the new flood of rumors that a betrothal would soon be announced.

Lysette pitied the lovelorn pair and told Max as much. "It seems so ridiculous to put them through such trials merely to preserve

Monsieur Clement's pride. It makes something very simple into something so complicated."

"It isn't so bad for Alexandre to want something he cannot have immediately." Max smiled and leaned down to kiss her. She was sitting at her dressing table, braiding her hair before they went to bed. "The best things are worth waiting for. Such as you."

"As I recall, you did not have to wait long for me at all."

"I waited my entire life for you."

Touched, Lysette smiled and rubbed her cheek against his hand. *"Bien-aimé,"* she whispered. "You do have a way with words." She began to unbutton the front of her dress and gestured to the dresser. "Will you bring me a nightgown, please?"

"Later," he murmured, easing the dress from her shoulders.

One of the largest balls of the season was being held at the Leseur plantation to honor the betrothal of one of the three Leseur daughters to Paul Patrice, the last unmarried son of a well-to-do New Orleans physician. Usually a doctor's son would not have been considered a suitable match for a planter's daughter, but Paul was a handsome lad with exquisite manners and gentlemanly bearing. Only three years older than Justin and Philippe, he was perfectly willing to surrender his bachelorhood in exchange for marriage into a wealthy family.

"Eighteen years of freedom, and now Paul wishes to shackle himself!" Justin had commented sourly. "Next year, probably a baby . . . *Mon Dieu,* hasn't he thought about what he is doing?"

"He could not do better than Félicie Leseur," Philippe replied, a touch dreamily. "Marriage is not as bad a fate as you seem to think, Justin."

Justin looked at him as if he'd gone mad. Then his mouth curled in a ridiculing sneer. "I suppose *you'll* be married before too long."

"I hope so. I hope I will be able to find the right girl."

"I know what kind of girl you'll choose," Justin continued. "Bookish and sensible, with spectacles pinching the end of her nose. You'll discuss art and music, and all those boring Greek tragedies."

Affronted, Philippe closed the Latin book before him. "She will be beautiful," he said with dignity, "and gentle and quiet. And you will be jealous."

Justin snorted. "I'm going to sail to the East and have my own harem. Fifty women!"

"Fifty?" Lysette repeated with a laugh, having just come into the room. "That will keep you very busy indeed, Justin."

He dropped his sneer and gave her an angelic smile. "But if I find someone like you, *petite Maman*, I'll have only one."

She laughed at his outrageous charm, and her smiling gaze turned to Philippe. "Tonight, *peut-être*, you will catch sight of the girl you dream of. Are you leaving in the carriage with Bernard and Alexandre?" She did not mention Irénée, who was afflicted with a touch of rheumatism and would not attend the ball.

Philippe nodded. "Yes. Father made it clear you and he were going alone in the first carriage."

"Alone?" Justin mused thoughtfully. "Why would Father want to be *alone* in the carriage with you, when he could have Philippe and me there? Well, I suppose he might try to —"

"*Justin!*" Philippe exploded, mortified at his brother's impudence. He threw a pillow cushion at Justin's head. Justin ducked it with a protest.

Lysette's mouth twitched with amusement. "I will see you at the Leseur plantation," she said gravely, and went back to the entrance hall, where Noeline waited with her bonnet and gloves.

Built facing one of the smaller bayous in the region, the Leseur home was large, simply designed, and stately. One side was bordered by a massive oak that was estimated to be at least three centuries old. Garlands of roses covered the house inside and out. The glitter from intricately prismed chandeliers danced in the most remote corners of the house. Guests filled the outside galleries, while servants moved among them with silver trays of refreshments.

Nearby was the *garçonnière,* separately constructed quarters for male guests or family bachelors who required privacy. Several gentlemen accompanied by personal attendants had been in the *garçonnière* since early afternoon, drinking, smoking, and discussing the latest events in the city. The ladies had been resting inside the house, and now were appearing in the ballroom in their most extravagant gowns. A special orchestra had been summoned from New Orleans to supply the music, and the lively strains of a quadrille filled the air.

"Lysette," Max said as he helped her from the carriage, "a word of warning."

"Yes?" She looked at him with wide, innocent eyes. Too innocent. "What is it, *bien-aimé?*"

"It hasn't escaped me that Alexandre has been trying to persuade you to help him spend a few minutes alone with Henriette tonight. You're planning something, aren't you?"

She appeared to be surprised. "I don't know what you're talking about."

Max gave her a warning glance. "If they

manage to give a convincing show of indifference to each other, they'll be married in a matter of months. If, however, they are discovered in a clandestine meeting, there will be nothing I can do to help them."

"They won't be caught together," Lysette assured him.

"Alex could lose Henriette over such a trifling thing. You do not understand the extent of Diron's pride."

"I do, I understand perfectly." Lysette tried to move away, but he kept his hands at her waist, staring down at her. "Max," she protested, "I haven't done anything!"

"Keep it that way," he advised, and let go of her.

Max kept his gaze on Alexandre and Lysette for the next two hours, but neither of them made a move to leave the ballroom. He relaxed after a glass or two of the fine wine being served to all the guests. The vintage had been made from vineyards on the Leseur plantation.

Max congratulated Leseur, both on the excellent wine and on the match between Félicie and Paul Patrice, and the two of them engaged in a casual conversation as others joined them.

From a distance, Lysette stood with Alexandre and watched her husband with a rush of pride. Max was dressed in stark black and white, a wine glass poised between his long fingers as he conversed with the men around him. He was elegant, virile, and devilishly handsome . . . and he was hers.

Alexandre followed her gaze. "It's not easy," he remarked, "having Max as a brother."

Lysette frowned at him, thinking of all the times she had seen Max smooth the way for his brothers, doing what he could to ensure they had whatever they desired, assuming their debts and responsibilities without one word of reproach. Alex's statement struck her as being singularly ungrateful. "Max does many things for you, *non?*"

"He does, but for years Bernard and I had to contend with the standards Max set. Everything he did was perfect. And then, when he fell so utterly in disgrace — it was a disaster for all of us. The Vallerand name was blackened, and Bernard and I suffered, as well as Max."

"And you resent him for that?"

"No, no. I might have, once, but not now. But Bernard . . ." Alexandre stopped, evidently thinking better of what he had been about to say.

"What?" Lysette prompted.

He shook his head. "It's nothing."

"Tell me, Alex, or I will not help you with Henriette."

He scowled. "I was only going to say that

Bernard seems to find it difficult to completely forgive Max. But then, Bernard is the next oldest son. He has always been compared to Max and found lacking."

"That is hardly Max's fault," Lysette said coolly. "*Vraiment,* Alex . . . you and Bernard must stop using him as a convenient excuse. You must take responsibility for your own actions. Max has quite enough to contend with."

"All right," he said, holding up his hands in mock self-defense. "I won't say any more. But why is it, *ma soeur,* that you are allowed to criticize Max, but you won't let anyone else?"

She grinned suddenly. "Because I'm his wife."

Max did not notice the exact moment when his wife disappeared. As he gradually became aware of her absence, he politely separated himself from the group in the ballroom and wandered past the open doors leading to the outside galleries. There was no sign of his wife.

"Dammit, Lysette, what are you doing?" he muttered softly. He went to the garden, knowing that if Lysette had engineered a meeting between Alexandre and Henriette, it would probably take place there.

The Leseur garden was large and intricately designed, filled with exotic trees, flowers, and plants from Europe and the Orient. Its artificial lagoons were stocked with fish and crossed by charming bridges. An indignant peacock scuttled out of the way as Max strode through the rose-covered arch that marked the entrance to the main path. The way became darker, the lanterns more infrequent, until he reached the corridor of tall yews. A fountain of cherubs and spouting fish marked the center of the garden, from which several paths branched off.

Max cursed softly. There was little chance of finding his wife, or her fellow companions. His only recourse was to return to the drawing room and wait.

Suddenly he heard footsteps on the graveled path. Withdrawing into the shadows, he watched the approaching figure.

It was Diron Clement. Evidently the old man had noticed his daughter's absence. He tromped past Max without seeing him. Max grimaced, taking note of the belligerent set of Diron's head. There would be hell to pay if he found Henriette with Alexandre. The old man headed to the left, on a path which — if Max's memory served him — led to a tiny pagoda. An unwanted smile pulled at his lips. In his younger days he had made use of the pagoda himself. He still retained a fond memory or two of the place. No, Alexandre would not conduct his tryst there. It was too obvious.

Taking a chance, Max chose the opposite direction, a path which led to a hothouse filled with exotic fruit trees. Keeping to the shadows, he drew closer until he saw Lysette standing at the corner of the hothouse. An owl hooted in the distance, and she jumped, looking from side to side.

The sight of her there, after she had promised not to take part in any illicit meeting between Alex and Henriette, made him grin ruefully. He was going to have to teach her that she could not tweak his nose and dance away without fear of retribution.

Lysette sighed, wishing she were back in the ballroom. She wondered if Max had noticed yet that she was missing. A night owl gave a low cry, and she started a little.

Suddenly a hard arm snaked around her waist from behind. A large hand covered her mouth as she yelped with fright. She was dragged back against a surface as unyielding as a brick wall. As she pried frantically at the hand over her mouth, she heard a familiar voice in her ear.

"Had I known you desired a tour of the gardens, sweet, I would have offered to accompany you."

Lysette sagged in relief, gasping as the hand was removed from her mouth. "Max . . ." She turned and wrapped her arms around his neck. "You startled me!" She

371

dropped her forehead against his chest.

"I intended to."

Lysette winced as she saw his ominous expression.

"Where are they?" he asked.

She bit her lip and looked at the hothouse. The door opened, and Alexandre stuck his head out. His hair was wildly mussed, and his lips were suspiciously moist. "Lysette? I thought I heard —" He froze as he saw Max. They were all silent.

Max was the first to speak. "You have one minute to say good-bye to Henriette. Make it meaningful. Your separation may be permanent."

Alexandre disappeared inside the building.

Lysette decided to explain as quickly as possible. She spoke without pausing for breath. "Max, they only wanted five minutes together, and I had already promised them I would help, so I couldn't go back on my word, and if you had only seen how happy they were when I brought Henriette here, you would have understood why I had to —"

"When we get home, I'm going to take you over my knee and ensure that you will not be able to sit comfortably for a long time."

Lysette blanched. "You wouldn't."

"I'm going to enjoy it immensely," he assured her. Her arms dropped from around his neck. "Max, let's discuss this. . . ."

She paused as she realized that Max was

not listening; he was gazing into the distance, his eyes alert. "What is it?" she asked.

Max yanked her against his body without warning, fitting his mouth over hers. Lysette squeaked and wriggled in surprise, but his arms were too tight, and his mouth absorbed all sound. He angled his head more deeply over hers, his tongue plunging into her mouth. His hand moved down to her bottom, cupping the soft flesh and pulling her high against the swelling bulge of his sex. Her vision blurred, and her struggles died away. Convulsively she swallowed and strained to press even closer to him. Suddenly he lifted his head, ignoring her soft protest.

"Ah . . . good evening, Monsieur Clement," he said thickly.

Lysette's head snapped around, and she saw Dion Clement's craggy face not five feet away. His subdued glare seemed to bore right through her.

"I was told my daughter Henriette was with you, Madame Vallerand," the old man barked. "Where is she?"

Lysette turned back to Max, glancing at him helplessly.

"It seems that we are unable to help you, sir." Max's thumb brushed lightly over the top of Lysette's spine. "I came here with my wife to share a private moment."

"Then you have not seen Henriette tonight?"

"I swear upon my honor that I have not."

Lysette closed her eyes, hoping fervently that Alex and Henriette had the sense to stay inside the hothouse.

14

Clement considered them both carefully, noting Lysette's flustered expression and disheveled gown, Max's unreadable face and obvious state of arousal. They had not been married long — it was hardly implausible that the couple had sneaked out to the garden in search of privacy. Giving them a last suspicious stare, he harrumphed and turned his back, walking away to renew his search for Henriette.

Lysette regarded her husband with dazed gratitude. "If you hadn't been here, he would have found them. Thank you."

"Straighten your gown," he said curtly. "And take Henriette back without delay."

The star-crossed lovers crept out of the hothouse. Lysette glanced at the girl's guilt-stricken face and forced a reassuring smile to her lips. "*Allons,* Henriette — we must go find your *tante,* quickly."

Timidly the girl drew away from Alexandre and preceded Lysette on the path back to the main house. Alex bit his lip, apparently wanting to call out to her, but not daring to anger his brother further.

Max watched until his wife disappeared from view, while thin vales of displeasure appeared around his mouth.

Alex gave him a mutinous glare. "Don't you understand anything about love, Max? Don't you know how it feels to want someone until your arms ache to hold her? Are you going to claim that had you been in my place you wouldn't have done the same? I know how you compromised Lysette in order to force her to marry you. And I feel —"

Mockingly Max held up his hands in self-defense. "Enough, Alex. I don't give a damn if you see Henriette or not. The risk is yours. But when you enlist the help of my wife, it is my right to interfere."

Alexandre's self-righteous anger vanished. "Of course," he mumbled. "But Lysette *wanted* to help."

"Of that I have no doubt. She is a soft-hearted creature, and easily entreated. It presents little difficulty to take advantage of such a generous nature, *n'est-ce pas?* Don't involve her again, Alex — I won't tolerate it."

Alexandre nodded, shamed by his brother's words. "I'm sorry, Max. All I have been able to think about is Henriette and —"

"I know that," Max interrupted.

"You are angry with Lysette. Please don't blame her. She only did what Henriette and I both begged her to do. You won't punish her, will you?"

Max lifted his brows and smiled derisively. "Why, Alex . . . you seem to believe that my wife needs protection from me."

Having returned Henriette safely to her aunt, who had promised she would not betray them to Diron, Lysette withdrew to a dark corner of the outside gallery. Guiltily she half hoped Max would not find her, though she knew she would have to face him sooner or later. The crowd of guests inside the house was moving toward the dining room, where midnight supper was being served. For her the ball had lost its glitter; she felt distinctly uneasy.

She had stung Max's masculine pride, and she regretted that. Although he was an indulgent and understanding husband, he was also a Creole male, and she had gone against his express wishes. Frowning, she considered various ways to appease him.

Lysette heard footsteps, and saw a dark form approaching. "Max?" she asked, knowing that he had come to find her. The footsteps halted. She kept her gaze averted as she spoke. "Forgive me. I couldn't bear to see Henriette and Alexandre so unhappy. But you were completely right, and I should have listened to you. Let me make amends, d'accord?" She approached him with a coaxing smile. "I want very much to please you, bien — aimé —"

She stopped with a sharp gasp as his face became visible. It was not Max. It was Etienne Sagesse.

There was a bright, glazed look in his eyes and she could smell the liquor on his breath. "What a tempting offer," he murmured. "I can guess how you make amends, with your sweet mouth and your clever little hands. I envy your husband, Lysette . . . I've made no secret of that."

Lysette's skin crawled as she saw the expression on his fleshy face. He was very, very drunk. She tried to walk around him, but he moved to block her. "Let me pass," she said in a low voice.

"Not yet. I want a little of what you give to your husband. You were mine first, after all. You should be in my bed each night. I should be the man rutting between your legs, not Vallerand."

"Don't be a fool," Lysette said shortly, her thoughts racing. She couldn't allow him to cause a scene. It would create a scandal, and another duel. She must get away from him quickly, before someone discovered them. "I didn't want you then, and I certainly don't now. Get out of my way, you drunken ass."

He smiled, his lips gleaming wetly. "What fire and spirit you have. Perhaps you are not the most beautiful woman in New Orleans, but you know how to keep a man's cock satisfied, don't you?" He lurched toward her.

"Poor Lysette. You could have been my wife, and instead you share a bed with a murderer."

"I think *you* killed her."

Sagesse smiled. "No, it wasn't I. Corinne was no threat to me. She had given me all I desired — more, actually. Aside from acute boredom, I had no reason to kill her." His arms stretched out, and he flattened his hands against the wall above her head.

Lysette stared at him, transfixed by the expression on his face. "You know what happened to her, don't you?" she asked softly.

His sour breath wafted against her face. *"Oui."*

"Tell me."

His gaze slid over her. "And if I do? What will you offer in return?"

As she remained silent, still staring at him, Sagesse reached for her breast and squeezed it roughly. Lysette struck him hard enough to turn his face to the side, then twisted past him. He caught her hair and pulled her back. She gave a muffled cry of pain and dug her nails into his hands, trying to pull her hair free.

His words struck her cheek in rapid bursts. "For once I'll know what it is to hold you in my arms."

"No —"

"You should have been mine." He shoved a knee between her thighs, and his wet mouth and teeth grazed her cheek. A cry broke from her lips, and his hand covered her mouth while his other felt for her breasts. Shuddering in revulsion, she bit his hand and screamed again.

Suddenly there was a furious shout from behind her, and Lysette was yanked away with a force that snapped her head back. She stumbled as she was released, and steadied herself against a narrow wooden column. Shivering, she watched Justin launch himself at Sagesse, going for his throat. As the pair fought, Lysette flinched at the sound of each blow.

"No, Justin!" Frantically she looked for help. The guests had noticed the disturbance and a crowd gathered around them. Someone pointed to her. She drew as far back into a shadow as possible, pushing back her tumbled hair, pulling up the front of her gown to cover her breasts.

A man darted forward from the crowd and dragged Justin away from Sagesse. It was Bernard. "Calm down, you fool!" he muttered, struggling to restrain the writhing boy.

"Damn you!" Justin cursed. "Let go! I'll tear him apart!"

Several Sagesse relatives appeared, among them Etienne's brother-in-law, Severin Dubois. They gathered around Etienne, arguing fiercely as they began to drag him away to the *garçonnière*. Etienne's behavior

380

had disgraced the entire family. Humiliated, they wanted only to conceal him before more damage to their honor could be done.

Lysette shrank back in embarrassment as she felt a multitude of gazes upon her. She wished she could disappear. Did they think she had brought this on herself? That perhaps she had allowed Etienne to seduce her, as he had seduced Corinne? She started as she heard a voice close by her ear.

"Lysette?" Philippe was beside her, looking down at her with concerned blue eyes. He put an arm around her shoulders, as if he thought she might faint. She leaned against him, taking comfort in his presence. Philippe was so calm and steady . . . so unlike his hotheaded brother, who was still swearing and fighting to be free of Bernard's grasp. Following her gaze, Philippe glanced at his red-faced brother. A faint smile touched his mouth. "He will never forgive Bernard for pulling him off Sagesse," he commented.

"I agree," Lysette said with a shaky laugh.

"Are you all right?"

She nodded briefly. "Where is Max?"

"Someone went to find him —" Philippe broke off as the chattering crowd fell silent. The congregation parted to make way for Max as he pushed his way through their midst. There was no sound. Even Justin was still.

Max stopped, his gaze darting from

Lysette's flushed face to Justin's. Turning, he saw Etienne Sagesse, propped up in the midst of relatives, and Lysette went cold as she saw the bloodlust in her husband's eyes.

"Max, no," she said sharply.

He didn't seem to hear her as he stared at Sagesse. "By God, I'll kill you," he said in a murderous voice that curdled everyone's blood, including Lysette's. Before anyone could react, he had reached Etienne in two strides.

Lysette put her hands over her mouth to suppress a scream as she saw her husband turn into a stranger. Tearing through the Sagesses, Max leapt on the drunken man and smashed his head against the floor. It took the combined efforts of Bernard, Alexandre, Justin, and Philippe to pull him off.

Severin Dubois broke through the tumult, while Max strained against the arms that held him back. Dubois spoke in a calm, authoritative voice that reached through Max's blind fury. "There is no excuse for the insult to your wife, Vallerand. Etienne was entirely at fault. On behalf of the Sagesse family, I offer the humblest apologies. All I can do is swear that it will not happen again."

"No, it won't," Max sneered. "Because this time I won't make the mistake of letting him live. Get him a sword. I'll finish it now."

"You cannot duel with him," Dubois countered. "He is not in a fit condition. It would be murder."

"Then tomorrow morning."

"It would be murder," Dubois repeated, shaking his head.

Suddenly Etienne's slurred voice interrupted. His relatives had helped him up from the floor. His nose was bleeding, but he made no effort to blot it. "But Max has a taste for murder."

Max's arms struggled against his brothers' restraining hands. "Let me go," he growled, but Bernard and Alex only tightened their hold on him.

"Etienne," Dubois said sharply, "be quiet."

Sagesse staggered forward with a half grimace that resembled a smile. "For years you've lied to yourself about what happened to Corinne," he said to Max. "Why can't you stand the truth? The pieces are all there. And yet you've never put them together. You could find the answers under your own roof, but *you don't want to.*" He cackled as he saw the sudden blankness on Max's face. "What a fool you are —"

"Etienne, enough!" Dubois snapped, taking hold of Sagesse's collar and dragging him away.

Max stared after them as if in a dream. Abruptly he shook off his brothers' hands and glanced around wildly for Lysette. She stood alone near the gallery railing, her hair falling from its pins in wild curls. He reached her at once and seized her narrow shoulders in his hands.

Lysette could not control her trembling. "I believe he knows who killed Corinne, Max."

Max gripped her head in his hands and spread rough kisses of reassurance and ownership across her face. "Did he hurt you?" he asked hoarsely.

"No, not at all."

His large hand roamed over her shoulders, back, and hips. Lysette knew that people were staring, but she relaxed against him, not caring what anyone thought. His body was rigid, his heart thundering with alarm and aggression.

"This won't happen again," came his scratchy whisper. "I'll kill him if I have to."

She jerked her head back, startled. "Don't say that. Everything is all right, Max."

His eyes were black and fathomless, his face pale beneath its swarthy tan. "It's not," he replied softly. "But it will be."

Her lips parted to reply, but he eased her away from his body and pushed her toward Alexandre. "Take her home."

"What are you going to do?" Lysette asked.

He refused to explain. "I'll be home soon."

"Come with me now," she begged.

Exchanging a glance with Alex, he turned and left.

"Max!" she cried, following him.

Alexandre caught her arm. "Don't worry, Lysette. Max is only going to talk with Severin and one or two of the Sagesses. I am certain that Jacques Clement will be there to help mediate." His attention turned to Bernard, who was standing nearby. "Are you going with him?"

Bernard shook his head. "I'd be of little use," he said, and added venomously, "especially since I wish we had let Max kill the insolent bastard."

Justin's voice cut through the silence. "If Father doesn't, I will."

They glanced at the boy, who had been forgotten in the disruption. Alex frowned, while Bernard laughed scornfully. "Little braggart," Bernard said.

Lysette went to the boy immediately, taking his hand and pressing it between her own. "Justin, don't say such things."

"I watched Sagesse all evening," he said roughly. "While *he* was watching *you*. When you disappeared, he went to look for you. That was when I followed him, and —"

"Thank you," she interrupted gently. "Thank you for rescuing me. Now it is all over, and we can —"

"I saw him go out to the gallery," Justin continued, his voice falling to a whisper, so that no one else could hear. He turned until his back was to the others. His intense stare did not waver from her face. "By the time I reached one of the doors, he had taken hold of you. I ran forward, and brushed past someone who was standing at the side of the gallery. Standing and watching the two of you. It was Uncle Bernard. He wasn't going to lift a finger to help you."

She shook her head, not understanding what he thought was significant. "Justin, not now —"

"Don't you understand? Something is wrong when a man won't defend a member of his family, no matter what feelings are between them. It was not only an offense against you, but against Father, and me, and —"

"I am tired," she whispered back, unwilling to hear more. Tempers were too high, and the boy was clearly incensed. All of this could be sorted out later.

Lysette huddled in bed alone, her teeth chattering. Her gaze moved restlessly through the dimly lit room. The events of the night kept churning through her mind, and she could not rid herself of the feeling that something terrible had been set in motion, something neither she nor Max could change.

She had never seen Max out of control, as he had been tonight. For a moment she had thought he would kill Sagesse right before her eyes. She pressed her hands to the side of her head to drive away the dark images.

But they persisted mercilessly, as did the echo of Max's vow: *By God, I'll kill you.*

Lysette groaned and turned over, burying her face in the pillow. The house was silent. The Vallerands had all retired, except for Bernard, who had chosen to spend the night somewhere else. They had all agreed not to mention anything about the evening to Irénée.

It seemed that hours dragged by before Lysette heard the sounds of someone's arrival. She bolted out of bed. As she reached the bedroom door, Max stepped inside. He did not appear surprised to find her awake.

"What happened?" she asked, slipping her arms around his waist. She felt the tension in his body, a simmering, barely contained violence. His hand swept down her back, and he hugged her briefly before holding her away in order to look at her.

"*Ça va?*"

"Yes, I'm fine. Now that you're here." A furrow gathered between her brows as she tried to read his mood. "Is there going to be a duel tomorrow?"

"No."

"Good," she said, infinitely relieved. "Come to bed, and we'll talk about —"

"Not yet, *petite*. I'm going out again."

"Why?"

"I have an errand to take care of."

"Tonight?" She shook her head in protest.

"No, Max, you must stay here. I don't care what business matters you have or what the errand is. I need you. Stay with me —"

"I'll return soon," he said firmly. "I have no choice about this, Lysette."

She could not let him go anywhere tonight, not in this dangerous mood. All her instincts insisted that she keep him safe with her. "Don't go," she said, gripping the front of his coat.

As she saw that he was about to refuse, she played a card she had hoped would not be necessary. "You told me once that if I asked you not to do something, you would oblige me. Now I am asking. Don't go."

Max let out a growl of frustration. "Dammit, Lysette, I have to. Don't do this to me tonight."

"Are you refusing me?" Lysette asked, staring into his narrowed eyes. She sensed his dilemma, his desire to please her clashing violently with his urgent need to accomplish whatever task he had set for himself. His mouth was taut with exasperation.

The silence stretched like a cord about to snap. Rather than allow Max to suffer another moment of torturous inner debate, Lysette decided to tip the balance. Her slender hands dropped from his coat and smoothed over the front of his breeches. She felt his body start at the unexpected touch. Finding the stirring shape of him, she cupped and squeezed gently, bringing the heavy shaft to pulsing life. She pressed the tips of her breasts to his chest.

His voice had lowered to a deep, unsteady timbre. "Lysette, what are you doing?"

"Distracting you." The shaft beneath her hands was full and thick now, and she plucked at the carved onyx buttons of his breeches to free it. With the help of the straining pressure beneath the thick cloth, the buttons popped easily from their holes.

Lysette made a sound of pleasure as her fingers slid around the rigid length of him.

Max gasped and staggered backward a step, and she followed readily, her teasing fingers slipping to the silken place beneath his testicles. "Lysette," he said gruffly, "if you think that is going to keep me here, you're wrong."

"What about this?" Her head lowered, and she took him into her soft, hot mouth. Her tongue searched delicately until she found a pulsing vein on the underside of the tumescent shaft.

She heard a strangled sound above her, before he found the breath to reply.

"*That's* going to keep me here." He leaned against the wall, breathing raggedly as she used her mouth and hands to arouse him thoroughly. When he could stand no more, he scooped her in his arms and carried her to the bed, consuming her with ravenous passion.

New Orleans was ablaze with gossip. The rivalry between Etienne Sagesse and Maximilien Vallerand was well known, but the events at the Leseur ball were outrageous. The story of Sagesse's drunken advances on Vallerand's red-haired wife was recounted until the wildest rumors scattered from one household to the next.

It was said that the young Madame Vallerand had been half naked out on the gallery. One witness was certain he had heard Vallerand swear to take revenge on every member of the Sagesse family. Someone else claimed that Vallerand had threatened to strangle his second wife as he had the first, if she was ever caught even looking at another man.

As Max went to his small shipping office in town, he was well aware of scurrying excitement in his wake. Not since before his marriage had women given him such glances, as if he were some dangerous animal to be avoided. Men regarded him with measuring gazes, like boys facing the schoolyard bully. Filled with disgust, Max concluded his business as quickly as possible. Obviously, it was his lot in life to be hounded by scandal whether he deserved it or not.

When he returned to the plantation, he saw several carriages stopped on the long drive in front of the main house. It was not Irénée's usual at-home day. Frowning, he walked in and removed his gloves and hat. There was a steady hum of voices coming from the parlor.

Before he went to investigate, Lysette appeared. "Irénée's friends," she whispered with a conspiratorial smile, taking his arm. "Don't show yourself. We don't want anyone to faint." She led him to the library. Max allowed her to tug him forward, while he filled his eyes with the sight of her. She was dressed in a vivid blue day gown trimmed with frothy white lace.

"Your mother has had a wonderful morning," she informed him, closing the library door. "Everyone from far and near has visited to hear her version of last night. It matters not in the least that she wasn't even there."

Max smiled reluctantly, reflecting that whereas any other wife would be strained and upset, Lysette was making light of the situation. He bent to kiss her, relishing the sweetness of her lips. "Don't worry," he said wryly. "The scandal could fade in as little as ten, twelve years."

Lysette smiled and pulled his head down again. "We'll just have to keep to ourselves until then."

"Madame Vallerand," he breathed, his lips sliding to her throat, "you could make hell itself seem appealing."

"Wherever you go, *bien-aimé*, I'll be certain to follow."

Late that night Lysette was awakened as Max lifted his arm from her waist and left the bed. She mumbled in protest, missing the warmth of his body "What are you doing?"

"I have to leave for a little while."

"Leave?" Sleepy and irritated, she pushed her hair out of her face. "Didn't we discuss this *last* night?"

"We did." He pulled on his breeches and hunted for his discarded shirt. "And I should have taken care of my business then . . . but I was distracted."

"Can't this business be attended to in the daylight?"

"I'm afraid not."

"Are you going to do something dangerous? Illegal?"

"Not entirely."

"Max!"

"I will return in approximately two hours."

"I do not approve," she muttered. "I *hate* it when you go out at night."

"Go to sleep," he whispered, pushing her back down, kissing her forehead. He tucked the covers around her. "When you wake, I'll be here beside you."

A light, drizzling rain greeted Lysette in the morning, and she dressed more warmly than was usually required for a September day. Her simple velvet dress was made of a rust-colored red that brought out the color of her hair. She parted her hair in the middle and gathered it loosely at the back of her head.

A faint groan came from the bed, and she looked over her shoulder at the mass of tangled sheets and long hair-dusted limbs. As he had promised, Max had returned during the night. Refusing to give any explanation of where he had been, he had shed his clothes, smothered her questions by making love to her, and promptly gone to sleep. Lysette had been irritated by his evasiveness, but also relieved to have him back.

She walked to the bed now, her hands resting on her hips. "So, you're awake," she said pertly.

"I'm tired," he muttered.

"Good, I hope you're *exhausted*. Maybe tonight you will stay in your own bed instead of going on some mysterious errand that you can't even explain to your own wife."

Max sat up, the bed linens falling to his waist as he rubbed his face. As annoyed with him as she was, Lysette could not help but appreciate the sight of his tawny, muscular body. "All right," he muttered. "I'll explain everything to you, as it is clear that I'll have no peace otherwise. Last night I —" He stopped as he heard heavy footsteps racing up the stairs.

Frowning curiously, Lysette stepped into

the hallway and saw Philippe. The boy's face was blank with panic. "Where is Justin?" he cried as soon as he saw her. "Is he home?"

"I don't know," she said, partially closing the bedroom door while Max pulled on a robe. "I think he is roaming about town with friends. Why? What is the matter?"

Philippe fought to catch his breath. "I went to my fencing lesson," he gasped. "I h-heard . . . news about Etienne Sagesse. . . ."

Lysette was gripped by an ominous chill as he paused. She felt Max's presence behind her, and she leaned back against him. "Go on," Max said, opening the door wider. "What about Sagesse, Philippe?"

"I heard that he was found last night in the Vieux Carré near Rampart Street. . . . Etienne Sagesse has been murdered."

CHAPTER

15

The full weight of the suspicions cast on Max was revealed by the visit of Jean-Claude Gervais, the captain of the *gens d'armes*. Gervais, the highest-ranking police official in New Orleans, would not have come himself unless the situation was extremely grave.

Captain Gervais fervently wished to be in anyone's shoes other than his own. He had not forgotten the favor Maximilien Vallerand had done him not long ago, putting a few words in the right ears to ensure the *gens d'armes* were provided with new arms and equipment. And now he was repaying the man by intruding on his privacy and questioning him in regard to murder. Suppressing his discomfort, Gervais assumed an impassive expression as he was welcomed into the Vallerand home.

"Monsieur Vallerand," he began, standing ramrod-straight as Max closed the library door to afford them privacy. "The reason I am here —"

"I know why you're here, Captain." Vallerand walked to a set of crystal decanters and held one up with an inquiring glance.

"*Non, merci,*" Gervais said, although he sorely desired a drink.

Vallerand shrugged and poured himself a brandy. "Sit down, if you wish. I expect this might take a while."

"Monsieur Vallerand," Gervais said, lowering his bulky frame into a deep leather chair, "I must begin by saying this is not an official —"

"I know that you have many questions, Captain. To save time, let us both be direct." Vallerand smiled slightly. "We'll save small talk for a more pleasant occasion, *oui?*"

Gervais nodded. "Is it true, monsieur, that you threatened Etienne Sagesse's life the night before last, on the premises of the Leseur plantation?"

Vallerand nodded. "Sagesse had just insulted my wife. Naturally I wanted to beat him to a pulp. But a fight was prevented by both our families. And I was persuaded not to challenge him to a duel because of his condition."

"Yes. I have been told that he drank." Only a Creole would understand the delicate significance Gervais placed on the last two words. The phrase was an indictment of his masculinity, honor, and character. It was unpardonable for a Creole to drink more liquor than he was able to hold.

Gervais clasped his hands loosely, resting

them on his plump thigh. "Monsieur, your wife and Monsieur Sagesse were at one time betrothed, were they not?"

Vallerand's sable eyes narrowed. "They were."

"The Sagesse family claims that you stole her from Etienne. How exactly was that accomplished?"

Vallerand was about to reply when there came a gentle knock, and the door was pushed open a crack.

"*Oui?*" Vallerand said abruptly.

Gervais heard a woman's quiet murmur. "I would like to listen, *mon mari*, if it would not displease you. I promise not to interfere."

Vallerand sent a questioning glance to Gervais. "If the captain has no objections. Captain Gervais, my wife, Lysette Vallerand."

Gervais bowed politely, discovering that the young Madame Vallerand was a striking woman, with her exotic red hair and vivid blue eyes. She possessed a wholesome quality, but at the same time she summoned images of rolling naked among fresh white bed linens . . . and her soft, carnal mouth brought startlingly lurid thoughts to mind. Even with her imposing husband in the room, Gervais felt his face begin to glow, and he was relieved to resume his seat in the leather chair.

"Captain?" Vallerand prompted.

Gervais started. "Monsieur . . . the questions I must ask may be distressing to Madame Vallerand."

"We may be frank in front of my wife," Vallerand said, sitting beside his wife.

"Ah, yes. The, ah, theft of Etienne Sagesse's betrothed."

"*Theft?*" Madame Vallerand repeated incredulously. "I would hardly call it that. When I first arrived in New Orleans, I left the Sagesse home of my own accord — because of Monsieur Sagesse's ungentlemanly behavior toward me. At the invitation of Maximilien's mother, I came to stay here — she was an acquaintance of my mother's, you see — and then I took ill. During my convalescence, I fell in love with Maximilien and accepted his offer of marriage. I was not stolen from anyone. It is very simple, *voyez-vous?*"

"Indeed," Gervais muttered. "Monsieur Vallerand, you dueled with Monsieur Sagesse over this matter, did you not?"

"Yes."

"Would you say it deepened the enmity that already existed between you?"

"No," Vallerand said shortly. "In fact, I ended the duel prematurely."

"Why?"

"I pitied him. Any man who was there will concur that I could have easily killed him on the spot, in legitimate defense of my honor. But I have finally reached the age, Captain, when a man desires a measure of peace. I even dared to hope that the feud between the Sagesses and Vallerands might come to an end." His brows quirked as he saw that even his wife was looking at him skeptically. "It's true," he said mildly.

"Even with the knowledge of Sagesse's relationship with your first wife?" the captain asked.

"Hatred is a draining emotion," Vallerand replied. "It leaves room for little else." He glanced at his wife with a slight smile. "I finally began to relinquish it when I realized how much richer life could be without it." His attention swerved back to the captain. "Not that I forgave Sagesse, you understand. His betrayal struck deep, and I have as much pride as any man. But I became tired of nursing the old bitterness, and I wished to put the past behind me."

"But Sagesse made that impossible?"

"I wouldn't say that. There was virtually no communication between us after the duel."

Captain Gervais asked several more questions about the affair between Corinne and Etienne, and then he changed tack. "Monsieur Vallerand, you were seen by two witnesses in the Vieux Carré last night. Your purpose there?"

Vallerand's expression became guarded, and he hesitated before replying.

"I was visiting my former *placée*."

Both Lysette and Captain Gervais flushed. *Mariame?* Lysette thought wildly. What in God's name had he been doing with Mariame? She blinked as she realized Captain Gervais was speaking to her. "Madame Vallerand, if you wish to leave the room —"

"No, I'll stay," she said tonelessly.

Clearly dismayed, Gervais resumed the questioning. "Your mistress?" he asked Max.

"Yes, for several years."

Lysette only half listened to the rest of the interview. Her mind buzzed with distasteful possibilities. Either Max had lied to her and was still keeping Mariame as a mistress, or he was lying to Captain Gervais in order to cover up the true reason he had been in the Vieux Carré.

Finally Captain Gervais stood up to indicate the questioning was over. "Monsieur Vallerand," he said solemnly, "I feel obligated to bring certain facts to your attention — unofficially, of course."

Max inclined his head, his gaze fastened alertly on the captain's face.

"It is important for the people of New Orleans to feel the law is being executed as competently now as it was before the American possession," Gervais said. "The public has little faith in any of the institutions of government — including, I regret to say, my

400

own force. Etienne Sagesse was of an old and recognized family, and his death is considered a great loss. People demand quick retribution for such a crime. Moreover, a fair trial cannot be guaranteed to anyone. The court system is in turmoil. One would be a fool to hang his life on the hopes of fairness and justice."

Max nodded slowly.

"Especially," Gervais added, "when several prominent men in the community have come forth to denounce you. One of these men is the judge of the County Court. They are calling for your arrest. It is more than simple saber-rattling, monsieur."

"Do any of these men, by chance, belong to the Mexican Association?" Max asked.

"Most of them, I believe," Gervais replied, a bit surprised by the question.

Burr's friends, Lysette realized in outrage. The associates of Aaron Burr were calling for his arrest, most likely having promised Burr they would do what they could to take revenge on Max for his disdain of their cause. There could be no better opportunity than this.

"I am giving you time to make plans, monsieur." Gervais looked at Max squarely. "Because I shall be forced to arrest you quite soon." He paused. "Have you any questions for me, monsieur?"

"Just one," Max said tersely. "How was Monsieur Sagesse murdered?"

"He was strangled," Gervais replied. "It

takes great strength, monsieur, to kill a man of Sagesse's size in such a manner." He looked pointedly at Max's deeply muscled chest and shoulders. "Not many men could have accomplished that."

Lysette could not make a sound as Max guided the captain to the front door. She pressed her fists against her stomach. She felt as if she were in a nightmare, and she longed to wake up from it.

A minute that seemed like a year went by, and then Max returned to her. He dropped to one knee beside the chair, taking both her cold fists in his warm hand. "Sweet," he murmured. "Look at me."

She gave him a fixed, frantic stare.

"I did see Mariame last night," Max said. "I had to make arrangements for her son — by another man — to flee the territory. He's of mixed blood, and last week he was discovered having an affair with a white woman. His life is in jeopardy. You may have heard what they do to . . . well, we won't go into that. A few days ago Mariame sent me a message asking for help. Knowing what the boy means to her, I could not refuse."

Lysette had barely listened to the explanation. "What Captain Gervais said about allowing time to make plans . . . he has given us time to get away. He meant escape, didn't he?"

"Yes." Max sighed. "That is what he meant."

"We must be gone by tonight, then. It won't take long for me to pack. Mexico? No, France —"

"We're not going anywhere," he said gently.

Lysette gripped his coat lapels. "Yes, we are! I don't care where we live, as long as I can be with you. If you stay, they'll —" Her voice cracked. "I believe what Captain Gervais said, Max."

"I did not kill Etienne Sagesse."

"I know that. But we will never be able to prove it, and even if we could, no one would listen. The American authorities want to show their power over the Creoles, and to take down a man of your position would make them feel as if they were finally in control of the city. We *have* to go. They *will* convict you. Don't you understand? If anything happens to you, Max . . ."

"We're not going to run. That's no life for you, or me."

"No!" she said, jerking away as he tried to comfort her. "No, don't say anything else!" Rapidly she gained control of herself. "I am going upstairs to pack for both of us and the boys. Tell Noeline to have the trunks brought out. No, no, I will tell her." She jumped back as he reached out for her. "Don't touch me!"

"We're staying, Lysette," he said quietly.

She steadied her quivering chin, and rapidly considered ways to force him to go. "*I* am leaving for France tonight, and you can either stay and be hanged with your principles, or go with your family and be happy. It shouldn't take you long to choose!"

Lysette began to storm out of the room, and then, lightning-swift, reappeared at the doorway. "And while you are considering your options," she added, "you might think about the fact that by now I am very likely pregnant. Our child will need a father! And if *that* doesn't perturb you . . ." Her eyes slitted. "Then I swear by all the saints that if you stay here to be hanged, I'll *still* go to France, and find someone else to marry! Does *that* motivate you to come with me?"

As she left and hurried upstairs, Max sat heavily in his chair. Despite his grim worry, he couldn't suppress a rueful grin. He could search the world over and never find a woman who understood him half so well. In a few concise sentences, Lysette had managed to hit him in every place he was vulnerable.

The house was still as a tomb, except for the sounds of Lysette's hasty packing. Heavily veiled and grief-stricken, Irénée had taken Noeline with her to the cathedral, where she spent several hours taking counsel from an old, familiar priest, and praying brokenly for forgiveness for her son. She had not been able to speak to Max, or even look at him, as she left the plantation.

Of course, Max reflected, it had not crossed Irénée's mind that he might *not* have killed Etienne Sagesse. For years she had lived with the belief that he had ended Corinne's life. He wondered bleakly how Irénée could still love a son she thought to be a cold-blooded killer.

Prowling in and around the house until early evening, Max pondered the idea of escape and rejected it. Long ago he had acquired holdings in Europe, in case his property in Louisiana was ever jeopardized. If forced to flee, he had the means to keep himself and Lysette in comfortable style for the rest of their lives. But the years of exile, being haunted by his reputation, always looking over his shoulder in fear of retribution from the Sagesses or their kin . . . he and Lysette would never be happy. And the vendetta the Sagesses would declare would be extended to his children. His sons' lives would be in danger, until someone paid for the crime Max was accused of. He had to stay and fight to prove his innocence.

Halting at the foot of the double staircase, he glanced at the second floor. Philippe had closeted himself in his room. After returning home and being told about Max's imminent arrest, Justin had left on some mysterious errand. A maid scurried by Max and went up the stairs carrying a leather valise, while

Lysette urged her to hurry. Max shook his head ruefully. No one could fault the woman he had wed for lack of spirit. He set his foot on the first step, intending to go up and put a stop to the useless packing.

He stopped at the explosive sound behind him, as Justin threw open the front door and burst into the house like a madman.

"Father!" he shouted. "Fath—" The boy skidded to a halt in front of Max, all tense, trembling energy. The drizzling mist from outside had soaked into his clothes and hair, and he stood there dripping on the rug.

Automatically Max reached out to steady him. "Justin, where have you —"

"F-following . . ." Justin stammered, clutching at Max's arms, "Following U-uncle Bernard." He tugged impatiently. "He is in town, drinking and gaming at La Sirène."

Max was hardly surprised. "He has his own ways of dealing with family misfortune, *mon fils*. God knows he's had to suffer through enough of it. Let him be. Now —"

"No, *no!*" Justin pulled at him tenaciously. "You have to talk to him."

"Why?"

"There are some things you must ask Bernard."

"Such as?"

"Ask him why he resents Lysette so much. And why he was willing to let her fall from the attic. Ask him why he stood on the gallery, watching her with Sagesse, and didn't try to help her! Ask him where *he* was last night!"

"Justin," Max said impatiently, "it is obvious that, for whatever reason, you and Bernard have quarreled. But right now there are more important —"

"No, nothing is this important!" Justin clung to him obstinately. "Ask him how he felt about my mother! And then ask what Etienne knew that made him so dangerous to Bernard!"

Max shook the boy roughly, startling him into silence. "No. *Stop it!*"

Justin closed his mouth.

"I understand that you want to help." Max's hands bit into the boy's wiry arms. "You don't want me to be blamed for the murder. But that gives you no license to cast accusations at others, especially members of your own family. You may not be fond of Bernard, but —"

"Come with me," Justin begged. "Talk to Bernard. If you do, you'll see what I'm trying to tell you. It is the only thing I will ever ask of you. Damn you, don't try to claim you haven't the time! What else were you planning to do tonight? Wait to be arrested?"

Max studied him, his face implacable, while Justin held his breath. Then Max nodded slightly. "All right."

Justin threw his arms around his father and

buried his head against his chest, then jumped away abruptly. "I don't want to come across any of the Sagesses. We must avoid the main road —"

"We'll have to use it," Max said. "By now the other routes have turned to mud." He strode to the door, while Justin scampered after him.

Renée Sagesse Dubois sat alone in the parlor with the sealed letter in her lap, staring at it with red-rimmed eyes. It was addressed to Maximilien Vallerand. She remembered watching Etienne write it just before the duel. Etienne had sealed it himself, adamantly refusing to tell her the contents. He had told her to give the letter to Maximilien, if Vallerand proved the victor.

Numbly Renée wondered why Vallerand had spared Etienne's life then, why he had ended the duel without real bloodshed. Etienne had mentioned it more than once in the months afterward, seeming to have even greater contempt for Maximilien.

Since the duel, Renée had tried to return the letter to Etienne. He insisted each time that it remain in her possession, with the same instructions. Upon his death, he wanted her to place the letter in Maximilien's hands.

But she could not. In spite of the promise she had made, Renée could not face the man who had killed her brother. "I am sorry,

Etienne," she whispered. "I cannot do it." Beginning to cry, she knocked the letter to the floor and hunched over in grief.

After a long spasm of sobbing, Renée regained her composure. Her eyes were drawn again to the letter. What could Etienne have written? What were his true feelings for the man who had been his friend, enemy, and ultimately his murderer? Leaning over, Renée snatched the letter up and broke the scarlet wax seal.

She began to read, using her fingers to wipe the stream of tears from her cheeks. The first page was too cryptic to understand. Frowning, she turned to the second. "Oh, no," she murmured, the letter trembling in her hand. "Etienne . . . how can this be?"

While Max rode along the mist-shrouded road with his son, he wondered grimly what madness had possessed him to head to town with Justin. He would gain nothing by talking to Bernard, who was probably too deep in his cups by now to form a complete sentence.

Why was Justin so determined to involve Bernard in this unholy mess? Max had to grit his teeth to keep from telling his son that he was going to turn back. But as Justin had pointed out, the boy had never asked for anything from him.

Justin increased their pace until the horses'

hooves were slogging a desperate canter through the mud. They came to a curve and slowed, seeing four riders a short distance ahead. The riders fanned out instantly, forming a half circle as they approached the pair.

Max recognized Severin Dubois, Etienne's two brothers, and a Sagesse cousin. It wasn't difficult to figure out their purpose — they had formed a lynching party to avenge the death of one of their own. Max's hand flew instinctively to his side. He swore under his breath, realizing that he had left his brace of pistols at home.

Justin cut his horse sharply to the right, preparing to flee.

"No, Justin," Max said hoarsely. The riders were too close; it was useless to run. Either not hearing him or ignoring the command, the boy continued on his reckless path. One of the Sagesses held his rifle by the barrel and used the heavy maplewood stock as a club.

A hoarse shout was torn from Max's throat, and he was seized with panic. "Damn you," he raged at the Sagesses, jumping from his horse. Running through the mud, he managed to reach his son in time to catch his limp form as it slid from the saddle.

The horses stamped and shuffled. Severin Dubois watched calmly as Max lowered his son to the ground. "Justice is uncertain these days," Dubois remarked. "We felt it best to take matters into our own hands."

Cradling his son's long body, Max turned Justin's head and smoothed back the damp black hair to view the injury. He shook with violent anger as he saw the gash and the bruise on his son's temple. The boy groaned and stirred, his lashes fluttering.

"I'm sorry," Max whispered, kissing his pale cheek. "*Je t'aime,* Justin. You'll be all right. Don't move, *mon fils.*" He stripped off his cloak and wrapped it protectively around the boy.

"He won't be harmed any further," Severin said. "Unless, of course, you try to make things difficult."

Max stared at Dubois with cold hatred, and he gently lowered Justin to the ground. Standing, he did not resist as one of the Sagesses began to bind his wrists.

Etienne Sagesse's sister was the last person Lysette had expected would call that evening. Still, she welcomed her with irreproachable politeness. She was sorry for Renée's loss, even though she had no liking for the woman.

"Where is Monsieur Vallerand?" Renée demanded without preamble. Lysette could not help staring in amazement. From what she remembered during her brief stay with the

Sagesses so many months ago, Etienne's sister had possessed an icy composure that had been unshakable. At the moment she seemed to be an entirely different woman, flushed and trembling with emotion. "I must speak to your husband," Renée said rapidly, refusing to go into the parlor. *"Immédiatement."*

"I am afraid he is not here," Lysette said.

"Where is he? When will he return?"

Lysette gave the older woman an assessing glance, wondering if the Sagesses had sent her for some malicious purpose. "I do not know," she said truthfully.

"I have something for him. Something from my brother."

"What is it?" Lysette did not bother to hide her mistrust.

"A letter. Etienne wished it to be given to Monsieur Vallerand when he died."

Lysette nodded coolly. No doubt the letter was some last bit of insulting nonsense. Only Etienne would find a way to taunt Max from the grave. "If you wish to leave it with me, I will see that my husband receives it."

"You do not understand. It tells everything, all about the past . . . the affair . . . *everything.*"

Lysette's eyes widened. "Let me see it." She hastily snatched it from the other woman's hands before it could be offered. Turning away, she read the scrawling lines

412

rapidly, a few of them seeming to leap from the page.

> What a blind fool love makes of you, Max. I understand you well enough to know you would rather shoulder the blame for a crime you did not commit than believe your own brother was capable of such betrayal.
>   . . . I gave you what you wished . . . I watched you wallow in self-delusion, while I . . .

Lysette broke off and looked at Renée. "Bernard?" she said wildly.

Renée regarded her with reluctant pity. "So the letter claims. After Corinne's affair with Etienne ended, she began a liaison with Bernard. She admitted as much to Etienne, and also told him of her plans to expose her affair with Bernard, if Bernard did not agree to run away with her."

Lysette scanned the rest of the letter frantically.

>   . . . there is no doubt that Bernard found the idea of doing away with Corinne much more appealing than enduring her companionship in a lifetime of exile. Given the same choice, I might have strangled the bitch myself. But making it appear as though the cuckolded husband

had done the deed . . . that was a master touch worthy only of a Vallerand.

"Etienne writes that your husband was a fool for not considering the possibility of an affair between Corinne and Bernard," Renée said. "Etienne scorned Maximilien for ignoring what he could have seen, if he'd only cared to look."

"But Max believed that Bernard was very much in love with someone else."

"Yes, an American girl."

"Bernard made her pregnant, and she ran away — oh, what was her name —"

"Ryla Curran," Renée interrupted. "In the letter Etienne makes a different claim. Bernard was interested in the girl, but *never* had an affair with her."

"How did Etienne know?"

"Because it was Etienne, not Bernard, who seduced her." Renée smiled bitterly. "Unfortunately she wasn't the first young girl Etienne ruined — or the last. But it served Bernard's purpose to pretend that he had been Ryla's lover — people were less likely to suspect the true nature of his relationship with Corinne."

Lysette went cold, wondering what it would do to Max to discover what his brother had done. Her mind reeled. "Bernard killed Etienne," she said.

"I believe so. Of course, there is no proof, only —"

"He did!" Lysette insisted. "Bernard must have been convinced the night of the Leseur ball that Etienne would not keep his silence much longer, not with his drinking, and . . . yes, Bernard *must* have killed him! Only, for this second murder, Max will pay in full measure."

"Do not panic," Renée said. "There is time. All that is necessary is to show the letter to the authorities when they come for your husband." Her lips thinned. "Unless Maximilien has already fled the territory. Has he?"

Lysette responded with a scathing glance.

Renée began to ask something else when they were distracted by a sudden intrusion.

"Max?" Lysette asked, whirling around. "Where —" The words died away on her lips.

Justin was leaning against the doorframe, gasping and panting, having run for miles without stopping. His face was bluish white under its tan, and his forehead was bruised and bloody. Every inch of him was soaked and spattered with mud. "I need help. Where is Alexandre?"

"With Henriette and the Clements," she answered automatically. "Justin, what —"

The boy interrupted her with a hoarse call toward the stairs. "Philippe! Philippe, come here!"

Philippe appeared at the top of the stairs, took one look at his brother, and began to hurry down. Justin glanced beyond Lysette to Renée Dubois. "How neighborly of you," he said, his mouth spasming with hatred. "Keeping my stepmother company while your husband and your brothers butcher my . . ." Dizziness overtook him, and he sagged against the doorway, holding his head. "My father," he finished with a gasp, and reached out to Lysette as she went to support him. He held her tightly, oblivious to the mud on his clothes and hands. "They took him," he gasped, struggling to stay conscious. "I don't know where. They'll kill him. Oh, God, they might have already."

The small group led Max's horse off the main road and through mud-bogged side avenues. The Sagesses were determined to punish the man they were certain had murdered Etienne. In this territory, where power seemed to change hands almost monthly, the definitions of right and wrong were variable. In their minds the only certain means a man had of extracting justice was to rely on his own family.

Hands bound behind him, Max waited tensely while they took his horse's reins and rode to a remote corner of the Sagesse plantation, out among fields left to lie fallow for the season. When they stopped near a grove of trees and began to dismount, Max took action, kicking his horse into a sudden leap

416

sideways, hoping the reins might be yanked out of Severin Dubois' grasp.

Dubois took the end of the rope binding Max's wrists and pulled, toppling him to the ground. Max landed on his side with a grunt of pain. There was no laughter or jeering at the ignominious descent. This was a serious business, and the Sagesses were acting not out of petty vengeance but moral obligation.

Although he knew it was hopeless, Max struggled as he was lifted to his feet. The first strike came with blinding force, whipping his head back and sending a burst of pain through his skull. Before he could draw breath, he was battered with a torrent of blows that cracked his ribs and drove the breath from his lungs. His head was snapped to the side, and he felt his body begin to sag. Dark and light swirled around him, and all sound dissolved in a roar.

Renée looked blank with surprise. "You say my husband has taken him?" she asked. "Severin and —"

"Yes!" Justin snarled at her. "Your entire accursed family!"

"How long ago?"

"I don't know. Half an hour, perhaps."

Renée came forward, lightly touching Lysette's shoulder. "I didn't know about this."

"Like hell you didn't," Justin muttered.

She returned his glare. "Your insolence won't help anyone, little man." She returned her gaze to Lysette. "I might know where they have taken him, but I am not certain. My carriage is just outside."

"Why would you want to help me find him?" Lysette asked woodenly, barely taking notice of Philippe as he joined them.

"It was wrong of Etienne to keep silent all those years, when he knew that Maximilien was innocent. No one can make reparation for what Etienne has done, and no one —"

"Perhaps," Justin interrupted icily, "we could make speeches later, and try to find my father before your family stretches his neck." Grunting with pain, he pushed open the front door and gestured to the carriage.

Philippe escorted Lysette outside, and Justin took Renée's elbow in a hard grasp. She glared at him. "You are ruining my gown with your dirty hand, boy!"

Justin did not let go of her, using her to maintain his precarious balance. "Tell me where we're going and why you think my father is there," he said as they went down the front steps. "You're probably leading us on a merry chase to keep us from finding him."

"I have already explained," Renée said haughtily. "And we are going to a field on the northwest corner of my plantation, a private and secluded place." A trace of malice entered her voice. "With trees aplenty for hanging. Severin killed a man there once before. I know, because I followed him."

"And the man's offense?"

They stopped at the door of the carriage. Renée shoved his hand away from her elbow. They faced each other, and she decided to shock the arrogant boy into silence. "Severin suspected him of being my lover," she said. Pleased with her own boldness, she waited for a youthful blush that never came.

"Was he?" Justin's dark eyes were far too adult for a boy his age.

"Yes," she said, hoping to shock him.

His gaze slid over her with a purely sexual speculation. "You must be good, to make a man risk his life for it."

To her annoyance, Renée was the one who blushed as she climbed hastily into the carriage.

The Sagesses had gathered underneath an ancient oak tree and wrapped a rope around the thickest limb.

"We'll wait until he comes to," Severin Dubois said, and the men grunted as they lifted Max's slumping body onto the saddle of the fidgeting black stallion. Sensitive and fiery-natured, the horse could not tolerate the nearness of anyone other than his master. Max was the only one who could ride him.

Tomas Sagesse, Etienne's youngest brother,

slipped the noose around the unconscious man's neck, tightened it, and gingerly took hold of the stallion's reins. "I will not be able to stay him for long."

"You must. I want Maximilien to be awake," Severin replied. "I want him to know."

When the horse was allowed to walk away, Vallerand's body would come to dangle in midair. His neck would not be broken. He would hang there with his windpipe closed, choking and strangling. Severin wandered closer to the agitated horse and stared into Vallerand's bloodied face. "Open your eyes. Let's have done with this!"

At the sound of the unfamiliar voice, the horse sidestepped, and the noose tightened. Vallerand stirred, his eyes half opening. His head lifted from the stallion's withers, easing the constricting pressure of the rope. Severin had expected to see anger, resentment, pleading in his face, but the dark eyes were emotionless.

Painstakingly, Vallerand parted his swollen lips. His voice was a mere scratch of sound. "Lysette . . ."

Severin frowned. "I shouldn't worry about your wife, Vallerand. I suspect she'll rejoice at being rid of such a cold-blooded bastard as you." He motioned for Tomas to release the horse's reins. "Now, while he's still awake."

All of a sudden, they heard a woman's desperate cry. *"Nooo!"*

From a distance they saw one of the Sagesse carriages, its wheels mired in mud, and a woman stumbling across the field toward them. Tomas raised his hand to slap the horse's hindquarters, but Severin stopped him with a curt command. He had just seen Renée emerge from the carriage. Stormy anger appeared on his face as he watched his wife and Vallerand's sons follow.

Lysette fell and picked herself up quickly, hurrying across the soft, sinking earth. Terror seized her as she saw that no one was holding the reins of the horse. There was a noose around Max's neck, secured to the tree limb above him. He was badly beaten, and his eyes were closed. Ripping her gaze from the sight, she spoke to Severin Dubois in a shaking voice. "You've made a mistake." She held out the letter to him. "Look at this — please — don't do anything until you read it."

Tentatively Tomas reached for the reins of the horse, but the stallion flinched, walleyed, ready to explode with movement. Lysette thrust the letter at Severin and stared at the horse, mesmerized, realizing that her husband's life was hanging by a fragile thread. A thousand prayers flashed through her mind. The paper rustled as Severin turned a page, and the stallion tossed his head impatiently. Max no longer seemed conscious, and she expected him to slide from the horse's back at any moment.

Suddenly she was aware of Justin's quiet voice behind her. "I'll cut the rope. Don't move."

The boy's thin, dark form moved behind the horse to the oak tree. He began to climb, a knife held between his teeth.

"Stop, boy," Severin Dubois said, pulling a flintlock pistol from his breeches. Justin continued shimmying up the tree trunk as if he hadn't heard. "Boy —" Dubois said again, and Lysette interrupted.

"Put away the pistol, Monsieur Dubois. You know that my husband is not guilty."

"This letter proves nothing."

"You must believe it," Lysette said, staring at Max's slumped form. "It is written in your own brother's hand." She had never thought she would feel such agony in her life. Everything she held dear, her only chance at happiness, was poised precariously before her.

"A hand that was none too steady, by the look of it," came Severin's reply. "Etienne was drunk when he wrote this. Why should I accept a word of it?"

Renée confronted him. "Stop tormenting her, Severin! For once be man enough to admit that you are wrong."

A breeze caught the folds of Lysette's cloak

and caused it to flap. The movement was enough to make the stallion jerk and run. Lysette heard a hoarse scream — her own — as she saw her husband's body fall from the saddle with nightmarish slowness.

But the rope was no longer tethered. Justin had sawed through it.

Max's body hit the soft earth and was still. A chilling breeze ruffled his black hair. Lysette reached him at once, falling to her knees beside him with a sob of terror.

CHAPTER
16

After glancing at the prone form on the ground, Severin turned back to Renée. "And if this letter is true, Renée?" he asked with a sneer. "What if Bernard was indeed the one who killed Corinne? That still doesn't change the fact that Maximilien murdered your brother because Etienne could not leave his pretty little wife alone."

"Why would Maximilien have resorted to murder if he desired Etienne's death?" Renée demanded. "Etienne gave him every opportunity to do it honorably! Maximilien could have killed him at the duel — but he did not. He could have demanded satisfaction at the Leseur ball and ended it with a sword right then, and no one would have thought the worse of him. But he did not. Severin, be reasonable for once!"

After prying the rope from his neck, Lysette pillowed Max's head and shoulders in her lap. His shirt was in tatters, his clothes wet and muddy. She searched beneath his jaw and found the weak rhythm of his heartbeat.

"You're safe now," she whispered, using a fold of her gown to wipe the blood from his face. There was an annoying trickle of hot liquid over her cheeks, and she wiped at it impatiently but the salty tears continued to leak from her eyes. Max groaned faintly, and she reassured him with a murmur. "I am here, *bien-aimé*."

His shaking fingers clenched in her velvet skirt. Instinctively he strove to bury himself deeper against her warm body. "Lysette . . ." He tried to roll to his side, then recoiled in shock and pain.

"No, no, be still," Lysette said, cuddling his head against her breasts.

"I love you," he whispered.

"Yes, I know, *ma cher*. I love you, too." She glanced at Justin, who was standing just a few feet away, seeming dazed. Her expression hardened with determination. "Justin, tell Monsieur Dubois that we are taking your father home now."

Justin nodded shortly and went to Dubois, who was still quarreling with his wife.

"What purpose do you have for defending him?" Dubois demanded, his face reddening.

Renée discarded her aggressive posture. "I am not defending him," she said, her voice noticeably softer. "It is just that I desire the *real* murderer of my brother to be punished. Won't you try to find Bernard? *There* is your justice, if you are able to pry the truth out of him."

"Perhaps we will," Severin said harshly, and raised his voice for all to hear. "Where *is* Bernard?"

No one answered. Lysette thought quickly, wondering what was best for Max's sake. If there were only her own desires to consider, she would encourage them to find Bernard and do as they pleased with him, as long as she never had to see his loathsome face again. But Bernard was Max's brother, and it was Max's right to decide how to handle him.

"Bernard is at home," Lysette said coolly. "He accompanied his mother to church today."

Justin and Philippe glanced at her discreetly, knowing that she was lying. "She is right," Justin said. "You'd better go now, if you hope to find him."

Lysette continued to stare at Severin Dubois. "Monsieur, I will keep the letter, if you please. It is the only thing that will prevent Captain Gervais from arresting my husband."

"First I must know," Severin replied, "what you intend to tell Gervais about what happened today."

In other words, she could have the letter if she gave her word she would not tell Gervais or his lieutenants how the Sagesses had brutally beaten her husband. Lysette swallowed back her impotent fury, thinking that the authorities would do nothing in any case. But her hatred of Dubois and the Sagesses would last the rest of her life, and she promised herself that eventually they would be paid in full for their actions. She did not have to look at Justin to know that he was thinking the same. "We'll keep our silence in exchange for the letter," she said. "Now I must take my husband home quickly, or you may yet have succeeded in killing him."

"Of course," Severin said, his brusqueness concealing his discomfort. He was not a soft-hearted man, nor was he capable of real contrition. But something about the way Vallerand's young wife stared at him elicited an unwanted feeling of shame.

"She is quite young to have such a sharp tongue," Dubois muttered to Renée sotto voce, turning away and gesturing the Sagesse brothers to the mired carriage. "I see why they call her *la mariée du diable.*"

"She is a strong girl," Renée replied, a shadow of melancholy crossing her face. "I wish she had been Etienne's — she might have been able to change him."

The Sagesses and their brother-in-law rode away toward the road leading to the Vallerand plantation. Renée's carriage moved along the side of the field and came to a stop nearby, and she opened the doors herself, giving rapid orders to the coachman.

Philippe came to crouch by Lysette. "I don't understand," he said. "You know that

Bernard is at La Sirène. Why did you tell them he was at home?"

"To allow us time," Lysette replied, using her cloak to shield Max's face from the rain.

"Time for what?" Philippe asked.

"To warn Bernard before they find him."

"No," Philippe said in outrage. "Why should Bernard be warned? Why shouldn't we allow the Sagesses to have him?"

"Because your father would not want that. Now let us move him to the carriage."

Despite the twins' lankiness, they were strong boys, and they managed to carry their father's unconscious form to the carriage. He did not make a sound, and Lysette wondered with growing dread how badly he was hurt.

After Max was safely inside, Justin took Lysette's arm and drew her a short distance away. His face was lined with exhaustion, but his expression was hard and sober. "I'll go to Bernard," he said quietly. "What should I say to him?"

"Tell him . . ." Lysette paused. "Tell him that the Sagesses are looking for him. For tonight, at least, I believe he can safely hide in the new warehouse Max built on the riverfront." She frowned. "How will you reach town?"

Justin nodded back in the direction of the black stallion, which had bolted only a short distance away and was grazing warily underneath a tree. "I'll take Father's horse."

"You can't," Lysette protested, knowing how volatile the stallion was.

"I can," Justin said flatly.

Lysette knew that he would not make the claim unless he was certain. She would not give her consent, however, until one point was made. "I am placing my trust in you," she said. "That you will do as you say, and not allow your own temper to best you. Give the message to Bernard and leave. No accusations, no arguments. I am trusting you not to lift your hand against him, Justin. Will that be too difficult for you?"

His blue eyes did not move from hers. "No." He took her slender hand, lifted it to his lips, and pressed the back of it against his cheek. "Take care of him," he said huskily, and walked her back to the carriage.

La Sirène was filled with all the noise, music, and good-natured brawling of any slightly disreputable drinking establishment on the waterfront. On any other occasion, Justin would have relished the opportunity to visit the place. It was the kind of tavern he liked, making no pretense at sophistication, yet discriminating enough that the vulgar, blustering Kaintocks from upriver were not allowed.

Entering the tavern, Justin pushed through the crowd to the gaming rooms in the back. He located his uncle easily. Bernard was sitting at a table with a group of friends, idly rearranging a hand of cards.

"Bernard," Justin interrupted, "I have a message for you."

Bernard looked up in surprise. "Justin? *Bon Dieu* — you are a mess. You've been fighting again." His dark eyes snapped with dislike. "Don't bother me here, boy."

"The message is from Lysette." Justin smiled coolly as he saw that the other gentlemen at the table were beginning to lend their attention to the exchange. "Would you like to hear it in private, or should I say it in front of everyone?"

"Insolent whelp." Bernard threw his cards down on the table and stood up, yanking Justin to the corner. "Now tell me, and then be gone with you."

Justin shook off his hand and stared at his uncle with hot blue eyes. "It would have been three murders," he murmured. "Because of you, they nearly killed Father this evening."

Bernard's face went blank. "What nonsense is this?"

"Lysette's message," Justin said, "is that the Sagesses know you killed Etienne. They are looking for you. If you value your life, you'd better find a way to disappear. Lysette suggests that you hide at the new warehouse on the quay."

Bernard did not react, except for a violent twitch at the corner of his mouth. "It's a lie," he said softly. "It's a bluff to make me admit to something I —"

"Perhaps it is," Justin replied. "Why don't you stay and find out? I think you should." He smiled thinly. "Really."

Bernard stared at the boy in incredulous fury. He lifted his hands as if he would throttle Justin.

Justin did not move. "Don't try it," he said softly. "I'm neither a drunkard nor a helpless woman — not your favored sort of victim at all."

"I regret nothing," Bernard said hoarsely. "The world is better for being rid of Sagesse . . . and your whore of a mother."

Justin flinched. Silently he watched as his uncle staggered from the room.

After Max had been attended to by the doctor, Noeline satisfied herself by adding yet more bandages and salves of her own, and then hung an array of charms over the doorway. Lysette did not dare remove them, having been assured by Noeline that they were very powerful.

To Lysette's relief, Max finally regained consciousness, his bruised eyes slitting open. "What happened?" he demanded, cursing in pain as he held a hand to his battered ribs.

Lysette hurried to the bedside with a glass of water. Gently she lifted his head and helped him to drink. She explained all that had occurred after his near-hanging, and showed him the letter that had saved his life. "Renée Dubois brought this earlier today. Etienne told her it was to be given to you upon his death."

"Read it to me," he said hoarsely, setting down the glass.

Lysette read the letter without inflection, trying to keep her voice steady. When she finished the first page and came to the first mention of Bernard, she did not look at Max's face, but sensed the torrent of outrage, fear, and fury that swept over him.

"No," he croaked.

She continued to read. Before she reached the end of the letter, Max had taken it from her and crushed it in his fist.

"Sagesse was a lying drunkard."

"Max, I know that you don't want to believe it, but —"

"But *you* do," he sneered. "It makes things much easier, doesn't it? Pin the blame on Bernard — someone you have no great liking for in the first place — and then the mystery of what happened ten years ago is over. Never mind that Sagesse had no more honor than a gutter rat. It's obvious you're perfectly satisfied with a drunken bastard's explanation of it all. But it didn't happen that way, damn you!"

"And why are you so certain of that? Simply because Bernard is your brother?"

"Damn you," Max repeated harshly. "Where is Bernard now?"

Understanding his anger, and the anguish behind it, Lysette replied without heat. "It's possible Bernard is hiding in the new warehouse on the waterfront. He knows the Sagesses are looking for him. He may already be on his way out of the territory."

Max pushed back the bedclothes and tried to move his legs over the edge of the mattress.

"Max, what are you doing?" Lysette exclaimed. "You are not well enough to go anywhere, you stubborn ox! *Nom de Dieu,* you were beaten within an inch of your life today."

He gasped in agony, clutching his ribs. "Help me get dressed."

"Absolutely not!"

"I have to see him."

"Why? You know he'll deny everything!"

"I'll know when I see him if it's true or not."

"I won't let you kill yourself, Max!" Filled with determination, Lysette pushed him back down as hard as she could. Although her weight was a fraction of his, his injuries had weakened him considerably. Groaning, Max collapsed to the pillow, briefly losing consciousness.

Alerted by the commotion, Noeline appeared at her side. "Madame?"

Lysette was grateful for the housekeeper's competent presence. "Sedate him, Noeline, before he is able to rise again. Give him enough to put an elephant to sleep — he won't stay put otherwise."

"*Oui,* madame."

"I am leaving for a little while," Lysette said, striding to the chair where her muddy cloak had been draped. "Yes, I know it's late — I'll take Justin with me."

The outlines of boxes, furniture, and bales of cotton were briefly illuminated by moonlight as one of the warehouse doors swung open. A woman's voice cut through the stifling air.

"Bernard? Are you here?"

The silence was broken by a shuffling and scraping in the corner. "Lysette?" Bernard's voice was laced with wary surprise. A match was struck.

Standing with Justin by her side, Lysette watched as her brother-in-law lit an oil lamp. "Be careful with that," she said tersely. "After what I've been through today, I have no wish to deal with a warehouse fire."

"After what *you've* been through," Bernard said, sounding shaken. "My God, I've been hiding here for hours, actually in fear for my life."

"You should be," Lysette assured him.

Bernard glared at the two of them. "What

are you doing here? What happened to Max?"

"He has been badly injured," Lysette replied, "but the doctor says he will recover."

"No thanks to you," Justin could not resist adding, and Lysette elbowed him to keep him quiet.

She met Bernard's hate-filled gaze without blinking. "Your life is in danger, Bernard. The Sagesses want to kill you, and if they don't find you first, you'll be arrested by Captain Gervais and his men. Etienne Sagesse left behind a letter that explained everything he knew about Corinne's murder. I'm certain you won't be surprised to learn that you are implicated."

"You red-haired bitch —" Bernard began, starting for her. Justin stepped forward immediately, pulling out his *colchemarde* with a bloodthirsty flourish. Confronted with the gleaming weapon, Bernard retreated and glared at Lysette. "What do you want from me?"

"Just the truth," Lysette replied. "Max will never come to terms with any of this unless you confirm what the letter says. Answer my questions, and I will help you to escape with your life."

"What do you want me to say?" he asked, quivering with fury, white with guilt.

"Why did you have the affair with Corinne?"

Bernard's gaze fastened to hers. It seemed he took great care to avoid the sight of Justin's pale face. "It just happened. I had no control over it. No harm was done, as Corinne had already cuckolded Max with Sagesse. And then I realized Corinne was half mad. She wanted to run away with me, leave everything. . . . I told her I couldn't, but she persisted. And one day she drove me into a rage. Before I knew it, my hands were around her neck. Max was better off without her — she made his life hell —"

"Please," Lysette interrupted acidly, "don't try to claim you were doing Max a service. He was unfairly branded a murderer, and he suffered for years. You let him take the blame for what you did."

Beads of sweat trickled down Bernard's face. "You must help me. No matter what I've done, you know that Max wouldn't want me to be killed."

"There's a ship that leaves for Liverpool at dawn," Lysette replied. "The *Nighthawk*. I spoke to Captain Tierney not an hour ago. He will allow you aboard, no questions asked." Untying a small pouch from her waist, she tossed it to him. Bernard caught it automatically in one fist. "There is enough money to help you establish a new life somewhere else. Don't ever return, Bernard." She turned to Justin, who still held the *colchemarde*, his hand shaking visibly. His blue eyes glittered with tears. He blinked in an effort not to let them fall. "Come, Justin," she murmured. "Take me home."

They left the warehouse, neither of them looking back.

In spite of the clamoring of Aaron Burr's associates, Max was not arrested. Etienne's letter, combined with a discreet nudging from Governor Claiborne and a most unexpected silence from the editor of the *Orleans Gazette*, convinced the Municipal Council and the *gens d'armes* that the absent Bernard Vallerand had indeed been guilty of the crime.

Perhaps those influential men in conspiracy with Aaron Burr could have pressed the issue further, but they were occupied with more demanding matters. By that summer of 1806, Burr had gathered men and supplies at a small island on the Ohio River in preparation for his conquest of Mexico and the West. However, the rumors that had dogged Burr ever since his trip to New Orleans proved his undoing.

Abandoning what he saw as a sinking ship, General Wilkinson changed sides and added his warnings to those President Jefferson had already received. The president eventually issued a proclamation calling for Burr's arrest, at the same time that one of Burr's coded letters to Wilkinson was published in a prominent newspaper.

When Irénée was told about what Bernard had done, she was as grief-stricken as if he had died. It was difficult for a mother to accept that her child could be capable of such evil, and the shock of the news seemed to age her immeasurably. However, she possessed a core of inner strength that sustained her, and she informed the household with dignity that Bernard's name was never to be mentioned in her presence again.

Max recovered from his injuries with remarkable speed, soon regaining his former vigor. Although the truth about Bernard had dealt him a severe blow, it had also relieved him to finally know what had happened to Corinne. With his name cleared and his reputation restored, Max was finally at ease with himself and the world. And Lysette kept him far too busy to dwell on his dark past, engaging him with her warmth and love until he could find no room in his heart for anything but happiness.

In the spring, Alexandre married Henriette Clement, and the wedding proved to be an occasion of great happiness for all concerned. For a while it had seemed that the scandal of Etienne Sagesse's death would prevent Diron Clement from allowing his daughter to marry a Vallerand. However, the old man was persuaded to see the rightness of the match, and he gave his consent with a show of calculating authority, terrified that someone might see the softhearted motives beneath all his scheming.

Lysette was thrilled when she received a letter from her sister Jacqueline, a gentle-spirited letter asking her forgiveness for the long silence between them. It led Lysette to hope that Jeanne and Gaspard would relent soon and recognize her marriage to Max. At Lysette's insistence, Jacqueline and her elderly husband came to stay at the plantation for nearly a month. Although Max disliked the intrusion on his privacy, he endured the visit because it brought Lysette such happiness.

Soon after Alexandre's wedding, Philippe left for France to continue his studies and visit all the places he had read and dreamed of for so long. Although the family begged and prodded Justin to go as well, the boy chose to stay behind, declaring that he had no interest in moldy museums and ancient ruins. With his brother gone, Justin often prowled around New Orleans alone, sometimes standing at the riverfront for hours and gazing after every departing ship as though it were his only chance of escape.

Justin had changed after the events of the past autumn, becoming a far more mature and considerate young man, the defiance of his boyhood finally slipping away. He spent much of his time in his father's company, the two of them deepening their relationship and becoming closer than anyone ever could have expected.

It was not long before Lysette discovered she was with child. She was amused by Max's attitude that she had accomplished something quite remarkable. "*Vraiment,* it is not all that unexpected," she teased him. "As your mother says, the only remarkable thing is that it took this long!"

"If you give me a daughter," he had told her, enfolding her in his arms, "I'll lay the world at your feet."

"I might decide to give you a son," she said. "Wouldn't you like another son?"

He shook his head with a grin. "No, *petite,* we need more women in the family."

Max had been excluded from Corinne's pregnancy, as was the usual way, and in truth, none of it had been significant to him until the twins had been born. With Lysette, however, he took an indelicate interest.

If there had been a question in anyone's mind about whether or not Maximilien doted on his wife, it was forever banished. Each time Lysette experienced a twinge of discomfort or a trace of nausea, the family physician was summoned, and soundly berated if he did not arrive immediately. Irénée told one of her friends in strictest confidence that despite the doctor's protests, Maximilien insisted on staying in the room while Lysette was being examined. The elderly ladies exclaimed over it with horrified delight during an entire Thursday afternoon.

To Lysette's disgruntlement, she was compelled by convention to enter confinement when the baby began to show. As was the Creole custom, she had to withdraw from public view and attend only small gatherings at home or private parties with close friends. To relieve Lysette's boredom for the last two or three months of the pregnancy, Max curtailed his activities in town and spent most of his time at the plantation. He brought her books, games, engravings, and on one Saturday evening he even hired actors from the St. Pierre to perform a play in their drawing room.

On the night of that memorable occasion, Lysette was feeling particularly content, marveling at the fact that her husband would go to such lengths to please her. She smiled and snuggled in Max's arms as he carried her upstairs, resting her hand on the taut curve of her stomach. "How lucky I am to be your wife," she said.

Max smiled sardonically. "Not long ago, you wouldn't have found anyone to agree with you."

"Well, now they all see how they misjudged you, and they realize what a wonderful man you are, *bien-aimé*."

"I don't give a damn what anyone thinks of me," he said, his eyes dark and warm. "Just so long as you are happy."

"I could be happier."

"Oh?" His brow raised. "Tell me what you want, my love, and it's yours."

Lysette played idly with the knot of his cravat. "I will let you know when we're in bed."

Max laughed softly. "For a woman who is *enceinte,* you are remarkably passionate, *petite.*"

"Is that a problem?"

A wicked gleam entered his eyes. "A problem I will gladly take care of," he promised. Lysette laughed and kicked her slippers off, letting them thump down the stairs as he carried her to the bedroom.

ABOUT THE AUTHOR

Lisa Kleypas is the *New York Times* best-selling author of sixteen historical romance novels that have been published in twelve languages.

After graduating from Wellesley College with a political science degree, she published her first novel at age twenty-one.

Later, she was named Miss Massachusetts and competed in the Miss America pageant in Atlantic City. Her books have appeared on bestseller lists such as the *New York Times*, *USA Today*, and *Publishers Weekly*. Lisa is married and has two children.